Cauldron

Once & Future Book 2

Meredith R. Stoddard

Erkita Press

Ruther Glen, Virginia

Erkita Press
10551 Gallant Fox Way
Ruther Glen, VA 22546
www.meredithstoddard.com

Publisher's Note: This is a work of fiction. Names, characters, places, and incidents are a product of the author's imagination. Locales and public names are sometimes used for atmospheric purposes. Any resemblance to actual people, living or dead, or to businesses, companies, events, institutions, or locales is completely coincidental.

Book Layout © 2014 BookDesignTemplates.com

Cauldron/ Meredith R. Stoddard. -- 1st ed.
ISBN 978-0-9904333-5-4

For my children

CONTENTS

CHAPTER ONE

Chapel Hill, North Carolina
December 9, 1995

"Who are you from?"

This was the question that had kept Sarah MacAlpin up all night. In English you might ask a new acquaintance where they are from. In Gaelic, that question is translated as, *"Cò às a tha sibh?"* But *cò* isn't the Gaelic word for where. It means who. Who are you from? This is likely a holdover from the era of the clan system, when one family and its adherents controlled a certain region of land. So, someone might answer, "I'm from MacKenzie territory." Or, "I'm from Campbell country." Maybe it went back further than that to the ancient kingdoms when tribe and family equated to territory. "I'm from Cat." Or, "I'm from Fortriu."

Sarah glanced over at the small, care-worn wooden trunk that held what was left of her grandmother's possessions. It didn't look dangerous, but what she had found inside had been like an electric shock to her exhausted system. It had also blown the crux of her dissertation right out of the water, setting her research back by weeks. Her body was more tired than any time she could remember. Her brain, however, was roiling with questions she should have asked Granny when she'd had the chance.

Sarah cursed herself for doing her best to forget the details of her childhood. She had made a career out of studying the people who had lived nearby in the holler and in the mountains beyond. Part of her wanted to preserve a way of life that was being steadily assimilated into a modern, bustling society. But if she was honest with herself, a big part of her choice to be a folklorist was to obscure the strangeness of her own upbringing. If she could make it fit into the larger context of Appalachia and specifically the Scots people of Appalachia, maybe her own childhood wouldn't seem so strange. She had done her work too well. Now, she had difficulty separating the legends she had learned through work with the ones she had learned at Granny's knee.

Somewhere around four in the morning, she gave up on the idea of sleeping. She dug out the boxes of index cards that held all of her research and began laying them out on her bed. She would have to take out the research on "The River Maiden," at least for the time being. Then she would survey what she had left and come up with a new plan. She would have preferred to do this on the table in the dining area, but Fleming Sinclair was asleep on her couch. Even if she couldn't sleep, she didn't see any reason to disturb him. Hopefully she could lose herself in work and forget about the other questions swirling around just below the surface.

**

From the front of her apartment came a pounding like someone was trying to knock down her newly replaced door. Sarah massaged the back of her neck and stretched her shoulders until her bruised ribs protested

"Sarah! Are you in there?" came the distant muffled voice from outside.

Barrett! She'd forgotten all about her friend. He'd gone to visit his mother in Mebane as soon as he'd finished his exams, but was planning to move into her apartment next semester.

Sarah made a beeline for the door and was almost there when Fleming stepped in front of her. She found herself eye level with his bare, leanly muscled chest. She glared up at him. A corner of his mouth ticked up in a quick smile.

"It's just my friend, Barrett. He's probably worried sick." She made to step around Fleming as the door rattled in its frame.

He blocked her again. "Still, it's best if ye let me make sure it's safe first. Why don't ye wait in the kitchen?"

"Sarah!" Barrett hammered on the door several times.

"Fine," Sarah seethed. "But could you do it before he breaks my new door?"

"Right." Fleming eyed her as she stalked to the kitchen.

He checked the peephole, careful not to get too close in case Barrett rattled the door again. Undoing the new chain and locks, he opened the door just enough to talk to the nearly frantic man in the hall. "Are ye alone then?"

"Who the fuck are you?"

"I'm a friend of Sarah's, and sh—"

"No, I'M a friend of Sarah's," Barrett cut him off. "You don't look like one of our friends."

"Look, mate—" Fleming said, holding up a quelling hand.

"Is she in there?" Barrett demanded. "Sarah?"

"I'm here, Bear." Sarah stepped into the living room. Barrett was leaning into the apartment, barred only by Fleming's arm.

His usually spiked hair was mussed, and his clothes looked like he had thrown them on in a rush.

Fleming rolled his eyes in frustration and let Barrett pass before checking the hall for anyone else.

"What the hell is going on?" Barrett crossed the room in two strides and wrapped her in his arms. It surprised her how good it felt. Barrett was the exact person she needed. He was the first person she'd seen since Thursday who didn't have his own agenda. He was her friend pure and simple, and that was all he wanted to be.

She rubbed her cheek against the soft cotton of his shirt. He smelled faintly of incense and smoke, but she really didn't care. Clinging to him, she whispered, "Oh God, Bear. I'm so glad to see you."

"I came as soon as I could. I almost had a heart attack when I heard. You weren't answering your phone." He rested his cheek on the top of her head.

"I stayed at Dermot's and then I was avoiding reporters," she said into his chest. "How much do you know?"

"I know it was Ryan, and that he's dead. That's about all I could get through Amy's sobbing." With a hand on her cheek, he turned her face up to him. His warm brown eyes searched hers. "Just tell me you're okay."

Sarah blinked against the sting of tears and words clogged in her throat. There was so much she wanted to tell him, and most of it she couldn't say. She would've loved to say she was fine, but that would be a lie. She just shook her head.

He nodded and pulled her close again. "Okay, honey. Let's sit down and you can tell me all about it. You can start with telling me about your new guard dog."

As he led her to the couch, Sarah looked back at Fleming. He had put on his shirt and stood at a polite distance. "I'll just be in the kitchen then," he said.

"Thanks." She sat next to Barrett and let him pull her close enough to rest her head on his shoulder. "That's Fleming," she said. "He's a cousin of Dermot's, and he saved my life the other night. He's been nice enough to stick around so I feel safe."

Barrett looked over her head toward the kitchen. "Is it working?"

"A little." She sighed. "At least I know someone else is in the apartment."

"He's pretty hot. Any chance he likes guys?" She could hear the laughter in his voice and loved him for the attempt to lighten things up. She peeked over his shoulder at Fleming puttering in the kitchen. Barrett had a point. Fleming was easy on the eyes in a rough-and-tumble sort of way. His brown hair was on the scruffy side and his nose looked like it had been broken once or twice. But his easy manner and laughing gray eyes made the overall effect rather nice.

"We haven't really gotten that personal, but you're welcome to ask him." Sarah couldn't stop a little giggle from escaping as she imagined that conversation.

"Eh. He's not really my type, way too good-looking." He gave her shoulder a reassuring rub. "So, tell me what happened."

She spent several seconds thinking over what she should and shouldn't tell him. "Did you ever meet Ryan?"

"Mmm, couple of times," he muttered.

"You sound like you weren't crazy about him. Was that your first impression or hindsight?"

"Hard to tell now," he said. "I think there was always something that didn't sit right with me, but I couldn't put a finger on it. He seemed to make Amy happy, though."

"That's exactly how I felt. Something about him gave me the creeps, but he really seemed to care about Amy. And she seemed happy. It was nice to see her with someone for more than a couple of weeks." Amy wasn't promiscuous, but she was always looking for love. Sarah had held her friend's hand through a few short and ill-fated relationships.

"Then he started acting aggressively toward me…nothing too blatant, just enough to put me on edge," Sarah said. "I actually caught him coming out of my room once. I told Amy about it, but she defended him. She even gave him a key to the apartment. Eventually, I went to where he said he worked, but the foreman had never heard of him. When I told Amy, she laid into me about being paranoid and self-absorbed and nosy. When her granddad got sick, they made a big show of Ryan handing me his key.

"But he must have kept a copy. Thursday night, I woke up and Ryan was on top of me with a knife to my throat…" Sara heard her voice crack and fought for control. She wasn't going to fall apart over what Ryan had done. She had to be stronger than that.

"He didn't…" Barrett let the question trail off, but Sarah took his meaning.

"No." She shook her head and gave his waist a reassuring squeeze. "No, he meant to kill me. He wasn't interested in anything else. But he wanted it to look like a suicide. He'd tried to arrange an accident before that night."

Barrett leaned his head back against the wall. "Halloween."

Sarah looked up at him and gave a short nod. "Yeah. He meant to push me in front of that bus. He used the crowd as cover."

"Thank God I was able to pull you back." Barrett kissed the top of her head as she settled her head back on his shoulder. "But why? Because of Amy?"

Sarah shook her head. "This is where it gets really weird."

"Because it wasn't weird enough?"

"I never really got a clear reason out of him. He babbled a lot. After Dermot arrived, he started making even less sense. Dermot attacked him and I ran outside to get help. Ryan chased me and caught me in the intersection on my way to the blue house. Fleming had already called the cops. He stalled Ryan until the police came. The rest...I'm sure you saw it on the news."

"So you think it was suicide by cop?" He looked puzzled.

She nodded, and he went silent. His hand rubbed absently on her shoulder. After a few minutes, he asked, "So if he's dead and the threat is over, what's with the bodyguard?"

"Ah, well..." Sarah eyed the frayed seam on the arm of the couch and fished around for a reason that her perceptive friend wouldn't see right through. After a minute, she said, "He's spelling Dermot. They're mostly sticking around for moral support. And to keep reporters away."

"Have they been harassing you?" Barrett sounded ready to take on any reporters who might try.

"I've ignored a couple of calls, but..." She took a long breath and lowered her voice to a whisper, "You can't tell anyone this."

When he nodded and leaned closer, she went on. "Do you remember the woman I told you about from Nova Scotia, the one who was murdered?"

He nodded again.

"Well, Ryan told me that he killed her. He followed me here from Canada. We're afraid that if someone in the press connects us, they will start hounding me. Serial killers make sensational news."

"Mmhmm." He sounded skeptical, but gave her shoulder a squeeze. Sarah rested her head back on his shoulder and enjoyed the comfort of his arms for a few more minutes.

"Well, I guess Amy and I will have to hunt down a new apartment," he said.

"Yeah."

Sarah looked around the living room that she and Amy had called home for the last two years. They had spent countless evenings chatting on that same frayed blue couch, laughing with friends over a few beers, comparing notes from folklore classes. It hurt more than a little to think that not only were their days in the apartment behind them, but maybe their friendship was too.

***

"It's in the paper," Dermot announced as he let himself into Sarah's apartment carrying a tray of coffees and a bag of scones. He scanned the front room and stopped short. He hadn't expected to find Sarah cuddled up on the couch with Barrett. "Hey, mate. Didn't know ye were here or I would have brought ye a coffee."

Barrett nodded to him over Sarah's head. "No problem. I've had enough of a jolt this morning."

Sarah, who had been leaning her head on her friend's shoulder, stirred. Rising from the couch, she shuffled toward Dermot. Her curly hair was twisted up into a messy bun held with a pencil, and there were dark circles under her eyes. She wore an old T-shirt and sweatpants that hung dangerously low on her hips. She looked exhausted and yet unbelievably beautiful. He wanted to wrap his arms around her and cradle her as Barrett had just been doing. But he couldn't allow himself to do that again. Sarah was meant for James Stuart.

"Thanks," she mumbled, reaching for the tray of coffees. Only then did he realize that he'd been standing next to the door dumbly staring at her. She took the tray and gave him a weak smile before turning to set it on the table.

"Didn't ye sleep?" He followed her, depositing the bag of scones on the table in front of her.

Sarah didn't look up at him, but shook her head. Her attention was focused on the pastries as she unrolled the top of the bag and reached inside.

Fleming came out of the kitchen with a glass of water in hand. His hair was mussed from sleeping on the couch, but at least he looked like he'd gotten some sleep. "How much?"

"Mm?" Dermot grunted, confused.

Fleming gave him an odd look. "News. How much was in the paper?"

"Oh." Dermot gave his head a shake before pulling the folded newspaper out of his back pocket. He held it out to his cohort. "No names, just the basics. Hopefully, no one will get too curious. There's coffee."

"Ah. Cheers, mate." Fleming glanced at Barrett, who waved a hand at the coffee in invitation. Fleming picked up one of the coffee cups and drank while scanning the article. When he finished reading, he tossed the paper onto the table. "Well, the boss said there would be press. As long as they accept that it's a domestic dispute, we might be able to avoid anything further."

Sarah pulled another scone out of the bag and put it on a napkin. She handed it to Fleming. He took it from her with a smile.

Dermot gritted his teeth against a stab of jealousy. She was all knowing smiles and nods with the other two men, but couldn't even spare him a look. He supposed he deserved that. He picked up his coffee and a scone before going to sit on the couch. He reckoned that after the last couple of days he should probably give her some space. "Maybe the local press will just move on."

"Let's hope so," Fleming said around a mouthful of pastry.

The four of them enjoyed their breakfast in silence, each lost in their own thoughts. When Sarah finished hers, she took the bag into the kitchen. Barrett followed her. Dermot called Fleming over with a jerk of his head. "Did she get any sleep?"

"Dunno. She cleaned this place top to bottom. I offered to help, but she wouldna have it. Then she gave me a blanket and pillow and went to her room. I heard the shower running for a bit."

"Mmmph. It's been a rough couple of days."

***

"You wanna tell me what that's all about?" Barrett whispered as he reached over Sarah's shoulder to get a glass from the cabinet.

"What?" She hoped he hadn't noticed Fleming's mention of "the boss."

"Oh, you all close-mouthed and Dermot all hang-dog. I thought he saved your life. He should be your hero." The sound of running water covered his voice.

Sarah tried not to let her face show just how miserable that topic made her. "It's complicated."

"Oooo…Do we need to go to your room so you can tell me all the juicy details?" Barrett leaned in close as he turned the water off. "Are you two a thing now?"

Sarah groaned. "We were and then we weren't in very rapid succession."

"What did he do?" Barrett's voice dropped an octave, and when Sarah dared to glance at him, his look was full of menace.

"Oh, Bear. I love you so much." She wrapped an arm around his waist. "Why couldn't you be straight?"

He returned her embrace. "Even if I was, honey, I wouldn't be good enough for you. Although my mother still holds out hope for us."

Sarah couldn't help laughing. Barrett's mother was a tough lady, but she'd always had a soft spot for Sarah. "I hate to disappoint her."

"You still haven't answered my question."

She smiled at him, her tenacious friend. "He didn't do anything that you could fix for me. We'll figure it out. I hope."

He studied her closely. "So you want to work it out."

Sarah hoped he couldn't see the tears pooling in her eyes. Not trusting her voice, she nodded.

"You love him."

Another quick nod.

Barrett gave her shoulder a squeeze and kissed her temple. "I hope he deserves you, baby."

"When are you leaving for New York?" Sarah asked Barrett as they left the kitchen.

"I don't have to go," he said.

"Yes," she insisted. "You do."

"I can stay here with you. I probably should anyway. Amy's not exactly in a state to go apartment hunting."

"Afraid you'll run into Stephen up there?" Sarah asked.

Barrett cleared his throat and looked uncomfortable. "Maybe a little."

"And that's exactly why you should go." She nudged him with an elbow. "You can't let fear of an awkward situation take away the holiday you planned. You should go and have a fantastic time without him."

"Are you sure you don't want me to stay?" He looked half-hopeful. She was tempted.

She nodded toward Dermot. "I've got two watch dogs now. I think I'll be fine. Don't let me rain on your plans…and don't make excuses."

Barrett glanced over his shoulder at Dermot. "I thought he was going home soon."

"He is, but Fleming will stick around. Apparently, he works for my new benefactor." Her tone turned dry.

"The one Amy calls Hottie MacMoneybags?"

Sarah laughed at her roommate's nickname for James Stuart, Scottish oil baron and chief funder of the fellowship that was taking her to Scotland in a few weeks. "The very one."

"Does he do this kind of thing for every academic he gives money to?" Barrett asked with an arched eyebrow.

Sarah looked over Barrett's shoulder to find Dermot looking hard at her. "Who knows? At the moment I'm not complaining."

Barrett watched her for several seconds. "Well, if I'm still going to New York, then I'd better do something about finding a new apartment. This late in the game we'll probably be stuck on the other side of Carrboro."

He was right. All of the apartments close to campus had likely been rented before exams started.

Barrett took his leave. Sarah was glad he was going to attempt to find something. She was sure that Amy wasn't up to the task just then.

"I'll be working for another hour or so, then I'll want to go to the library," she told Dermot as she walked past him to her room.

CHAPTER TWO

"Fleming's gone for the day," Dermot said from the bedroom doorway a little while later.

"Mmhmm," Sarah muttered without turning around. Her back was stiff, shoulders tight. She was still upset with him.

"Listen, I ken ye're angry with me. But can ye be a little less obvious about it in front of Fleming?"

She had plenty of reason to be angry. It had been little more than twenty-four hours since she had confided her painful past to him. Sarah's mother had tried to drown her when she was only six. Then her mother's death, which most people believed was accidental, had actually been suicide. Little Sarah had been the one to find her in a pool of blood with a cryptic message scrawled on the wall. She had trusted him with her most painful secrets, and just a few hours later he had broken her heart while adding to her list of secrets.

She still didn't turn around, but lifted her eyes to the ceiling. "Well, you can imagine it's just a little hard to contain."

"Right." He stepped into the room. "The problem is that Fleming works for James, and ye have to expect that anything he hears or observes is going to get back to the boss."

"So I went from living with a stalker to living with a spy." She said over her shoulder. "No. I forgot. You've been spying on me for months."

"Not by choice."

She finally turned to look at him, her green eyes shooting sparks. "You keep saying that, but I don't see anyone holding a gun to your head."

"It's not that simple," he said through his teeth.

"Oh right. Because it's your *duty*, and he's your *king*, and I'm some magical *princess* who's going to liberate the Scots," she said with obvious skepticism. "I. Don't. Believe. That."

"You don't have to believe it. James believes it. Walter believes it and whoever sent Ryan Cumberland to kill ye believes it." He sighed, searching for patience. "Ryan's attempt on your life proves that someone outside of James's circle knows who you are. If they think that they can get to James through you, they're going to keep trying."

"Sounds to me like I'd be safer staying as far away from James Stuart as possible. Maybe I shouldn't go to Scotland after all."

"Really?" He cocked his head. "Ryan was here before ye ever met James. He killed Bridget and she had never met James. James Stuart is the only person with the resources to protect ye."

Her lips pressed into a firm line. "Mmhmm…And who's going to protect me from James?"

"It may be hard to believe, but James doesna mean you any harm."

She arched an eyebrow at him. "No, he just wants to force me into a marriage I don't want. No, thanks."

"And a life on the run from him and his enemies sounds better?" Dermot stepped closer, trying for a calmer tone. "He doesna want to force ye into marriage. He would much rather woo ye. That's why he can't know that I told ye about his intentions. I convinced him that it's worth his while to win ye, to make ye love him without all of the extra baggage. I told him not to tell ye about everything else, because I knew you would resist it. If he finds out now that I told ye, he'll want to move on getting married right away. Ye'll never have time to finish yer dissertation. Ye won't even have time to get to know him."

"And you really think that I'll be able to continue working on folklore while married to James?" Her face said she was sure she wouldn't.

"I think ye'll have a better chance with him than without him. If ye don't go to Scotland, ye'll have to spend the rest of yer life hiding from James and whoever sent Ryan, and anyone else who believes in the legend. Ye'll have to leave behind everything ye've worked for."

"I'm not going to do that, and I'm not going to marry James Stuart," she growled.

"Well, ye can't stay here." He took a few steps closer. "Look, I know that ye probably hate me right now. But I'm trying to buy ye some time, to find a way to make the best of this. I'm trying to make it hurt a little bit less."

She sighed studying him for several seconds. "You know he can't win me. Not when I'm already in love with you."

He closed his eyes and breathed deep. When he opened them, he was struck by the hope and determination in her eyes. He felt gutted to have to crush that hope. "I've already told ye, we can't have that." He lifted his hand to cup her cheek. "Please just let me do what I can for ye?"

Her eyes glistened with tears. "I'll think about it, but no guarantees."

Dermot leaned closer and planted a chaste kiss on her forehead. She wrapped her arms around his waist and hugged him.

He rested his arm on her shoulders and tried not to think about how good it felt to be so close.

He glanced down at the bed cluttered with index cards. "Where's the rest of yer outline?"

"I had to pull some things out." Sarah pulled away from him and turned to the dresser. She picked up a photograph. "Last night I was looking through Granny's things and I found this."

He looked closely at the old black and white photo of two girls on a beach. "What's this?"

Sarah sipped her coffee. "Notice anything about the one on the left?"

He studied the girl on the left more closely. Both girls appeared to be happy. Their smiles were genuine, but the one on the left was looking slightly off camera. Her eyes were flat, unfocused. "Is she blind?"

"Ding, ding! Got it in one." Sarah's voice was grim. "Not only that, but I know her. That's Isobel MacKenzie, and the girl on the right is my grandmother."

"Wait." He looked up at her, his brow creased. "They knew each other?"

"Looks like it." She shrugged taking the photo back. "Of course, that means they probably learned 'The River Maiden' from the same place, or one of them learned it from the other."

The reason for the drastic changes in her outline clicked. "So their versions of the song didn't evolve independently."

"Exactly. That was the linchpin of my argument. Now I have to find a different angle for my dissertation. It's set me back weeks at least." Sarah rested her hip against the dresser, looking defeated. Part of him was glad she had something to get her mind off the events of the past couple of days.

"Maybe not as much as ye think. Ye still have the Budge recording. That developed independently from them." He nodded at the picture on the dresser. "And it's in English."

Sarah nodded thoughtfully. "That's true, but I don't know if Isobel taught it to Granny or vice versa. So I have an American English version and maybe a Scottish, maybe Cape Breton version. It's just not as strong as showing three versions of the same song influenced by three different environments."

They went back to puzzling over the cards on the bed. After a few minutes, Dermot asked, "Where do ye think ye go from here?"

Sarah took a deep breath. "I think I have two angles to work. First, I need to search more of the transcriptions here to see if there is another song that crosses communities like that. Second, I need to determine the origins of the two versions of 'The River Maiden.' I'm going to have to trace the Budge version as far back as possible, and I have to find another Scottish version."

"It would be great if ye knew which of those girls taught which." He glanced at the picture again.

"It would," she agreed. "I would write to Isobel and ask…but this soon after Bridget's death? That just feels wrong. So, it's back to research, research, research."

"Mmmphmm," he agreed.

"Isobel said her grandmother taught her, but I don't recall Granny ever saying where she learned it," Sarah shrugged. "The funny thing is, Isobel never mentioned knowing Granny. She talked about knowing a Jamie MacAlpin, but not a Maggie or Margaret. And Granny never mentioned being in Cape Breton. I'm sure of that."

"Maybe yer gran's name wasn't MacAlpin when she was there. Didn't she change it when she married?"

Sarah shook her head. "She never married. Said she never needed a man. She told people in the mountains that she was a widow."

He studied her. "Moonshiner, farmer, feminist. I'm sorry she's gone. She sounds like quite a lady."

Sarah's lips curled into a half-smile. "She was something, alright."

CHAPTER THREE

A sharp knock on the listening room window almost made Sarah jump out of her skin. Heart racing, she looked out the glass to find Dermot on the other side of the glass, looking guilty. She opened the door and gave him a withering glare.

"Sorry. I wasna thinking," he whispered.

She would have given him a hard time about sneaking up on someone who had been snuck up on and held hostage just a couple of days ago, but since the incident she had no idea what things were likely to set her off. "S'okay. What's up?"

"My appetite. I'm starving and we both need a break."

Sarah stretched her neck, rolling her head from side to side. "Yeah, I guess I could use a break."

"Come on. I'll buy you a burrito." He leaned into the tiny room and snatched her backpack from the back of her chair.

Sarah turned to gather her tapes and headphones. She couldn't help thinking of the last time they'd been in one of the library's listening rooms together. She'd been a nervous wreck from lack of sleep and visions and he had pulled her into his arms and held onto her long enough for her to stop falling apart. That had only been three months ago.

When she turned for the door, his broad shoulders filled the frame. By the look in his eyes, she could tell he was remembering the very same moment.

***

God help him, he should have waited for her to gather her own things. The second he had leaned across the threshold of that tiny cubicle he'd been swept back to that day when he'd caught her in mid-panic and held her until the shaking stopped. Most of the time, she fought so hard to keep her vulnerabilities hidden. But she had needed help that day and he'd been there. It hadn't been the first time he'd helped her, but it was the first time she had willingly allowed it. He'd felt twelve feet tall. It was also the day he'd known he was truly in danger of falling for her.

He moved out of her way, but she stepped closer, too close. She whispered, "It doesn't have to be this way."

He breathed in her scent. He would have to content himself with that. "Aye, it does."

The look she gave him was full of challenge. If she touched him now, when the memory of her in his arms was so fresh, his willpower would crumble. She didn't. She moved aside and returned her tapes to the collection desk.

Dermot stood rooted to the spot and counted to ten. When that wasn't enough, he started counting to one hundred.

"You coming?" she asked as she stopped by the door to shrug on her jacket.

"Right."

The dining hall was nearly deserted as they slid their trays onto a table in the corner. Dermot liked this vantage point. No one would sneak up on them here.

"So, have you found anything that sounds familiar?" Sarah began before attacking her burrito. On her first bite, the bottom fell out and landed with a plop on her plate. She looked down at it with a sigh and went to get a fork.

When she sat back down, he answered her question, "All of it sounds familiar, but nothing that's similar to "The River Maiden". I found some familiar elements that cross form Gaelic to English like *'mo nighean donn'* to 'nut brown maid', but no other whole songs. You?"

"Nah." She pushed the scattered contents of her burrito around with the fork. "I was just starting to listen to some of the tapes recorded in the same area as the Budge recording. I'm hoping there will be something more, or maybe something I missed before."

"How many times have ye listened to those tapes?"

She looked up. "Enough that there's a pre-echo in my head."

"Maybe I should have a go at them. New set of ears and all that," he offered.

She shrugged. "Sure. At this point I'm willing to try just about anything."

They spent the rest of the meal in stilted and awkward small talk. He didn't want to acknowledge that tense moment in the library, and from the way she kept her eyes trained on her plate neither did she. He remembered her prescription for survival: keep eating, keep breathing, keep going about your life, and someday it wouldn't hurt so bloody much.

***

They were in the foyer of the dining hall when she let out a gasp. He was putting on his jacket and whipped around, expecting a threat, only to find her staring at the bulletin board that covered most of the wall. It was wallpapered with a semester's worth of notices, flyers seeking roommates or selling things, and calendars for various clubs pinned several layers deep on the cork board. But Sarah's eyes were trained on a poster for a play that had been presented the month before. It was *Macbeth*, performed by a traveling group of British actors. The image they had chosen for the ad was of the three witches lit from beneath as they stood around a cauldron with mist spilling down its sides. Sarah moved in closer to the poster. She seemed transfixed.

"How did I not see this?" she breathed. She looked back over her shoulder, her eyes sparkling.

He shrugged and stood next to her. "I've seen that play a dozen times. Haven't you?"

"Not the play, the Weird Sisters." She turned back to the poster, shaking her head. "Think about it. Three sisters around their cauldron who told Macbeth that he would be king."

He shook his head. "They're not in 'The River Maiden.'"

"No, but the cauldron is, and the king uses it to unite the people," Her eyes were bright, and he could almost see her mental wheels spinning into overdrive. "And they were in my storybook."

"What storybook?"

"Ugh." She groaned and clenched her fist in frustration. "I meant to show it to you. I found it in Granny's trunk along with the photo of Granny and Isobel. It's a book that I made when I was a little girl, before Mama died. It tells the story of a tribe of people older than any other. When they had a conflict with a newer tribe, the queen and her two sisters led them to safety on the hidden island. In the book, it seemed like they were the same tribe from 'The River Maiden', but I don't know how much of that was actual legend and how much was a little girl's imagination."

He cocked his head to the side in thought. "But it does connect the cauldron and three women. You still need something to prove it's legend and not made up."

"Right." Sarah waved her hand at the poster. "Shakespeare called them witches because that's how people thought about them at the time. In my book, they're the keepers of the cauldron."

"And ye think an English playwright knew that story?"

"He must have heard some version of it. The three witches aren't unheard of in Scottish folklore. It wouldn't be a surprise if the stories filtered to the south. The real question is, how old are those stories."

"Just playing devil's advocate here, but they could just be a theatrical device, like a Greek chorus. He used those in other plays as well."

She sighed and grabbed his hand, pulling him out the door. "I'm not saying you're wrong, but I don't think it's an either/or proposition."

She pulled him down the steps and across the courtyard to the student bookstore. She stopped right next to the checkout desk, where a spinning rack was loaded with small paperbacks of plays, novellas, and poetry. She turned the rack to a side that was full of Shakespeare's best known plays. "Look at these. *Julius Caesar, Henry V, Richard III*...all histories. *The Tempest, A Midsummer Night's Dream*...these come from legends. *Macbeth* is a combination of history and legend. Shakespeare was prolific, but I would be surprised if any of his plots were original. Audiences like familiar stories. That's as true now as it was then. He wrote to appeal to the masses. So why not borrow from stories they already knew?"

"Alright, but how well did they know these stories and for how long?"

"Exactly." She pulled a copy of Macbeth from the rack and flipped to act III, scene 1. She scanned the lines. "There is plenty of strange superstition and theatrical embellishment, but this scene is focused on the cauldron." She pointed to specific lines and read: "Round about the cauldron go," and then a few lines later, "Boil thou first i' th' charmed pot." She turned the page and pointed to three more mentions of the cauldron. She quoted another line, "Like elves and fairies in a ring, enchanting all that you put in."

When she looked up at him, her grin was infectious. "It's the cauldron of the auld folk, just like the storybook."

"That thread might be a bit thin," he said.

Despite her excitement, there wasn't enough connection for a strong academic argument. Sarah bobbed her head. "Okay maybe, but you do see the connection, right?"

"Yeah, I can see it," he conceded.

"Then we just have to find something to make it stronger!" She slapped the book down on the counter and pulled out her wallet.

A clerk who had been somewhere among the shelves glided in and rang her up. Sarah tucked the book into her backpack.

"So, back to the library?" he asked as they left the store.

"Yep, but this time we need to be looking for anything to do with the three witches, three sisters, or the cauldron.

CHAPTER FOUR

By the time they returned to her apartment, Sarah had a new stack of index cards loaded with research notes on the three witches and the cauldron. In addition to occurring in Scottish folklore, they had found trios of supernatural women in Norse and even Greek mythology.

They spent the long walk home discussing their findings. Dermot continued his role as devil's advocate, picking apart her theories all the way through the door. "But every storyteller worth his salt knows the rule of three," he said.

"Sure," she answered as she stepped into her apartment and slid the backpack from her shoulders. "But the Norns, the Fates, and the three from my story are so similar, and they cross cultures, the English Channel, the Alps…They have to be based on something older."

"A lot of your old-school academics will say the Rule of Three comes from the Holy Trinity."

Sarah gave him her best side-eye. "And any religious scholar who has looked up from his Bible in the last forty years would say that like everything else about Christianity as we know it, the Trinity is an appropriation of an older tradition."

Dermot smiled down at her, his eyes sparkling with laughter. "Somehow I dinna think calling them old-fashioned is a winning argument."

A throat cleared in the room in front of them. They had been so involved in their discussion that they hadn't noticed anyone else there. In a flash, Dermot pulled her behind him and drew a gun from the small of his back. He leveled the pistol at the dining area, where a well-dressed man was sitting calmly at the table next to Sarah's telephone.

"Ye have five seconds to identify yerself," Dermot said with quiet menace.

Peeking around Dermot's arm, Sarah saw the man rise slowly from his seat, his hands in the air. "My name is Martin Carol. I work in public relations for Alba Petroleum. I'm going to give you my card. It's in my jacket pocket."

Sarah felt Dermot tense, reminding her of a snake posed to strike. His gun hand didn't waver. Carol reached into the inside pocket of his impeccably tailored suit coat and pulled out a white card between two fingers. He cautiously stretched his arm past the gun holding the card so they could read it.

Alba Petroleum

Martin Carol

Media Liaison

"Mr. Stuart sent me," he said, and Sarah got the impression that those four simple words held a lot of meaning where Carol came from.

"Then ye willna mind if I call him," Dermot challenged.

The man's mouth spread into a confident smile, showing his perfectly straight, perfectly white teeth. "Not at all."

Dermot pulled Sarah with him as he went to the phone on the table. The gun stayed trained on the intruder as he dialed. Dermot knew the number by heart. "Miss Lennox, this is Dermot Sinclair."

Sarah kept an eye on Carol, not that Dermot had stopped watching him. The man seemed completely unfazed by Dermot's suspicion. After a couple of minutes, Dermot spoke again, "Yes, your man, Carol is here. He says that ye sent him."

Dermot listened to the quick response. Then, "Can ye describe him to me?" He listened again to the voice on the other end. Eventually, he nodded. "Right then, that's him. Cheers."

His shoulders relaxed and he let his arm drop so the pistol pointed at the floor. He hung up the phone. "Sorry, mate. Canna be too careful."

Sarah felt the tension drain from her shoulders. She watched Dermot return the gun to the holster at the small of his back and pull his sweatshirt over it. On principle, she wasn't a fan of guns—but a very small, primitive part of her was glad that he had it.

Carol smoothed his unruffled hair. "That's quite alright. I've been briefed on recent events. I can't say that I blame you for being cautious."

"Right. What do ye have for us?"

Carol shifted his gaze to Sarah. He indicated a seat at the table with a wave of his hand. "Miss MacAlpin?"

Sarah went to take a seat, but as soon as her hand touched the back of the chair, she was hit with a flood of memories from the last time she had sat down at that table with Dermot, just days ago. They'd been at gunpoint, sitting across from each other, when Dermot had told her who she was for the first time…and who he was. She said, "You know what? Let's sit over there."

They moved to the living room. Sarah and Dermot sat on the couch while Carol looked askance at the worn green upholstery of the adjacent chair before deigning to lower himself into it. He pulled a folder from his leather attaché case and handed it to Sarah. "What we have is a tiered strategy for responding to press enquiries. Ideally, we would prefer not to say anything more. As yet this appears to be a domestic dispute, or at worst a case of stalking. If the police don't release any further information and we say nothing more, then the story should simply die down."

"Sounds good to me," Sarah agreed, still holding the folder.

He nodded toward the folder. "In case someone in the media connects this incident with the murder of Bridget MacKenzie, we've prepared a narrative for the press. You'll find in there a version of events that explains the connection between you and Miss MacKenzie and how this monster followed you from Nova Scotia. As Miss MacKenzie never met Mr. Stuart, his name has been left out of the narrative. Your stance should be that you would like to get back to normal life as soon as possible and are not interested in giving interviews."

He paused and smiled as if this were the simplest thing in the world. But then again, Sarah imagined he did this sort of thing all the time. "If it becomes necessary to talk to the press, our strategy will be to provide any interested journalists with more than sufficient information. If we present this as a serial killer who stalked you and was killed by police, then there should be little further interest. By combining a strategic release of information with a plea for privacy, we should be able to deflect any undue media attention."

Sarah was skeptical. "You might be underestimating the amount of ghoulish curiosity people have for stories about serial killers."

"That could be true," Carol conceded, but he seemed unperturbed. "Still, we only have to keep the local press at bay until you leave for Scotland. I understand that will be less than a month from now?"

Sarah nodded. "Just a little over three weeks."

"What about the national media, or even international?" Dermot cut in. "If the word gets out about the connection with Bridget MacKenzie, then won't we have to deal with Canadian press as well?"

Carol tilted his head to the side as if granting a point. "So far, the story has garnered no more than local interest in the communities involved. You may get a call or two from outside the local media, but that's where the plea for privacy will be effective. You can simply tell them that you prefer to speak only with the police."

Sarah opened the folder and perused the bullet points of the statement that he'd given her. He certainly appeared to have dotted all the i's and crossed all the t's. It was a tight, believable story that gave enough truth to answer the main questions a reporter might ask, but left out any connection to James Stuart or Alba Petroleum. Carol's smooth confidence suggested this wasn't his first foray into media manipulation.

"This looks to be in order, except for this part." Sarah pointed to the description of how Ryan had stalked her for months. "You can't mention Amy."

Carol's gaze sharpened on hers. "She's your flat mate. People are going to ask, and what's there is true. Is it not? Ryan Cumberland duped Amy Monroe to gain access to you."

"Sure, but no one needs to know that. She's had enough trouble with this. She doesn't need the press calling her too. If you can keep James Stuart out of it, you can keep Amy out." Sarah tossed the folder onto the coffee table and leaned back, folding her arms across her chest.

Carol leaned forward in his chair. His voice was even and firm. "Mr. Stuart was only tangentially involved in this situation. Miss Monroe, on the other hand, had direct involvement with both you and Cumberland."

Sarah studied him. Carol was unflappable and clearly bent on his narrative. Sarah wondered what it would take to change his mind. She glanced at Dermot. His look said he understood why she wanted to protect Amy, but he wasn't sure it would work. He laid a hand on her knee. "People all over town knew she was dating him. Someone will likely talk about it."

"It doesn't have to come from me," Sarah said. She eyed both men. "I can't control other people, but I will not give Amy's name to any reporter, and I won't answer any questions about her. As far as they're concerned she had nothing to do with it."

Carol looked past her to Dermot as if he was looking for support. Sarah felt Dermot shrug. "Don't look at me, mate. This is her show."

The only sign that the PR man was less than pleased was a flexing of the muscles in his jaw. He looked thoughtful and blew out a long breath. "Alright. I'll give you a revised narrative in the morning without any reference to Miss Monroe. But you should keep in mind that the further the story is from the truth, the easier someone will see through it."

Sarah gave him a steely-eyed look. "I'll convince them."

Carol took the folder back from Sarah and made a note on the sheet inside. Beside her, Dermot cleared his throat. "Is there a contingency plan for this? What should she say if someone asks about Mr. Stuart?"

"I'm glad you asked." Carol turned to Sarah. He seemed happy to be back on solid ground. "You, Miss MacAlpin, had no real reason to know that Miss MacKenzie was connected to Alba Petroleum at all, that is without Cumberland telling you."

"She just said she'd been offered a job by an oil company. She never said which oil company," Sarah said as if responding to a reporter's question.

Carol grinned. "Just so, and your answer to any questions about the connection should be exactly that. If anyone asks, we will acknowledge the offer. Alba Petroleum employs many geologists and recruits them from top universities. There is no reason to believe that the threads connecting both of you to Mr. Stuart are anything more than coincidental."

"You seem to have a plan for everything." Sarah rose from the couch, effectively ending the conversation.

Carol smiled smugly. "It is what we do."

"And are you doing this for Bridget's family too?" Sarah asked.

"Indeed. One of my colleagues is there as we speak." The smile he gave her didn't quite reach his eyes.

"Good. Thank you." She extended a hand to him.

"Of course." Carol shook hands. "I'll have the revised narrative to you in the morning. In the meantime, I suggest you continue screening your calls."

"We will," Dermot said from behind her.

Carol nodded to Dermot before turning to the door. When he was gone, Sarah let herself sink back down to the couch. She'd been so energized when they arrived home, but Carol's visit had brought all of the questions about her life and her future crashing back with a vengeance.

"Right." Before she knew what was happening, Dermot was pulling her up from the couch and ushering her into the bedroom. "Ye're going back here and ye're going to sleep for at least eight hours."

"That's a lot easier said than done, you know," she mumbled.

Dermot took her face in his hands and waited for her to meet his eyes. "Ye're safe. I'll stay here all night if that's what it takes for ye to get some rest."

"Here in the apartment…" she cut her eyes to the bed, "or here with me?"

The look he gave her told her what she already suspected. He wouldn't be sleeping with her. Sarah let her eyes drop to his mouth. His lips were pressed into a firm line. She gave a wistful sigh, wanting badly to go back forty-eight hours to the morning she had spent in his bed, before he'd broken her heart.

"Sleep. I'll be right outside."

He retreated to the hallway and closed the door with a soft click.

CHAPTER FIVE

Granny's soft, clear voice echoed off the cracked plaster walls as wood smoke filled Sarah's nostrils. Granny was singing one of her favorites about a piper who went to the fairies to fetch back his love. The chorus was full of stags and heather, and Sarah always thought that Granny sang it when she was feeling homesick. When the song was done, Granny let the silence stretch out. There was only the creak of the rocker and the crackle of the fire.

"Why did you leave your home?" Her voice was small and drowsy. She leaned her small head against Granny's shoulder and fingered a ruffle of flannel on the yoke of Granny's nightgown.

Granny leaned her head against the back of the chair, her eyes turned to the ceiling. When she spoke, her voice was quiet and thick with memory. "There was war coming. We had reason to think that it would come to us. Some of our people chose to stay, but my cousin Eilidh and I were sent away. When the war followed us, we moved again, and I came here."

"Where is Eilidh now?"

"Och, she went back to our home when the war was over." Granny rested her cheek on top of the little girl's head.

With the simple logic of children, the small voice asked, "Why didn't you go home too?"

Mòrag felt Granny's shoulders lift and sag in a long sigh that ruffled her curls. When she spoke, Granny's voice was softer, the words cut short as if she was pushing them out past something in her throat. "It was decided that I should stay here."

"That doesn't sound fair. Why did she get to go home, and you didn't?" Mòrag lifted her head to face her grandmother.

Granny wrapped her arms tighter around little Mòrag and pressed her head back down. "Dinna worry over me, a'lean-abh. This life suits me fine."

The screen door creaked on its hinges and Mòrag thought better of asking more questions. She shifted to look over Granny's shoulder. Granny just kept singing quietly.

Mama came in slowly, moving like she was trying to be quiet. The rocking chair creaked and Mama turned her head sharply. Their eyes met, and Mòrag could almost hear Mama's teeth grinding from across the room. She knew Mama didn't like for Granny to tell her the old stories. Mòrag didn't understand why.

Mama let the screen door swing back with a crack that made Mòrag jump. She took a little more care with the other door and sauntered into the parlor. A sneer marred her once-pretty face. "Fillin' her head with fairy tales again. Hmm?"

"Never ye mind, a Mhàili." Granny's voice was weary.

"Right. Did she tell you about the cauldron again?" Mama asked the little girl. Her dark eyes were wild with fury as she spat out each question. "Did she tell you how it always gave food and never let the people go hungry? Or about the giants?"

"A Mhàili! Ye're scaring the lass," Granny barked, and she was right. Little Mòrag was shaking, clinging to Granny.

Mama kept hammering her with questions. "Did she tell you how the people lived on the hidden island where the sluagh ùr couldn't find them?"

"Molly!"

"Why don't you tell her the truth?" Mama turned her eyes to Granny. Her tone was softer, almost pleading. "Why do you let her think she has a future?"

"A Mhàili…" Granny's voice cracked, and she tried to say more, but the words just wouldn't come out.

***

"Wake up, princess!" The voice was loud and sharp in Sarah's ear. Her eyes flew open and her chest seized. Ryan Cumberland was right there, sitting on her chest like a sneering incubus. "I know what you are. That's why you have to die."

It wasn't possible. Ryan was dead. She had seen him lying in the street with a bullet hole in his forehead. Sarah tried to breath, but she couldn't make her chest rise under his weight. Not real. He could not be real.

He leaned closer, his nose almost touching hers. His breath smelled of stale beer. "Poor Sarah," he said in that same mocking tone he'd used with her the other night. "She just couldn't take the stress."

"Not real!" she screamed in her mind. Her lungs were starting to burn and her head spun. "Slit her wrists," he sneered, leaning even closer. Sarah's vision was going black around the edges. She felt his breath on her lips. "Just. Like. Her. Mother."

***

Then Ryan was gone like a puff of smoke. Sarah was left wide awake and blinking into the dark. She sat up, pulling in a throat-tearing gasp. She was still gulping for air when Dermot burst into the room.

"Are ye alright?" He grabbed her shoulders and searched her face.

Sarah nodded, still stunned. He pulled her tight against him, and she snuggled close, turning her head to rest her ear over his heart. He held her for several minutes. Sarah was content to stay that way, matching her breath to his and listening to his heartbeat steady and sure.

"Was it the dream again?" his voice rumbled under her ear.

"What dream?" she asked without lifting her head.

"The one ye were having in the mountains, when ye couldna breathe. I got the feeling it wasn't the first time ye'd had it." His hand rubbed slow, comforting circles on her back. "That really is why I climbed into bed with ye that night."

"And here all this time I thought you just wanted a cuddle." She pulled back and pushed her hair away from her face. "No, I woke up. At least I think I was awake and saw Ryan. He was lying on top of me. He was so real…I could even smell his breath. Some kind of flashback. Haven't had that happen in a while."

He shifted to sit more firmly on the bed and leaned his back against the wall. Sarah fit herself under his arm, enjoying the solid feel of him. "I knew some blokes in the army who came back from the Gulf War or the Falklands with post-traumatic stress. They had nightmares, sometimes waking flashbacks that seemed so real they attacked people nearby."

"But not you?" she asked softly.

"Not me." There was a hint of regret in his voice. "I was barely there long enough. I got wounded almost as soon as the SCUDS started falling."

"How did you get injured?" She glanced up at him. He had his eyes trained on the open closet across the room. It was dark inside, but Sarah had a feeling it was the darkness of the desert that he was seeing. He had never explained the injury that had ended his army career. It clearly still bothered him.

A cloud of memory gathered in his eyes, but he stayed silent until it passed. "It really wasna all that bad. It was just so frustrating. All that training, there in the war zone, and I got injured in camp."

"When the Iraqis were bombing?" she asked.

"Mmhmm." He grew quiet again, as if lost in the memory.

Sarah was silent for a while, leaving him to his thoughts. "The dream, the one I had in the mountains, was about my mother. It's a recurring one. I can't breathe because I'm in the bathtub." She paused, deciding how specific she should be. "She's holding me under the water, but not like she did that day. It's like she's in the tub with me, whispering to me. She says, 'They can't have you,' and, 'I won't let them take you.' I guess it's meant to be soothing, but there's an edge to her voice, an urgency…I can see the windflowers floating on the surface above us."

He listened silently, his fingers playing with her curls. They were each lost in their own memories. Sarah had a sudden thought that sent a laugh bubbling up from her chest.

Dermot looked down at her as if she'd grown another head. "What's funny?"

"I've traded a nightmare where I can't breathe for a hallucination where I can't breathe," she said, her shoulders shaking with quiet laughter. "I don't know whether that's a step up or a step down."

He chuckled. "I suppose if ye canna laugh…"

"Right," she sighed, mentally finishing the adage, "you'd have to cry."

They stayed there, snuggled together. She was nearly asleep when he spoke again, "Sarah?"

"Mmm?"

"Have ye ever thought about talking to a professional? About the dreams I mean."

She sat up to look at him and smiled. "Oh, I did. Several in fact, when I was an undergrad. Most people in the holler turned to the church for counseling. That wasn't an option for us. I only had the nightmares for the first few months after Mama died. Then they just seemed to go away. But when I went off to college and Granny died, the nightmares started up again. After scaring the bejeezus out of my roommate for three nights in one week, I went to the counselors offered by the student health department. Once word got out about what I'd been through, I got to be something of a curiosity among the mental health professionals of Boone. In some cases, I use the term 'professionals' loosely."

She rolled her eyes and looked down. Her fingers fidgeted with the hem of her nightshirt. "A couple of them wanted me to pray on it. They didn't last long. One of them told me I should go back to where it happened to confront the memories. Of course, I had sold the farm and the house had been torn down, so that wasn't an option. Another put me on antidepressants, but that just made me jittery about everything. It also made the dreams worse. After I stopped taking the pills, the dreams seemed to go away on their own. At least for a while."

His big hand covered hers, and he gave it a gentle squeeze of silent support. She went on, "They seem to come back when I'm anxious about something. They were really bad when I graduated from Appalachian and moved down here, when I was wrapping up my master's thesis, and last summer. Seems like whenever I'm leading up to a big event, I conjure up my own private boogie man, or boogie mama in my case. And now I have a new demon."

He made one of his speaking grunts that might have been confirmation and pulled her back under his arm. "So what do you want to do about it?"

Sarah relaxed into his hold. "Same thing I did in the holler, same thing I always do. Keep breathing. Keep eating. Keep sleeping until I'm strong enough to face it, or it goes away."

"Well," he said, kissing the top of her head, "dinna be afraid to ask for help when ye need it."

Sarah smiled and snuggled closer, once again listening to his heartbeat against her ear.

CHAPTER SIX

Dermot focused on the long stream of coffee gathering in the pot. The huffing noise of the steaming coffee maker drowned out the sound of the shower running down the hall. He braced his hands on the counter and pressed his fingers into the laminate until they hurt. He was not going to think about her lips parting in a sigh as the hot water ran over her skin. He was most definitely not going to imagine her hair, heavy and wet, clinging to the curves of her neck and back and breasts. No, he was going to stand here in the tiny, cramped kitchen and become an absolute expert on the operation of this particular brand of cheap, drip coffee maker.

His neck ached from spending half the night propped against the side of Sarah's bed. After their talk, he'd simply held her. She'd been through so much, and she still managed to be stronger than anyone he knew. Hell, he'd spent more months than he cared to think of feeling sorry for himself over the knee injury that put him out of the army. Here she was, having survived more heartache than most people could imagine, mostly on the strength of her own will. What he wouldn't give for that kind of strength.

In spite of all his instincts telling him not to, he had stayed with Sarah all night. When her breathing had slowed and he was sure she was asleep, he'd lain her down in the bed and covered her with the blanket. He didn't want to leave her in case she had another dream or flashback. After a minute of indecision, he had settled for sitting on the floor next to the bed. He leaned his head against the mattress and drifted in and out of sleep for the rest of the night. At some point he recalled surfacing to feel her fingers threading through his hair and grazing the whorl of his ear. He'd closed his eyes and allowed himself the luxury of enjoying her touch. When he'd opened his eyes again, it was to catch sight of her walking toward the bathroom, the T-shirt she slept in just barely covering the curve of her ass.

The coffee maker sputtered its last, loud puffs of steam, pulling him from his thoughts. He was pouring himself a cup when a quiet knock came at the door. After checking the peephole, Dermot opened the door to Martin Carol, who presented him with the manila folder from the day before. "I have the updated statement for Miss MacAlpin."

"Cheers." Dermot took the folder and stepped back so the other man could come in.

Carol gave him the once-over. Dermot had no doubt he looked a mess after sleeping in his clothes, first on the couch and then the floor. "How is she this morning?"

Dermot rubbed the back of his neck with his hand. "Well, I havena exactly talked to her this morning."

Sarah's voice, raised in a skirling puirt a beul, drifted from the back of the apartment. Both men turned to look down the hall, but the shower was still running and the bathroom door was firmly closed. "But I think she's doing quite well all things considered."

Carol hummed thoughtfully. "I'm sure you know that Mr. Stuart is very concerned about her welfare. He seems to have taken a fancy to her."

"Yes, I know." Dermot wondered just what Carol might be getting at. He generally assumed that no one outside his inner circle knew of James's aspirations. It could make for difficult business dealings if it was common knowledge that the CEO of Alba Petroleum wanted to be king.

"I'm surprised," Carol said, arching an eyebrow in obvious speculation. "I thought starlets and heiresses were more his type."

Dermot shifted uncomfortably. "Well, ye never know. His interest might not be romantic."

"I've been asked to look into her background. That suggests more than a casual interest," Carol said, casting a sideways look down the hall.

"But not necessarily a romantic one." Dermot shifted to block the other man's view of the hallway, deciding he would not offer Carol a cup of coffee. He had to remind himself that this man worked for James.

"Would you be able to answer a few questions about her?" Carol asked.

Dermot grunted. "Miss Lennox said you might have some."

"I can't seem to find any of the expected documents on a Sarah MacAlpin…birth certificate, school transcripts, the like."

"Her given name is Mòrag, Mòrag NicMhàili MacAlpin," Dermot said. "Sarah is just the English name she uses."

"Ah." Carol took out a small notepad and pen from the pocket inside his jacket. "Could you spell that for me?"

Dermot did, glancing over his shoulder to make sure the bathroom door was still closed.

"And do you know the county where she was born or grew up?" Carol didn't look up from his notepad.

"Mitchell." Dermot had learned that when he'd been looking into her background last summer after Walter Stuart had given him a dossier and told him where to find her. Dermot was surprised that Carol didn't seem to have the same information.

"Any family left there?" Carol asked.

Dermot narrowed his eyes at the man. He thought about the policeman who'd shot Ryan Cumberland and had introduced himself as Doug MacDuff. Dermot was almost certain that he was the same MacDuff who had been like a father to Sarah. "No, no family at all."

Carol creased his brow. "None?"

"Her mother died when she was young and her grandmother died a few years ago." He cocked his head to one side. "I'm surprised ye don't know this much already. It's public record."

"Of course I received a brief with the basic information, but with the name difference, it's been difficult to verify." Carol cleared his throat nervously.

The bathroom door opened down the hall, and Dermot glanced back to see Sarah's towel-clad back as she entered her room.

Carol didn't look, but took that as his cue. "That should be enough to go on for now."

"Right, cheers." Dermot watched him as he made a beeline for the door.

***

Sarah walked out of her room to find Dermot absently drinking coffee. "Who was that?"

"Carol. He dropped off the updated file." He handed her the folder that had been dangling from his fingers.

She opened it and scanned the information inside as she strolled to the kitchen. Just as she had asked, Carol had removed every reference to Amy. He had even included a draft of a press release that could be issued if necessary. It came complete with a sticky note listing the circumstances that would make it useful, as well as an admonishment to only use it should the connection with James Stuart come to light. It was sort of an "in case of emergency, break glass" media fire extinguisher. Sarah hoped like hell she wouldn't need it.

Humming to herself, she pulled two slices of bread from the bag on the counter and put them in the toaster.

"Ye're awfully cheerful this morning," Dermot said as he lounged in the doorway. He looked so good all mussed and drowsy, like he'd just rolled out of bed.

She shot him a dazzling smile. "Why shouldn't I be? I've got not one but two handsome men at my beck and call, a billionaire in my back pocket, and I'm in love."

He pushed away from the door frame looking squeamish. "Sarah—"

"Relax," she cut him off with a giggle. She'd known exactly what kind of reaction that last point would get. "I need your help with something."

"What's that?" He looked wary.

"Nothing sordid or even romantic, so take it easy." Sarah shook her head and reached for the peanut butter. "It was something you said to me last night. You reminded me of what one of the therapists said to me about confronting the thing that was causing my nightmares."

"Yeah, ye mentioned that last night."

She nodded. "Of course, by that time I couldn't go home, because I had already sold the farm." Her toast popped up with a clang and they both jumped. Sarah got a plate and retrieved the hot toast with quick, careful fingertips. "So, I was thinking, maybe that's why the nightmares didn't bother me so much before I went to school. When I was younger, I had to live with Mama for months after she tried to kill me. I lived in that house for years after that. I had to face what happened, and it didn't become a problem until I left."

"Which suggests that it was triggered by some other anxiety."

Sarah tipped her head in his direction. "Right. The thing is, the bathtub dream always gets more frequent when something is about to happen, like a move…or my thesis being due. I can't even count how many times I've had it since you showed up."

"Great." He rolled his eyes. "D'ye think it's a coping mechanism, a way for your subconscious to say, 'Remember this awful thing? Whatever ye're afraid of now is nothing.'"

She bobbed her head back and forth in a "maybe" gesture. "Or, and this may sound sick, but it could be that the familiarity of my mother's madness is somehow more comforting than whatever anxiety I have at that moment. Mama is the devil I know."

He gave her a sympathetic look.

"Of course, whenever the thing I'm worried about happens or doesn't, the dreams stop." She lifted the knife as if demonstrating a point.

"When was the last time ye had the bathtub dream?" he asked.

She shrugged. "I'm not entirely sure. So much has happened, but I haven't had it since Ryan attacked me."

"That fits yer theory then."

She smiled at him. "Exactly."

"So, what is it ye want to confront?" His eyebrows creased in concern.

"You might not like it. I was hoping that if I confront what happened with Ryan, I would at least silence that particular boogie man…for now." Sarah finished preparing her toast and turned to him. "Have breakfast with me?"

He shrugged. "Sure."

"No, I mean at the table. I can't let memories of the other night chase me out of my home, and I don't want them to follow me. I want to take back my apartment before I leave."

He studied her for several seconds. Sarah could see the wheels turning in his head. She wondered if this would be as hard for him as it would be for her. "Alright. Can ye make me some of that toast?"

CHAPTER SEVEN

Breakfast and coffee in hand, they went to the dining area. Dermot pulled out a chair at the head of the table, but Sarah interrupted him, "No, I think we need to sit in the same places that we were sitting in the other night."

He nodded and moved to the correct seat. He cast a long look at the room behind him before he turned to face her. Sarah could tell he was uneasy with his back to the room, even when there was no one else there.

"I know," she said softly as he turned back to her.

They held each other's gaze across the table as they both pulled out their chairs and sat down slowly. Ignoring the first prickle of tension that tripped like icy fingers across her shoulders, Sarah lifted her coffee cup and took a deliberate sip. It was hot, rich, and comforting. She inhaled and focused on relaxing her back as she exhaled. She forced herself to lean against the back of her chair, something she couldn't have done the other night when Ryan Cumberland had tied her hands behind her back and held a gun to her head.

Just as her shoulders touched the chair back, she could have sworn she felt a breath on her ear. Before she could panic or hear his voice in her head, she sprang upright again. She quickly picked up her toast and took a bite. She hoped that would keep Dermot from seeing how nervous she was—and that the crunching would drown out Ryan's voice in her head.

She hadn't counted on the peanut butter sticking her mouth closed. Her breath caught and she struggled to swallow.

"There's no one behind ye," Dermot reassured her as she coughed.

Sarah washed the toast down with a gulp of coffee. "I know that in my head, but I still have that cold, twitchy feeling like he's standing right there."

"I expect it'll be a while before that goes away." His smile was gentle. "Take another deep breath."

She inhaled slowly through her nose and blew out a long, slow breath. She settled herself more firmly in the chair and forced herself to lean back. There it was again, the hot breath on her ear.

"*Poor Sarah,*" the voice hissed. She closed her eyes tight, willing him away, but that only made the specter of Ryan Cumberland more solid, more alive.

Her eyes popped open and met Dermot's comforting blue gaze. "I think…I think, I should talk about what I remember. I never did that about Mama, not until I'd left home. Maybe that'll be the difference."

"Alright."

"He…" the words caught in her throat and she reached for her mug again, "he was going to slit my wrists in the bathtub, make it look like suicide."

"*Poor Sarah. I guess she just couldn't take it anymore.*" Ryan's voice was like a fly buzzing in her ear.

"Ach, love." Dermot reached a hand across the table.

"I need to do this," Sarah said, shaking her head and not taking his offered hand. "I told him no one would believe that, told him I almost drowned when I was little. I had just convinced him when you banged on the door."

Her chest tightened with the same emotions she'd felt that night, that powerful mixture of relief at not being alone and terror at what Ryan might do to Dermot. *"One sound out of you and he bites it."*

"I was so glad to hear your voice, but I was so afraid for you." She leaned forward and laid her hand on his. He turned his hand and gripped hers. Sarah blinked back tears. "I don't know what I would have done if you'd been hurt."

"The game is up, Sinclair. You might as well confess," came the voice from behind her. The words hit Sarah like a kick to the chest. She leaned back, pulling away, leaving Dermot's hand empty on the table. For several heartbeats her breath fluttered like a candle flame as she remembered Ryan's declaration. *"He's as big a liar as I am. James Stuart hired him to come here and watch you…He's your bodyguard."*

When she found her voice again it was little more than a whimper. "I…I think I need to hear you say it."

Dermot pulled his hand away and squared his shoulders. "Say what?"

"Oh princess, you really don't know do you? Stuart is going to own it all. But you…you're going to make him a king." Sarah felt the barrel of the gun drilling into her temple. *"Tell her right now, or I'll shoot…Look her in the eyes and tell her you're not her friend, you're her keeper."*

"You know what," she whispered as she felt a tear track down her cheek.

Dermot squirmed in his seat. Sarah held her breath, watching him and waiting. Seconds ticked by in grinding silence.

That night, he'd kept his voice even. This time it was pained. His accent was thick with emotion, but he didn't falter as he said, "I am yer keeper. Ye're a princess, and James sent me here to protect ye."

She drew in a long breath as if she were drawing the words inside her, tasting them, testing their truth against what she knew. She had dismissed them before. She was less sure now.

Then she remembered Dermot's next words: "*Na bith eagail ort. Cuir earbs' annam.*" Don't be afraid. Trust me. Trust him when he'd been lying to her for months. But she had trusted him that night. When he'd made his move, she had run just as he'd meant her to. Dermot hadn't been able to stop Ryan, but in the street he'd been in a much more vulnerable position. Without the cover of the apartment, she'd had a chance.

Later, she'd trusted him with her secrets, with her heart, and in a matter of hours he'd broken it. Sarah closed her eyes and felt the soul-deep pain of the other morning. Dermot had proved Ryan right. "*He's not your friend. He's your keeper.*"

Sarah shot out of her chair, almost knocking it into the wall behind her. "I think that's enough for now."

He rose and started to come around the table to her, but she shied away from him. "Are ye alright?"

She held up a hand to stave him off. "I'm fine. Really."

"Ye're sure?" At her nod, he stepped back. "D'ye think it helped?"

She wrapped her arms around herself and gave him a steely look. "I think it clarified some things."

He frowned, eyebrows drawing together. "Right."

"I think I should do it again. Probably a few times, but that's good for today. Let's take our breakfast over there and talk about something else." She waved in the direction of the couch.

"Yeah…" He wavered, looking like he wanted to say more, but then turned and picked up his coffee and breakfast. He followed Sarah to the sitting area and sat down. By the time he'd settled into his chair, Sarah was sitting cross-legged with her plate beside her and her mug balanced on one knee.

She smiled at him, though it didn't quite reach her eyes. "So what's your plan for today?"

He sighed heavily. "I need to make some progress on packing up my flat."

"Mmm." She nodded. "When do you leave again?"

"I've been meaning to talk to you about that." He slid forward in the chair and rested his elbows on his knees. Giving her an earnest look, he said, "I'm scheduled to leave Thursday morning, but I can stay if…well, if you want me to."

She wasn't sure what she wanted. In the short months they had known each other, he had by turns charmed, frustrated, and supported her. She had come to depend on him. She loved him, and she had believed him when he'd said that he loved her—until he'd told her why they couldn't be together.

She had trusted him with things that she'd only ever told to Amy, Barrett, or a professional therapist. And he had told her exactly what she needed to hear. Had that been real, or was it another manipulation? In spite of everything, she still felt drawn to him, connected at a bone deep level. After the trauma of the other night, she was afraid to let him out of her sight, but every time she looked at him it hurt.

Sarah didn't know if she wanted him to stay or go, but she did know that the constant push-pull of being near him was exhausting at a time when she needed all the resources she could muster. Would she feel differently if she had some space, some relief from the tension? Could she feel safe without him nearby? "Who would be minding the king's business if you left?"

"That's not fair." He looked at her sharply.

Sarah arched an eyebrow at him. "I really don't think you want me to start listing the things about this situation that aren't fair."

Dermot pressed his lips together and set his mug on the coffee table. "Fleming would stay. He can move in here and be with you twenty-four/seven so you won't have to be alone."

"And if I do want to be alone?" Sarah asked.

The look he gave her was almost fatherly. "D'ye think that's a good idea?"

"I don't know," Sarah said, bristling. "But I don't much like the idea of trading one prison for another."

He massaged the back of his neck with one hand as he ground out, "Ye're not a prisoner."

"Really?" She stood and stalked around the coffee table. Turning back to him, she said, "And what would happen if I just picked up and left without a word to anyone?"

He shifted his shoulders as if he was squaring up for a fight before saying in a carefully even tone, "James would find ye."

"And what would have happened if I hadn't wanted the fellowship in Scotland? What if my application hadn't been good enough?" She took a step closer to him. She knew his temper. It felt a little like poking a bear.

"James would have found another way to get ye there, or he would have approached ye here." She could see the muscles flexing in his jaw. He didn't like her questions.

"Mmhmm." She picked up her mug from the table and headed for the kitchen. If she didn't get out of there, this was only going to escalate until they were verbally shredding each other.

She was passing him when he sprang from the chair, clearly at the end of his patience. "Look, I ken well enough how it seems, but no one wants ye to feel like ye're being forced into anything."

She put her dishes down on the dining table and spun on him. Her own temper was almost at its limit. "How on Earth could I feel any other way?"

He took a step toward her. His face looked thunderous. He held out his arms bent at the elbows and hands straight as blades and parallel. Sarah couldn't help thinking he looked like he was measuring the exact size of the box they were trying to put her in. "Ye know, if ye could for one second stop focusing on the negative, ye might see this as a real opportunity. Think about all the good ye could do with his money."

"Do you really think I'm that mercenary?"

"Of course not," he snapped. "But you could make such a difference. Look at Princess Diana."

"I don't want a life like that, always being photographed and prodded here and there. No, thank you!" The very idea had the muscles in her shoulders knotting with tension. She had to get out of this. "And I've been making my own opportunities for a while now. It might take me a bit longer, but I think I can get where I want to go without his help."

She stalked back to the bedroom and slammed the door just as the phone rang.

***

"What?" Dermot barked into the phone as he glared down the hall at Sarah's closed door.

"Am I interrupting something?" came the smooth cultured voice of James Stuart. Speak of the bloody devil.

Dermot huffed in frustration. "With Sarah around? Always. The woman never stops."

"Well, let's hope she brings us some of that boundless energy." Dermot could hear the grin in James's voice, and there was very little in the world that could have irritated him more at that moment than James Stuart taking Sarah for granted. When he didn't respond, James sobered and said, "It sounds like she's taking it all in stride. Is she truly doing well?"

Dermot ran a hand through his hair and sighed. "Better than most would. She's already back researching her paper."

"That's a good sign, right? Then you'll be coming back on schedule?"

Dermot massaged the back of his neck. "I'm not sure. I'm not convinced she doesna need me here."

"Mmm." There was a note of skepticism in James's voice. "Naturally, we want her to be comfortable, but I have important work for you here."

"I thought taking care of Sarah was my priority." Dermot could hear a sharp edge creeping into his tone.

"It is of course, and you're doing a fine job." James's sarcasm couldn't be missed.

"Don't you start, cousin," Dermot's voice cut like cold steel. "If you lot had told me about Bridget MacKenzie earlier, Cumberland never would have gotten that close."

James's tone was cool, unflappable. "And if you had asked for that background check earlier, we'd have known he was a problem much sooner."

Dermot had nothing to counter that. There had been failures of communication all around, and the result had almost cost Sarah her life. He growled in frustration.

James continued, "Part of taking care of Sarah is paving the way for her here. I need you to set up the security for your building, and I'm sure you have some work to do with the research team."

"I do, and I would hate for us to get behind schedule." He looked down the hall at her closed door. "Still, I'm not sure I can leave her."

"What does she think?" That was a first: James asking for Sarah's opinion…or anyone besides Walter Stuart's for that matter.

"I don't think she knows. She doesn't like to admit when she needs help." He thought back to this morning's session at the table. "And I'm not sure I can offer the kind of help she needs."

"Well, you'll need to figure it out soon, so that we can send back-up for Fleming." At least Dermot knew that Alba Petroleum had a security department big enough to spare a man or two to replace him if he did go home.

"Right. I will," Dermot said through his teeth.

"Did Martin Carol get things all sorted?" James asked, moving on.

"He did," Dermot confirmed. "He said you asked him to look into her. Didn't we already do that?"

"Only to verify that she is the one we were looking for. Now we need to make sure we know of any potential skeletons in her closet. Eventually, her role will be a public one. We can't have any unfortunate surprises."

Here was Lord Caledon, the politician. Of all the faces of James, this was the one that Dermot was the least comfortable with. He could at least respect when his childhood friend was being a ruthless CEO, but politician James was always working an angle, keeping up appearances and triangulating positions. It made Dermot want to take a very hot shower. "Wouldn't it be better just to ask her?"

"I'm sure it would, but you said yourself she's not ready for that yet. We're merely trying to be prepared."

Which sounded reasonable when he put it that way. Still, Dermot couldn't help feeling a bit like a sneak.

"Aye well, if she sees him gadding about town when she thinks his work is done, she'll figure out someone's hiding something." Dermot could just imagine Sarah's reaction to knowing that Carol was vetting her. "She's got a suspicious nature to begin with. After everything that's happened, she's on high alert."

"Of course she is, which is why Carol has instructions to keep a low profile."

Dermot hated feeling like he was being handled. He was starting to understand Sarah's aversion to it.

"Your concern for her is commendable, but you're not the only one looking out for her," James said.

"Right, but I'm the devil she knows." He stopped for a breath before he raised his voice. "She's not just going to trust someone new because you say she can. And she doesna want to feel like a prisoner."

"Fleming will still be there, and you've said she trusts him. We can manage it." James's tone put a stamp on that topic. Discussion over. "Now, may I speak with Sarah?"

No. Not now. Dermot quickly thought of an excuse. "Em…no. She's in the shower just now."

"Ah, well then carry on." James's disappointment came through loud and clear.

It meant nothing, but Dermot enjoyed feeling that little bit of control over the situation, even if it was only for a moment. He responded with a satisfied, "Mmph."

"And Dermot?"

"Yeah."

"I'll be expecting you in my office Monday morning."

So much for that little moment of control. James rang off, leaving Dermot back where he'd been when the conversation began: staring down the hall at Sarah's closed door.

CHAPTER EIGHT

Sarah paced back and forth in her room, frustrated. She was getting seriously tired of Dermot's refrain of, "You're in danger and we're the only way out." For all she knew, James had sent Ryan after her to trick her into whatever his crazy plan was. A few months ago, she had been like any other grad student, working like crazy and paying precious little attention to her social life. She really just wanted to finish school and get a nice job teaching at a university, publishing the occasional paper, maybe making a couple of documentaries. She just wanted a nice, quiet nerdy life. Was that really so much to ask?

Now here she was with bodyguards and billionaires. And the man she thought she loved, who could have been up for spending that quiet academic life with her, was telling her that dream was over. She had cried her eyes raw on Friday when Dermot had told her why they couldn't be together. She had raged her way to a spotless apartment, and then tried to distract herself with more research. The situation wasn't changing, and she was running out of ideas for getting her life back on track. Now she was just left wondering why. Why her?

On one of her passes across the room, the paper bag containing her mother's journal caught her eye. It was on the corner of the dresser, right where she had put it after Duff gave it to her the other day. She hadn't planned to read it. No doubt it was full of her mother's teenage dreams and disappointments. She didn't need to read that Mama had had a crush on Russ

Corbett or anybody else from Kettle Holler. Worse, it probably contained mad ramblings about whatever it was that made Mama go crazy, or what had sent her life careening off the rails like Sarah's seemed to be. It was probably full of how much she hated being saddled with a baby when she should have been enjoying her youth.

Looking at the bag lying amid the clutter of her dresser, something flashed in Sarah's memory: her mother sitting at the small desk in her room with her back to the open door, head and shoulders bent over something. At six, Sarah knew what it looked like when someone was focused on writing. She did the same thing when she was writing at school. Mama must have been writing something. She had knocked on the door timidly.

Mama's head popped up and she turned to look at Sarah over her shoulder. Her eyes were hard and she looked angry. She rose and stalked forward. Sarah took a couple of quick steps back. Mama slammed the door in her face. Maybe Mama hadn't been a teenager when she wrote this.

Her hand hovered over the bag, hesitant, as if opening it would open up the mental doors she had tried to keep shut for so long, a Pandora's Box of emotional scars that were better left locked away. With trembling fingers, she unrolled the top of the bag and pulled out the journal. Its leather binding showed less wear than you would expect from a book made in the Sixties. Sarah opened the cover and flipped to the first page.

Mama gave me this book when I left home years ago, but I was too young and busy then to write things down. I know now that I won't be around to tell you these things when you're old enough to hear them. So I reckon Mama knew what she was about back then. She still does most of the time even if we don't always agree. So. I'll use this book she gave me to tell you why I can't be there.

There is something broken inside me, baby, something I've been trying to fix for years. It's like I fell into a hole somewhere along the way. Every time I think I've licked it, every time I think I might find a way to climb out, I just tumble right back to the bottom. For my own sake, I could find a way to live down here, but it ain't about me anymore.

I'm afraid, baby, that the same thing that happened to me is going to happen to you. I can already see it, and you can too. You told me so yourself that day in the bathtub. I hope someday you can come to forgive me for that day and all the days after. I don't want to hurt you, but sometimes I just think it would be better if you were spared the kind of heartache that I've seen.

If I can't stop it for you, then I'll have to stop for myself. I can't sit by and watch you be robbed of the life you want like I was. You are the most precious thing in this world to me and I would rather die than watch you sink into the same hole that I'm living in. That's why I have to leave you. It's the only way I can protect you. I hope that after you read this, you can forgive your poor, broken mother.

Sarah's scalp tingled and the hairs stood up on her arms. She quickly flipped through the rest of the pages checking how much her mother had written. The book was almost completely full of her mother's neat looping script. In some parts, the curves stretched vertically and the angles got sharper, as if Mama had been writing faster. Some pages were tidy and clear, and some pages had writing around the edges and in the margins. But almost every page was full, and none of them were dated.

This wasn't a journal. It was some kind of memoir or one insanely long suicide note, and it might just contain some of the answers she was looking for.

**

Dermot went to the door and stood there with his head cocked, listening. Sarah had been in there for the better part of an hour, no doubt fuming about their argument. All that came from the other side of the door was silence punctuated by the occasional sniff and what sounded like pages being shuffled. He wondered if she knew that nothing brought him low like her silence. He could dry tears, soothe rage, and calm fears, but silence left him nothing to work with. Silence gave him time and space to examine his own role in this hijacking of her life.

He leaned a shoulder against the frame and rapped on the door with a knuckle. He waited, but there was no answer. "Sarah?"

Nothing.

"I'm sorry. I hate this. I hate what this is doing to ye. If I thought even for a second that I could get all of them to leave ye alone, I would do it. I'd take back every minute of the last six months." He felt the unaccustomed sting of tears building in his eyes. He leaned his forehead against the door.

After the silence stretched on, he said, "I tried, ye know. Last June, after I kissed ye that first time. That's why I left. I called James with the taste of ye still on my lips, and I told him they were wrong, that ye weren't the one. But then ye went to Cape Breton and ye saw Isobel MacKenzie. She knew ye for what ye are. She told them, and they sent me back. Ye have to believe, I didna want this."

He trailed off, not trusting his voice, not knowing what more there was to say. For all he knew she was asleep on the other side of that door…or she was beyond his reach now. He had nearly given up hope when he heard the faintest creak of the knob turning. He lifted his head as the door cracked open.

Sarah peered up at him, her eyes shining like peridot and swimming with tears. Without a word, she slipped out of her room and into his arms. She pressed her face against his chest and wrapped her arms tight around him.

He held her close, bending to rest his cheek on top of her head. They stood that way for several minutes, just breathing in each other's arms. There was no more conflict, no more tension, just comfort. Dermot thought that if this was all he could have of her for the rest of their lives, he'd take it.

"I think you should go," she said softly, her ear still resting over his heart.

He wondered if she could hear it break. Did it sound like glass cracking or just a stutter in its usual rhythm? "Hmm?"

She still clung to him, as if she was afraid to look at him when she said, "On Thursday. I think you should go home, like you planned."

He cleared his throat, hoping to get past the sudden tight feeling. "Are ye sure?"

He felt her nod and closed his eyes tight.

"I know you have work to do there, and I have some things I need to finish up here," she said. "It's better if we get on with them."

"I see." He didn't.

"And," she paused, "I think a little distance will help us get used to the way things are now. We...we need to find our feet again. And I think we need to do that separately."

It made sense. Of course, it did. That didn't make it hurt any less. He tightened his arms around her. "If that's what ye want."

"It's what I think is best." She didn't pull away or loosen her grip, as if her arms disagreed with what her mouth was saying.

"Right." He cleared his throat and tried not to sound like he'd just been carved up. "Then I reckon I'd better get packing."

She nodded again. "Okay. I've got some reading to do. But first I'm going to take care of the dishes."

"Go on." He kissed the top of her head before letting her go. "I'll be there in a tic."

Sarah dropped her arms and went to gather the breakfast dishes. Dermot braced his hands on either side of the door frame for support. He took several labored breaths, trying to gain control. Trying to fill the hollow space where his heart had been.

CHAPTER NINE

From Molly MacAlpin's Journal

You'll learn that this story goes back a long time, but my part of it started in the spring of 1968. I was seventeen years old and America was at war. There was the war in Vietnam, and a culture war at home. In the mountains, the government was fighting a war on poverty, and in Kettle Holler poverty seemed to be winning. You would think all this conflict might bring a person down, but I was near to graduating high school and full of expectations.

One day Russell Corbett dropped me off at the end of our road. I was never too keen on Russ, but he had his own car and that made him a good person to know. I got our mail out of the mailbox and there was one of those Airmail envelopes in it with the edges striped like a peppermint. The return address said it was from Scotland. I knew Mama missed her home, but we hadn't ever gotten anything from there before. I hoped this wasn't bad news.

I set off up the road walking fast. I was curious and a little worried. I caught up with Mama in the back yard hanging up the laundry. I held out the letter to her, and she just looked at it for the longest time, like she thought it might bite.

"Well, don't you want to know what it says?" I asked.

She finished pinning up a dress and dried her hands on her apron before taking the letter. She slid a long finger under the corner and tore open the top of the envelope. She pulled out a letter written on thin paper and another smaller sheet. I could see the writing through the back of the paper, and I watched the blood drain from Mama's face as she read it.

"Is it bad news?" If she heard me, she didn't show any sign. "Mama?"

"Hmm?" She looked up at me like she'd forgotten I was there. "No, my cousin Eilidh had invited ye to visit."

"In Scotland?"

"Aye. Our village is having a sort of celebration, like a festival for the young people, and they would like you to be a part of it." Mama put the letter in the pocket of her apron and went back to hanging the laundry. She shook out a shirt with more snap than usual.

"When?"

She pushed the pin down over the shirt and clothesline sharply. Her answer was short, "In June, midsummer. Ye'll need to go as soon as ye're out of school to make it in time."

"Me? What about you, you're going too, aren't you?"

She shook her head, but didn't look at me. "They've only bought the one ticket, besides there's too much to be done here for me to be haring off to the Highlands on a lark. Someone's got to tend the farm and malt the barley."

I couldn't believe what I was hearing. "But you've wanted to go home forever."

She finally met my eyes and hers were so full of heartbreak, it made any other argument clog up in my throat. "This is my home now."

I tried to talk to her about it time and again over the next few weeks, but she wouldn't have it. She made arrangements for me to go. They had sent a voucher for a ticket from New

York City to Glasgow. But we had to get me to New York, and then there was the issue of a girl my age traveling alone.

"Why do I need an escort? I'll be eighteen," I said to her one night after dinner.

"Because it's not safe for a lass of yer age to go traveling that far alone," she said over her shoulder without taking her hands from the dishwater.

"Why can't you escort me? I know you want to go."

"I'm nae goin, and ye'll be safer with a man along." Her voice got sharper.

"But if I don't know him, how is that safer?" It didn't make sense.

"He'll be someone we can trust. I'll make sure of it."

And that was the end of that conversation. She wouldn't hear another word about it. It was near the end of school that my dance teacher, you might remember Ms. Silvie Anders, she was still teaching when you were a little girl. I should have taken you to her. Well, Ms. Silvie was a Rockette, and she heard about an audition in New York that she thought I should try for. It was in August. So I asked Mama if she thought I would be back from Scotland in time for that audition. She wouldn't ever give me an answer. It was always some dodge, "Ye dinna know what ye'll want to do when ye get back," or, "Things change, lass." I just thought she didn't want me moving away to New York, or she didn't think I was good enough and didn't want me to be disappointed. I should have known something was up.

***

The ride to Boone was long, bumpy, and mostly silent. I had graduated from high school the day before. I barely had time to catch my breath. My friends who could find jobs would be starting work soon. Russ Corbett and some of the other boys had joined the army and were heading off to basic training. A couple of my classmates were planning to go to college, but for most of us that was just a dream. My dream was another story, and as I watched the cloud of dust settle in the road behind Mama's old rattle-trap pickup, I couldn't help thinking that I never wanted to see Kettle Holler again.

Mama seemed lost in her thoughts. I know I was lost in mine. So we were content to ride along, Mama driving and me watching the hills and hollers roll by outside the window. I remember resting my elbow on the sill and letting my hand move with the wind, skimming the tops of the mountains on the horizon. When we got to the bus station, she helped me get my suitcase out of the back of the truck. We went to the ticket counter and bought a ticket for the 2:15 bus to Raleigh, then went over to the chairs to wait.

I have to admit, for all that I was looking forward to leaving, I was nervous as all get-out. I'd never traveled by myself, not this far from home anyways. I'd been as far as Asheville, but that was with Ms. Silvie and some of the other girls. This was a whole other kettle of fish. I sat in my blue cotton travelling dress and folded my hands on top of my shoulder bag in my lap. Mama sat beside me fishing in the patchwork sack she used as a purse. The more time passed, the more fidgety she got.

Finally, she started to talk as she kept digging. "Now, ye mind yer Aunt Eilidh. She can be a bit hard, but she means well and she's family."

"Okay, Mama."

"And dinna be tarrying in the city too long. Ye're expected to be there by midsummer." She jabbed a finger at me to make her point.

"I won't."

"Now yer escort will meet ye in Raleigh as he's coming from Jacksonville. He'll be taking ye all the way to Làrachd an Fhamhair."

"I'm sure it'll be fine, Mama." We had gone over all of this before, but I knew she was going to miss me and worry until she heard I was there safely. I know it seems like your Granny doesn't worry about much, but she does. She hides it well most times. That day was not most times, and when the announcement came for my bus, I thought she was going to jump out of her skin.

"Och. That's it then." She stood, looking from me to the door and back to me.

"That's it." I stood and bent to get my suitcase.

"Dinna forget the ham biscuits." She handed me a paper sack that she'd been carrying. Then she pulled this book out of her bag. "I got this diary for ye. I…I thought ye might use it to write down the things ye see…and yer feelings."

"My feelings?" Mama and I didn't generally talk about feelings, unless you count tired or hungry as feelings. I'm sure you know, when you live like we do there ain't much room for going on about feelings. We've always been more worried about getting food on the table and clothes on our backs than talking about how we felt about it. Maybe we should have talked about those things more.

"Just take it. If ye need to talk to someone and I can't be there, maybe this'll help ye." She shoved the book at me. I took it and put it into my purse.

"*Tha gaol agam ort, mo chridhe,*" Mama switched to Gaelic to say she loved me as if we were at home. She usually spoke English when she was in public. People in the hills get testy when they can't understand you. I'm sure you know that from experience.

"*Tha goal agam orbh, a Mhami.*" I dropped my suitcase and hugged her. It might be hard for you to believe with all the fighting we used to do, but I did love her. I was going to miss her. I still didn't understand why she couldn't go with me. "*Beanachd leibh.*"

"*Mar sin leat.*" She looked as though she wanted to say more than just good-bye, but another call went out for the 2:15 passengers. I would have waited, but she patted my arm and pushed me toward the door. "*Mar sin leat, a nighean.*"

I went through the doors and handed my suitcase to the porter and turned to climb onto the bus. On the bottom step, I looked back into the terminal. Mama was still there, but her head was hanging down. She looked so alone, I almost decided to forget the trip and go home to the holler.

She turned away and started walking to the doors that led out to the street. With every step, her shoulders got a bit straighter and her head a bit higher. By the time she hit the street, she was the same straight-backed, hard-working woman that everyone knows. She was alone, but she had been alone for as long as I or anyone else could remember. Back then, I thought she was hard. Now I wish I had just an ounce of her strength.

***

I met Grant MacDuff at the bus station in Raleigh, and right away I wished I hadn't. He wasn't the same man then that you know. It was late at night and I was achy from sitting on the bus for hours. The bus I caught in Boone had blown a tire somewhere around Hickory, and I had spent about an hour sitting on a grass bank on the side of the road waiting for a tire change. I was tired and hot and sure I had missed the train I was supposed to take to New York.

I had no idea what he looked like. I only knew his name and that he was a U.S. Marine from Jacksonville. I collected my suitcase from the porter and went inside. There were only a few people in the terminal waiting for their buses. I didn't see him when I walked in. I stood there looking around. I don't know where he came from, or where he was waiting for me, but he just appeared at my elbow. "You Molly MacAlpin?"

"Yes, are you Grant MacDuff?" He looked like something out of a spaghetti western with his cowboy hat and worn jeans. He had that hard, squinty-eyed look like Clint Eastwood, and it made me wonder if I should go with him. The only thing that broke the image were the combat boots he wore. I reckoned he wasn't much older than me, but his tanned skin and deliberate movements made him seem more mature.

He nodded once, pulled my suitcase from my grasp and started walking toward the door. "Come on."

I followed him out to the street where an old Mercury was waiting with another man in the driver's seat. "This the girl we've been waiting for?"

"Mmmhmm," said my escort as he held the back door open for me. I hesitated for a second. "What are you waiting for, an engraved invitation?"

What else was I going to do? I slid into the back seat of the Mercury. Duff put my suitcase in the trunk before getting into the passenger seat.

"Alright, train station, here we come," the driver said with some enthusiasm. A little part of me wished he could be my escort. He certainly didn't seem to be in as foul a mood.

Within a few minutes we pulled up in front of the boxy gray train station. Duff retrieved my suitcase from the trunk and opened the door for me. Then he leaned back into the front seat and shook hands with the driver. "Thanks, Len."

"No sweat, man. And, hey," the driver cast a look my way and I pretended not to be listening while he whispered, "go easy on the girl. It ain't her fault."

Duff grunted and closed the door. I watched as the only friendly face I'd seen since the holler drove off into the night.

Duff picked up our bags and jerked his head toward the door. I followed him inside to the ticket counter. Sure enough, that flat tire had caused us to miss that train to New York. There was another one leaving at eight o'clock the next morning. I turned around as Duff changed our tickets and surveyed the inside of the train station. The waiting area was filled with rows of tall wooden benches that looked a little like church pews, empty at that hour. Next to the ticket counter was a news stand that was closed. But in between was a Coca-Cola machine. It was one of those that has the bottles lined up in a column behind the glass door. I dug out my change purse and started counting out change.

Because your Granny taught me that you catch more flies with honey, I put in thirty cents and pulled out two Coca-Colas. Duff carried our bags over to the benches. I used the bottle opener mounted on the side of the machine to pop the caps off. Then I took the bottles over to where he sat and held one out to Duff. He looked surprised for a second before taking it with a quiet, "Thanks."

"Anytime." I moved my suitcase in front of the bench, then I sat down and put my feet up on it like a stool. I was beat, but it felt so good to stretch my legs. I wasn't looking forward to the long train ride. We sat there drinking our soda pops in silence. I was starting to nod off when I heard his stomach growl. I reached into my purse and pulled out the sack of ham biscuits Mama had given me. I had barely eaten anything all day for nerves. I was still more tired than hungry, but there was no reason to let him go hungry when I had food. I held out one of the wax paper wrapped biscuits to him. "Ham biscuit?"

He looked at it, doubtful.

"It's homemade. My Mama sent me this whole bag, but I'll never eat them all." I smiled at him, trying to be friendly.

He didn't smile back, but nodded and said, "If you're not going to eat 'em."

I smiled even bigger. I kept the biscuit in my hand and gave him the bag with the rest of them. "Here you go."

He looked at the bag, then back at me. I unwrapped mine and took a bite full of salty ham and Mama's buttery biscuit. It tasted like home, and for a second made me so homesick I could barely swallow. Duff unwrapped a biscuit for himself. We sat there in the silent train station eating our biscuits and washing them down with Coca-Cola.

CHAPTER TEN

December 12, 1995
Chapel Hill, North Carolina

Greenlaw Hall had been teeming with students and humming with conversation punctuated by the slamming of stairwell doors just weeks before. Now the halls were dim and empty. Even the smallest sound echoed.

Sarah waved toward the corner of the fourth floor hallway. "Just stand over there. The less explaining I have to do, the better."

"Alright, give a shout if ye need me." Fleming waved over his shoulder as he walked away.

Sarah gave him a second to get around the corner before knocking on the door of Donald Campbell, her academic adviser and friend.

"Sarah!" Donald's round, freckled face lit up when he spotted her through the window in his office door. "Och, I'm that glad to see ye. I've tried calling a couple of times, but yer machine seems to be full."

"Yeah." Sarah stepped inside and pulled off her jacket. "I've been getting calls from local reporters about the incident. I'm trying to screen them, but the machine fills up pretty fast. I should have called you. I'm sorry."

"Never mind that. How are ye?" The look he gave her was filled with concern.

"I'm doing pretty well, all things considered. Trying to get things back to normal, or as much as they can be while getting ready to move."

"It might not be a bad thing that ye're leaving." He gave her a fatherly nod. "A change of scene might make it easier to get on with things."

"I think you're right." Naturally, she didn't mention that she wasn't sure she was going to Scotland anymore. "In the meantime, I've been trying to wrap up some research before I go, and I wanted to ask you some questions."

"Shoot," he said with an inviting wave as he made his way around the desk piled high with papers.

"I was actually wondering about the occurrences of three witches in Gaelic songs and legends. I had a bit of an epiphany the other day about the witches in Macbeth, and ever since, I've been looking for correlations between Shakespeare's play and the appearance of trios of women in songs and legends."

He pursed his lips in thought. "Well, I imagine ye've found more than a few."

"I have, but none that are quite like what's in the play. I'm sure Shakespeare took some license, but I was hoping to find a more obvious correlation."

"Why this sudden interest in the Weird Sisters? I thought 'The River Maiden' was the crux of yer argument." Donald shifted a stack of papers on his cluttered desk to see her as he returned to his seat.

Sarah sighed. "Well, as it turns out, I recently discovered that two of my sources knew each other."

"Ach. Let me guess...yer Granny and Alex Budge? I canna say that's a great surprise."

"Actually, no. I mean they knew of each other, but I don't think they ever met. No, I was going through some of my grandmother's things and I found a picture of Granny arm in arm with Isobel MacKenzie."

Donald's russet brows drew together in confusion. "The woman from Cape Breton? Are ye sure?"

Sarah nodded. "I recognized the scenery in the picture as being near Isobel's house. One of the women appears to be blind, and the other is definitely my grandmother."

"Mmm, that does complicate things." Donald cocked his head and appeared deep in thought for several seconds. "Although I dinna think it makes the song completely useless."

Sarah shook her head. She had gotten over the initial panic about her dissertation, but she was still trying to find a new angle. "No, but I'd like to bolster it with some additional comparisons. I was following this trail to see if it led me to something useful."

He leaned forward, resting his forearms on the desk between them. "Just what about Shakespeare's witches caught yer attention?"

"Well, you know Shakespeare liked to borrow plots from other sources." When he nodded agreement, Sarah pulled her pocket copy of Macbeth out of her bag and opened it to act I, scene 3. "I've marked the passages that I thought sounded like he lifted them from traditional songs."

Donald took the book from her and began to scan down the lines. "Ye're right. Some of this does sound very traditional."

Sarah nodded, waiting. She'd been working with Donald long enough to trust that he would follow her train of thought.

"This bit here," he said, tipping the book toward her and pointing a finger to some lines toward the bottom of the page,

"'Thrice to thine, and thrice to mine, and thrice again to make up nine.' That's verra familiar to me. And then, 'The charm's wound up.' Wound up…wound up like a string. Like the three Fates…"

Sarah listened patiently.

"Have ye thought about expanding yer search beyond songs?" He eyed her over the rim of his glasses, which had slid down his nose as he was reading.

"I hadn't really. What are you thinking?"

"Well, they're witches, yeah? So ye might want to look at some charms." He gave her a look that said she should have thought of that.

"Gaelic charms?"

He lifted the fingers of the hand that had been skimming the page and waved them about as he explained. "They fell out of use with many other superstitions, but they were fairly common for a time. A person who needed a bit of extra reassurance about something would pay a wise woman for a charm. There are charms for different health conditions, safe journeys, warding off the evil eye. It was usually some lines of poetic invocation written on a piece of paper and tucked under someone's pillow or rolled up and sewn into their clothes. That's why the line of being wound up sticks in my mind." He thought for several seconds, looking down to the page. "The bit about thrice and thrice and thrice again sounds like it might come from a charm. They're always talking about threes and nines."

"Is there a record of those kinds of charms being used in the New World?"

"There's better than that." A broad grin spread across Donald's face and his eyes sparked with enthusiasm. "Most of these charms that we know were told to collectors in the last hundred years. The only charm that I know of that survived in its original form, on the paper that was actually used to carry it, is in Raleigh."

"Here, in the States?" Sarah couldn't believe the luck of an original Gaelic artifact practically in her back yard.

"In the state archives. Wallace Purdy's charm. It's from the late eighteenth century. It mentions the nine and a trio of things as well. It's a fascinating mix of Christian iconography and pagan folklore. Ye might start there."

Sarah muttered almost to herself, "How did I not know that was there?"

Donald gave her a fatherly smile. "Ye've a great mind, Sarah, but sometimes yer focus can be a bit narrow. Ye've been concentrating on music for so long, ye've missed some of the other evidence."

"It sure looks that way." She slumped back in her chair and pulled a notebook and pen from her bag. "Can you tell me more about these charms. Maybe point at some collections?"

"Of course! Though most of the collections are in Scotland," Donald said.

"Then it's lucky I'm heading over there." She was still weighing her options, but this was another piece on that side of the scale.

"That reminds me. When are ye leaving us?" Donald asked.

"January fourth," she said, thinking of the packet of documents that included her passport, student visa, and one-way plane ticket sitting on her dresser. "So I'd better get over to the archives as soon as possible."

Donald glanced at his watch. "Well, I don't think ye'll make it today, but they should be open tomorrow."

"Then I'll have to be there bright and early." Sarah smiled as she put her copy of Macbeth back in her bag. "Do you have plans for the holiday?"

"Indeed I do. I'll be meeting my brother in Jamaica. Will ye be spending the holiday with the Monroes again?" he said, rising and coming around the desk to see her out.

Sarah stopped short. She hadn't thought about how she would spend Christmas. She had spent the last few years with Amy's family. "No, I don't think so. I'm not sure what I'll be doing."

"I'm sorry to hear that," he said, his brows creased.

Sarah opened the door and was about to step out, but she stopped and turned back to him. "Donald?"

"Mmm?"

Sarah hesitated, not quite sure how to ask the question that had just occurred to her and how much might she give away by asking. "Em, how much did you know about Dermot when you introduced us?"

If she hadn't known him so well she might have missed it. But for a fraction of a second, he seemed to freeze. He recovered quickly. "Och well, I didna know the lad himself, but his mother and I are old friends…small academic world and all that."

"Right." That was probably true, but Sarah doubted that was the whole story. Still, she smiled and stepped into the hall. "Well, thanks. I suppose I'll see you after this next semester then."

"Indeed." He returned her smile with just a hint of relief and patted her shoulder again absently.

***

"Wait here," Fleming told Sarah when they got to the bottom of the stairs.

She sighed in irritation. Just a few days of having a proper bodyguard and she was already chafing at the inconvenience of it. Still, she waited quietly in the stairwell while Fleming checked the U-shaped gallery on the first floor. Smack in the middle of the busiest part of campus, Greenlaw presented all manner of security issues, as Fleming had pointed out in no uncertain terms. Sarah had listened to a laundry list of them as they had climbed the stairs to Donald's office.

She had also listened to his instructions for the exit procedure with minimal eye rolling. The building was surrounded by students when classes were in session, but during the holiday break people on campus were few and far between.

Sarah was completely unsurprised when Fleming opened the stairwell door to tell her that the gallery was clear. Of course, as soon as she left the stairs he instructed her to "stay put" while he checked outside.

Sarah watched him through the plate glass as he checked first in the direction of the quad. When he walked to the opposite corner and peered around the building cautiously, Sarah had had enough. She pushed through the door and strode confidently for Wilson Library.

"Damn," she heard Fleming mutter from about thirty feet away. She glanced back over her shoulder to see him speed walking her way and looking downright thunderous.

"Sarah," a woman said. Coming from behind one of the huge oak trees, she stepped into Sarah's path. She appeared to be in her twenties. Her blonde hair was loose and blowing in the December breeze. She wore fashionable boots, a light jacket, and a teal paisley scarf with her jeans. Sarah supposed she could be a graduate student, but she looked more put together than most grad students Sarah knew.

"Sorry, have we met?" Sarah asked as the woman fell into step with her. She heard Fleming break into a run.

The woman put her hand into her purse as Fleming arrived beside her. He would have tackled her, but Sarah put a hand on his arm to stop him, not wanting another scene like the time James's bodyguard had attacked Jon for waiting in front of her apartment.

"I'm Beth Cartwright, with the Triangle Times newspaper. You're a hard lady to get a hold of." She pulled her hand from her purse and held out a microcassette recorder. "I'd like to ask you a few questions about the hostage situation last Thursday night."

Sarah glared at the woman and turned away without a word, walking toward the library. Fleming maneuvered himself between Sarah and the reporter.

The woman jogged around him and held out the recorder as she kept pace with Sarah. "Was it really a domestic dispute? What set him off?"

Sarah picked up her pace, but the woman stayed right beside her. "What about your roommate? Where was she when this was going on?"

Sarah reached the library steps and hoped Miss Cartwright would take the hint. Fleming again tried to position himself between them. This time he held up an arm to ward the woman off, but she ducked under it. "Were you sexually assaulted?"

That caught Sarah up short. Clearly, this woman wasn't going to stop. Sarah turned to face her. "No. All I'm willing to say about the other night is that it happened, it's over, and I want to get back to my life now."

"Was he a stalker?" The woman stepped up next to Sarah, extending the recorder closer.

"You'll have to ask the police about that. You know, if you're keen for a story, maybe you should look into the prevalence of sexual assault on campus, or how the housekeeping staff is trying to get a living wage. There are a lot more interesting stories in this town than mine." With that, she turned and went up the stairs. This time when Fleming stepped in front of the reporter, she let them get away.

Sarah stopped in the library's entry hall to catch her breath. Fleming was right behind her and pushed the heavy door closed. He stood in front of it to make sure they weren't followed. The look he gave her spoke volumes. Sarah found herself feeling like a petulant teenager who had just learned the hard way. "Sorry."

"I reckon ye'll listen next time, right?" His hard grey eyes pinned her to the spot.

She nodded sheepishly. "Yeah, I'll listen."

***

Sarah handed her driver's license across the security desk of the Search Room at the North Carolina State archives. She smiled at the stern gray-haired woman behind the desk. Sarah had left her coat, backpack, and bodyguard outside by the lockers. Fleming had looked decidedly frustrated when she pointed out to him that only researchers were allowed in the Search Room, and no one was allowed to take bags, coats, notebooks, folders, or really anything that might cause damage or facilitate theft of any precious artifacts inside. He had huffed, but she had pointed out that if she couldn't take so much as a pencil inside, then neither could anyone else. It was probably the safest room in Raleigh. She had left him disgruntled at the door, admonishing him to keep her notebook and pen handy so she could write down her impressions as soon as she came out.

"One moment," the woman at the desk said after looking at Sarah's ID. She turned and went back into an adjoining office.

Puzzled, Sarah waited while the woman had a brief hushed conversation with a man in the office. In short order, the man rose and came out with his hand extended, a welcoming smile on his face. He was thickening with middle age. A beard, glasses, and a sweater that was starting to look thin at the cuffs and elbows gave him a scholarly appearance. "Miss MacAlpin, I'm Richard Mangum, the director of the archives."

"Oh." Sarah was surprised by his effusive greeting and glanced around, hoping that the few other people quietly researching weren't disturbed. She gave him her hand, which he shook with enthusiasm. "It's nice to meet you."

"Always glad to help another Tarheel." He lifted his right hand to show a large but not obtrusive class ring with a topaz of just the right shade of Carolina blue. "Class of seventy-two."

Sarah hoped her face looked suitably impressed as Mangum rounded the counter and held out a hand in the direction of the main Search Room. As Sarah followed him, he leaned toward her and quietly said, "I'm glad you called ahead. The document you're looking for was in the vault where we keep the oldest artifacts. It's not every day that someone calls asking about our Gaelic documents."

"I don't imagine it is," Sarah said as they walked past rows of tables with comfortable looking high-backed chairs and bookshelves lined with volumes and indexes. "Do you have many Gaelic documents?"

"Just a Psalm book and a couple of sermons. This document is pretty unique." Mangum led her to a door off the main room, which he unlocked using a key on a ring attached to his belt with a retractable cord. He held the door for Sarah.

It was sparse inside, with nothing but a simple rectangular table. In the middle of the table was a gray cardboard box with metal reinforced corners. It was the size of a sheet of letter paper and not more than an inch deep. The label on the side showed its bin number and reference categories.

Sarah waited for Mangum to take his position on the other side of the table. "You can see it's a little thing. I almost missed it in the bin."

"Yes, I can see how it might have gotten lost among all the other documents," Sarah said.

"You ready?" Mangum asked with an eager grin.

She smiled and nodded before returning her eyes to the box. Mangum lifted the lid of the gray box to reveal a white card-stock folder. He set the lid aside and lifted the folder out. Every movement was done with the utmost care, and Sarah noticed that his hands were impeccably clean. He shifted the box aside with the back of a hand, careful not to bend the folder. Then he placed the folder in the center of the table and pulled back the protective layers of paper. First the sides opened one by one, then the top and bottom. When the document was finally revealed, it was so small, Sarah was amazed it had survived.

It was only a few inches square, nestled into the corner of a clear protective sleeve. She remembered what Donald had said about charms being sewn into clothes. That must have been how such a small scrap survived for almost 250 years. The paper was yellowed, and the ink had long since turned brown. The edges of the paper were frayed in places, and there were creases where it had been folded.

Mangum lifted the tiny document in its sleeve and held it out to Sarah. She went to take it from him, but looked up for permission before touching the sleeve. He nodded, "The polyester sleeve protects it."

Sara slid her hand under the document and lifted it from his hands. She looked closely at the long, scrawling handwriting. At first it seemed incomprehensible, but after a minute of study the shapes resolve themselves into letters, and Sarah recognized words.

As with much of the lore of Scotland, it was a blend of Christian and pagan references, although the Christian references seemed to stop after the first few lines. It was almost as cryptic as anything Shakespeare's witches might have said, but the imagery it used was becoming familiar.

"Can you read that?" Mangum asked.

Sarah looked up to find him watching her with open curiosity. She smiled. "I can make out most of it."

"And you understand it?" He looked surprised, as if Gaelic speakers were as rare and mythical as unicorns.

"Well, I know what the words mean. My focus is usually on folk songs. I'm just starting to study charms like this one." She wished she could copy down what she was reading, but of course she had nothing to write with. She understood they didn't want any documents damaged or stolen. Still, here she was trying to translate an amazing document, but unable to write anything down. "Is there a way I can get a picture of the document?"

Mangum smiled. "I've already got some photos and information for you. You can take them with you."

"Oh, that's perfect. Thanks." She looked back at the scrap of paper.

"I had a feeling you would want to take a longer look at it." Mangum fidgeted a little as she continued deciphering the handwritten lines.

"What is it?" she asked gently.

"It's only," he gestured at the document, "I've never heard the language. I'm from Scotland County, and I know some of my ancestors spoke Gaelic, but no one remembers it now. Would you...I mean, would you mind reading it out loud?"

Sarah gave him a sidelong smile. "You know this is a spell. You're not superstitious are you?"

"Only when it comes to basketball."

Sarah chuckled. Most Tarheels were superstitious about basketball. She cleared her throat and prepared to read. She skipped the typical invocation at the beginning and read the part that had caught her attention. The words came smoothly. Sarah always loved the way that Gaelic sounds flowed together, leniting and slenderizing words to work with the words around them like a progression of musical chords.

Na naoinear de an Làrachd

Bha sgath air Calum Cille

Air lèirsinn den fhirinn

Air an bean-luirg

Seun sibh fo-duine agaibh

Thoir luathachadh air turas

Le dùrachd tri-fhillte triuir

"That's just beautiful," Mangum whispered, as if he didn't want to break the spell. He had a look of wonder on his face. "What does it mean?"

"Ah…" Sarah wasn't entirely sure of the meaning herself, but she could make an educated guess. "That will probably take some more study. Some of these terms are new to me. Basically it invokes 'the Nine of the Footprint.'"

Sarah laid the sleeve on the table between them and pointed to the line about the Nine. Then she moved her finger down the page, indicating lines as she translated, "By vision of the future, By vision of the truth, By the…and here is a term that's new to me, *bean-luirg*. It basically means 'finder woman.' Then comes the request. Protect your humble servant, speed his journey, with the goodwill of the three-fold three."

"The three-fold three…" Mangum looked thoughtful. "Do you know what that is?"

Sarah shook her head. "No. That's one of the reasons I wanted to look at the charm. I've seen similar references, but I'm not sure. Could be something to do with the Holy Trinity, or something else. Do you know anything about the history of the document?"

Mangum pulled some more papers from the box and handed them to Sarah. "These are the provenance documents."

She read through the papers. The charm had been donated to the archives by the estate of Elnora Purdy of Robeson County, a descendant of Wallace Purdy. It seemed that when Elnora died, her family had gone through her house and found some belongings of Wallace, who had been a cooper in the colony in the mid-eighteenth century. When they had opened the trunk, the charm had been at the bottom.

The state archives had catalogued it as Irish until a scholar from Canada had come down to view it in the 1960s and informed them that it was, in fact, Scottish Gaelic. Sarah was thankful for that, otherwise she might never have known it was there.

"I made copies of all of those records too," Mangum put in.

"Thank you so much," Sarah said.

He nodded proudly.

They replaced the documents in their box, locked the small room, and returned to the main desk. As Sarah retrieved her driver's license, Mangum got the file from his office and handed it over the counter with a genial smile. "Here you are. I hope that helps you."

Sarah smiled back. "I am sure it will. Thanks again."

She found Fleming sitting on a bench in the hall, looking bored nearly to tears. Not for the first time this week, she wished Dermot had been her daytime guardian, but he was packing up the last of his things for his return to Scotland. Fleming was an easy guy to like. He was witty, friendly, and thoughtful, but Sarah missed the partnership that she and Dermot shared when they were working. She never felt bad about spending hours in the library or the Folklife Collection, or dragging him to Raleigh to look at an old scrap of paper, because Dermot understood what she was doing.

The three of them had fallen into a routine this week, with Dermot taking the "night shift" in Sarah's apartment. That suited her fine. She was still having nightmares, though they were getting less intense. If she took every opportunity to tempt

Dermot, well, she couldn't be blamed for that. He had lit that fire, and Sarah wasn't about to let the smoldering embers go out.

Each morning Fleming would arrive rested and ready to accompany her through her day while a tired and grumbling Dermot would trudge off to get some much-needed rest and pack up his things. He was leaving tomorrow, and Sarah still wasn't 100 percent sure that was what she wanted. She'd thought it was what she needed in order to sort out her feelings, but the closer they got to him actually leaving, the more she wanted to cling to him.

"All set, then?" Fleming asked as she approached the bench where he was sitting next to her bag. At her nod, he practically vaulted from the bench. "Where to now?"

"Home." She held up the file Richard Mangum had given her. "I've got some copies in here to study."

"Home it is." He ushered her out the door and down the block to where they had parked Sarah's car. She stood aside while he checked over the car. When he gave her the all-clear, she got in and started the engine.

The drive back to Chapel Hill wasn't especially long. By the time she got to the highway, Sarah's mind drifted back to the words of the charm, and a line she hadn't translated for Mangum: "*Bha sgath air Calum Cille.*" [Saint Columba was afraid.]

Afraid of what?

CHAPTER ELEVEN

"That's practically blasphemy," Dermot said as he brought the dinner dishes into the kitchen. As she often did when chewing on a puzzle, Sarah had detoured to the grocery store on the way home from Raleigh. Dinner was a chicken and rice casserole with loads of cheese and broccoli...pure comfort food. When Dermot had arrived, she sent Fleming off with a healthy serving in a leftover whipped cream tub, and she and Dermot sat down to talk about the charm. She had let him peruse the photos of the document over dinner in the hopes that he might see something she didn't.

Sarah took the dishes and started rinsing them in the sink. "I didn't think that sort of thing bothered you."

"It doesna bother me." He shrugged. "But Columba is credited with Christianizing Scotland. He's been turned into a folk hero. I doubt half the stories about him are true, but he's larger than life to some Scots. There's even a story about him seeing the Loch Ness monster. It's strange to see a line about him being afraid. Did your Granny never tell ye anything about him?"

Sarah shook her head. "Not really. I mean I know who he was and all, but I learned that later. Granny never had much time for organized religion."

Dermot made a tsk-ing sound and shook his head in mock jest. "And her a Highland lass."

Sarah rolled her eyes and opened the dishwasher. She handed him the glass she'd been rinsing. "Here make yourself useful. What about the 'Nine of the Footprint' or the three-fold three? Do those sound familiar?"

"Well, the kings of Dàl Riada used a stone footprint in coronation ceremonies." He took the glass and placed it on the top rack of the dishwasher.

"That's what I was thinking. But I don't remember anything about the Nine." She handed him another glass. "Do you agree that it's *naoinear* and not just *naoi* something?"

"It's hard to tell. That smudge in the middle could be an 'n' or it could just be a smudge. There aren't many other things it could be, though. *Noainear* or *noai ear* most likely."

Sarah moved on to rinsing plates, puzzling over the words. "*Noai ear*. The construction there is weird, nine east?"

"Nine of the east? I agree the grammar is weird, but that's not the only spot in this charm where the grammar is a bit off." He took the plate she held out for him and bent to put it in the bottom rack. Sarah paused her rinsing to cast a brief glance at his backside.

"Mmhmm," she hummed in acknowledgement or appreciation. It was rare to find perfect grammar or even consistent wording in oral traditions. It made translating things a challenge. "But the Nine of the East of the Footprint?"

"Or the Nine of the Eastern Footprint," he suggested.

Sarah turned back to the sink. "So, what's to the east? The Orkneys, Shetlands, Norway?"

Dermot paused in loading the dishwasher and said thoughtfully, "It could be land that's not there anymore."

"What, like a lost island?"

"Yeah, exactly like that." He turned to face her. "For decades, fishermen in the North Sea have been pulling up tools of stone and bone from the ocean. And now that oil companies are exploring, they're finding even more. The theory is that there was a landmass between Britain and the continent that was flooded after the last ice age. I believe there are actually some teams working on mapping it."

"That's a bit of a stretch. How many thousands of years are we talking about? Do you really think this tradition could have lasted that long?"

"Who's to say? Vedic traditions in India go back to 1500 BCE."

"Yeah, but you're talking about even further back than that. For an oral tradition to have survived that long, it's…" She trailed off, searching for the right words.

"It would have to be well tended, yeah."

"Or completely isolated," she said. "What are the odds of that?"

"Och, there are plenty of settlements in the islands and highlands that were isolated for centuries." He leaned back against the counter, bracing his hands on either side of him. He seemed to take up all of the extra space in her tiny kitchen, but Sarah didn't mind a bit.

"You'd be talking millennia."

"Certainly before any recorded history in that part of the world."

"In the time before time…Before our land became an island…" The words of her childhood storybook came back to her. Could that be what it meant? Dermot had a point that the story seemed to be describing a North Sea landmass, which would have lain to the east of southern Britain, joining it to mainland Europe. "So we're talking about *noainear*, nine people, or *noai ear*, nine somethings from the east."

"If it's people," Dermot said, "there were three sisters."

"Sure, and maybe that three times three is the Nine they're talking about, but where do the other six come from?" Sarah wiped her hands on a towel and leaned back against the counter. Her mouth was set in a grim line.

He stared off into space and sighed heavily. "Yeah, dunno."

Sarah arched an eyebrow. "That's your expert academic opinion?"

"Aye well," he shrugged, "I said I was a folklorist. Didna say I was a good one."

He gave her a familiar wry smile and warmth spread through her. It reminded her of the fall break when they had spent several days in a cabin in the mountains. They had been there for research, but it had been so cozily domestic that she had hated to leave. She smiled back at Dermot and the memory of those evenings in the mountains, wishing they could go back there and hide away from everything. But of course that wasn't possible. He was leaving tomorrow.

"Who am I going to bounce these things off of when you're gone?" she asked, her voice almost a whisper.

He drew in a deep breath. "Ye told me to go."

"I know." She bowed her head and focused on neatly folding the dishtowel. "I still think that's the right thing to do, but that doesn't mean I'm not going to miss you."

He pushed away from the counter and pulled her into his arms. Sarah leaned her cheek against his chest. He murmured. "It's only for a few weeks."

She nodded. "But it's not going to be the same, will it?"

He tightened his arms around her. "No, *mo ghraidh*, it willna be like this again."

Sarah pulled back so she could look at him. His eyes met hers, and she saw her own longing reflected there. She slowly slid her hand behind his head and pulled his mouth down to meet hers. He didn't protest, but she could feel him tense as if every muscle was poised for a fight.

By contrast, his lips were soft on hers, tentative. Sarah skimmed her tongue along his bottom lip, and he opened to her. They tasted each other in small sips, as if they were afraid to go too deep. Sarah was so relieved he hadn't stopped her, that he was kissing her again. When she sighed into his mouth, he took control.

With his hands under her arms, he lifted her to sit on the counter and stepped between her knees. Sarah wrapped herself around him. Her arms gripped his shoulders and she hooked her ankles behind his back as he set to devouring her. This was the passion she remembered. This was the man she needed like air. He pulled her hips closer into his. Sarah felt the evidence of his arousal through his jeans and ground against it.

He groaned. She arched her back, and his teeth skated down the side of her neck, nipping her sensitive skin. Sarah pulled his mouth back to hers, hungry for more, "Make love to me."

He grunted and ground his hips against hers.

"Yes," she said. "Make love to me again."

Her words must have cut through his fog of need. He pulled back from her to rest his forehead against hers. His arms shook and his breath came in quick pants. "I can't."

"Yes, you can," her voice cracked with disbelief. He wasn't going to deny her again.

"No." The word sounded like it hurt him to say it.

"Will you take me away from this place, *A Dharmuid*?" she pleaded. Her hand on his jaw, she pulled his eyes up to meet hers. "You said yourself that it's not going to be like this again. We'll never have this kind of freedom in Scotland. We should take advantage of it now."

He shook his head slowly. "It's not just about us. And you ken how that worked out for Darmuid and Grainne. That's exactly how it would be for us, chased everywhere we went."

"Fine, but we can still have tonight. There's no one else here. No one is watching us. This is the last chance we'll have to really be alone." She hated the urgency in her voice, hated having to beg.

He just shook his head and pulled away. He couldn't even look at her as he stalked out of the kitchen, leaving her sitting on the counter. Her chest felt tight, and her shoulders curved forward as if they could protect her heart by curling around it.

She slid down from the counter and turned. She could see Dermot standing in the middle of the living room. His back was to her, every muscle rigid with tension. She watched him and waited, hoping he would turn around, change his mind, come back to her.

He didn't.

Sarah tried not to make a sound as she left the kitchen and made her way back to her room. She closed the door with a soft click. That was when the tears started. She didn't sob and wail as she had done the last time, the time he told her about James and why they couldn't be together. These tears were silent, but lasting.

She made her way blindly to the bed and laid down. Wrapping herself in the quilt, she let herself cry, careful not to let him hear.

CHAPTER TWELVE

June 1968

From Molly MacAlpin's Journal

My first impression of New York City was a blur. Because we had to take the later train, we arrived in New York the same day that our flight was leaving for London. So all I got to see of the city was Grand Central Station, LaGuardia Airport, and whatever I managed to glimpse out of the window during the taxi ride in between. I wanted so bad to jump out of that car and explore. It was the noisiest, busiest, most exciting place I had ever seen, and I wanted to dive right into the middle of it. As I sat in the taxi next to Grumpy MacDuff, who'd been barking orders at me since before we got off the train, I wished the whole trip was behind me so I could get started finding a place to live and some kind of work until August.

"Grand" is exactly the right word for Grand Central Station. Even churches in the mountains weren't that grand. The only building I had seen that was anywhere close was the Biltmore, and I only saw that from a distance. But this building was huge and lively. I felt like the country mouse walking around in the middle of all that bustle. I know Duff got fair cross with me because I kept slowing down to gawp at every new thing I saw.

LaGuardia was much the same, but in a different way. It's so modern. Grand Central looks like a temple of some kind, but the airport is more like a cross between a bus station and a spaceship. Thanks to Duff's hurrying me along at every step, we got to the gate with time to spare. I sat down in the rows of chairs to wait.

Across from me was a woman who wasn't like anyone I had ever seen before. She wore a beautiful white A-line dress with a boat neck and a diamond shaped cutout just below the collar. It wasn't revealing, more suggesting. Her hair was bobbed and curled prettily at the ends. She kept it back from her face with a wide white band that was the same material as her dress. She wore white tights and white shoes that were so spotless they looked like they'd never touched the ground. She sat elegantly with her legs crossed at the ankles and tucked beneath her chair. In her lap was a magazine that she slowly flipped through with long, perfectly manicured, pink-tipped fingers.

Between the bus, train, and rushed cab ride, I hadn't had a chance to change since leaving home. I looked down at my bare knees and wrinkled blue flowered traveling dress that I had put on the day before in my drafty old room back in the holler. I had thought myself no end of fancy in a new dress that I had made. My brown shoes were scuffed and worn but still serviceable, and my socks that had come to my knees when I left home were drooping around my ankles. My stick-straight hair hung down over my shoulders. I was used to being a big fish in the small pond of Kettle Holler, but this woman made me feel like the lowest creature around. I know I shouldn't have cared about such things. I should tell you that clothes and fancy living don't make one person better than another, but I was young then. And sometimes when we're young, we don't understand what our priorities should be.

The announcement came over calling for first-class passengers for our flight, and the lady in the white dress stood up. A handsome man dressed just as nicely as she was came over and picked up her bag. I tried to look away, like I hadn't been staring at her.

"Miss?"

I looked up to find her smiling and holding her magazine out to me. "I'm done with this magazine. Would you like it?"

"Oh! Thank you." I was surprised and a little embarrassed. She had obviously noticed me watching her. I took the magazine. It was *Harper's Bazaar*, full of fashion pictures and ads for fine things that I would never own. At least it gave me something to read on the plane, since I was pretty sure Duff wasn't going to be much for conversation.

"Have a nice day," the lady in the white dress said, still smiling as she strode away.

A few minutes later, they called for the other passengers for our flight. Duff strode up with a newspaper under his arm and picked up his knapsack. "Well, come on."

I pulled my bag onto my shoulder and followed him toward the gate, wondering how a stranger could manage to show me more kindness than this man who'd been sent to travel with me.

We found our seats and got settled and ready for takeoff. I was getting more and more nervous as the minutes ticked by. When we finally started down the runway, I thought I might jump out of my skin. I gripped the arm of the seat so hard my fingers hurt, and I watched out the window as we picked up speed. I thought we were going to end up in the river. The runway is that close to the water. It was the most exhilarating thing, that feeling of going faster and faster and the plane shaking all around you till you think it might fall apart. Then suddenly it lifts off the ground and you're floating. I only know one other feeling like that.

We broke through the clouds and leveled off. I opened the magazine and began flipping through it. Duff opened his newspaper and set to reading. When they came by to serve us dinner, he noticed the magazine. "Where'd you get that?"

"A lady in the airport gave it to me. Said she was done with it." I flipped it closed and put it in pocket in front of me so I could lower the tray.

The cover was facing us, and he glanced at it as he was letting his own tray down. He practically sneered when he said, "What do you want with a magazine like that? Gettin' ready for when you're rich and famous?"

"Maybe." I tried not to let on that his attitude bothered me. He'd done little more than grunt and growl at me since we met. The rest of the time he'd been a big glowering presence at my side. "I'm going to be a dancer, like Cyd Charise."

He let out the closest thing to a laugh I'd heard since I laid eyes on him. "I'll bet. Well, you won't need fancy clothes at the ass-end of nowhere we're going to."

I know it wasn't nice, but I couldn't take any more. "You know. We've got a lotta ornery hillbillies where I come from, but you might be the orneriest person I've ever met."

He looked startled for a second. Then he picked up his paper and folded it so it showed an article about the war. "If I'm ornery, it's because I've spent the last year training for Vietnam. But when my brothers were getting ready to ship out, I got pulled in by some higher-ups and told I had a different mission. I don't much like sitting here while my fellow Marines are getting shot at. I trained for war, not escorting some kid to Larrick Awar or whatever you people call it."

"*Làrachd an Fhamhair*," I muttered in Gaelic. "It means the giant's footprint. And what higher-ups?"

"It doesn't matter." He waved my question off. "Look, I knew I might be asked to do something like this eventually, but I didn't expect it to be now and I don't have to like it."

With that, he braced his arm on the tray, blocking me out, and tucked into his food. I nibbled at mine and watched the blue sky darken out the window. I'm not sure when I fell asleep, but when I woke up, I had been covered with a blanket and was leaning on his shoulder. He didn't seem to mind.

***

After the flight from New York to London, a train to Edinburgh, and another to Inverness, I was once again riding in a car through the mountains. The car was waiting for us in Inverness, a tiny blue thing called a Mini, arranged by whatever mysterious benefactor was responsible for Duff being there. We drove from Inverness to Ullapool, then up a winding road through the Highlands toward Làrachd an Fhamhair.

The mountains in Scotland aren't much like the mountains at home. Oh, there are things that are the same. You can see the stone peeking out where the soil is washed or blown away, like the rocks just don't want to stay hidden under the dirt anymore. The people seem to be much the same, though the accents are different. There's no such thing as dry weather there. It's all just varying degrees of wet. There's a reason why there are thirteen different Gaelic words for rain, and I used every one of them while I was in Scotland. There aren't as many trees there either. There are some forests, but it's mostly bushes and heather.

The hills rolled past in a patchwork of bright green, brown, and stone gray. Inside the car it was less tense, but somehow worse than my ride to Boone had been a few days before. Mama might have been jumpy, but at least she cared. I was pretty sure Grant MacDuff didn't give a fig what happened to me. After that conversation on the plane, he only spoke to me when necessary. He wasn't as ornery as he'd been before, just remote. I wished I could open the windows while we drove along, but the weather was dreich, as your Granny would say. So, I had to content myself with watching the scenery through the rain streaks on my window.

We stopped for a bite at a little village and the eastern end of the loch. We had brought some sandwiches before leaving Ullapool and ate picnic style on the hood of the little blue Mini. Duff spread out his map on the hood, examining all the little roads that led away from the loch. There weren't many.

"The orders I got said the turn is near the castle. Did your Mama tell you anything about this place?" he asked in frustration.

"Plenty, but none of it was about the village or how to get there," I said.

"Hmmph." He went back to perusing the map. "Looks like we go up this way a little further and we'll see some ruins. There are a couple of other roads that lead away from the loch on this side, but that's the only one that's near the castle. It's almost an immediate turn to the right."

I followed his finger along the road that ran by the loch. There wasn't anything on the map to indicate there was a village anywhere near there. "It doesn't look like there's anything on the map."

He nodded. "That's what I can't figure out. The directions I got make it seem like it should be around here." He drew a small circle with his finger on the map near the road he had just shown me. "But there's nothing on the map. It doesn't even look like there's a road that goes back there."

"Mama did say it was remote. I just thought she meant it was in the mountains." I stared at the map, trying to see if there were any indications of villages on that side of the loch. "Are you sure that's where the turn is?"

He blew out a long breath, letting his shoulders slump. "That's what the letter said. Would have been nice if they'd marked it on a map for us."

I crumpled up the paper my sandwich had been wrapped in. "Well, there's only one way to find it. Let's move, soldier."

"Marine," he grumbled.

"Hmm?" I asked.

"Soldiers are in the army." He pulled his shoulders back and raised his chin, giving me that squinty-eyed look down his nose. "I'm a marine."

"Right, then. Let's go, marine," I said with an exaggerate eye roll.

It must have been an hour later when Duff pulled the little car to the side of the road near the ruins of an old stone house. He practically jumped from the car and slammed the door. By the time I got out, he had the map spread out on the hood again. He was muttering under his breath and shaking his head. We had driven up and down the loch at least a dozen times, even taking a few side roads, but had only found a few houses. The only village we had come across was the tiny one where we had stopped for lunch.

While Duff was busy muttering to himself, I strolled up the rise and looked around. I thought that higher ground might help me find what we were looking for, but I got distracted by the loch. Baby, you'll never see anything as blue as Loch Assynt.

The sun had come out and it struck that water like flint, making thousands of little sparks of light reflect off the cobalt blue. I've seen a lot of beautiful things in this world, but you're the only thing I've ever seen that matched the beauty of that loch in the midsummer sun.

I heard a curse come from the direction of the car and looked back to see Duff scanning the rocky hills across the road and looking back at the map. His temper wasn't great to begin with, but it was getting downright frayed. I took a deep breath and sat down cross-legged on the ground facing the loch. I closed my eyes and listened to the water lapping against the stones. I sat there just breathing, until I could feel everything around me from the ground to the sky. Then I cast out, just like Mama taught me. I know she taught you too. I guess it can't hurt for you to know how.

I felt the circle of awareness around me expand further and further. I felt the road behind me and the loch in front of me. Then the hills on the other side of the road, then the hollow behind. It was there that I found the narrow track that led between the ridges of stone.

I came back slowly. When I opened my eyes, I just sat there watching the water glint off the loch for a minute. I don't know if it was nervousness or outright fear, but something in me rebelled at the thought of getting up and finding our people. It was so relaxing sitting there by the water.

"Molly," I heard Duff calling from what seemed like far away. I got to my feet, smoothed my skirt down, and walked back to the car. He was stalking back and forth like a caged animal looking in every direction.

He sighed when he saw me, and if I hadn't known better I would have thought he was happy instead of just relieved. "Don't run off like that."

"Sorry." I waved at the driver's door. "Get in. I know where we're going."

He looked at the map in his hand and at me. I could tell he was building up a head of steam. "Do you mean we've been driving around for an hour and you knew where we were going?"

"Of course not." I gave him my best smile. "I mean, I just figured it out."

He lifted an eyebrow at me, not moving toward the car. "How?"

"Magic." I winked. "Now, do you want to get in the car and let me tell you where it is, or would you rather stand here cursing at your map until the rain comes back?"

He folded the map and folded himself into the tiny car. He was silent, but I could practically hear him grumbling on the inside. "Which way?"

"To the right, and go slow."

We practically crawled down the road, heading toward the old ruined house. There were two long ridges that ran almost parallel to the road and overlapped at just the right spot. The track that went between them was just that: two dirt tracks just the right width for car tires. Duff pulled onto the track when I pointed it out.

"Are you sure about this?" he asked, leaning forward and looking skeptically the road ahead. "I hope this little car is up to this."

I wondered the same thing, but there wasn't much choice in the matter. We crept along the track as it wound between the ridges until you couldn't see the loch behind us, nor anything ahead but the little trail. We were walled in by the hills on each side. Just as we were starting to feel trapped, the hill to our left ended in a sharp drop and the hollow opened up. Below and around us was the village. A small bunching of stone houses lined a stream running through the hollow bottom, with one good-sized building that seemed to be a communal hall. There were more houses scattered up the surrounding hillsides. It looked like any mountain town, except that the houses were made of gray stone instead of clapboard and the roofs were covered in moss. Anyone spying on Làrachd an Fhamhair from a distance would think it was nothing more than a pile of rocks no different from all the other piles of rocks around it.

We followed the track across the hill and down into the holler. It ran through the village and came to a circle in front of the largest of the stone buildings. Duff parked near the front door. There didn't seem to be any other cars in the village, and the sound of our engine had brought a number of curious faces peeking around doors and out windows. A round, squat man with a thick gray beard came strolling out of the big building, wiping his hands on a clean but well-worn apron. He eyed us with suspicion.

Duff and I got out of the car and walked around to meet the man. "Hi," I said, conscious that my accent might make me sound like someone from another planet. Truth to tell, I felt like someone from another planet. "I'm looking for my aunt, Eilidh MacLeod. Do you know her?"

The man's beard split into a wide grin and he laughed. If his beard had been just a little whiter, I would have sworn he was Santa Claus. "Och! Ye mun be here for the feast, aye?"

I couldn't do much besides smile and nod.

"Would ye be Maighread MacAlpin's lass, then?" His black eyes twinkled at me with such open joy that I felt the prickle of tears in my own. Mama and I were so alone in the holler. Sure, we were accepted as part of the community for the liquor that Mama provided, but we weren't part of their church or their society. We lived among them, but we weren't of them. We were of these people. I felt it in this man's joy at my arrival. I was home, and I wished like hell that Mama had come with me.

"Jock MacLeod, Maighread's cousin, which I reckon makes me yers too." The smiling man in the apron pointed to his chest. "We're mostly kin here."

"I'm Molly." At the throat clearing behind me, I turned and waved Duff forward. "This is Grant MacDuff. He brought me here."

Jock looked Duff up and down. Duff straightened his shoulders and gave Jock what I'm calling his Eastwood look. After several seconds, Jock chuckled and extended a hand. "Ah reckon ye'll do."

He turned back to me and said, "*A bheil Gàidhlig agaibh?*"

I gave him my most winning smile and assured him that I did speak Gaelic. "*Tha, gu dearbh!*" I nodded in Duff's direction, "But he doesn't."

"Right, right." Jock nodded. Then he waved over a little boy from the smattering of people who were slowly coming out of their houses and drifting over to us. He told the boy in Gaelic to go fetch Aunt Eilidh. The boy went running up the side of the holler between houses. Standing in the middle, we could look about and see there were about twenty houses dotting the hillsides.

"Come into the hall then, ye dinna need to wait out here." Jock ushered us toward the door of the building he had come out of.

It was dim inside. There were a few windows, but most of the light came from a big fireplace in the middle of the room. On the fire was a big iron pot that had a stew bubbling away. There were tables and benches lined up around the room. The air was close, warm, and smelled of peat smoke.

"We've only one more lass to wait for, and then we'll have the feast. Och, it'll be a great day," Jock said, bustling around the room. He waved us to a bench near the fire.

Duff and I sat, and Jock quickly put cups of water in front of us. "Ye'll be hungry nae doubt."

"Um, we ate earlier," I said, not wanting to trouble him. "But this water is refreshing."

"Aye, grand." He nodded with enthusiasm.

"Can you tell us more about the feast? It's a midsummer celebration, right?" That was pretty much all Mama had told me, that it was a kind of homecoming.

He stopped his bustling and gave me a puzzled look. "Did your ma not tell ye? It's ma—"

He was cut off when the wind blew the door open. I jumped from the loud crack when it hit the stone wall. There was a woman silhouetted in the doorway with the afternoon sun shining around her. She was tall and willowy, wearing a light dress that swirled about her knees. Her hair was picked up by the wind and blew around her head in tendrils, twisting in the air like snakes. I thought she seemed like something from an old story: half fairy, half gorgon.

She stepped inside and closed the door behind her. In the firelight, she lost some of that supernatural quality. She was a woman like most others, though she was beautiful. Her auburn hair was streaked with white, and she had green eyes and skin like cream. She was like the mountain forest in the fall, all dramatic colors and angles. It was her eyes that clued me in. They were so much like Mama's that I knew this had to be Aunt Eilidh.

She didn't bother to introduce herself, but gracefully sat down across the table from me without looking at the men. She spent several seconds examining me before saying in Gaelic, "How is my cousin, Maighread?"

"Heartbroken that she couldn't be here," I replied in the same language. "She misses her home."

"And you? Do you miss your home?" She watched me closely.

"I haven't found my home yet." And that was the truth. I didn't want to call Kettle Holler home, nor yet Làrachd an Fhamhair. I hadn't been anywhere else long enough.

Whether that answer pleased her or not, she didn't show it. I got the feeling Aunt Eilidh didn't show much of her feelings. She switched her gaze to Duff. "This is yer steward."

"Steward? He escorted me here."

"What did they tell ye to do?" She asked Duff in English.

"I was told to go where she goes and make sure no one interferes with her." His voice showed none of the emotional turmoil I'd been hearing from him since we met.

Eilidh gave a thoughtful nod. "Did ye have any trouble?"

Duff shook his head no.

"Good, that's good." She nodded again before standing gracefully. "I expect we should get you settled. Ye can meet the others for tea. Come."

We followed her out of the large building to one of the smaller stone houses nearby. Aunt Eilidh waved at the house and turned to Duff, saying, "This is where the lads will be staying. Ye can bide there with them."

He made a short nod. "Aye, ma'am."

She nodded to the highest of the cottages on the hillside across the stream that ran through the middle of the village. "We'll be in yon blackhouse. When ye're settled, ye can bring the lass's things."

Duff just nodded and went to the car to fetch his bags. I followed Aunt Eilidh up the hill to the blackhouse she had pointed to. It was a little bigger than the one she said the "lads" would be in. She led me inside and turned to watch me, like she was waiting for me to turn my nose up or something.

Aunt Eilidh's house was like the others in the village, though a little bit larger. They were all made of dark gray stones that appeared to be stacked dry. The roofs were all made of rushes and covered with turf. The door was solid wood, worn by years to match the color of the stones. The windows had shutters that stood open. Inside, the walls were whitewashed and the furnishings were simple.

Going to Làrachd an Fhamhair was like stepping back in time. Aunt Eilidh's house was probably the finest in the village, but even then it was right primitive. There was no electricity or plumbing. There was a fireplace at one end for heat and cooking and a bed piled with quilts at the other end next to a washstand. Above the sleeping area was a loft with more pallets for sleeping. There was a work table by the window near the fire, with a small settle on the opposite wall. A side-by-side cabinet along the back wall held most of her belongings. I noticed there wasn't much in the way of cooking tools or food stores.

It reminded me of the old cabin on the ridge above the holler, the one Duff uses. You'll know it wasn't much different than the way some mountain people live. There was no newspaper on the walls to keep the drafts out, or tar paper repairs to the outside. A turf roof looks a far sight better than a tin one, though it doesn't make any sound in the rain. Compared to some of those shacks, Aunt Eilidh's house was cozy. I couldn't help smiling.

She must've liked that. When she spoke again her tone was friendlier. "Ye'll be sharing the loft with the other lasses. Right now, it's just my Sheila, but the MacKenzie lass should be here any day."

"I'm sure it'll be fine," I said, looking up toward the loft. "Sheila is your daughter?"

"Aye, and yer cousin forbye. She's gone to Lochinver wi' Davie Lyall and Willie Cross to fetch supplies for the fete. She'll be home tonight. In the meantime, ye can unpack yer things and have yer tea. It'll be down in the hall." She tilted her head back in the direction of the big house.

***

We were back down in the hall having our "tea," which is really a sort of early dinner, when the others returned. Most of the village ate their meals in the hall. It was like a communal kitchen and dining hall, with its great pot bubbling over the fire. I was sitting with Aunt Eilidh and Jock MacLeod at the table nearest to the pot. It seemed to be a place of honor. Duff was at a table near the door. We were all enjoying a hearty mutton stew and homemade bread with our tea when we heard an engine. The younger ones went out to see who it was, but Aunt Eilidh and the older folk stayed where they were. I reckon they knew the particular sound of their own truck. I took my cue from them.

A few minutes later, they all came spilling back into the hall around a younger version of Aunt Eilidh. She was tall and willowy with green eyes. Unlike her mother's auburn hair, Sheila's hair was fiery red with glints of strawberry blond. She walked with a fluid grace and confidence as if she owned the place, and I suppose she did. It was her home after all, and she was the daughter of the village matriarch. The children milled around her as she held court over them, handing out sweets. They were followed by a man broad enough to fill the doorway and tall enough that he had to duck to come in. His blond hair was shaggy, but not unkempt. His sharp eyes looked out from either side of a beaked nose. The man who came behind him was smaller and thin and seemed almost lost in the big man's shadow.

Aunt Eilidh rose and motioned for them to join us. She had looked fairly stern since we'd arrived, but she beamed at her daughter. Sheila waded through the children and came to our table. Eilidh wrapped an arm around her waist and said, "This is my Sheila. *A nighean*, this is your cousin Màili from America."

Sheila looked down at me with a smile so sweet it would make your teeth hurt. "Well hello, cousin. You've come a long way."

I stood up to shake her hand. "I have. I'm pleased to meet you."

"And this is Davie Lyall, her steward," Eilidh said, indicating the big man. I nodded hello to him. He nodded back before going to sit with Duff near the door. "And this...Och. Where is that lad?"

Eilidh and Sheila looked around behind them. They found the other young man in the shadows away from the fire. I'm not sure if he was hiding or lurking, but it seemed that he didn't want to be seen. Aunt Eilidh waved him forward. "Come on, lad, and meet the lass."

The "lad" stepped out of the shadows. He was a young man about the same age as Sheila and me. He looked presentable enough with short dark hair, and his clothes were neat and clean if plain. He held his thin shoulders high up by his ears like he was nervous, and his dark eyes shifted side to side before they settled on mine.

Eilidh grabbed his hand and pulled him closer to the table. "This is Willie Cross. Say hello to young Màili, Will."

The corners of his mouth tipped up in a quick smile and he bobbed his head. He might have whispered hallo, but I didn't hear it. He pulled his hand from Aunt Eilidh's and walked around the table to sit next to Jock. Jock got up and fetched him some stew, and Willie kept his attention on his bowl. Aunt Eilidh got some food for Sheila and we all sat down and went back to our tea.

Aunt Eilidh asked, "Did ye get all the things from the list?"

"Aye, and the post," Sheila said, dipping a crust of bread into her stew.

"And I dinna suppose there was any word from Rab," Aunt Eilidh said, her tone cooling several degrees.

Sheila took a bite of bread and shrugged. Aunt Eilidh gave a soft huff that sounded like frustration. After she had chewed and swallowed, Sheila said, "I did hear that he was seen playing his fiddle in a pub in Ullapool two days ago. You know Rab. He'll be here when the time comes and not a minute before."

"Aye, I ken that well enough," Aunt Eilidh muttered, looking disgruntled.

We continued talking about my trip from the States, some local gossip Sheila had gathered in Lochinver, and general plans for the next few days. I was nearly done with my stew when I felt a little prickle on the back of my neck. I looked up to find Willie Cross watching me. When I smiled at him, he quickly shifted his gaze back to his bowl and didn't look up again.

When we were done and had cleared away the dishes, Sheila threw her arm around my shoulders and said, "Come along, cousin. I'll give ye the tour."

We walked out of the hall and along the lane by the creek, just as I had earlier with Aunt Eilidh. This time Sheila pointed out the different buildings and what they were for. She waved toward the house that Duff had been shown to. "That's the lads' house. The unmarried men stay there. It's usually just Willie and Davy, but it'll be gey full soon with everyone coming in."

"How many are coming?" I asked, following her lead around some large rocks.

"Oh well, there's you and your steward. We have another cousin coming from Canada. She'll have a steward with her." She ticked people off on her fingers. "There's Lachlan Morse. His family moved to Ullapool when he was little. Then there's Rab Ballantyne. Ye heard my ma mention him. Always comes in on his own time, but he'll be here."

"Won't their families come with them? I thought this was a homecoming feast," I said.

She looked puzzled at me. "Homecoming?"

"You know, when relatives who've moved away come back for a visit. Churches at home have them every year," I explained.

"Em, not exactly." Her brow crinkled and she looked at me sideways. "Did yer mam not tell ye?"

I started to get a little nervous. "Tell me what?"

"Didn't she tell ye about the giant's footprint and the story of our people?" She slowed as we arrived at the small stone bridge that crossed the creek.

You know the story. Granny taught it to you too. The one about our people coming from a giant's footprint in stone and his wife making the cauldron of plenty. "Sure, but that's just a fairy story."

"No, it's not." Sheila looked insulted. "That's why we live in this hidden glen. We're protecting that legacy and protecting our people."

"Protecting them how?" I hadn't heard that story since I was a little girl, but I was fairly certain there wasn't anyone trying to invade the village.

She gave me a look like she thought I was the dumbest creature on Earth. "We're a verra special tribe, *a Mhàili*. You have…a skill, do ye not? Ye probably used yours to find yer way here. Well, I have a skill too and I expect when she gets here, we'll find that our cousin Rona has one as well. Ye canna learn these things."

"Sure you can. My mama taught me." And she had, when I was a little girl. It had been a game, but I hadn't really used it in years before that day.

"She was able to teach ye because ye're one of us. Ye couldna teach these things to new folk, *sluagh ùr*. Even our own people can't learn these things, only *na triuir peathraichean*."

"The three sisters?" Sounded a bit too much like religion to me. I could picture the sweaty, red-faced preacher back in Kettle Holler talking to people on the street as he unlocked his new Cadillac, calling every person he saw struggling to buy shoes "Brother This" and "Sister That" and telling them all how Mama and I were the sinners. I wasn't sure I wanted that kind of sisterhood. "We're not sisters."

"Och, but we are in the ways that count, just like our mothers are." She shook her head. "I still can't believe she didna tell ye this."

Neither could I. I would have said Sheila was pulling my leg, but everything she was saying fit with the things I knew. Mama just never connected those things for me. "What about the feast then, if it's not a homecoming?"

"Aye, well, we have to keep the line going, so there will always be three sisters. So every generation we have to," she smiled like she had some secret joke and her cheeks started turning pink, "plan for the next."

She gave me a significant look, as if I should know what she meant. I was starting to get an idea, but I needed for her to say it outright. I set my jaw and spoke through my teeth. "Just tell me exactly what you mean."

Sheila looked right smug at knowing so much when I knew so little. I wanted to like this new cousin, but it seemed to me she was enjoying this conversation too much. There was definitely laughter in her voice when she said, "It's a matchmaking ceremony, or a mating one at least."

I could feel my blood starting to boil and my skin turning red from the neck up. "What do you mean, mating ceremony?"

Sheila started strolling again and stepped up onto the bridge. "It's just that ye dinna have to marry the lad if ye dinna want to, just have a child."

That stopped me in my tracks and had the mutton stew rising in my throat. I covered my mouth and muttered under my hand, leaning toward the side of the bridge. "I think I'm gonna be sick."

Sheila looked like butter wouldn't melt in her mouth. "Not in the burn. The privy is over there."

I followed the direction of her elegantly pointed finger to a small turf-covered hut that did prove to be an outhouse. As I ran to keep ahead of my roiling stomach, I heard her call after me, "Dinna be out too late. The green man'll get ye."

CHAPTER THIRTEEN

December 12, 1995
Chapel Hill, North Carolina

Dermot put his feet up on the arm of the couch, having finally tired of kicking himself over kissing Sarah. He really had to gain some control. Giving in to those impulses was only going to hurt her more. Not to mention that he couldn't protect her if he kept acting like a bloody teenager.

He'd spent the last couple of hours castigating himself. Now he tried to relax while mentally reviewing everything he needed for the next day. His passport and ticket were in his backpack. He had packed all of his clothes. Fleming and whoever was coming to help him would be using the flat, so he'd left the measly collection of household things he had acquired. They would donate them before they left. Fleming and Sarah would drive him to the airport in the morning.

He closed his eyes and moved on to a mental list of things he needed to do once he was home. Topping the list was visiting Mum. It had been months since he'd seen her. He had to work with James's security team on the building they would be living in. He needed to get the research team office up and running, and then help plan their first fundraiser.

She was standing in the upstairs hallway, naked and shivering. Water dripped from her hair, making tiny puddles on the worn pine floor boards. Afternoon sunlight stretched into the hall from the rooms on either side, peeking through the cracked door at the end of the hall.

Behind her, the bathroom light glinted off the water puddled around the feet of the old bathtub. Wet footprints tracked from the tub to where she stood. White, star-shaped windflowers were scattered across the floor. Sarah knelt to pick one up. Another blossom fell from her hair and landed with a wet plop at her feet.

A grunt and gasp somewhere behind her had her turning back toward the door. She stood up and took a cautious step in that direction. She heard the first whispers. Voices she had heard so many times they were part of her sounded low and urgent near her ears. It was like someone was standing behind her whispering over her shoulder.

…never get to you…

Sarah whipped around to see the source of the whisper, but there was nothing to see but walls and wet floor.

…an righ air chall's a…

Another voice sounded over her other shoulder, but again when she looked no one was there.

…not my baby, I'll…

…banoan chann ur afoinn…

The voices continued. Mixing and talking over each other, growing louder.

…Eirichidh e a-rithist…

…won't let them take…

More grunting and panting came from down the hall, as if someone was laboring hard and painfully. The grunts occasionally turned to sobs. Sarah didn't know if it was better to follow the awful sounds coming from the room, or to get away *from the voices behind her, but she slid one foot in front of the other, slowly moving down the hall. Her heart was racing; goosebumps rose on her cold skin. Water dripped from her hair, trailing in icy tendrils down her back.*

...Shnàmh mhaidean air an ...

...can't have you...

With his eyes closed and deep in thought, he didn't hear Sarah come out of her room. He opened his eyes to see her standing where the hallway opened into the main room. She was shivering, her teeth practically chattering, and her breath was shallow and fast. "Sarah?"

The voices rose as she moved toward the door, their confused messages gaining urgency. Sarah's heartbeat sounded in her ears, adding to the crowded noise in her head. And still came the grunting and sobbing from the room in front of her.

She lifted her hand to push open the door. Her fingers were shaking, and she snapped her fist closed, tightening all the muscles in her hand to gain control. She opened her fingers again and pushed the door open.

Sarah didn't acknowledge him. She lifted her arm, her hand shook, and she balled it into a tight fist before she opened it again and made a pushing motion.

Dermot sat forward on the couch. She had to be sleepwalking. He'd seen her in the throes of a nightmare before, but never like this. He wondered if he should wake her.

The voices grew even louder, mixing with other sounds, the cacophony almost drowning out the familiar creak of the hinges. Her mother was there, kneeling on the bed and frantically digging at an open vein in her wrist. Sarah watched in icy horror as Mama reached up to drag two bloody fingers in a line down the wall, making part of a "t." Most of the letters were already there. Bloody drops slid from the "r," "u," and "i." Mama returned to her wrist, covering her fingers in more blood like dipping them in some macabre inkwell.

The voices went on muttering. Sarah had heard about all she could take. She tried her best to ignore them and reached out to Mama. She had to stop her. She grabbed her mother's shoulder.

Sarah gasped. Her arm raised again, she seemed to pull something toward her. Dermot held his breath

Mama whirled around, and her dark, frantic eyes met Sarah's. Suddenly, there was silence. No more voices, no sobbing, no shivering. Mama lifted her bloody hand to caress Sarah's cheek. She was lost in her mother's eyes, so brown they were almost black. Mama was looking at her with such love that Sarah's heart ached with it. She tried to recall a time when her mother had looked at her like that, but any memories had been blotted out by her mother's illness.

Mama nodded slowly in understanding, as if she knew what her sickness had done to her little girl. Tears streamed down her face. Then she drew in a deep breath, and broke the silence. Her voice was full of desperation, "Run."

With a speed that he'd only seen in her once before, she took off like a shot. Running. She crashed into the door before he could reach her. By the time he got his arms around her, she had recovered and her fingers were scrabbling to open the lock.

He pinned her arms to her side and tried to pull her away from the door. She fought him with every bit of strength she had. She didn't scream or cry. She wasn't looking for attention; she was desperate for escape. Her feet found purchase on the carpet, and she pushed with all her strength toward the door. When that didn't work, she relaxed until he loosened his grip slightly, then she threw all her weight toward the door.

He caught her around the waist and lifted her off the floor. He whirled around to the couch and sat down, pulling her with him. She tried to spring back up, but he dumped her onto the cushion and pressed her into the couch.

"Sarah!" he shouted directly into her face. Her eyes were open, but her only response was to struggle harder to break free. Memories flashed in his mind of him lying on top of her in the dirt and leaves of a forest on Grandfather Mountain a few months before. It was worse this time. Understanding more of her history gave him insight into what she might be running from. Maybe she was running from him. "Sarah!"

All her resistance stopped. Dermot froze, not knowing if she was awake and not wanting to risk letting her go. The only sound was their ragged breathing. He watched awareness come over her like a curtain being lifted. Her eyes darted around in confusion, taking in the details of her surroundings. When her eyes met his, they were full of a pain that nearly gutted him. Tears filled them and slid into her hair. She didn't make a sound.

"Ah love." He lifted a hand to wipe the tears away. "Was it Ryan?"

She tried to speak. The words backed up behind her lips, which were pressed together in a hard line. Part of her seemed to want to talk, but she also seemed scared. In the end she could only shake her head.

Then the dam broke. She began to sob. Sarah buried her face in his neck, and he held her while she let the flood take her. He shifted so he was lying beside her and let her weep.

When the storm had passed, she pushed away from him and sat up. She propped her elbows on her knees and let her head fall into her hands.

"It was Mama," she said after a few shuddering breaths. "I told you I found her, right?"

"Aye."

Sarah scooted away from him. Dermot shifted to give her room and watched as she folded herself into the smallest possible space at the corner of the couch, "This was god-awful. Sh…she was…"

She swallowed hard, shaking her head. "There was blood everywhere. She wasn't dead, though. She was…ugh…she was smearing it on the wall. She told me to run."

Dermot slumped back on the couch. He couldn't bring himself to imagine the things that Sarah had gone through with her mother. Surviving the things that she had would have wrecked a lesser person. He wondered if it was the Stuarts that her mother was warning her about…or herself. He waited for her to say more, but she was quiet.

"You know she was dead by the time she was my age?" Sarah said after a while. Her voice was quiet, but more steady. "She was only nineteen when I was born, and here I am. I've lived longer than she did."

He didn't know what to say to that. He wanted to tell her a thousand things, but they wouldn't be anything more than platitudes.

"Sometimes I feel like I'm on a timer." She put a hand to her head, as if she could keep those thoughts from spilling out. "She was just a sad, young mother trapped by a child she didn't want until one day she snapped."

"And here I am. I survived living with her and living without her. I survived Ryan. I've lost everything, and I might lose it all again. I can't help wondering, when am I going to snap?"

He stood up and paced around the coffee table. He'd never heard her sound this defeated. He gritted his teeth and said, "Ye're not her."

"Aren't I?" She looked directly at him for the first time since she'd started talking. Her face was full of uncertainty. "How can a child grow up around that and not be damaged? How much of this could be genetic?"

"Will ye stop talking shite," he whispered sharply, dropping to his knees in front of her. He gripped her by the arms and tried to resist the urge to shake her. "Ye said yerself. Ye've survived more, lived longer. Could she have fought off a killer? Could she have built the life you have? Ye're the strongest person I know."

"But it's always there." Her voice got quiet and small as she shrank further into the corner of the couch. Her eyes were red. She looked wrung out. "I'm always wondering where that threshold is. How many times am I going to get knocked down before I stop getting back up?"

He took her hands and held them tight between his. His eyes bored into her. "And every time ye do get back up, ye're stronger than ye were before. You're. Not. Her."

Her eyes searched his, probably searching for the truth after all the lies he'd told her. She shouldn't have to look far. Those words were some of the truest he'd ever said. She took a deep breath and nodded. "Not today."

He smiled and choked back the lump in his throat. "Like ye said, keep eating, keep breathing, keep sleeping."

"Keep living." She gave him a watery smile.

"Aye, that's right." He kissed her forehead and wrapped his arms around her. She embraced him and held on tight. He wanted to drag her away and protect her from the Jameses and Walters and Ryans of the world for the rest of their lives. But he knew that even if he threw his entire life away, Mum and all, they would still be found eventually.

CHAPTER FOURTEEN

The sun sliced through the blinds and across her face as Sarah blinked away sleep. Awareness came slowly and with it the dawning realization that she was sleeping on Dermot. Her legs were thrown over his lap and she leaned against his shoulder, her face resting just below the spot where his ear met his jaw. It was a favorite spot of hers. She knew just what a kiss placed in that very spot would do to him.

She breathed in his scent, marking it in her memory and wondering when they would be this close again. He was resting his head against the back of the couch, his mouth slightly open in sleep. One arm supported her back while the other rested across her legs. His hand loosely splayed across her thigh. From the steady rise and fall of his chest, Sarah thought he must still be sleeping. He couldn't be comfortable with her leaning on him so heavily.

Resisting the allure of her favorite spot on his neck, Sarah gently tried to get up without waking him. She had barely shifted when the arm around her back pulled her closer. The hand on her thigh slid higher, his fingers pressing into her skin. He turned his head to rest against hers. His voice rumbled low but urgent, "Not yet, *a graidh*."

His mumbled endearment was enough for Sarah. She nuzzled the spot under his ear and let her body melt into his. The world could wait.

***

Sarah pulled her hair back and twisted it into a tight bun. She secured it with an elastic band before using conditioner to smooth back any stray curls. She slid into her favorite pair of jeans and opted for a pretty fitted sweater rather than the usual T-shirt and flannel. She even swiped her cheeks with a hint of blush. Checking herself in the mirror, she was satisfied with the look: put together, but not obviously trying to make an impression.

Of course, no amount of hair elastics, makeup, or a push-up bra could stop the roiling ball of snakes that had taken up residence in her gut. She would have thought that spending half the night curled up on the couch with Dermot would have helped her relax, but his impending departure had her even more on edge than usual. She'd be damned, though, if she was going to let Dermot get on a plane with the image of her sleepwalking or crying or freaking out fresh in his mind. As it was, she wasn't convinced he really would leave—or that she really wanted him to.

As she stepped into the hallway she heard Dermot asking nervously, "And ye won't leave her alone for even a minute?"

"I was there too, mate. I know the threat is real," Fleming said with more calm.

"I dinna have to tell ye how important—"

"No, of course not."

"If anything happens—"

"We won't let anything happen." Fleming lost some of his usual good humor.

Sarah went into the room, not wanting their conversation to escalate into an argument. Dermot was standing by the door, his duffel bag at his feet. Fleming stood near the table, coffee mug in hand. Dermot looked like he'd already downed a few cups. He was practically vibrating with agitation.

Sarah looked down at his bag and back up to his eyes. "In a hurry to get away from me?"

He huffed and set his hands on his hips. "Of course, not."

"My backup is a touch late in arriving," Fleming explained. "Yer mother hen here isna taking it well."

"And ye can bet I'll be reporting that to Shaw," Dermot said, pacing away from the door.

"Who's Shaw?" Sarah asked.

"My boss," Fleming said.

Dermot was on his way back to the door when a knock sounded from outside. "Ah. Let's hope that's him."

Fleming checked the peephole before opening the door just wide enough to view the identification the person on the outside held up. A deep voice with a Georgia accent said, "Mark Shaw sent me."

Fleming whispered something that Sarah couldn't hear. The voice from the hall returned as little more than a rumble, but it must have been the right answer because Fleming let the door open wide enough to let the man in. Sarah's first impression was that he could have been a student. He was dressed in relaxed jeans, a hooded university sweatshirt, and high-topped sneakers. He looked like he was heading for class or the next basketball game. He was tall, but not too tall. He was good-looking, but not too good-looking. He seemed perfectly suited to blend in with almost any crowd he would encounter. He stepped into the apartment and extended a hand to Fleming. "Curtis Blake."

Fleming gave his hand a brief shake. "Fleming Sinclair."

"You're late," Dermot snapped.

Curtis raised an eyebrow at him. Fleming cleared his throat. "My colleague, Dermot Sinclair."

Curtis held out his hand for Dermot. "Family business?"

"Ye might say that." Dermot shook his hand.

"Actually, I was early. I've been scoping out the street, getting the lay of the land." Curtis walked toward the front window and motioned for Dermot to follow. "Did you know there's a woman sitting in a parked car half a block away? She's been there for the last couple of hours."

Dermot followed and parted the blinds with two fingers. Evidently he saw the same thing Curtis had, because Sarah could hear his teeth grinding from across the room.

Then a hopeful thought struck her, and she rushed to the window with her heart in her throat. "Is it Amy?"

Dermot caught her before she could look. "I dinna recognize the car."

"It could be one of her family's cars. I should talk to her." She turned for the door, excited by the thought that her friend might be ready to talk, might have forgiven her.

Dermot stepped in front of Sarah as Fleming blocked the door. "We don't know that it's Amy. It could well be a reporter or the next Ryan Cumberland."

That stopped her. She had been so excited at the prospect of making peace with Amy that she hadn't thought about the other possibilities. She looked at Curtis. "Do you have a description?"

He shook his head. "Couldn't get a good look. She's wearing a hat and sunglasses."

Sarah felt deflated. Dermot looked at Curtis. "Did ye get the license plate?"

"Do you have a pencil and paper?" he answered.

Sarah went to the kitchen pass-through to get a pad and pen. She brought them back to Curtis.

"Thank you, ma'am." He wrote down the license plate before handing it to Dermot.

Dermot glanced at the paper and smacked the pad against his thigh. "It'll take at least a day for Alba Security to get this checked out."

"If we were in Georgia, I could have it checked," Curtis shrugged. "But I don't have any police contacts here."

"I might," Sarah said.

The men all looked at her. She could tell immediately that Dermot understood who she was talking about. "Do ye think he'd help us?"

Sarah waggled her head from side to side and drew in a hissing breath. "I think he'd help me."

"Might be worth a shot," Fleming put in.

"Do we just call the police department and ask for him?" Dermot asked.

"I have his number. Hang on." She went back to her room and retrieved the business card that was stuck in the frame of her mirror. She returned to the front room where the men were waiting and held up the card. "Let's hope he's there."

After three rings a gruff voice answered, "MacDuff."

"Umm, hi," she said stupidly.

"Yeah?" he barked.

She cleared her throat and went on with more confidence, "Sorry, it's Sarah. I could use your help."

All the impatience that had been in his voice was gone when he said, "Are you alright? What can I do?"

Sarah couldn't help smiling. Now he sounded like the Duff she knew. "There's a woman sitting in a parked car near my apartment. She's been there for a couple of hours, and it's making me kind of nervous. Is there a way for you to check her out?"

"Do you have a plate?" His tone was business-like, but not unkind.

"Yes." Sarah read him the plate that Curtis had written down.

"Right, give me thirty minutes."

She didn't have time to thank him before she heard the click of the line going dead.

Sarah looked up to find all three of her bodyguards, staring at her in expectation. It wasn't the kind of scrutiny she enjoyed. She told them, "He said give him thirty minutes."

They all nodded silently. After a few seconds, Curtis extended his hand to Sarah, giving her a warm smile that sparked in his dark brown eyes. "In the meantime, we haven't been properly introduced. I'm Curtis Blake."

Sarah shook his hand and smiled back. His confident demeanor went a long way toward putting her at ease. "Sarah MacAlpin."

"I know." His smile grew. "I'm going to be your shadow for the next few weeks."

"Okay," she said. "What do you need from me?"

"I think that's going to depend on who that is watching your place and where we go." His voice was smooth and reassuring. He cut his eyes over to Fleming. "I'll be on the day shift while you have the nights, right?"

"That's the plan," Fleming answered.

"Great." Curtis looked back to Sarah. "Then I'd appreciate it if you told me each evening where you plan to go the next day. It'll give me a chance to scout the buildings and routes."

"Okay. I can't always promise I'll know the day before, but I'll try," she said. "I hope you like libraries. I spend a lot of time in them."

He laughed a low, sexy rumble. "I'm sure it'll be fine. We should work out a signal for when you get nervous about anything around you. Maybe a tug on your ear or something like that."

Sarah nodded. "I can do that."

She looked over at Dermot, who was watching the new guy closely. Curtis followed her eyes. "You're leaving today?"

Dermot nodded. "I just have time to clear up this issue of the woman in the car, and then we have to be going. Ye'll have to forgive me, but ye seem very relaxed. Did Shaw explain the situation to ye?"

Curtis lifted his chin a notch. "You seem mighty tense, man. I find that a calm demeanor puts clients at ease."

"She was nearly killed a week ago. She's not at ease." Dermot's voice took on a new edge as he stepped closer to Curtis, who squared his shoulders. "And ye shouldna be either."

Curtis moved closer to Dermot, his brows drawing together and his eyes going hard. "I have a track record that proves my methods work. That's why I was hired."

The two men seemed ready to face off right there in her living room. Sarah inserted her arms between them and pushed both men back. "Okay, guys, we're all on the same team here. Remember?"

"He's not serious. He doesn't understand," Dermot seethed to her in Gaelic.

Sarah turned to him, responding in the same language, "You don't know that and you're nervous. Calm down."

"You're too precious. I'm not going." He waved his hands in a gesture of finality.

"Yes, you are. You need to go." She took a step closer to him and lowered her voice. This wasn't a conversation that needed an audience, even if they had no idea what she and Dermot were saying. "I need you to go. I can't make any decisions about how to move forward with you near."

His blue eyes held hers for a long, tense moment. "Will I see you again?"

Sarah took a long breath of her own. "I don't know."

He closed his eyes and absorbed her answer. She hated hurting him, but she wouldn't lie. She turned to Curtis. "You'll have to forgive Dermot. He's a friend and a colleague. He doesn't have your objectivity on the situation."

"I can tell." He looked at Dermot. "It's all good, man. I'll take good care of her."

Dermot didn't speak. He could only nod before stalking into the kitchen, leaving Sarah to stand in awkward silence while he very loudly searched for a clean mug.

Roughly twenty minutes later, the phone rang. For once, Sarah answered it, something she hadn't done in a week. "Hello?"

"That car is registered to an Elizabeth Cartwright of Wake County," Duff's voice said without preamble. "And a patrol car should be paying her a visit any minute."

Sarah didn't know what else to say except, "Thank you."

"It's no problem." She could picture his wry smile. "You take care now, Sarah-girl."

"I will." Again he cut off the call before she could say goodbye, but Sarah couldn't help smiling. He always had her back, even when she hadn't known he was there. The guys were watching her. She tilted her head toward the window.

Fleming was closest this time. He peeked through the blinds and grinned. "There's a police car pulling up behind her. His lights are on."

"It's that reporter who tried to talk to me the other day, Beth Cartwright."

Dermot grumbled, "Ye'd best keep that press release on hand."

"I've got it," Sarah said. "But I don't think we want to use it for one reporter at one very small paper."

Fleming stepped back from the window, and Sarah saw the shadow of a car pass by. He turned and looked out the blinds again to follow Ms. Cartwright's progress down Ransom Street. After several seconds he turned back to the room. "She's gone for now."

***

Raleigh-Durham International Airport was not what people generally thought of when they thought of international airports. Rather than bustling and crowded, it worked at a steady but relaxed pace and, though small, there tended to be plenty of room for travelers to sit while waiting for flights. Sarah shifted in the standard-issue black leather chair. Flanked by two of her guard dogs, she couldn't help feeling self-conscious. Of course, anyone else would simply think that two friends had given a third a ride to the airport. Sarah had to keep reminding herself that no one else knew any differently.

They'd been sitting in awkward silence punctuated by occasional flights of small talk for nearly an hour. Sarah had to admit that Fleming was pretty good at small talk, and he was carrying most of the weight on that front. He had a quick wit and a friendly disposition that made him easy to be around. She was grateful for something to diffuse the tension that was crackling between her and Dermot like static electricity.

Still, they had exhausted most avenues of conversation some time ago. Sarah had tried to distract herself by imagining stories behind the people they saw walking by or milling about the gate. There was a family reunion taking place at the gate across the aisle as a college-aged young man got off an arriving flight to be surrounded by parents and younger siblings. She smiled, watching the two younger kids hopping and talking over each other in their excitement. Then she made up a story about the tired looking couple who were leaning on each other at the end of one row of benches. They'd been in Raleigh to visit friends and had too much fun the night before.

Sarah was willing to grab at any straw that would help her forget why they were there. Yes, she had told Dermot to leave. She had wanted some peace, if only for a few weeks, but she was painfully aware this may be the last time she ever saw him.

"We are beginning the boarding process for Flight 1438 to London, Gatwick. We'll start with first class passengers and anyone needing assistance boarding," a pretty blond gate agent announced over the public address system. She was primly dressed in the practically designed uniform with its scarf tied neatly at the collar. Sarah was both relieved and terrified to hear the announcement.

Fleming was the first to stand. He offered his hand to Dermot. "Well, mate, it's been grand. I'll see ye in a few weeks."

"That ye will," Dermot said, shaking his hand. He jerked his head in Sarah's direction. "Take good care of her, aye?"

Fleming nodded, showing he understood full well the importance of keeping Sarah safe. He jerked his head toward a newsstand near the gate. "Of course. I'll just be over there."

He walked out of earshot, though not out of sight, and pretended to be interested in the Raleigh paper.

Sarah stood and nervously wiped her hands on her jeans. "Well, I guess this is it."

Dermot looked down into her eyes. "Is it?"

"For now." She stepped closer. For all her words telling him to go, she wished that he would put his arms around her. She wished he would tell her again that he loved her. "You'll call or send me an email when you get there, so I know you're safe?"

"I will." He reached for her and pulled her into a chaste hug. Sarah breathed in his scent, a combination of soap and musk. She clung to him. "I don't have to go. I mean, if ye need me."

Sarah let out a quick, sharp laugh. "Oh, I need you, but I don't think you should stay."

He gave her shoulders a squeeze. "I wish it could be different."

"Yeah." Try as she might, she couldn't help the tears pooling in her eyes. She pulled away, not wanting to let him see just how much this hurt. "Me too."

He picked up his backpack from the chair where he'd left it and slung it over his shoulder. "Right, I'll see ye in a few weeks then."

Afraid the tears would spill over, Sarah backed away. She didn't trust her voice, so she tried to smile and gave an equivocal, "Mmhmm."

He turned to the gate and presented his boarding pass. Sarah felt like a lovesick puppy standing in the middle of the aisle watching him walk away. She was reminded of the part in Jane Eyre when Rochester tells Jane that he feels like there is a string tied around each of their hearts, and that if she goes too far from him it will snap. The tugging she felt from her ribs was that string pulling tighter, stretching thinner.

She had to remind herself this was for the best. If he was here, if he waited for her to come with him, she would never choose anything but to be near him. Whether that was the best thing for her or not, she would always go where he took her. His very presence tethered her to him. Without him near, she could think, she could look at all the angles. Without him near, she could choose.

He stopped just before stepping on the gangway and looked back at her. He raised an eyebrow in question, as if to say, "Last chance. Still want me to go?" She tried to smile, but knew she probably failed so she gave a short nod. He nodded back and turned to walk down the ramp to the plane.

Sarah stood rooted to that spot as the few stragglers boarded behind him. She watched as the gate agent closed the heavy metal door after the boarding stopped, and then as the plane disconnected and rolled away from the gate. All the while feeling that cord stretch further and further.

She wasn't sure how long she would have stood there staring at the spot where his plane had been if she hadn't heard Fleming clear his throat behind her. She turned to find him waiting there with a newspaper tucked under his arm. "Ready?"

"Yeah." She took a step toward him before looking over her shoulder again at the gate. No.

CHAPTER FIFTEEN

June 1968

From the journal of Molly MacAlpin

The next morning after our porridge, I found Duff stacking peat behind the hall. He looked like he'd been up and working for a while. His hair was damp and his sleeves were rolled up. He wasn't alone. Davie Lyall was helping him. They were laughing and joking like they didn't have a care in the world.

I didn't want an audience so I grabbed Duff's wrist and pulled him out of earshot. "How soon do you think we can get out of here?"

He took my arm and turned me to face him. "Now hold on a minute. These are your people."

"I don't want to claim kin with these people," I said, glancing around his shoulder to make sure we weren't attracting attention. "You didn't want to be here to begin with and now I don't either. We need to go before the feast."

Anger clouded his features, and for a second I thought he might be mad at me. He growled, "Has somebody hurt you?"

"What? Not yet." I shook my head and tried to keep my voice down. "Do you know what they want me to do?"

"I have a pretty good idea. They're matchmaking, right?"

"That's a nice way of putting it. They mean for me to have a baby! Me and Sheila and this Rona girl when she gets here. And we don't get any say in the matter."

"Wait. Do you mean to tell me you didn't know that's what we were coming here for?" He bent his head closer to me.

"Do you mean you did?" It's a good thing I don't have heat vision like Superman, else I'd have burnt a hole in his skull with the look I gave him.

He put his hands up to ward me off. "Now, hold on. I didn't know anything about this baby business or about you not getting your pick. All I knew was that you needed to get here for the matchmaking, and I was the one to do it."

"And you didn't think to say anything?" My voice rose higher.

"How was I supposed to know you didn't know anything?" he whispered through his teeth, glancing back toward where Davie was still stacking peat.

"I told you I have plans! I'm going to be a dancer, and I'm not going to be dragging along a man I didn't choose or a baby I don't want." I could feel my blood pressure rising.

Duff pulled me further away from the hall. "Listen, I didn't know about that. I swear. But I do know that we don't have a lot of choice. I didn't want to leave my life either, but I'm pledged to protect you. I've known since I was a little boy that I might get picked to do something like this. But when they came and told me, I tried hard to get out of it. They told me that I either came here with you or I'd get a dishonorable discharge. This is bigger than you think, and these people will get what they want."

None of what he was saying made sense to me. "What people, and what do you mean you've known since you were a little boy?"

He sighed, and I could tell this answer was not going to be a quick one. He looked around and extended a hand toward a large rock further up the hill. "Let's sit down."

Duff ushered me to the rock, and we sat side by side. He took a deep breath and turned my way slightly. "I'm from a little town down east, outside of Fayetteville. You probably wouldn't even know the name. It ain't got much but hogs, tobacco farms, and MacDuffs. We're all related there, and just about all of us know our duty."

"I still don't know what you're talking about." I was feeling like such a fool for being the only one not to know any of this.

He raised an eyebrow at me. "How much Scottish history did your Mama tell you?"

"Enough." Not that I had listened much. "I thought."

"Do you know about the Sinclairs?" he asked patiently.

"The king's stewards," I gasped. "That's what everyone means by calling you that?"

"Right. Well, when there wasn't a kingdom anymore to take care of, a branch of the Sinclairs turned to taking care of things that were in the interest of the king-in-exile, or in the interest of restoring the kingdom. Well, the MacDuffs, at least mine, are part of that branch of Sinclairs. We grow up knowing that someday we'll be called on for service. That's why I'm here. Your family is very important to the kingdom."

I huffed in exasperation. "Duff, there is no kingdom anymore."

"Wrong." He looked around us and kicked the rock we were sitting on. "Scotland didn't go anywhere. It's still here. Just because it doesn't have its own king or its own government doesn't mean that it's any less than it was. The people are just as strong as ever, and there are some who understand that that's what matters."

"Even to a boy from Tobaccoville, North Carolina?" I gave him the look your Granny always gives when she thinks I'm fibbing. "Can you really say that matters to an American? To a marine?"

He pressed his lips together and took a deep breath. "When I've been told about it from the cradle. It's like…what do the Catholics call it…Cata—"

"Catechism?" I supplied.

"That's it." He looked back toward the hall. "I won't lie. It ain't been easy. You know how angry I was when you met me. I didn't want to leave the marines for this, that's for damn sure." He leaned forward, propping his elbows on his knees, and picked up a stone. He began tossing the stone from hand to hand.

"We were about done with boot camp at Parris Island and fixin' to ship out when I got called into the colonel's office. The colonel was in there with some suit who introduced himself as senator something or other. Of course, I wouldn't know my senator from a hole in the wall. Whoever he was, he knew just what strings to pull. He had that colonel dancing like a marionette. They told me they had a special mission for me and only me.

"Now, you tell a marine you've got a special mission just for him, and he's gonna jump at it. I left that colonel's office feeling happy as a pig in shit, like I was something special. Then a couple of days later they told me I was escorting some girl from up in the mountains across the wrong ocean to Scotland instead of going to Vietnam." He hit my shoulder with his, and I heard a little smile in his voice.

He sobered and said, "I respectfully told them that I didn't think that was the best use of my training. To which the senator said he was sorry, but he was sure my uniform read MacDuff, and he just knew I didn't want to shame my family by not only refusing my sacred duty but also being discharged from the Corps. So I could refuse and lose everything I'd been working for and never go home again, or I could fall in line. Well, if you'd ever met my daddy, you would know that there was no choice at all."

"And here you are," I said.

"Here I am." He looked around the glen like he still couldn't quite believe it. "The reason I'm telling you this is to show you that this is important to more than just the people in this glen. There is a whole network of people working to make this happen, and some of them are pretty powerful. You might get out of here. You might even get out of Scotland, but they'll track you down."

I studied him for a long minute. "Are you pledged to protect me, Duff, or to keep me in line?"

He leaned back and looked at me. "I'm pledged to protect you, even if sometimes that means protecting you from yourself."

"Hmmph." I didn't much appreciate that. I never really thought Duff was my friend. He sure hadn't acted friendly, but I had thought he was supposed to be there for me. "What about me, Duff? Doesn't what I want matter?"

"It ain't about you, Molly." He laid a hand on mine where it rested in my lap and gave it a gentle squeeze. "This is a lot bigger than either of us."

"I still don't understand why," I grumbled. Nobody ever seemed to want to give me a whole answer.

"I reckon you'd better ask your aunt about that. She can tell you more than anybody else." He patted my knee and went off to catch up with Davie and the work they were doing.

***

"Och, I expect she's preparing for the feast day," Jock said when I found him on the outskirts of the village digging up potatoes in a small patch. They weren't in rows like a garden, but bunched in a clump.

"Do you think she could use some help?" I offered, hoping he would tell me where to find her.

"No, lass." He gave me a significant look. "I dinna think anyone can help with that. But ye can give me a hand wi' these tatties."

I couldn't do much else without being rude, so I helped Jock harvest potatoes, herbs, and greens. He had them planted in little patches all over the hills around the village just like Mama does with her barley. You wouldn't know there was that much food growing around there if you didn't know where to look.

I was dropping a handful of radishes into his basket when it struck me that there didn't seem enough to feed the whole village. "Is this going to be enough food?"

"Och, sure." Jock glanced at the basket. "We dinna really need this. But it's nice to have some variety. Ye canna always be eating stew and parritch."

I'd had two meals so far, and there never seemed to be a shortage of food. I had watched Jock dish out stew and porridge to everyone in the hall and not run out, even when I didn't think the pot could hold any more. "Where does it all come from, Jock?"

He looked at me like I must be joking. Then his beard split into a grin. "From the cauldron of course."

I couldn't tell if he was teasing me, but I let it pass and went back to digging for radishes. It felt good to have my hands in the dirt for a bit, like home. And the work helped to sooth my temper. Jock was humming to himself as he worked. It reminded me of Mama. "How well did you know my mama?"

He gave me a fatherly look. "Ye see the size of this glen? Everyone here knows everyone else, and well."

I smiled. "Right."

"Your mam was my friend, if that's what ye're asking."

I stopped digging and studied him. "Do you know why she left here?"

"Och, that's easy, but it's not a happy tale." He swiped the back of a meaty hand across his forehead. "It was the Nazis, or at least we think that's who they were. It was late in the fall of 1938. We were due to have the matching feast the following summer. We only have it once a generation, ye ken."

I nodded, eager to hear more. Mama never talked about why she left, only that it had been necessary.

"Well, things get fair quiet here late in the year as ye can imagine. We're all sitting around the hearth in the great hall when someone notices a lantern coming over the ridge from the loch. Needless to say, we were surprised." He made a gesture toward the nearest cottage with its turf roof, stone walls, and minimal windows. "Ye can see we dinna advertise our presence here. Even when we go to Lochinver or Ullapool, we tell them we're from somewhere else. No one wanders into Làrachd an Fhamhair, unless they're looking for it. But that's just what this laddie claimed when he staggered into the village half frozen and starved. His clothes were soaked to the skin.

"We canna turn away a body who's hungry and lost, but we were suspicious. He claimed to be on a fishing trip to the loch. Said he'd gotten separated from his mates in a fog and couldna find his way back to Inchnadamph. Of course, we didna believe that story. We couldna see anyone who wasn't local fishing that late in the year. And we could tell by his accent, German I think, that he wasn't a Scot. So we invited him in, fed him, and let him warm himself by the fire while we pondered what to do.

"The next morning he was too sick to move. We let him stay in the lads' house and continued treating him like a guest. It was on the third day that he started asking questions. At first they were innocent, like, 'What's the name of your village?' and, 'Are ye all the same clan?' We answered what we could, but stayed canny mind ye. The next day I was taking him his breakfast and he asked me about the three witches. Had I heard of them? Did I think they were real? Weel, I didna let on that I had ever heard of sich a thing and left him to his parritch.

"Meanwhile I fetched the sisters, that would be yer grandmother and wee Sheila's as well. The other had already gone to Canada by then. I told them what the German had said. We set to debating whether to stonewall his questions and send him on his way, or to make him disappear. Ye ken?" He waited for me to respond.

I nodded, knowing perfectly well what Jock meant by "disappear."

"In the end it didna matter. The next time someone went to check on him, he was gone. I dinna ken if he'd been pretending from the start or had a miraculous recovery. Either way, he was gone and he knew the location of the village. We had to protect the sisters. There was naught else to do but send them away. So we sent them to Nova Scotia to be with the third sister. They had moved there a generation earlier for similar reasons.

"They left early one morning. I'll never forget the look on your Mam's face. She was sore grieved, she and Eilidh both, but they had to get out before yon German could come back with," he paused, looking for the right word, "reinforcements. I was never sure why Maighread didna come back when Eilidh did. We were told they'd decided to spread out to make it harder to find them all. I suppose that's why Maighread went to America instead of staying in Nova Scotia with Isobel."

I was getting confused. How would I ever keep all of this new family straight? "Isobel is the mother of the third girl we're waiting on, right?"

"Aye, that's right." He grinned. "I met her once. She came here for the feast after the war. Sweet lass, Isobel. We had to wait until nearly 1949 to have the feast that we'd been planning before the war."

"Why so long?" I asked.

"Och weel, there were some camps around the Highlands where they kept some high level Nazis. There were a few escapes. A couple of times they headed this way." He paused, looking away. I thought I saw some memory flicker behind his eyes. Then he shook his head and went back to digging. "We thought it better to be safe and wait."

I did the math in my head. Born in 1950, that meant that I was likely the product of whatever matchmaking feast they'd had in '49. "Did Mama come back for that late feast?"

He shook his head, and I could see his regret. "No, we sent a lad and a steward to her in America."

I never knew my father, and I never remembered Mama having a steward or any other man hanging around. "What happened to them?"

Jock shrugged. "Don't know. I didn't know them well, and they never came back after going to America, like yer ma."

I took his hand. "I know she misses it, misses all of you."

He sniffed and looked away, "Aye, I miss her too."

I made myself busy digging while Jock sat back for a few minutes. We had finished that patch and moved on to the next when another car puttered over the ridge. Jock picked up his basket. I carried the tools, and we headed back to the hall. We were walking past the lads' house when we were overtaken by Willie. His strides ate up the trail and the village center. He didn't say a word to us as he passed.

Jock must have noticed my eyes following him. He watched Willie before leaning toward me to say quietly, "He isna simple minded, ye ken. He's just shy."

If it was shyness, it was the worst case I'd ever seen. He never seemed to speak when I was around. If he talked to anyone else, I didn't see it. I didn't think he was simple either, but he was definitely odd. "I haven't really talked to him, so I'll have to take your word on that."

As we neared the hall, the little green car came to a stop and a girl my age opened the passenger door. She wasn't striking like Sheila, but a softer sort of pretty, with wavy blonde hair and bright blue eyes that looked around the welcoming crowd with a mix of wonder and nerves. I had probably looked the same when I arrived the day before. I wondered if she knew. Had her mother prepared her?

***

We approached the crowd and Jock waded in, basket and all. What followed was a similar conversation to the one I'd had with him the day before. She was indeed Rona MacKenzie and the steward with her, Gavin Sinclair, was a stocky fireplug of a man. His weathered and sunburned face made him appear older than I think he was.

"Go and sit ye doon by the fire," said Jock with a tilt of his head toward the hall. He lifted the basket full of our harvest. "We'll just put these away and have a wash."

When we had washed up, we sat down with a cup of tea to hear about Rona and Gavin's trip and wait for Aunt Eilidh to make her way in to welcome them.

In the end it was Sheila, not Eilidh who showed up. She waltzed in like the queen of the manor with her cool smile. "My mother is preparing herself for the ceremony, ye'll have to forgive her for not welcoming ye. I'll show ye where ye'll be staying."

We took our leave of Jock and Rona, and Gavin fetched their bags from the car. Just as Eilidh had, Sheila led us first to the lads' house. "Gavin, ye'll be staying here with the lads and the other stewards. They should be around here somewhere." She looked around as if they should magically appear.

"They were stacking peat this morning," I put in.

"Ah, yes. Everyone chips in here, especially around feast days." Sheila looked at Gavin like she was assessing his ability to chip in.

"A lot like a fishing boat, no shirkers." He puffed out his chest. "I'll put these inside and see what I can do to help."

He opened the door and found Willie Cross on the other side. He was sitting on the bed and holding something in his hands, something he was looking at intensely. When he saw the light from the door, he slid whatever it was under the mattress and stood up awkwardly, rubbing a nervous hand on his thigh.

"Hallo, Willie," Sheila said, her voice turned sharp. "Come and meet Rona and Gavin."

He stepped forward into the light from the doorway, and I could see the sweat beading on his forehead. His eyes darted back and forth between the four of us.

"This is my cousin, Rona MacKenzie from Canada, and this is her steward, Gavin Sinclair." Willie made eye contact with each of them and nodded, but that wasn't good enough for Sheila. "Say hallo, Willie."

His cheeks turned pink, and I remembered what Jock said about him being shy. I felt right sorry for him. His mouth worked a bit like he couldn't quite get the words out. Finally, he said in a soft voice, "Hallo, Rona, Gavin."

They both smiled in return while Sheila rolled her eyes. Willie saw it and looked down at his shoes, blushing harder. Rona bent down to look into his downcast eyes, her voice full of kindness as she said, "I'm pleased to meet you, Willie."

He gave her a ghost of a smile and another nod.

"Come on, Willie." Gavin put a companionable arm around his shoulder and steered him back into the cottage. "You can show me my bed and then help me find the other stewards."

Willie turned with Gavin, but looked back over his shoulder at us. His eyes met mine, and I smiled at him. Just as they had when we met, the corners of his mouth flicked upward in a tentative smile. Then the door to the cottage closed and Sheila led us on. We crossed the burn and climbed up the hill to Aunt Eilidh's house. "This is where we'll be staying for now.

The three of us are sharing the loft. It's quite comfortable, is it not, *a Mhàili?*"

"Very comfortable," I said.

Sheila looked around the cottage as if she didn't know what to show next. Suddenly her face brightened. "Let me show you where the ceremony will be, at the pool." She arched an eyebrow, looking at me sideways. "You should come too. Our tour was cut so short yesterday."

Sheila waltzed out the door, leaving Rona and I to follow. Rona fell in behind me and whispered, "Is she always like that?"

"I just met her but so far, yes," I whispered over my shoulder.

We followed Sheila down the hillside as she chattered about how the village was run, where and when we ate, the privies, the laundry. It reminded me a little of those communes people talked about in America. Everyone chipping in and everyone benefiting. Still, from the way she lorded her position over all the newcomers and Willie, it didn't seem like any kind of Utopia to me. She took us down along the burn to the bottom of the glen.

There we turned up a steep rocky path that wound back up into the hills. The path ended at a plateau that was surrounded by ridges on all sides and backed by a high rock face. In the middle of it was an almost perfectly round pool of green water. The edge was rimmed with mossy stones. A stump rose in one spot where a tree had once stood. "This is the scrying pool. It'll tell my mam who our matches are."

I stood back while Rona stepped close to the pool and looked at the surface. "Your mom, eh?"

"She is the only sister here," Sheila said, shrugging as if that answered everything.

"Where is her mom?" Rona asked, nodding my way.

"She wasna needed, and it's a long journey from North Carolina. Of course, your mam couldna see it even if she were here," Sheila said before I had a chance to say anything.

I couldn't believe how rude Sheila was being. Rona was surprised too from the hard look she gave our cousin. "My mother sees just fine when she's looking at the future."

Sheila eyed her from across the pool. "Is that so?"

"It is." Rona walked along the edge of the water. "There are supposed to be at least two sisters here. This power shouldn't belong to one. Where did you say your mother is?"

"She's preparing herself for the ceremony." Sheila seemed a little less confident when she said, "In any case, it's a bit late to do aught about that now."

"Mmhmm." Rona seemed unimpressed. She looked my way and said, "This doesn't bother you?"

There was so much about it that bothered me, I didn't know where to begin. "I don't know enough about this to know what should bother me, but I definitely wish my mama was here."

"Oh?" Sheila practically sneered. "Because she did such a fine job of preparing you for the feast?"

Rona and I both looked at her stone-faced. After several seconds, she backed down and mumbled, "Sorry, I'll leave you two to get acquainted."

When she'd been gone long enough for us to believe she was out of earshot, Rona asked, "What did she mean by that?"

"My mother didn't tell me anything about this ceremony, or mating, or…" I heaved a sigh. "Anything. She said it was a homecoming feast for midsummer, and Eilidh only sent the one ticket. We couldn't afford for both of us to come."

"That sounds familiar. They only sent one ticket for me too." We started walking back down the path. "Your mom didn't tell you anything?"

"She told me the story of the giant and his wife and the cauldron, but not like it was our story. It was just another fairy story." I waved as we picked our way down the trail. "I don't understand any of this. It's like y'all are talking a different language."

We walked on, each of us deep in our own thoughts. Eventually Rona asked, "You remember in the story of the giant's footprint how the new folk almost killed the king while they tried to destroy it? And the king's wife and two sisters moved the whole tribe away from the new folk overnight?"

"Yeah, in the boats made from the roofs of their houses." I had always admired their quick thinking.

"Mmhmm. And they were considered the auld folk then. Our people have been protecting the giant's footprint for longer than human history, longer than even legends remember. And the three sisters are the leaders of our people." She looped her arm through mine. "We are descended from those three sisters, and we've been advising kings, at least in this land, since before anyone can remember. And every generation we have to pick mates that will help us maintain our talents without causing the potential problems that come with inbreeding."

"This sounds too bizarre to be real," I couldn't help saying. "It's like the Twilight Zone."

She laughed at that. "I know. Nova Scotia isn't the most modern place in the world, but it's not Làrachd an Fhamhair. I don't know anything I can tell you to make you believe this, except that it would be a mighty elaborate hoax. I've been told this all my life, and the older I get, the harder it is to believe. But whatever doubts I have, I also have talents that other people don't. Don't you?"

You know we do, baby. I know you have them. I had never described them to anyone but Mama before that day, but I said, "I can find things, and people sometimes. I helped the sheriff once find a little boy that got lost on our mountain."

Her smile grew, and I could tell she had similar skills. She said, "I can see some things before they happen. I've saved a fishing boat or two by warning them when not to go out. You see, if everyone was making this up, there would be a lot of people in on that lie, and they can't make up the things we can do."

She had a point. It was hard to imagine all of these people working together on some big lie. And what would be the point of tricking some poor girl from Kettle Holler? It didn't make the situation any easier, but talking with Rona did take away some of my doubt. It even started to make me feel like I was kind of special. "I wonder what Sheila's talent is."

Rona giggled and gave me an arch look. "Being smug and bossy?"

CHAPTER SIXTEEN

December 15, 1995
Chapel Hill, North Carolina

Sarah closed the journal and let it fall to her lap. She sat in her bed staring gape-mouthed through the dark at the opposite wall, trying to process what she just read. Just like her, Molly had been trapped by a strange tradition. It all sounded too familiar. Làrachd an Fhamhair meant Giant's Footprint. Sarah thought of her storybook, "Our people sprang from the footprint of a giant left in stone." She should have noticed that before, but she had been distracted by Mama and Duff. It had taken Rona MacKenzie laying it out like that to connect the village with the legend. Rona MacKenzie. Jock had called her mother Isobel, and Sheila had made that crack about her not being able to see. Rona's mother must have been the same Isobel MacKenzie who Sarah had met in Cape Breton.

"My mother sees just fine when she's looking at the future," Rona had said. Their talent was seeing the future. Suddenly, Sarah's encounter with Isobel took on a whole new dimension. She reviewed it in her mind, settling on the last thing they had talked about when Isobel had given her the stone.

"You're alone in the world. You need something to remind you of your family," the old, blind woman had told her. When she protested, Isobel had said, "I can feel it in the air around you. I can hear it in your voice. You guard yourself well, wee Mòrag. Don't stop. You will know who you can trust."

Sarah had just taken it as the ramblings of an old woman. She'd had no reason to imagine that she had any connection to a blind woman living in a cottage in Nova Scotia. That was, until she found the photograph, and now read her mother's account. This meant there was a lot more to connect Sarah to Bridget MacKenzie than just James Stuart. They were family. Sarah wondered how much Bridget had known when they talked about the stone and where it came from. "The heart of our people," she'd said.

But if Bridget's talent was seeing the future, how had she not known that Ryan Cumberland was after her? Sarah remembered how Bridget had admitted not knowing what the future was. Her plans had been up in the air. Had she known she was going to die?

Sarah had no idea how long she sat there in bed pondering the implications of being able to see the future, but when she came out of her mental fog, the room was bathed in the silvery light of predawn. Unfortunately, Bridget wasn't around to ask anymore and Sarah doubted she would be able to talk with her grandmother, or even her mother, anytime soon, although it might be worth a try. In the meantime, she began to wonder about her own talent. Mama said she could find things or people.

As she described it, it reminded Sarah of something that she did whenever she moved to preserve the memory of a place. She had done it when she moved all of their things out after selling the farm. She would close her eyes and take a mental journey over a place. Mama called it casting out. Maybe it was more than just a journey through memory. She wondered if she could see the present if she tried.

She sat up straighter and folded her legs together as if she were going to meditate. She thought that was close enough to what Mama had done when she tried to find the hidden glen. Amy had talked her into taking some yoga classes shortly after they'd met. Sarah thought the breathing she'd learned should come in handy here.

She inhaled deeply. On the exhale, she focused on relaxing. She started with her face and neck. On the next breath, she worked on her back and core, then her legs. Then she started to listen. She could hear the apartment building around her, the hum of the appliances, the occasional knock of the radiators, and the soft warm sounds of her sleeping neighbors. With each exhale, the sights around her became clearer. The sound and blur began to resolve itself into a picture, and each breath expanded what she could see. Each time she breathed out, it was like she was pushing the walls of her vision further.

She needed something to focus on, somewhere to direct her vision. Fleming. He was on night duty in her apartment. She should be able to find him easily enough. She exhaled again and thought of him. Before she knew it she was looking at Fleming, sitting on the couch in her front room. The light of the television flickered across his face. He was awake, but sitting quietly watching. She didn't hear anything coming from the TV. Sarah wondered if that was a limitation of the vision or if he had the volume turned down. She looked him over again, noting that he was wearing jeans and a green Hibernian Football Club T-shirt under a dark flannel shirt.

Sarah looked around for something she didn't remember seeing before, something that would prove this was the present.

There was a newspaper on the sofa beside him. He had folded it back on itself and the part facing up had a story about the Carolina-Pittsburgh game and another about the upcoming college bowl games. Sarah didn't pay much attention to sports, and she was sure she hadn't seen that page of the newspaper earlier. That was the perfect test.

With one long inhale, Sarah pulled herself back, like sucking herself back into her own body. It took her a few beats to come to full awareness. Now she just needed to see whether that was memory or the present. She climbed off the bed and quietly opened her door. She didn't want to disturb Fleming. She wanted to verify that he was exactly where she had seen him. Sarah tiptoed down the hall and found him. He was sitting comfortably watching an almost silent TV, one leg stretched out under the coffee table.

When she came out of the dark hallway into the light, he sat up straighter and looked at her closely. "Everything alright?"

From his concerned demeanor, Sarah was guessing that Dermot had told him about her tendency toward sleepwalking. "Everything's fine, just came out for a glass of water." She quickly got some water from the kitchen before joining him on the couch. "You know, you can turn the TV up if you want to. I don't mind."

"Och, yeah. I didn't want to disturb ye." He smiled. "Dermot said ye sometimes have trouble sleeping."

So the volume was turned down. Sarah tilted her head in acknowledgment. "He's not wrong about that."

She glanced down at the sofa between them. There was the newspaper complete with the basketball and football articles she had noticed. It had been the present she'd seen. Sarah didn't know whether to be elated that she had this new skill to explore or terrified by the confirmation of that part of her mother's story. The more Molly was telling the truth, and the more similar they were, the more Sarah worried about her future.

What Duff had told Molly about this being bigger than them, and involving powerful people, sounded way too much like what Dermot had told her when he'd laid it all out. The more Molly's story was confirmed, the more it confirmed Dermot's story too.

CHAPTER SEVENTEEN

December 15, 1995
Edinburgh, Scotland

After fifteen more hours of drinking, fitful sleep, and fretful nail biting punctuated by an interminable layover in London, Dermot trudged through the baggage claim in Edinburgh. He was on his way out the door when she stepped right in front of him. Her perfectly polished black pumps blocked his path to the exit. With considerable effort he dragged his eyes up from the floor and took in a woman so put together that she could have walked out of a business magazine. Nothing was out of place, from her pencil skirt to her prim French twist, and she was holding a sign with his name on it.

"Mr. Sinclair." It wasn't a question. Her voice seemed familiar, but she confirmed it when she held out a hand and said, "I'm Audra Lennox. Mr. Stuart wanted me to make sure that you arrived safely and were able to find the house on Bernard Terrace."

So he wasn't to have a moment to collect himself. James clearly wanted him to hit the ground running, and he's sent his own personal assistant to make sure that happened. Dermot shook the woman's hand and tried to be personable. "Nice to put a face to the voice."

"Likewise." She smiled cheerfully before turning toward the door. "Our car is right this way."

Dermot followed her outside to where a sedan was waiting, driver already holding the door. Miss Lennox lowered herself into the car almost without breaking stride. She slid across to give him room, and Dermot gave his bag to the driver with a nod of greeting and got in.

"I hope your flight was smooth," Miss Lennox said. Her rounded vowels and soft consonants should have been soothing, but after so many months in America, he found the difference jarring.

Although he was sure the woman's cool efficiency was much valued by James Stuart, in his current jet-lagged and hungover state, her calm assurance grated on his nerves. His answer was little more than an equivocal grunt; it was rude to be sure, but he was past caring at the moment.

If she was at all put off by his bad manners, she didn't show it. "We should be there shortly."

They rode the rest of the way in silence, through the bustling streets of Edinburgh. Dermot watched the familiar city go by. He and his mother had been nomads most of his youth, moving from one university to another throughout the country. She had finally settled in Edinburgh when he'd been in his teens, and it had started to feel like home. They passed through residential areas where small square houses lined up in their small gardens so unlike the large Victorian and colonial homes of Chapel Hill. Soon the streets were crammed with row houses and larger buildings as they neared the university.

They turned from the commercial bustle of Nicholson Street and onto Bernard Terrace, a quiet block of houses across from a handful of offices. Dermot had no doubt that James Stuart owned the entire row. The car came to a stop near the middle of the row at one of the few houses that did not have the number painted on the transom above the door. There was nothing at all to distinguish number twenty-three from the houses around it.

Dermot got out when the driver opened the door and offered his hand to Miss Lennox, not that she needed it. She rose with the practiced grace of a woman who lived in high heels. In her hand was a file folder and a key ring.

She opened the solid front door, and Dermot noted the lack of any sort of extra lock or combination entry. That would have to be fixed. Inside a wide staircase rose to a landing before curling around to the next floor while a central hallway stretched to the back door.

"There are two flats per floor, although there will be just you, Miss MacAlpin, and another of our security staff. The rest will be vacant," Miss Lennox said.

Again Dermot could do little more than grunt a response. He was already thinking of the building in terms of security. The doors would have to be improved. The wide windows would all need glass-break sensors. "Are there skylights on the top floor?"

"No, I made sure there was no easy roof access. Mr. Shaw will be here tomorrow at two o'clock to meet with you about any additional security improvements," she added as she opened the door to a ground floor flat. "We've already furnished your flat."

The layout was simple. Front room with bay window leading back to an open kitchen and hallway with bed and bath. "Is there garden access from the flats?"

"Not at all from this one. The others are only via fire escape," she answered. "I have had the pantry stocked with the basics. There is milk in the refrigerator and of course a grocery around the corner. Can I make you a cup of tea?"

Dermot turned to find her next to the kitchen counter wearing a practiced cordial smile. He felt a moment's guilt at his gruff behavior and gave her an apologetic smile. "No, thank you. I'm sorry I'm not better company. The jet lag seems to have hit me much harder coming home than it did going out there. Everything looks fine. I'll talk to Shaw tomorrow about any changes."

"Very well, then. Here are the keys to all of the flats, front and rear doors, and the utility room." Her smile brightened into something genuine as she laid the keys on the counter next to the file. "I'll leave you to it."

With a quick nod as if she were checking "Drop Sinclair at rental property" off her mental to-do list, she turned and left. Dermot listened as her heels clicked on the hall floor and the heavy front door opened and closed. A movement by the door had him jumping until he realized it was the driver quietly depositing his ruck sack.

Once the man was gone, Dermot closed the door to his flat and took his bag to the bedroom. He needed a shower and some fresh clothes before what came next.

***

He got off the bus a block away from his destination. The weather was damp and cold, but not yet full winter. By the time Sarah arrived, it would be freezing. No doubt she would call it arctic. He pulled up the collar of his coat to block the wind and made his way to the modern building that housed the Leith House Rest Home. It's sharp lines and bright paint stuck out among the older stone buildings. He had stopped to buy a modest bouquet of flowers. Freesias…she had always liked freesias.

The automatic doors slid open into the reception area. He walked up to the long desk that covered the wall.

He half expected to see the stone-faced woman who had told him last June that his mother was just getting settled in and was not to be disturbed. None of his appeals or threats had moved her. Before he had truly lost his temper, she had simply shaken her steel grey head without moving so much as a hair and handed him the envelope. Inside had been a plain sheet of fine white paper with a phone number written on it.

He had waited until he got back to his old flat before calling. He hadn't trusted himself to make the call in public.

***

Six months earlier

"Mr. Sinclair," the polished voice said on the other end of the line. Dermot could picture the old snake sitting in some leather chair having a brandy and waiting for his call.

"I told you, I quit. I'm done doing your dirty work," he snapped, not bothering with pleasantries. They were wasted on Walter Stuart.

"And I believe I made it clear that quitting isn't an option," the old bastard said, sounding entirely too calm.

"I'm taking my mother out of that place, if I have to carry her out on my shoulder," Dermot seethed.

"I'm afraid I can't allow that." The bastard was too confident. "You see, while you were in the army, your mother gave me power of attorney. I can place her anywhere I see fit."

Dermot's blood was boiling. "She can't have been in her right mind."

"Well, son—"

"I am not your son," Dermot cut in, hating the very idea.

"No, you're certainly not." The older man's voice dripped with scorn. "You're welcome to find a solicitor and spend the rest of her life arguing your mother's mental capacity, but why waste the time that she has left?"

"You can't keep me from seeing her." He felt an early frisson of panic stirring in his chest. His fingers hurt from gripping the phone.

Stuart bit out the next words with the confidence that only came with the backing of millions of pounds. "Yes, by greasing the right wheels, I can, and I will until you do what I've asked."

"Does James know about your little extortion plot?" Dermot knew his cousin and childhood friend would never have agreed to a tactic like this.

"No more than he knows about your shameful disloyalty. Sinclairs do not *quit*. Not that we should expect anything better from the likes of you."

Dermot let that last comment pass. Stuart had always looked down his nose at Dermot and his mother. He wasn't sure if it was that Seonag was her own woman or that she'd had a child out of wedlock. "It's not disloyal to want to live my own life."

"It is when you refuse to do what your prince asks," Stuart spat.

Dermot sighed. He was sick to death of this Prince James madness. James would no more be king than Dermot would. "He's not asking, and he's not a prince. Lord Caledon can get his own lasses without my help. Let him go and fetch her."

"He has more important things to do than chase her or any of the others down. That's a steward's job."

"Why me? I'm not the only one."

"No, but you are uniquely suited to the task. She's a folk-lorist. You can bond over your studies while you vet her. If she's the one, convince her to come here." Stuart made it sound like the simplest thing to ask a woman to drop everything and come to Scotland.

"And if she won't?" Dermot ground out.

"She will. She's one of the sisters. It's her destiny," he said with an assurance that made Dermot feel sorry for a poor girl he hadn't even met yet. "In the meantime, your mother will be getting the very best of care, far better than the public home she was in before."

"I'll lose so much time. She won't even remember me by the time I come back." The pleading tone in his voice made him feel sick. But what else was he supposed to do?

"Oh my dear boy," the old man laughed, "she barely remembers you now."

***

"I'm hoping to visit my mother, Seonag Sinclair," he said to the politely smiling woman behind the desk whose name tag said Liz.

"Let me just check," she said, turning to a computer on the desk and tapping out his mother's name. After reading something on the screen, her eyebrows drew together, and she reached for the telephone.

Dermot held his breath, hoping that Walter Stuart hadn't found some new thing to hold over his head. They had better let him in. He'd done everything that Walter and James had asked, every bloody thing.

"Yes, alright then," Liz said into the phone. "Just making sure."

She turned to Dermot smiling again and pointed to a set of wide institutional doors to the left of the desk. "It's just through those doors, room 317. When you hear the lock click, you'll be able to open it."

His shoulders sagged in relief. "Cheers."

The electronic lock on the door clicked and he opened it, stepping from the comfortable, well-decorated reception room into the bright antiseptic hallway that seemed more like a hospital. Still, when he got up to the third floor, he found his mother's room was cozy enough with lamplight and her own quilt on the bed. A photo of him as a boy sat on the night table. His mother sat in a reclining chair facing the narrow window.

Dermot knocked on the open door. She peeked around the back of the chair, and her eyebrows rose above bight green eyes. "Oh, hello, young man."

So, she didn't know him today. He could rarely predict when she would recognize him. It was easier on the phone. He could tell her who he was and she believed him. They would talk almost like they used to, before she would eventually get tired or distracted and forget. In person it was harder to convince her that the grown man in front of her was actually the wee lad she remembered. "Hello, mum."

"Come and sit." She waved him to a simple chair next to hers. She picked up the knitting that was resting in her lap and continued the row she was on. She glanced up and nodded at the flowers in his hand. "Have you brought those flowers for your own mum?"

"I've brought them for you. They should brighten things up a bit." He set the flowers on top of the dresser.

"How sweet of you!" She beamed at him. "And what's your name, love?"

"Dermot," he choked out. He cleared his throat and said it again.

She tilted her head and grinned. "Och. My own lad's name is Dermot. I named him for the Irish hero. Do you know the tale?"

Tears pricked his eyes. "I do, yes. He ran away with Finn's wife."

"He did. He did." She patted his hand where it rested on the arm of her chair. "It was a great love he had. We should all be so lucky to have a love like that."

He couldn't help but think of Sarah. He was sure his mum would have liked her. He settled into his chair to make small talk, hoping that at any moment she would look over at him and know who he was.

And then he could tell her about Sarah and his time in North Carolina. He could tell her about the Preservation Scotland team and the project they would be working on. He knew she would be delighted. If things were different, she could have been on the team herself.

When he left here, he could rage at the thief that was stealing her memories, but as long as he was here, he needed to make his visit as pleasant as he could. So he quietly sat with her and talked about nothing until she grew tired.

CHAPTER EIGHTEEN

Date: 12/15/1995

To: SarahMac@uncch.edu

From: D_Sinclair@albapetrol.co.uk

Home safe. Settling in. Going to have a beer and a fry up and sleep off the jet lag.

Take care of yourself.

D

Date: 12/16/1995

To: D_Sinclair@albapetrol.co.uk

From: SarahMac@uncch.edu

Glad to hear it. Been hitting the library hard, but generating more questions than answers. Wish I could bounce some ideas off of you. Miss my sounding board.

Love always,

S

Sarah stood and stretched her arms behind her until her shoulder blades met. She had been hitting the library hard, but not in a way that she was used to. Instead of spending her day in the Folklife Collection in Wilson Library, she had spent the day pouring through volumes of comparative folklore spanning the last two centuries in the enormous and strikingly modern Davis Library. She was tired, sore, and practically cross-eyed from reading over tons of pages of tiny, splotched, and fading print. She was more than ready to go home—and she was sure that Curtis was too.

She had to give her bodyguard credit. He was certainly good at being unobtrusive. He managed to blend with the few other students who were still around after the semester's end while staying close enough to make her feel safe. It was a delicate balance of being constantly near her without appearing to follow her or being intrusive. Curtis was a pro, but Sarah was sure he was bored out of his wits on library duty. She just had one more thing to check.

Sarah logged out of the computer and gathered her things. She was no more than four feet out of the computer lab door when Curtis fell into step behind her. She headed for the stairs. They were five floors up, and as tired as she was she would have preferred the elevator. But as both Fleming and Curtis had told her on separate occasions, they were sitting ducks in elevators. Stairs offered multiple exits if needed. Not for the first time, Sarah hoped that having to constantly stress about points of entry, hidden corners, and strange cars on her street wasn't going to be the new normal.

She went down a couple of floors to the maps collection. This wasn't an area she usually researched. Luckily, there was an attendant at the desk. "Hi, I'm looking for maps of a couple of small towns in the UK. What kind of maps or atlases do you have that might help me?"

The young woman looked up from the book that she was reading. "Small towns?"

"Yes."

Her eyebrows drew together and she tilted her head to the side, thinking. "I think the Ordnance Surveys will be your best bet. They're pretty detailed. I'll show you."

She rose from the desk and walked over to a rack of large books that rested horizontally on rollers. There was a tilted stand on top of the rack with an incredibly thick book like a dictionary resting on it. She ran a hand down the spines of the books in the rack. "Here are survey maps." She rested a hand on the giant book on the stand. "And this is the gazetteer. If all you know about these places are the names, you want to start with the gazetteer. Find them in there, and it will tell you which map book and page to go to."

Sarah smiled at her. "Great. Thanks."

Sarah set her bag on the table in front of the rack and turned to open the gazetteer. It was one of those books you see in the library that never moves from its spot because it's just too heavy. She opened the front to see how it was organized. It was basically a giant index for all of the maps. She tried Làrachd an Fhamhair first, but didn't expect to find it listed. It wasn't. Next she decided to triangulate its location based on the towns and landmarks that her mother's journal had mentioned. Since she was already in the L's, she started with Lochinver. Then she looked up Loch Assynt and Inchnadamph.

The loch crossed a couple of pages on the map, but Inchnadamph was at one end of it. Sarah was amazed at how many of the names of the different features were in Gaelic. Not too far from Inchnadamph was a castle. That must be the castle Mama had mentioned when she and Duff were trying to find the village. What she didn't see was a road running away from the loch near the castle that led between two ridges, and none of those Gaelic names she saw was Làrachd an Fhamhair nor anything else to do with giants. When they said the glen was hidden, they weren't kidding.

Sarah slid the map book back into the rack and picked up her bag. She passed Curtis, who was sitting at the other end of the table, and he rose to follow her. She took the stairs down and headed for the door. That was enough work for today. On her way through the lobby she spotted a familiar polished figure in the open reading area for popular periodicals. She hadn't expected to see Martin Carol again after he had dropped off his PR brief. She would have thought he'd be back in Scotland, but there he was, comfortably ensconced in one of the low, well-cushioned chairs reading what appeared to be a celebrity gossip magazine.

Unable to contain her curiosity, Sarah approached him. "Mr. Carol?"

"Ah, Miss MacAlpin." He actually looked startled and made to rise from his chair, but Sarah waved him back down. "I hadn't expected to see you here," he continued. "I was given to understand that most of your work was done in Wilson Library."

Sarah sat down in the chair next to him. "It is, but I do occasionally come over here. I thought you would have gone home by now."

"Yes, well I was, but my boss decided that I should stay close by in case you needed some help." His eyes sharpened on hers. "Have you been getting any more calls from reporters?"

She shook her head. "They seem to have given up on the phone. Although there is one that tried to talk to me on campus and staked out my apartment."

"Really?" His eyebrows drew together in concern. "Who?"

"Her name is Beth Cartwright. She works for the *Triangle Times*. I checked it out. It's a small paper based in Raleigh."

"Hmm." He pulled a notepad from his briefcase and wrote down the name. "I'll have to look into that further. I'll do some checking. You have my card, just give that number a call if she bothers you again."

"I'll do that." Sarah nodded to the magazine in his hand. "Research?"

He started and his cheeks turned a few shades pinker. "Oh…well…yes, it does pay to keep abreast of the latest rumors."

"I don't really read those magazines. Do they print things about Mr. Stuart much in American tabloids?"

He shook his head. "Not nearly as much as at home, to be sure. Although they do print the occasional picture when he is seen with an American celebrity."

Sarah remembered the way James's bodyguard had tackled Jon Samuels a few weeks before, thinking he was a photographer. "I'm told the tabloids in the UK can be pretty aggressive."

"Indeed, though not nearly so bad as on the continent. One photograph with a single woman is enough to launch a week's worth of rumors." He leaned toward her in his seat and lowered his voice. "Last year, he was photographed over several days with the same model in Ibiza. Well, that was enough to set off countless articles speculating on when they would be getting married. One paper even claimed they were already secretly married. Of course, none of it was true, but it kept the PR department hopping."

"I can't imagine he appreciated it much either," Sarah said.

He dismissed that with a wave of his hand. "Oh, he hardly notices those things. He's much too busy to bother with what tabloids are saying. My department handles that for him."

Sarah wondered about that. "That seems like a personal topic for the PR department of an oil company. I would think you should be focused on the public image of the company."

"And we do, of course. We are a rather large department. But the public persona of our CEO does reflect on the company, so it also falls under our purview."

"I see." Sarah straightened and went to put on her coat. "It must be like living in a fishbowl."

"Indeed." Carol gave her a crooked smile. "But an incredibly posh fishbowl."

Sarah laughed. After spending an evening with James Stuart, she had to agree. He led a charmed life. He might not think so, but Sarah had been poor. She'd seen the other end of the spectrum. It did seem like a bit much to have an entire staff devoted to your public image when there were so many other things in the world more worth worrying about.

As she stood to leave, Carol interrupted her. "Em, Miss MacAlpin, there is one thing that I wanted to ask you."

Sarah lowered herself back into the chair. "Oh?"

"Yes." He shifted toward her. "I was reading your master's thesis on the use of religious themes in protest songs during the abolitionist and labor movements. It had me wondering about your views on worker's rights."

Sarah's brows furrowed, puzzled. "I believe that the profits of an employer shouldn't trump the basic human rights of their employees."

One corner of Carol's mouth quirked up in challenge. "That sounds a rather leftist point of view."

"I make no apologies for that," Sarah replied calmly, though inside she was bristling. It was strange enough that he had read the paper, but to be challenging her on her political views made her hackles rise. "You can travel anywhere through coal country and talk to the people who lived through the latter part of the labor movement there. Heck, there are some still living through it. You ask them what it was like before safety standards and child labor laws. Labor unions are responsible for those as well as weekends and minimum wage. Those aren't bad things."

His smile changed to one of approval. "You defend your position eloquently."

"I don't consider it a difficult position to defend." Sarah looked at him squarely. "Do you regularly go around reading obscure academic papers on labor lore?"

A short, nervous laugh escaped him. "Em, no. Of course not. I'm merely learning all I can so that I'll be prepared in case your name is linked with Mr. Stuart's…because of the murder."

"Right," she thought, "because of the murder." Sarah cocked her head to the side. "Sorry, but what does my master's thesis have to do with that?"

Carol went to stand, picking up his case. "Likely nothing, I'm sure." He gave her a reassuring smile. "Just due diligence."

Sarah wasn't buying that. After the last few months of being stalked and spied on, she was more than a little sensitive to strange people checking her out. She was, however, sure that she wasn't going to get anything else out of Martin Carol. She rose and slid her bag back over her shoulder. "Right, well I'll see you around then."

"Indeed." He smiled blandly. With a nod, he walked away, returning the magazine to a nearby stand before leaving.

Sarah watched him walk out of the glass doors and over toward the Pit.

"Friend of yours?" Curtis asked at her shoulder.

Still watching Carol walk across the brick courtyard and to the stairs that led to the street, Sarah shook her head. "Actually, he works for James Stuart." She looked at him, checking for his reaction. "Did Fleming say anything to you about him?"

Curtis shrugged and shook his head. "I don't even know who he is."

***

Later that afternoon Sarah was sitting on the couch going through the notes from her research when Curtis asked, "So what is it exactly that you're researching so hard?"

She studied him. Most people got bored pretty quickly when she was too specific about what she did. Curtis didn't seem the type to be interested in old Scottish songs and charms so she gave him her standard vague answer. "Folklore, myths, legends...anything that gets passed down by word of mouth. Sometimes the older stories make it into books like the ones I was looking at today."

"Like Grimm's Fairy Tales?" he said.

"Something like that." She returned her attention to her notes.

"But you're looking at legends about witches?" he interrupted again. She gave him a sharp look and he shrugged. "I was following you around all day. I saw some of the books you were reading."

Sarah tilted her head to the side, acknowledging his excuse. "Yeah, well, really I'm trying to solve this one question from something I translated the other day."

"About witches."

"Um, not exactly. It's more about a certain number that appears in a charm that I translated form Gaelic."

"A charm?" His eyebrows rose in question.

"Yeah, it's like a spell for luck or safety. It wasn't unusual in the last century and even before that for someone who was traveling or starting something new to purchase a charm from a witch, for lack of a better term, to ensure success."

"So not a broom riding, baby eating, devil worshipping witch," he said with a smile.

Sarah laughed out loud. Between church propaganda and pop culture, the image of witches had been pretty much ruined. "Uh, no. More like what folks today would call a root doctor, someone who practices traditional medicine and counseling."

He nodded. "I hear ya. You know my granddaddy was a root doctor."

"Really?" She was surprised he told her. That was something that was usually kept a community secret. Some root doctors had been prosecuted for practicing medicine without license.

"Yeah." His eyes glazed a little with memory. "His grandmother was a slave from Louisiana and she passed it down. I remember people used to come to the house. They would tell him their troubles and he would take 'em to the shed in the back yard. Later on, they would leave feeling better…happy, relieved, hopeful."

"He didn't teach it to you?" she asked.

"Naw. Some of the stories, but none of the practice. He might've taught us when we got older, but he died of cancer when I was ten. The kids were never allowed in the shed, because my Grandmama was afraid we would talk about it at school."

Sarah knew that dangers of saying things at school that were outside of the norm. She'd had more than one teacher talk to her Mama and Granny about her imagination. "Well, my Granny was a witch, but she didn't talk about it either. The more I study, the more I'm learning she kept a lot of things secret. Actually, maybe you can help."

She was about to ask Curtis about the number nine in the lore that he knew of when they heard a key in the lock. A second later Fleming came in holding a pizza box and a bag of sodas and looking rested. "I brought pizza."

"You didn't have to do that." Sarah stood to take the box from him and put it on the table. "I'll get some plates."

"I thought ye could use a break from cooking, but I'm not complaining."

"I'm kind of worn out," she said, getting the plates from the cabinet.

"Well, take a break and have a slice." He pulled three sodas from the six-pack and put the rest in the fridge. He leaned close to her ear and quietly said, "Mr. Stuart will most likely be calling ye this evening."

Sarah let that sink in. She knew James had been trying to call, but had missed her a couple of times. She hadn't bothered to call back partly because she had no idea what to say to him and partly to show him that she wasn't one of his lackeys who came running whenever he wanted. After today, she thought talking to James might not be a bad idea. "Good. I have something to ask him. Did you know that Martin Carol is still in town?"

Fleming didn't miss a beat. "The PR man?"

"Yeah. I ran into him at the library today." She watched his reaction closely.

He pursed his lips and shrugged before taking the plates to the table. "Dunno anything about it."

He seemed to be telling the truth, but Sarah didn't really know him well enough to be sure. She followed Fleming to the table.

Fleming was setting his glass down at the head of the table with Curtis to his left and his back facing the room. That left Sarah the choice of sitting awkwardly at the other end of the table or in the same seat she'd been in while being held hostage by Ryan Cumberland. She had been testing herself in the days since, working to desensitize herself. Still, she didn't relish the idea of having a panic attack in the middle of dinner.

She turned to Fleming. "Actually, do you mind if I sit there? It's a memory thing."

From the way he said, "Ah," Sarah guessed he'd been told some of what had happened inside her apartment that night. He immediately moved his glass to the vacant seat and walked around behind her. "Right. Here ye go."

She could feel her cheeks burning. She hated showing weakness, even to someone as friendly and accommodating as Fleming. "Thanks."

"No worries, I didna know what ye liked so I got one with everything." He opened the pizza box, and Sarah was hit with the delicious aroma of pepperoni, sausage, melted cheese, and yeasty crust.

She sighed before sliding a slice onto her plate. "I like pizza way too much. I don't even care what's on it."

Fleming took a bite. "Mmm…I'm going to miss this when I go home."

Sarah was content to let their conversation flow around her while her mind returned to the question of the Nine. She went over a mental list of what she had found.

She had started with Celtic lore. There were groups of nine maidens all over European folklore. There were nine maidens on the isle of Avalon, and with Ceridwen in Wales, and the Cailleach, Queen of Winter. There were nine sacred woods burned in Beltain fires that marked the transition from winter into spring, death to rebirth, dark to light. There was even more than one stone circle in Britain with nine stones, usually referred to as maidens or ladies. All of them representing transformation, generation, or healing. Sarah could imagine how Saint Columba might have bristled at any of these while he was trying to convert the pagans of Scotland to his particular brand of patriarchal Christianity, but she wasn't sure he would have feared them.

Christianity wasn't short of nines either. There were nine orders of angels, nine gifts of the Spirit. The ninth commandment, "Thou shalt not bear false witness against thy neighbor." It proved an interesting coincidence when she read that the number nine in Hebrew numerology was considered the symbol for "immutable truth." Maybe it was truth that Columba feared. From what Sarah had read about the historical man, he was very ambitious and not above switching allegiances to further his own ends.

In the Gospel of Luke, chapter seventeen, Jesus told a group of ten lepers to get cleansed by the priests. Only one returned to praise God. In verse seventeen, Jesus asks, "'Were not all ten cleansed? Where are the other nine? Has no one returned to give praise to God except this foreigner?' Then he said to him, 'Rise and go, your faith has made you well.'" Was the Nine symbolic of those nine, all "natives" who rejected Jesus? Could Columba have feared for his own countrymen who rejected Christianity and kept to the old ways?

Going further afield, Sarah had found nine prevalent in Norse mythology too. Heimdallr, who watches the gateway between the human world and Asgard, was said to be the "son of nine mothers," who are all sisters. There are nine worlds in the great tree of Yggdrasil, including Jotunheimr, the realm of giants. There were also the nine Muses of Greek mythology. She had even found a tribe in Kenya, the Kikiuyu, who believed themselves to be descended from nine sisters. Once she started looking for it, the number nine seemed to be everywhere.

Sarah had no idea how long she sat there, munching pizza and thinking, but she was drawn back to the present when the phone rang. She blinked a few times at the half-eaten piece of pizza in her hand. The guys were no longer at the table and their plates had been cleared. Fleming put a hand on her shoulder and bent his head to look in her eyes. "Ye back with us then?"

Sarah gave her head a quick shake to get through the cloud of thought. "Yeah. Sorry, I was thinking."

"Ye must be thinking pretty deep there." He smiled before extending the hand that held the telephone to her. "The boss is on the phone."

"Hmph, your boss maybe," she thought before taking the phone and lifting it to her ear. "Hello, James?"

"You, my dear, are a difficult woman to get a hold of." The buttery smooth and richly accented voice of James Stuart dripped from the other end of the line. Sarah thought he had missed his calling as a voice-over artist, something to fall back on if the whole oil executive, international playboy gig didn't work out.

"Well, I'm a busy girl," Sarah said, trying to sound all business. From here on out, that's how it had to be with James. Sarah liked him well enough. He was charming, generous, and so stupefyingly handsome that women tended to lose their train of thought just by looking at him. But Sarah did not want him thinking that he had a snowball's chance in hell with her romantically. "I have a lot of research to do, on top of getting ready to move. What can I do for you, James?"

There was the usual delay of a transatlantic call before he practically purred, "Well, I could say that I called to see how you were getting on with your bodyguards, but the truth is I just wanted to hear your voice."

Sarah wasn't sure what to say to that. Any girl with eyes in her head would have come running if James just crooked his finger, but Sarah was in love with someone else. She had a fine line to walk with James. If she wanted to continue with the fellowship in Scotland, then she was going to have to maintain a cordial relationship with its main source of funding. But she also didn't want to lead him on. Even before she knew about his plans, she had told him that their relationship needed to remain professional. "The bodyguards are just fine." She glanced up to see said bodyguards leaving the table for the kitchen. "Though they're probably bored out of their wits. I'm afraid sitting around in the library while I do research isn't a very exciting assignment. What time is it there? It's got to be late."

"Close to midnight actually, I'm ready for bed. It's been a long day full of tedious meetings." He did sound tired. No doubt, plotting to take over the country was exhausting.

She carried her plate to the kitchen and handed it to Fleming. Her tone was loaded with sarcasm. "Did you call me for a lullaby?"

"Would you? I've never heard you sing," he said, taking her literally.

Sarah made her way back to her room and closed the door. "Don't get excited. It's more of an academic exercise for me."

"I doubt that. I heard you're quite the performer." She had to hand it to him. He even flirted smoothly. She needed to shut that down.

"Sorry, I don't take requests." Part of her wanted to tell him that she knew everything, that she wasn't going to play his game. Then she remembered what Dermot said about James rushing things if he found out that she knew. "James, I ran into Martin Carol today at the library."

"Oh?" His voice gave away nothing.

"He said he had read my master's thesis and asked me a political question about it."

"I see." His voice was cool and even, but Sarah thought she heard a note of tension.

Suddenly she realized there was a little power in knowing something he didn't. After being swept along by recent events, she kind of enjoyed that feeling. "James, am I being vetted for something I don't know about?"

The only indication that she had surprised him was a soft throaty sort of grunt that he quickly followed up by saying, "Ah, well, the Preservation Scotland team is going to need to do quite a lot of fundraising and potentially some media appearances. Dermot was hoping that you would be a good spokesperson for the team. But as with everything involving the media, we wanted to make sure there weren't any skeletons in your closet so to speak."

A likely story. It wasn't her proudest moment, but she enjoyed hearing the powerful, supremely confident executive squirm just a little. "So you used an Alba Petroleum employee for that when you could have just asked me?"

"Yes, well...um," he fished around for an explanation, "Carol had already checked on information about you for the media packet. With everything you've been through, I didn't want you to be bothered."

"Right. I'm not sure what my support for organized labor has to do with anything."

"Do you support organized labor?" He actually sounded curious.

Sarah bristled. If nothing else, this confirmed some of what Dermot said about James's political ambitions. Why else would he be vetting her views? "My politics have nothing to do with my studies, and they're none of your business."

"You're right, of course." His voice was full of contrition. Sarah almost felt bad for snapping at him. "I'm sorry to have upset you. Please know that it was only an abundance of caution. I...well...I can't be too careful."

"You know, James, you might be the only person I know who's more paranoid than I am."

He laughed, instantly more at ease than seconds before. "I think we may have more in common than either of us knows."

She sighed inwardly. No matter how much she tried to push him away or hold him off, he kept pouring on the charm. She heard the anticipation in his voice when he said, "When are you coming to Scotland?"

"The date on my ticket says January sixth. I've still got some things to clear up here." She looked over at the one-way plane ticket that was lodged in the corner of the mirror on top of her dresser.

"I'll be counting the days," he said, making her cringe.

She was going to have to have another talk with him about keeping things professional. But she could leave that for another day. "It'll be here before we know it."

"Good night, Sarah." He sounded wistful and tired, which reminded her that underneath the perfectly polished exterior, there was a fairly lonely man. She had sensed it when they had gone to dinner a couple of months ago, and she knew that he had once been a regular if spoiled kid from the stories Dermot had told her of their childhood. She hated the situation they all found themselves in, not just for her sake, but for theirs as well.

Her voice softened to a friendlier tone when she said, "Good night, James."

"I'll see you soon," he said.

"Mmhmm…"

CHAPTER NINETEEN

June 1968
Làrachd an Fhamhair, Scotland

Lachlan Morse arrived late that night. Rona, Sheila, and I had all gone to bed, so we didn't see him until breakfast the next day. He was handsome enough to cause notice, at least for Rona and me. We were getting our porridge when she elbowed me and indicated the table across the hearth from ours. The newcomer was sitting across from Willie. He was attempting to make conversation with Willie, who was responding mainly by showing Lachlan the top of his head as he bent over his bowl. Where Willie was shy and tense, Lachlan was confident and relaxed. His eyes were a lively, intelligent brown, and in no time at all he turned them in our direction and smiled.

I heard Rona inhale sharply, and when I glanced her way, her cheeks were turning pink. I took her elbow and steered her toward our table. "Come on, cuz."

When we had settled down at our seats I heard raucous laughter near the door and looked up to see the stewards laughing and back slapping over who knows what. "It's like a school lunch room all over again."

"Amazing how quickly they revert to schoolyard behavior when left to themselves," Sheila said with a genuine smile as she sat down at the table with us.

Rona and I exchanged a look of surprise that she was being so friendly. "Well, I imagine all of them staying together has that effect."

The three of us went on talking about boys and being sociable like we were all friends right through breakfast. When we were done and on our way out of the hall, Sheila called to me. I turned around and she was smiling that soft smile that I'd first seen from her. "Listen, I'm sorry I was short with ye yesterday. It's a difficult situation we're in, and I can't imagine what a shock it must be to ye. We're sisters after all. We should be friends."

I was shocked. I hadn't expected an apology. "That right nice of you, Sheila. I agree. Squabbling doesn't help anybody."

Her smile grew even bigger and actually looked genuine. "That's grand. Maybe later ye can tell me more about what it's like in America."

"Sure."

She left practically skipping down the lane. I looked up to see Duff watching me from the doorway of the lads' house, a question in his eyes. I just shrugged and started walking. I strolled down the lane away from the hall. What I really needed to do was talk with Aunt Eilidh. Rona had helped explain some things, but that still didn't tell me what to expect from this whole situation. I couldn't figure out what to do next if I didn't know what was coming. Since Aunt Eilidh disappeared every time I went to look for her, I decided I was going to have to use my talent to find her.

I went to the most central place I could think of in the little glen: the footbridge across the burn. I stood in the middle of the bridge and breathed for a minute. Then, when I thought I was calm enough, I closed my eyes and cast out. My view went high above the bridge and the village, above the glen. It looked like nothing more than a green hollow with some large rocky outcroppings here and there. From above, you would never know there even was a village. But I knew what to look for. I could recognize every house and shed. I saw the horse paddock where the cars were hidden, and the privies. I even saw myself standing on the stone bridge that was barely more than a few stones across the stream. It looked as if it was there by some accident of nature. They had done a great job of hiding this place, just like Aunt Eilidh had done a good job of avoiding me...but I found her. I could see her sitting on a rock ledge uphill from the scrying pool that Sheila had shown us.

I pulled myself back in, opened my eyes, and headed straight down the path to where I had seen her.

***

Coming from the mountains like we do, we see a lot of beautiful places. But there is nothing like the highlands where we live. In the mountains you grew up in, there are so many trees you can't see the holler from most places on the hill. There aren't that many trees here, mostly bushes, rocks, and grass. The mountains at home are like a burlesque show, hiding their real beauty except in certain spots or at the right time of year. But the Highlands around Làrachd an Fhamhair are naked. They show everything from every angle, and they're not ashamed of it. It seems so funny when I think about it, that this is where our people would choose to hide, but that's exactly what they do. They live on the earth's naked skin here, camouflaged as well as a panther in the forest. And when our people don't want to be found by strangers, we won't be.

But as foreign as I felt there, I was no stranger. That ground felt good and solid under my feet and the wind on my face felt like an old friend. Mama taught me the trick of being silent as you go, and I did my best to be silent as I came up to the ledge where Aunt Eilidh sat. She had her eyes closed and her head tilted toward the rising sun. I didn't climb onto the ledge with her. If she was indeed preparing for whatever was coming, I didn't want to interrupt. But I did want answers, so I settled myself near the path to wait until she was done. I crossed my legs Indian style and faced the sun just as she did. I think if my head hadn't been so full of questions, I might have found some of the peace she seemed to be seeking. Like I said before, I was too young and busy then. All I could wrap my mind around was finding a way out of that glen and away from those people and their plans.

"I ken ye're there, lass," she said after a time. "Best come out with it."

I stood up and stepped out onto the ledge where she was sitting. It looked right down on the plateau and the pool. "I'm sorry to disturb you."

"Nae bother. I expect ye have some questions for me." Her tone was gentle, but I could tell she was a little annoyed by the interruption.

"Well," I hardly knew where to begin, "my Mama didn't really tell me much about what I'm doing here. I hoped you could explain what's happening."

"Aye, Sheila said ye were shocked when she told ye what the feast was for." She shook her head. "I canna think why my sister kept ye in the dark. It only makes this harder."

"You'll have to pardon me, ma'am, but it makes what harder?" I said.

She sighed. "Well, I gather Sheila told ye the basics. Ye're here to be matched wi' one of the lads to make a child."

I nodded. I still found that hard to believe, but I thought it would be better to let her talk than object outright.

"Aye, well. This is how we've done since before the new folk came to live on this land. The three sisters have always been charged with keeping the stone and the cauldron safe. Over time we developed our skills. They protect us. But to keep those skills, we have to choose who we breed with carefully. That's what the ceremony at the pool is for, selecting who would be the best mate for each of ye."

"What if I want to choose my own mate?" I really did mean to listen to her first, but that was one of the questions in the front of my mind.

"Och! Ye can." She smiled sweetly and patted my knee. "After ye've given us a girl child to carry on the sisterhood."

I must have looked bothered by this because she went on, "We dinna expect ye to marry the lad, though some do on occasion. Ye'll be handfast, which is like a temporary arrangement until a child is born. Then he's free to go and ye're free to find any man ye like."

I hoped my mouth wasn't gaping open. She talked like it was the most natural thing in the world to be bred like a mare. "And the child?"

"Weel, ye must raise the child yerself. Who else could teach her the skills that need to be passed on?" she answered.

"What if I'm not ready to be a mother?"

"Nothing can really prepare ye for a child, lass. Even those who think themselves ready aren't." She put her arm around my shoulders in a gesture that was meant to be reassuring. "Ye'll do fine. Ye have all the tools ye need. Ye can stay here, or go back to America, but we'll be sure ye have what's important."

It was like being run over by a very slow-moving train. There were a dozen reasons why I did not want to do any of this. When I said I wasn't ready I meant that I had plans and things to do that I didn't think I could do with a child clinging to me. I don't know if she didn't understand what I was saying or just chose not to acknowledge it. It was like the idea of me not wanting to be a part of this breeding didn't matter at all.

Don't get me wrong, baby. Once you were born, even before you were born, I loved you and I wouldn't have traded you for the world. You are the child of my heart. I hope when your time comes that you will love the child you are given, and I hope that you get to choose the father.

"Tomorrow at sunrise, we'll ask the pool which man is right for each of ye." It sounded like she meant for this to be reassuring. It only made me feel more alone. "Then ye'll have the summer to get to know each other. By Lammas Day, ye'll be ready to live together and in no time at all the next generation will be here."

My chest felt hollow and my head light. It was like that breathless feeling you get standing at the edge of a cliff, like gravity's pull might be too much to fight. "I don't think I can do this."

"Och, sure ye can. It's what ye were made for, and what I was made for, and yer mother, and our mothers before us and their mothers. These worldly modern things ye think ye want to do, they're nothing in the face of what we are, what we will be. What happens tomorrow will change the world someday, and ye'll be glad ye were a part of it. It's a great honor to be what we are. I hope ye'll come to believe that." She stepped around me and walked on down the trail. I stayed there for a while thinking about what she said: "It's a great honor to be what we are." I didn't believe it. I still don't. I hope you won't fall for that line either when they tell it to you.

I started my way back down the mountain. When I got to the pool, I stopped. I walked around it and eventually sat on one of the stones at the edge. I stared into that awful smelling green water so thick with algae that you couldn't even see an inch below the surface. She really thought this water was going to tell her who my mate should be. It was the craziest, dumbest, most superstitious thing I had ever heard. And you know we have some mighty superstitious things in our mountains. But this stinky pool and Aunt Eilidh's ancient nonsense took the cake.

And your Granny sent me here with not a word of warning, not an ounce of preparation. In all my years growing up in the mountains, she let me do what I wanted within reason. When I wanted to dance, she got me lessons. When I wanted to go places, she made sure I could. I did well in school because I thought I was going to build a life with that knowledge, and she never told me otherwise.

***

There was a boy I liked once, Kurt Mackey. He was the son of the local doctor and about the best boy in the county. He wasn't bad to look at. He was smart and would be going to Carolina the next fall. He could have gone out with any girl he wanted, but he asked me to the senior prom. Of course, I was tickled and couldn't wait to go. Well, there aren't many events like a senior prom, especially for the kids living around Kettle

Holler. It was the closest thing to glamorous that we would ever get, and I wasn't planning to miss it. So I asked Mama one day while she was working in the garden. It was always good to ask her about important things while she was doing something with her hands. I think she found the work soothing and she was less likely to get upset.

I used to think she was always pretty honest with me, and I had no reason to doubt her when she said, "I dinna want ye getting any ideas about this Mackey boy, or any other boy. Ye're too good for him and every lad in these mountains. Yer time will come, lass, but it willna be with the likes o' any of these lads around here."

Once I had convinced her that I didn't have any designs on Kurt Mackey or Russ Corbett or any other boy that Kettle Holler had to offer, she let me go to the dance. I thought she was telling me to save myself for the right man. Of course, what Mama said to me that day seems to mean something entirely different now. Maybe she was just telling me to save myself for this.

I sat there by that pool and I tried my best to figure out why she would've kept this a secret from me. I tried to think of any other times when she might have given me clues that I must have missed.

I remembered her telling me the story of our people—only I never understood what "our people" meant. I just thought she meant Scottish people, or people from the Highlands. She'd been telling me stories of her home and how much she missed her people for all my life. So many stories that, for a little while, being here felt like home. But she never told me about this.

Every day she watched me get closer to it. She listened to all my dreams. She let me make plans as long as they didn't involve boys like Kurt Mackey. She let me imagine a whole life for myself, and she never said a thing, not a word of warning, not even when that letter came with the invitation for this visit. I tried to think back through all my years to find a time when she might have hinted at it, but there was nothing.

Then I thought about that last ride to Boone, and how nervous she was, like she wanted to say something more. I remembered her standing there in the middle of that bus station looking like she didn't want me to go, like she wanted to tell me one more thing. But then she turned around and walked away. I hated her for letting me get on that bus. I hated her for letting me dream, when she knew what I wanted wasn't going to happen.

I looked around that pool and up at the hills, cursing the minute I set foot in this glen. The stone under me felt so cold through my skirt, and the smell of the earth and moss and sulfurous water was like to make me sick. I should have stayed in New York. I could've gotten away then. Now I was stuck here in the ass end of the Highlands with little money and no friends, and I was getting that prickly feeling on the back of my neck.

"Hello?" I sat there, practically holding my breath, but I didn't hear anything. I looked around to see if I was being watched. I couldn't see anybody. Still, I couldn't shake that feeling.

That was when I looked down at the pool. There was a shape in the water. It was a silhouette, like someone leaning over the edge with the sun behind them. It looked like a person's head and shoulders, but the head seemed to have horns like a stag's. From its position, someone should have been right across the pool from me. I looked up to where they should have been, but there was no one there. I felt a chill streak like an icy finger down my spine. When I looked back at the water, the reflection was gone.

I got to my feet and backed away from the pool. I slipped on some wet moss, but I caught myself before I landed flat on the stones. My heart was pounding. I still felt like I wasn't alone, but I couldn't see anyone else no matter where I looked, certainly not somebody wearing horns. I turned and ran back up the glen toward the village.

I was relieved to see a crowd gathered in front of the hall. I sure as hell didn't feel like being alone anymore, though I didn't feel much like being a part of this group either. They appeared to be celebrating another arrival. I guessed it must have been that Rab that Aunt Eilidh had been grumbling about. The children and young people were all surrounding the newcomer, and he appeared to be slapping the backs of Davie and Lachlan as if he knew them. Sheila and Rona were there too. Sheila was looking up at him with open admiration. When I came near the crowd, his back was turned to me, but I could see he stood taller than everyone except Duff and held himself with a definite swagger.

I skirted the group and was almost to the door of the hall before he turned around. Golden hair curled around a face so handsome it was practically criminal. His cheekbones and jaw were chiseled like a statue. His lips were perfectly shaped and just pink enough to look inviting without seeming feminine. And his eyes, well, they were the color of the mountain forest in the summertime, deep green and full of life. He was laughing and the sun sparked in them when they settled on me.

"And who is this?" he asked to the crowd in general. He stepped close to the door where I was standing.

Sheila followed close behind him and answered, "This is my cousin, Màili, from America."

"Hallo then, Màili from America." He grinned, holding out his hand. I placed my hand in his, expecting a brief shake, but he held my hand between both of his, stroking the inside of my wrist with his thumb. "I'm Rab from Inverness."

"Dinna believe him, *a Mhàili*. He's from right here in Làrachd an Fhamhair." Sheila pulled Rab's other arm toward the hall. "Come and have some tea, Rab."

"Aye, I will." He didn't take his eyes from mine, but made a look like he was sorry for the interruption. "Come and have tea with us, Màili."

I'm not sure why, but I just couldn't go and sit with them. Maybe it was leftover anger. Maybe it was the way he was looking at me, but I knew that if I joined in now when all the young people were laughing together that I would be lost. There would be no more resisting their plans. The Molly MacAlpin with plans of her own would disappear to be replaced by, what, a brood mare?

"N-no thank you," I stammered like a nervous little girl. I'm sure I blushed too. "I'm not that hungry."

I slid away from the wall and made to leave, but he still had my hand. I pulled on it, and he held it for another second before letting it go. I took a few steps away from the hall, but I could still feel his eyes on me. I looked back over my shoulder and, sure enough, those green eyes were still turned my way. He was watching me go with a look that I couldn't mistake for anything other than interest. And Sheila stood behind him in the doorway, face red as a beet. Great. Just when I was starting to get along with my new cousin.

I should have been paying attention to where I was walking because that was when I ran right smack into Willie Cross and we both nearly tumbled. He grabbed me by the upper arms to steady me.

"Thank you, Willie. I ought to watch where I…" I let my words trail off when I realized that he wasn't listening. He was looking past me at Rab, who still stood by the doorway to the hall with a smug grin on his perfect lips. Willie's hands tightened on my arms until it hurt, and I must have gasped because he looked down at me. His dark eyes bored into mine for longer than was comfortable before he relaxed his grip. He ran his hands down my arms and took a step back.

He went back to his usual nervous demeanor, looking at his shoes, the path, the houses, anywhere but my eyes. Eventually, he just nodded a couple of times and started walking toward the hall. I ran for Aunt Eilidh's house and slammed the door behind me when I got inside.

I half expected someone to come scold me for slamming the door, but the cottage was quiet. I looked around, listening for any movement, but there was no one. I was alone. Alone, because everyone was down at the hall. Now that Rab Ballantyne was here, the feast would go on, and the ceremony Aunt Eilidh had told me about would happen at sunrise just like she planned. Hail, hail, the gang's all here.

Or maybe not. If everybody else was at the hall, that meant no one was watching me. If I headed up the mountain instead of down, I could be over the ridge and gone before they were done with their tea. I pushed away from the door and quick as lightning climbed up to the loft. I started shoving everything I could get my hands on that was mine into my travel bag. The suitcase would be too much to carry.

I knew how to forage, I had been picking vegetables and wild greens with Jock yesterday, and Mama had shown me how to snare animals. Even if they caught me, I could delay things by a few days, and then it wouldn't be midsummer anymore. That would buy me a year to get away and convince them how wrong this all was.

Bag packed, I climbed down and tied some bread that was sitting on the table into a scarf and went to the door. I stepped out and looked down toward the hall. I didn't see anyone in the lane or outside. This was definitely the time to make a break for it. I turned the other way and walked around the house.

I got to the corner of the cottage, and that's when he grabbed me. I was spun around and pushed up against the wall. It happened so fast that it took me a second to focus on who had me. When my eyes cleared, they were looking directly into Duff's. Part of me wanted to sink down with relief that it was him and not some horned monster or anyone else.

"Where you going, Molly?" he asked.

I pushed at his shoulders just to give me a little room to breathe. "Anywhere but here."

"Just how far did you think you would get with nothing but a few rolls of bread?" He nodded at the scarf I had tied around the rolls.

"I can feed myself just fine, and I'm from the mountains. I can make it." I made to slide by him, but he put his arm up to block me.

"No. You won't. You're always followed. If not by me, then someone else. And even if you survived travelling alone through this wilderness, the minute you use your passport, they'll find you." His tone softened. "I told you, there are powerful people who have a stake in what you are doing. They won't just let you get away."

"Come with me. You don't want to be a part of this any more than I do. We could make it. We can go anywhere." I twisted to look around the wall. Everyone was still at the hall.

"No. That's what I'm trying to tell you. They will find us anywhere we go."

"I can't do this!" I hissed at him.

"You can. This isn't something you can get out of. You just have to endure it, and when it's over you move on."

"Maybe you move on. When this is over, I'll have a child to raise. This is my life we're talking about. Mine!" That's when I hit him. I ain't proud of it. I had so much anger and fear and frustration built up that I just let my fist fly right into his ribs. It felt so good to let some of that out, that I did it again and again.

"That's right," he said, holding his arms out to his side. I just kept raining blows on his chest and stomach and sides. "You go ahead, darlin'. Get it out."

I don't know how many times I hit him. I just kept going until I had punched myself out. He took every blow with nothing more than a grunt. I don't even know if I hurt him. All I know is when I couldn't lift my arms anymore, he was still standing in front of me. I was standing there gasping for breath with my arms hanging by my sides. A sob bubbled up from my chest. Then another, and pretty soon I was weeping like it was the end of the world. I guess in some ways it was.

I would have fallen to the ground, but Duff put his arms around me. They were strong and solid, and I clung to him. Minutes before he'd used his arms to trap me against the wall, but now they were my lifeline, the only thing holding me to the Earth.

"It's alright, Molly." I turned into him and buried my face in his shirt. He stroked my hair and made shushing sounds. When I had cried myself dry, he kept holding me.

"I'm sorry," I said into his wet shirt.

"You've got nothing to be sorry about." His voice was a soothing rumble. We stood there a long time holding on to each other. "Come on. Let's get you inside before anyone comes along."

He ushered me back into the house with his arm firmly around my waist. I didn't know what to do, I was so exhausted. It seemed like everything hurt, my throat, my eyes, my head, my heart. He went to the wash stand and wet a cloth. He brought it to me. "Hold this over your eyes while I get you something for your throat."

For once, I listened to him, and the cool wet cloth did soothe my eyes. A minute or two later, he brought me some warm water with a little honey in it. "I didn't have time to brew tea, but this should help your throat."

I didn't say anything. I nodded and took the cup. The water was sweet and the honey did ease some of the scratchiness in my throat. When I had drunk the water down, he took the cup and led me to the ladder. "Up you go. You'll need some rest. It's an early morning tomorrow."

I was too worn out to resist or to even say anything. I just climbed the ladder to the loft and went to my pallet to lay down. He pulled the quilt up over me and bent down to kiss my forehead. I turned to the wall and curled up. I slipped away into sleep, but I thought I heard him say, "I wish it didn't have to be this way, sweetheart."

CHAPTER TWENTY

December 17, 1995
Chapel Hill, North Carolina

"It could be worse," Sarah said, sliding into a booth at her favorite pizza place. Although maybe she was trying to convince herself. After what she had read in the journal the night before, she had needed a day to feel like a relatively normal person. Reading about Duff and Mama seemed entirely too close to Dermot and herself. She knew how they had turned out, and it didn't give her much hope. So she was spending the day studying how Curtis operated. If she was going to escape one day, she needed some ideas on how.

By now she was used to taking the seat that faced away from the door. She had become accustomed to Dermot's preference for facing the door long before he told her that he was guarding her or that she even needed a bodyguard. Now it was a given. Of course Sarah also knew exactly which stores on Franklin Street had back doors, including the restaurant they were in, and where most of the alleys led. She added, "I could have asked you to take me to the mall."

Curtis groaned and settled into his seat. "Well, I'm sure it's more crowded at the mall, but at least everyone is on foot. Here I have to worry about cars and pedestrians."

They had come to Franklin Street, the town's main drag, to finish the little bit of Christmas shopping that Sarah had to do.

With no family and a graduate student's budget, there wasn't much to get. She had gotten Amy a pair of earrings that she had been admiring for months, plus a Carolina sweatshirt for Dermot from The Shrunken Head. She still needed to find something for Barrett, but she expected she would find it in the record store a block away.

Curtis was staying closer than usual, actually walking with her as if they were friends. They had talked about the cover before leaving her apartment that morning. He hadn't liked the idea of "parading up and down the street like a target," but she had worn him down. "I can't be a prisoner. Besides, you're a pro. You must be used to a lot more activity than I'm showing you in the library."

He waggled his head. "Eh, you're a different animal for sure. I usually do celebrities who are only in Atlanta for a few days at a time for concerts or ball games or something. They come in, move from hotel to venue, maybe a restaurant or two. Then they leave. I'm not used to following someone in their everyday life and definitely not used to this much walking. Don't you people drive anywhere?"

Sarah giggled. "Parking is notorious in this town, and so much of the campus has none at all. No one drives around here, and if they do, they probably have a stack of parking tickets to show for it. Sorry, the campus wasn't built for people who need bodyguards. Not that I don't appreciate you, but I'm not entirely convinced that I do."

"Well, the 'boss,' as Fleming calls him, sure is." Curtis paused when the waiter came by to take their order. He went for a variety of meats while Sarah opted for her favorite spinach and feta. When the waiter left, he leaned forward and lowered his voice. "I just don't get what an oil executive wants with a folklorist."

Sarah's eyes widened, and before she could respond he added, "I know. I shouldn't be asking questions. It just doesn't seem to fit. It makes me curious."

She tried not to betray too much, but his questions were starting to make her a little nervous. Sarah liked Curtis. She didn't want to think that he had any hidden agenda. But weren't bodyguards paid to not be curious? "Are you sure you haven't missed your calling as a private investigator?"

He chuckled. "Actually, that is another part of my business. That's how I can follow you without seeming to be following you sometimes. I'm also just naturally curious. It's an asset and a hazard in my business."

"To be honest, I'm not sure what James's angle is." She hoped he bought her half-truth. Heaven knows he would never believe the whole. "I can only think it's some kind of paternalistic impulse. He recommended me for the fellowship in Scotland. I think he's trying to be sure I actually make it there."

Curtis tilted his head to the side and shrugged. "I guess. But a folklorist? I could understand a geologist for business reasons."

"There was a geologist," Sarah thought, remembering the pretty, athletic, and friendly Bridget MacKenzie. Out loud, she said, "Folklore is culturally important, and in Scotland, which has been subjugated to England for centuries, it's even more important for national identity."

"So James is some kind of Scottish nationalist?" he asked.

Sarah shook her head as the waiter returned with their slices. "I have no idea what his political leanings are, but there are people in Scotland who believe that they are essentially an occupied nation. The Gaelic language and culture are things that set Scotland apart from England."

"I thought Gaelic was an Irish thing," Curtis asked.

"A lot of Americans think that. Without giving you a long lecture on the evolution of Celtic languages, there are three Gaelic languages: Irish, Manx, and Scottish. They all come from the same root, but they're all different enough to be separate languages. It's sort of like the difference between Spanish and Portuguese. Plus, there are folktales and legends that are specific to Scotland. Preserving those things is important to James. I try not to question his reasons."

"So he funds this folklore preservation team that you're joining," he said.

"Exactly." She took a bite of her pizza, the tangy feta mixing with the creamy mozzarella and sharp flavor of the spinach. "Film and audio tapes cost money. Travel costs money, and I do occasionally like to eat, so I have to find funding somehow."

"Not to mention tuition," he suggested.

"That too. My grandmother left me some money, and I made some when I sold our farm. I've stretched it for a long time, but I know it's not limitless," Sarah said.

"I don't know how you do it. I'll take a simple transactional business any day. I provide service. I get paid. I don't have to go begging or cozying up to anybody for funding."

Sarah had to nod in agreement. "I can definitely see the attraction. I'm obviously not in this for the money. I would love to just study and collect stories and songs, but that's the nature of the beast."

They continued talking and eating, not touching on anything more serious. When Sarah thought Curtis had relaxed enough, she said, "I need to use the ladies room."

His brows knitted together and he gave her a chilling look. "It would be safer if you could wait until we get home."

She gave him a look that made it clear that wasn't an option. With a sigh, he slid out of the booth and waited for her to stand up. As he made his way to the restroom at the back of the restaurant, he told her the plan. His voice was low, but all business. "I'll have to check the ladies room first. You hold the door while I make sure it's clear. When you're done, knock on the door and wait for me to open it. I'll be right on the other side."

"Got it." This was her life now. Would it be like this in Scotland?

Curtis opened the door to the ladies' room and Sarah held it open as instructed. This would be the perfect kind of moment to slip away. His attention was in the bathroom, and she was less than twenty feet from the back door. She tucked that knowledge away for another time. The bathroom was small, but divided into one stall with a sink and mirror. There was a door on the wall opposite the sink. Sarah guessed it must be a closet of some sort. After checking the stall, Curtis knocked on the closet door. When there was no answer, he tried the knob, but it didn't budge. He pulled and twisted, but the door just rattled in its frame. The lock in the handle needed a key, which Sarah expected was probably kept by the manager.

"It's locked up tight," Curtis said, turning back to her.

Sarah went in. "Thanks."

She watched the door swing closed on his back. Curtis planted his feet and folded his arms at the door. She wasn't likely to sneak out of the bathroom to escape.

It was when she was done and washing her hands that she looked into the mirror to find Ryan Cumberland standing behind her. Sarah froze. His mouth curled into the knowing smirk that had always bothered her. She knew she should scream, run, lash out, do something, but her breath caught in her chest and she couldn't move. She managed to close her eyes tight as if she could wish him away.

When she opened them again, she was looking at the smirking face of Beth Cartwright, not her late stalker. The reporter stood blocking the door, hands in the pockets of her tailored coat. Sarah had no doubt that one of those pockets held a tape recorder. The woman tilted her blond head toward the closet. "The doorknob in the closet locks on the inside. Not sure why, but it certainly works in my favor today."

"It's probably not a great idea to sneak up on a woman who was just attacked," Sarah seethed.

"No doubt, but there wasn't much chance of me getting you alone without sneaking." The reporter smiled like a cat that had just gotten into the cream. "I hoped you would need the restroom. I came in the back door when I saw you go in the front."

"Congratulations, you must be the sharpest tool in the shed…or broom closet," Sarah deadpanned, turning to lean back against the sink as if she was completely at ease, even though heart was still in her throat. "I see you didn't take my advice about the housekeeper story."

Beth grinned. "Oh, I'll get to that. But there's no fun stirring things up on campus when most of the students are out of town. Your story, on the other hand, that's the kind of thing that sells papers to locals. They want to hear about sensational crime, as long as none of them are the targets."

Sarah ground her teeth so hard she was worried about losing a filling. "Except that you already have everything you're going to get of my story."

The woman circled Sarah like a predator. "I don't know about that. I think there are a lot of unanswered questions in your case. Like where did your bodyguards come from and who's footing the bill for those guys?"

Sarah continued, affecting an air of calm, "No one is footing the bill. They're friends who volunteered to help me feel safer and deal with harassment from people like you."

"Yeah?" Beth lifted a skeptical eyebrow. "I can tell you guys go way back."

Sarah shrugged. "You can believe what you want. Just watch what you print. I don't think your little upstart paper is ready for a libel suit."

"What I really find interesting is how you're linked with that poor Canadian woman who washed up in Maine a couple of months ago."

Sarah hoped her face didn't betray her surprise. The last she heard was that the police were keeping that connection a secret while the investigation was still going on. In the absence of any other motive, they were treating the case as if Ryan Cumberland was a serial killer. They were searching for any other victims. However, that wasn't supposed to be common knowledge. With a mental apology to the ghost of Bridget MacKenzie, Sarah opted to play dumb. "What Canadian woman?"

"You don't know?" Beth cocked her head and gave Sarah a puzzled look. "Looks like your stalker did the same thing to a woman in Nova Scotia before he showed up here."

Sarah shook her head. "First I've heard of it."

"I'd be happy to tell you all about it, if you'll give me an interview," she said with a predatory twinkle in her eye.

Sarah sighed. "You're assuming that I want to know about it. I don't."

"Aren't you a little curious? I mean he kills this woman in Canada and then comes all the way down here to target you? Doesn't that make you wonder?"

"No." Sara tried to sound as convincing as possible. "Believe it or not, I actually have more interesting things to do with my life than play the victim for other people's entertainment. He stalked me. He tried to kill me, and now he's dead. End of story."

"But it's not," Beth purred. "He didn't just do it to you. What about this other woman, or any other victims? Why you? Why her?"

Sarah pushed away from the sink and turned toward the door. "I've already told you that I'm not interested in questions or explanations. I just want to move on."

Beth pursed her lips and looked up in exaggerated thought. "I wonder if Amy Monroe feels the same. Do the police think she was working with him?"

Quick as lightning, Sarah had the woman pinned against the very closet door she'd been hiding behind. She pressed her forearm against the reporter's throat and leaned close. She growled slowly, making every word clear, "If I ever see Amy Monroe's name in your paper in anything but a wedding announcement, I will hunt. You. Down."

Sarah was shocked to see excitement sparking in the other woman's eyes as a triumphant grin spread across her lips. She cursed herself for letting this reporter goad her into an emotional reaction. Beth choked out, "I could leave her alone, if you give me that interview."

"Everything okay, Sarah?" The sound of the scuffle must have alerted Curtis to trouble. Like the professional that he was, he had come in so quietly that Sarah hadn't noticed. She was actually grateful that he hadn't jumped right into the middle of things.

"Sure," Sarah said, hoping to brazen her way through the situation. Without looking away from Beth, she said, "Miss Cartwright and I are just coming to an understanding, hopefully one that won't result in me needing a restraining order. Something tells me your editor wouldn't appreciate me including the paper's entire staff in that."

Beth inhaled sharply through her nose and Sarah hoped that was a flicker of alarm in her eyes. "No, I don't think he would."

"Then I think we understand each other just fine." Sarah pressed her arm harder against Beth's throat just enough to emphasize her point before stepping back. "I expect I won't be seeing you again. So have a merry Christmas."

Beth pushed away from the door and slid past them, giving as wide a berth as the small room allowed. She pulled the door open just enough for her to escape, and in a second she was gone.

Sarah went for the closet door and opened it. Sure enough there was a lock on the inside of the closet. She held the door open and pointed it out to Curtis. "It's not your fault."

Curtis looked furious. "Who the hell puts a lock on the inside of the closet?"

"It's probably just that a handyman or someone bought the wrong kind of knob and put it on anyway without thinking that it gives someone the opportunity to hide in here." And thanks to that mistake, the guys would probably keep an even closer watch over her. Damnit.

"We should point that out to the manager on the way out," Curtis said, obviously ready to leave, which suited Sarah just fine.

"Yeah, and I need to call the police when we get home. She asked me about something that she shouldn't know about. I think the police might have someone leaking information to her."

CHAPTER TWENTY-ONE

June 1968
Làrachd an Fhamhair, Scotland

"*A Mhàili.*" Someone was shaking me by the shoulder. I tried to pull the quilt back over my head, but someone grabbed it. "No, you can't go back to sleep. We have to get up."

I had no idea how long I had been asleep, but it was definitely not long enough.

Whoever it was grabbed the quilt again and yanked it further down. "I don't care if you're tired. It's the Solstice and we have to get ready."

I turned over and cracked one very puffy eyelid to find Rona kneeling over my pallet, looking only slightly cross. When I rolled onto my back, her brows drew together. "Oh! Your eyes are a mess. Sheila, give me a cold wet cloth."

I could hear Sheila moving around below, and before long a hand appeared at the edge of the loft with a wet cloth. Rona took it and approached me. "Lie back and put this over your eyes. I'm going to get dressed, and then it's your turn. Don't go back to sleep."

I kept the towel over my eyes and listened to Rona and Sheila getting ready. Whatever their opinions of each other, they were after all two young women getting ready for an important event. They helped each other, asked opinions, and traded tips with a minimum of words. I heard the shoosh of fabric sliding against skin as they put their clothes on and the crackle of static from a brush being pulled through hair. There was a gasp followed by an mmhmm of approval. I wondered if this was what it would be like to have sisters, other women with whom you had such an understanding that you didn't need words.

"Alright, Sleeping Beauty, it's yer turn," Sheila's voice called up. I lifted the cloth from my eyes and blinked into focus. They felt a bit less gritty, and the sleep had done wonders for my head. I peeked over the edge of the loft and saw the two of them bathed in the lamplight. They were both wearing simple dresses of saffron colored linen that swirled around their ankles. I climbed down and they set about getting me ready. Sheila brushed my hair while Rona dried my face and put on some foundation. "Can't have you looking like you've been crying all night, can we?"

"It's still night," I groaned.

"Well, we canna have ye looking like ye're going to hang." Sheila leaned forward. "Besides, tonight we feast and dance. This is a happy time. What will yer man think?"

I didn't really care what he would think, whichever one he was, but I didn't feel like arguing the point just then. It was actually nice being fussed over by the two of them, almost like we were friends.

"Close your eyes. I want to shade them a little to make them look less puffy." Rona was poised with a small brush near my face. I did as she said and the brush felt feather light on my eyelids.

The two of them stood back to admire their handiwork and smiled. Rona held up a mirror big enough for me to see my head and shoulders. I couldn't see much color in the lamplight, but the effect was enough. I didn't look like I had just rolled out of bed after a bender.

"Shall we then?" Sheila's eyes sparkled with excitement.

"Might as well, eh." Rona set the mirror aside and reached for my hand. When I put my hand in hers, she gave it a reassuring squeeze. Sheila opened the door and we headed out into the night. We could see the torches and wood fires in front of the hall from across the glen. Sheila took my other hand and led us down the lane toward the feast.

There were more people there than I had seen since arriving in the village. They were all gathered in the grassy circle in front of the hall. There were fires lit at both ends of long tables full of food. People clustered all around the green, talking, eating, and dancing. Musicians at the far end of the green played a reel.

"Ye were right, ye ken. It is a sort of homecoming. There are some of us who live all over, but they usually come home for midsummer. This is a big year because of us," Sheila said, practically bouncing across the foot bridge, dragging us behind her.

When we stepped into the firelight, the music stopped. All eyes turned to us, and I wanted to hide behind the other girls. I wasn't ready for whatever was going to happen tonight, and I knew it. The dress, the makeup, the connection to the girls on either side of me seemed like a sham. Just like earlier that day, I wanted to turn around and sneak off into the dark. And just like earlier, it was Duff who stopped me. I let go of Sheila and Rona's hands and was gripping my skirt like I was about to turn around and run for it when he strolled up to us and held out his hand to me. He stood tall, and his eyes shone like he was proud of me just for showing up. At that moment, I needed strength, and he gave it to me.

I smoothed my skirt before I put my shaking hand in his. He grinned at me and pulled me toward the dancers. I heard a celebratory yip, and the music began again. Duff and I joined the group of dancers and were soon swept along in the reel.

I realized a few bars in that Duff had no idea what he was doing. I kept having to turn him the right way and point him to where he needed to go. Your Granny taught me country dancing from about the time I could walk, so I fell right in with the locals. Duff stuck out like a sore thumb. He didn't mind, though, and pretty soon we were both laughing at his mistakes, and the rest of the group didn't seem to mind the Yank who was all elbows and knees. By the end of the first song, I was laughing so hard I forgot all about how intimidated I was.

Later, when I was getting some food from one of the tables, and Duff had gone to get me a drink, Rab Ballantyne appeared in front of me. He looked mighty fine standing there in the firelight with a fiddle braced on his hip. "Listen I'm sorry if I came on a bit strong earlier. I'm not so forward as a' that."

I smiled and probably blushed a bit. "It's okay. I just wasn't feeling very sociable."

"Aye." He smiled and took a step closer. "It's just that ye were a bit of a surprise. I wasna expecting to meet such a bonny lass in the auld village."

I gave him a little side eye to let him know I wasn't falling for it.

"Weel, word 'round is that this whole thing was a surprise to ye."

"Of course." I didn't like the idea of the whole village talking about me behind their hands, but I guess I should have expected it. "No one has secrets where I come from either."

His smile faded and he looked away in silence. In a few seconds, the wolfish grin was back and he leaned in closer like he was going to whisper in my ear. "Och, there are secrets and then there are secrets."

Just when I thought we were going to have a normal conversation, he was back to being fresh. I leaned back and looked at him. "Do you always do that?"

He looked back at me like he was surprised I hadn't melted. "Smile at pretty lasses? No' always but usually."

"I mean flirt when you don't know what else to say," I said with a knowing smile.

"Canna fool ye, can I?" He relaxed and didn't look too bothered by me calling him out.

"Well, I've recently had my eyes opened to a lot of things," I said, looking around the green. It looked so idyllic, with families playing and talking, people dancing. It looked like nothing more than a picnic. I almost forgot that it was the middle of the night, and come morning I would be handfast to a mate chosen for me by some mysterious process that I didn't understand.

"Aye. I expect ye have," he murmured.

I glanced at him as he looked out at the crowd. He was so handsome a girl couldn't help admire him, and despite his flirting he seemed to be an alright guy. It occurred to me then that he might well be the one I was matched to. "Tell me about Inverness. What do you do there?"

"Bit o' this, bit o' that, but mostly I'm a musician. Did ye not hear us earlier?"

"Oh I did. But I was dancing. I guess I didn't stop to see who was playing the music." I glanced the fiddle he was still holding.

"Weel, I reckon that means we were doing it right." He stood up straighter and laid his fiddle on the table. "Ye like dancing then?"

Suddenly my throat felt tighter, and an ache started just under my breastbone. I looked over at the dancers near the musicians. Their feet looked so light and they seemed free. My voice must have cracked when I said, "More than just about anything."

He reached for my hand. "Och no. I didna mean to—"

I slipped my hand from his and waved it in dismissal. "Don't worry about it. You couldn't kn—"

"Dance with me. Now." He picked up his fiddle and pulled me toward the dancing. His eyes were alight with mischief. "I canna let ye be maudlin. 'Tis a night to celebrate."

I hope someday that you meet a man who pulls at you the way Rab Ballantyne pulled at me. It started at that moment, or at least that was the first time I noticed it. But he was like a magnet for me. I had barely eaten anything. I was thirsty and tired, and I knew Duff would be back any second with drinks. But with Rab standing there with the firelight reflected in his laughing green eyes, well, I just didn't have it in me to resist.

I let him pull me over to where the musicians were sitting. He rested his fiddle and whispered in the ear of the other fiddle player. A few seconds later they began to play a waltz. It was different from the country dances, but the other young folk didn't mind.

"Yer light on yer feet," he said as we turned together.

"I had planned to be a dancer." I tried not to mentally add "until I came to this place."

"I saw that look. I willna let ye be sad tonight." He whirled me around some more. His arms felt so good around me we could have spun off the edge of the Earth and I wouldn't have noticed.

*****

We danced until the sky started to lighten. Then the music stopped, and we heard Jock announce that it was time. It was like someone had lassoed us and yanked us back down to the ground. I stood there in the circle of Rab's arms, trying to catch my breath. He seemed to be struggling to do the same, and we held on to each other. We were barely aware of the group moving around us.

Then there was a tap on his shoulder. He looked around to see Duff standing behind him looking like a suspicious big brother, which I guess isn't far from how he felt. Rab's cheeks reddened, and he backed away from me with a little bow of his head. He turned toward the hall where the other lads seemed to be gathering.

Duff silently stepped up to me and pulled my arm into the crook of his elbow. He walked me to the head of a crowd gathering in front of the hall. Rona and Sheila were there with their stewards, Davie and Gavin. Behind them in this odd procession were Lachlan and Rab, both smiling warmly, and Willie, who was busy examining the tops of his shoes.

"*Trobhad*," Sheila called as she took Davie's arm and started down the lane through the glen. Some of the younger boys took torches and hurried along the path to light the way. Rona took Gavin's arm and followed.

"You ready?" Duff asked as we fell into step behind them.

"Not really, but I reckon there isn't much to be done about it." I kept putting one foot in front of the other. I felt numb. It reminded me of a figurehead on the bow of a ship, beautiful, but motionless, expressionless even when heading into a storm. And believe me, I felt like I was heading right into a hurricane.

As we walked, the sky became lighter and lighter. By the time we reached the plateau where the pool was, we didn't need the torches anymore. Everything took on that blue tinge that you see just before the sun starts to come up. The crowd grew silent as we climbed the hill. The only sounds were the shushing of our feet through the grass and the torches crackling.

Aunt Eilidh was waiting for us, standing on the tree stump like it was a platform. She stood with her back to the cliff as everyone came in and took their places. The stewards and sisters stood at intervals around the pool. The lads and the villagers arranged themselves behind us. Eilidh kept her eyes trained on the mountain across the glen to the east as everyone arranged themselves properly.

Aunt Eilidh's shoulders rose and fell with a deep breath. When she spoke, her voice echoed off the hills around us. "Children of the auld folk. It's been a long time since we've celebrated a matching on the Solstice. Though we've become scattered like leaves on the wind, our tradition has brought us back here.

"The modern world no longer remembers us, and the few who do make up stories. But we know the truth. We have kept our line pure, and the day will come when the few who know what we are will come for our help. So we gather here to make

the next generation as strong as those that have gone before."
As she spoke, the sun began to peek over the mountain across
the glen. I watched the band of light track down the rock face
behind her.

With one hand, she waved the three lads forward. Lachlan
went first, walking to Aunt Eilidh and bending his head. Aunt
Eilidh reached up and plucked several strands of hair from his
head. She transferred that hair to the other hand while Lachlan
returned to his place. Next Rab repeated the process, wincing
when she yanked the curly gold strands from his head. Then
Willie bowed low and she took some from him as well.

When each of them had given their hair, Aunt Eilidh raised
her hand over the pool. She reached back, and a boy hastened
forward to give her a torch. Eilidh held the torch over the pool
and dropped the hairs into the flame, letting the ashes fall to the
green water below. She handed the torch back to the boy and
bent down to take up a staff, which she used to stir the sickening
green water. She continued stirring as the band of sunlight slid
down the cliff into the clearing and across the ground to the
pool.

"Come child, we havena got much time." Aunt Eilidh
waved to Sheila. The young woman stepped onto the stump just
as the first rays of sunlight hit the water. From her robe, Aunt
Eilidh produced a knife. She took Sheila's hand and sliced the
knife across her palm. Sheila grimaced, but didn't seem
surprised and the blood began to flow immediately. Aunt Eilidh
held Sheila's hand over the water. She gripped her daughter's
hand, turned it to the side, and squeezed so that the blood ran
into the murky green water.

Aunt Eilidh stirred the water again, keeping Sheila's arm
outstretched and dripping blood. The green and red swirled

together and the sulfur smell grew as the water was disturbed. The two of them stared into the pool as if searching the swirling colors for something. I have no idea what she saw, but I watched all the color drain from Sheila's face and her shoulders sink. Aunt Eilidh glanced at her, then back at the water.

"Robert Ballantyne," Aunt Eilidh declared in a rush.

Sheila gasped and stared at her mother. I saw Aunt Eilidh nod and pull Sheila's hand back. Rab stepped forward and held out his hand. Aunt Eilidh swept her knife across it. She placed Sheila's injured hand in his and wrapped a cloth around them, tying a knot underneath. Together, they went back to the place where Sheila had stood before.

Next Rona stepped forward and the procedure was repeated. This time Aunt Eilidh found the answer quickly. "Lachlan Morse!"

Lachlan came forward with his smiling eyes on Rona's. He didn't even flinch when Aunt Eilidh cut his hand. When they walked back to their place, Rona leaned comfortably into him.

"Come on then." Aunt Eilidh was looking crossly at me. The concentrated light of the sun over the mountain was starting to diffuse. We didn't have much time.

I guess she expected me to go through the ritual just the same as everyone else, though by process of elimination it was obvious which man was my match. I didn't see why it needed to be announced. But I suppose fair's fair. Duff gave me a little bump with his shoulder, and I stumbled forward a couple of steps before I managed to walk to where Aunt Eilidh stood.

She grabbed my hand and sliced. The cut burned across my palm like fire and I made my hand into a fist, wishing the burning would stop. It was made ten times worse when she wrapped her hand around mine and squeezed. I watched several large drops of blood spread across the surface of the pool. I waited for her to stir it, wanting to see what the others had seen. When it took so long for Aunt Eilidh to stir, I glanced up at her. She was staring hard at the ridge across the plateau.

I followed her eyes to find a figure there. The sunlight was so bright high up on the hill that I couldn't see more than a silhouette. It was almost the same profile I had seen in the water the day before, the man with the stag's horns.

"William Cross," Aunt Eilidh pronounced while I was still watching the figure on the ridge. At the name, the figure turned and walked down the other side.

Before I knew what was happening, Willie had come beside me and his bleeding hand was pressed against mine. His grip was strong, even painful. Aunt Eilidh tied the cloth around our joined hands, and Willie pulled me along to my place by the edge of the pool.

Aunt Eilidh faced the group from the village and raised her voice to announce, "Our matches are made. May they be fruitful."

Everyone cheered. Well, everyone but those of us who had really been involved. Rab looked as green as the water in the pool, and Sheila looked shell-shocked. Rona and Lachlan looked quietly pleased with each other. Aunt Eilidh looked nervously from one couple to the next. Meanwhile, Willie was still looking down at the ground. His grip on my hand had not lessened. I was starting to lose feeling in my fingers.

The villagers and stewards started making their way back down the hill. I turned to see them go. Duff looked back at me. His mouth was set in a grim line, and I was thinking that he looked about as unhappy as I felt. He sighed and turned to go. When we arrived back in the village, the people had gone back to eating, drinking, and dancing. The couples each sat down near the food table. I don't know if this part was some sort of tradition, but it seemed like the natural thing, like a wedding feast. Only I didn't feel married, and I didn't want to be.

We sat there, not saying a word. People offered to bring us food and drink. I didn't understand how they could go on with the party. All the energy had drained out of me.

"I ken what you're thinking," came a low voice from beside me. I turned to find Willie watching me from beneath his dark brows. His expression was closed off.

"I doubt that." I turned back to watch the party.

"Ye're thinking that ye're stuck with the village numpty." He turned away as if he didn't want to see my reaction.

"I won't lie to you. I'm not happy, but it has more to do with the whole situation than it does with you in particular." I gave his hand a reassuring squeeze.

He turned back to me and gave me the closest thing he had to a smile. It didn't last long. Quick as a wink, he went back to looking at anything else, but he squeezed my hand in thanks.

We stayed there, hands tied together while the village moved around us. The others even went to join in the dancing, but Willie and I kept our seats. When the dew had evaporated from the leaves, people drifted back to their homes or to the hall, where some of the visitors were sleeping.

The three sisters with our mates wound our way through the village and back to Aunt Eilidh's house. There she had warm water and washcloths waiting for us. We used the cloths to separate and clean our hands from where our blood had mixed together and dried. Willie wished me goodnight with a flurry of nervous nodding. Lachlan kissed Rona, who blushed prettily. Rab gave Sheila a buss on the cheek and she looked a little disappointed. As he was pulling the door closed, he lifted his eyes to mine with a look that I couldn't quite place.

CHAPTER TWENTY-TWO

December 18, 1995
Chapel Hill, North Carolina

"Hold the phone."

Sarah let the journal drop to her lap and stared at the wall of her room. Something was familiar. It was like a tickling feeling at the back of her mind. She ran through the key points of the ritual she had just read: pool, bloodletting, divination. She had heard about something like this before. She tapped her thumb on the book while her memory worked.

Sarah jumped up from the bed and was out of her room like a shot. She startled Fleming so badly he was already on his feet by the time she got to the front room. "Relax," she said, holding up a hand to forestall him. "Everything's fine. I'm just following a thread and got excited."

His shoulders sagged, and he gave her a look that said, "Don't scare a man like that."

Sarah waggled her eyebrows as she walked by him to the low bookcase under the front window. "Gotta keep you on your toes, right?"

His response was a low throaty grunt that reminded her so much of Dermot that her throat tightened with longing. She knelt by the bookcase and scanned the spines. When they had first moved in together, she and Amy had started pooling what textbooks they didn't sell into a home library that now stretched

234 · MEREDITH R. STODDARD

across the front wall of the apartment. Sarah was looking for a book on Northern European mythology. She usually stuck to folklore from the last few hundred years—ancient mythology wasn't really her area, but that was folklore too. Right?

She fluttered her fingers across the spines of the books on the bottom shelf until she found the one she was looking for, a compendium of Norse myths. She snatched it from the shelf and sat cross-legged on the floor. She flipped to the table of contents, trying to match the vague idea in her memory with the legends in the book. She lit on the chapter about Yggdrasil, the tree that provided the framework for the nine Norse worlds. Flipping to that chapter, Sarah skimmed until she found the legend she was looking for.

***

It was Odin's custom to ride his great horse, Sleipnir, along the trunk of the great tree of Yggdrasil. On these journeys he observed three women who appeared daily by the water at the base of the tree. Each day they tended the tree, drawing water and moving sand and carving the trunk. It was the last of these that puzzled Odin the most.

Every day as he passed these women, Odin grew more curious. One day when he could bear it no more, he paused to ask them, "Maidens, why do you tend the tree so faithfully?"

The woman gathering water said, "I am Urth. I gather the waters from the Well of Destiny to nourish the great tree of the worlds."

The woman who was shifting the sand replied, "I am Verthandi. I use the sands from the shore of the well to strengthen the roots."

When the third did not speak, Odin drew closer to where she was carving the trunk. "What of you, maiden? Why do you carve the tree? Surely that cannot help it grow."

"I am Skuld, and it is not only for the tree that I am carving. These are the fates of the children born each day."

"But who set you these tasks?" Odin asked.

"We came here from Jotunheim to protect the world tree from the petty battles of fickle gods," said Verthandi.

"How do you know what to carve?" he asked Skuld.

"I see their fates in the Well of Destiny," she replied.

Odin went to the edge of the well and looked into the water. He saw nothing but rocks and moss. He continued his daily rides and watched as the carvings on the trunk of the tree multiplied.

Each day he grew more curious for the knowledge of Skuld, until he determined to learn the meaning of the carvings. The next day, he brought a rope. He tied it to the strongest bough of the great tree, a branch that stretched over the Well of Destiny. Tying the other end to his foot, he suspended himself over the water. Then he took a dagger and cut his breast. He hung there and watched as his blood blended with the water of the well.

He refused all drink. He refused all food. He took no time to rest, but watched the water ceaselessly. The Norns continued their daily duties, and his frustration grew. Each day the women came and saw what he could not in the waters of the well. Each day Skuld carved the fates on the trunk of the great tree.

"Why can I not see what you see?" he cried when the Norns appeared after several days.

"Patience," they told him. "We have devoted our entire lives to seeking the truth. You have been here but a few days. When your sacrifice is great enough, the answers will come."

For days longer, Odin watched as the waters of the Well of Destiny were poured onto the roots and returned to the well each morning as the dew dripped from the leaves. His own blood was a part of that water and so now a part of the tree.

On the morning of the ninth day, in the gray light just before dawn, as Odin watched the dew drip down in to the pool and the ripples spread across the surface, he saw something more. Below the surface, faint shapes of runes began to appear, the same symbols he had seen Skuld carving every day. As the light of the rising sun hit the water, the meaning of the runes dawned upon him. He looked to the trunk of the great tree of Yggdrasil and he was able to read the story of the nine worlds and understand the role of every being in them. And that was how Odin gained the wisdom of the flow of time.

**

Sarah felt the hairs stand up on the back of her neck. Three women with different kinds of sight, and wisdom that comes from bloodletting into a pool…there were too many similarities between this legend and her mother's story to ignore. But what did it mean? Was her family part of some strange Nordic cult? Was this something that they brought to Scotland from Scandinavia, or was it from something older? Dermot had mentioned Doggerland, the landmass that had once connected Britain to mainland Europe. It had been swallowed by the sea after the last ice age.

"Find what ye were looking for?" Fleming's voice cut across her thoughts. Her head was spinning with so many questions that it took her a minute to answer.

"Uh, yeah." She returned her gaze to the book. "Yeah, I think I did." She rose from where she'd been sitting on the floor and blindly made her way back to her room while reading through the story again. When she finished rereading, Sarah found herself sitting on her bed. She barely remembered having gotten up from the living room floor.

"We came from Jotunheim..." the story said. Sarah flipped to the index. There were several references to Jotunheim, and each one made the connection stronger. Jotunheim was the land of giants, but not lonely giants with golden egg–laying geese. They were tricksters bedeviling the gods. These giants had families and foibles. Then she got to the story of Mimir's well. Here was another example of Odin sacrificing part of himself to gain wisdom. This time he gave up an eye for the privilege of drinking from a well in Jotunheim. Once again, the giant was the one who seemed to control knowledge or judgment.

Sarah laid the Norse mythology book on the bed and retrieved the storybook she had made as a child. She read it again. So much of it seemed to click. "Our people sprang from the footprint of a giant set in stone..." Sarah glanced at herself in the mirror above her dresser. At a perfectly average five-foot-six, she found the idea of being descended from giants unlikely. But then maybe they weren't actually descended. Maybe they were the keepers of some sort of legacy of knowledge. They weren't the giant's children, but the giant's wife had given them a gift.

That brought her back to the question of just how old the giant connection was. In her story she had written, "Long ago,

238 · MEREDITH R. STODDARD

before our land became an island…" That certainly supported Dermot's Doggerland theory, but that would make the giant legend over eight thousand years old.

"That's not even possible," she said to herself. But then legends evolved and were adapted to new cultures. What were the chances they could have been adapted from something that old? Sarah knew one person who might be able to answer that question. Before she thought it out, the phone was in her hand and she had dialed the number.

"Hello?" the voice on the other end was thick with sleep.

"Jon, I need to pick your brain for a few minutes." The words tumbled out. She wasn't entirely sure why she had called him, but she didn't want to wait for the morning to research the answer herself. As late-night calls to your ex went, she figured professional questions weren't completely pathetic.

"Sarah?" His voice sounded clearer, but there was no question that he wasn't exactly happy to hear from her. "It's two o'clock in the morning."

"Sorry, I know it's late. But what's the point of having an anthropologist friend if you can't call him with a question at two in the morning?" She tried to sound casual, as if their last conversation hadn't ended with her basically calling him a coward.

"We're not friends," he said curtly.

"Sure we are, we're just not dating anymore."

"The last time I was your friend it got me cornered and threatened late one night in the arboretum," he grumbled.

"You don't have to worry about that now. Dermot's gone back to Scotland, and I'll be out of your hair soon too. I just have a few questions. It's strictly professional."

"Then it can wait until office hours," he said.

"What were humans doing eight to ten thousand years ago?" she asked in a rush, afraid he would hang up on her.

"Which ones?" he asked with a sigh.

"European ones."

"Yeah," he sniffed. "They were shifting from hunting and gathering to farming, starting to domesticate animals. Getting into hand crafts like spinning and weaving."

"Okay. What kind of societies did they have?"

"Well, not too advanced. Agrarian settlements. Still mostly on the continent," he muttered.

"What about language and myths?" she asked.

He sighed again. "Well, Indo-European language didn't develop until about six thousand years ago. There was certainly language before that, but we don't know much about it, not enough to know any kind of mythology. But then there are things that appear in folklore across cultures that suggest either a shared experience or some kind of deeper subconscious connection, the deluge, dragons, giants—"

"Giants, huh? Which cultures had giants?"

"There seems to be at least one Goliath creature in almost every culture."

"Like Judaculla?" Sarah remembered hearing Cherokee legends of a giant that lived in the mountains. "Or Paul Bunyan?"

"Yeah, but those are one-offs. Some cultures have legends about races of giants. In North and South America, indigenous people have legends about a giant race. Early Christian lore talks about the Nephilim. The Vikings believed in a race of giants and spread that belief all over northern Europe," he said through a yawn.

"I think I read something about that." She could research the folklore aspect herself. "So is there any physical evidence of giants?"

He groaned. "Some amateur archaeologists claim to have found giant bones or fossils. There was one cache in Wisconsin I think that was supposed to have over a dozen skeletons, but none of it was ever confirmed. We're talking about the anthropological equivalent of Bigfoot sightings."

"Okay, I think you've given me plenty to go on." She grabbed an index card and began jotting down things to look up.

"Sure. Hey, Sarah?" He hesitated as if he was trying to find the right words. "Are you okay? I saw the…thing on the news. I wanted to call, but you know."

"Yeah, I know." She couldn't help feeling a little gratified that he had been worried for her. It might not have worked out between them, but he wasn't a bad guy. "I'll be alright."

"Okay. Next time could you hold your questions until a decent hour?" he asked, not unkindly.

"Sure, Jon. Thanks again," she said.

"Night." This click on the other end told her that he'd hung up. She eyed the books on her bed and wondered if she should keep reading or try to get some sleep. In the end, she picked up Molly's journal.

CHAPTER TWENTY-THREE

June 1968
Làrachd an Fhamhair, Scotland

The next evening was the first time we ran out of food. The dregs from the party had been cleared away, and the village had slowly gone back to normal life. Visitors had all returned to their homes in Lochinver, Lairg, and elsewhere. The remainder of us gathered in the hall for tea.

I was sitting at the table by the fire with the other sisters and our men, Jock and Aunt Eilidh. Sheila was making some fawning comment about Rab's fiddle playing at the feast while he was uncomfortably pushing his spoon through his stew when a little voice came from near the fire, "Uncle Jock? There's nae food in here."

Jock turned to look at the girl. "Of course there's food, child. Just use the ladle."

The girl dipped the ladle into the great pot. When she pulled it back up, it was empty. Jock got up and went to the pot. He put the ladle in, and we all heard it clang against the bottom of the cauldron. He gave Aunt Eilidh a pleading look.

She went to see for herself and gasped when she looked inside the pot. Her eyes darted to Sheila's before she turned to Jock. "Nae doubt the feast overtaxed our stores. It'll be right as rain tomorrow."

It wasn't, nor the next day. Soon some of the men had to go to Lochinver to buy supplies. We harvested more vegetables from Jock's wee garden patches and began foraging in the hills for more. It seemed strange to me that no one was prepared for the amount of food they needed. They'd been living here for who knows how long. They should have known how much it would take to feed them all. I said so to Rona one day when we were digging potatoes.

"Well, they've always had the cauldron. Eh?" She shrugged.

"What does that have to do with it?"

"You know, from the story? The cauldron of plenty. They've never had to tell how much food they'll need before, because they've always had enough."

"You mean it's real?" Some of the other aspects of the story I could believe, or at least understand how others could believe them, but the cauldron always seemed like too much magic to be real. Then I remembered what Jock had said when I asked him how the gardens could provide enough food for everyone. "Magic."

And now that magic wasn't working. "Why do you think it stopped?"

"I wish I knew." Rona thought for several seconds, her eyes on her dirty hands. She bumped my arm with her elbow. "Good thing we've been living with the *sluagh ùr*. We know how much food we need."

The next time we were in the hall, I couldn't help staring at the cauldron. It really did just look like a great big iron pot, a lot like the one Mama used for the washing. It stood over the fire on iron legs. Jock was still using it to cook in. I guess he hoped it might start producing food again. But every meal ended with the sound of the ladle scraping the bottom.

After a couple of weeks, I was sitting at the table eating a bit of porridge when Duff sat down across from me. I had slept late, so I'd been the one to scrape the bottom of the pot.

"Do you know how to smoke meat?" he asked without even a how-do-you-do.

I nodded. "Mama taught me. We used to buy a pig or two every fall and smoke the meat for winter."

He looked around like he didn't want anyone listening. "No one here seems to know how. If I got the lads to help me build a smokehouse, could you show them how?"

"I reckon I could." I pushed my bowl aside. "What are we smoking?"

"Deer, I guess. Maybe some fish." He glanced over at the pot. "We've got to do something. They'll never get through the winter if they can't put by enough food."

"Can you get the supplies you need?" Over his shoulder, I saw Jock at the back of the hall staring at the shelves and bins with their meager food stores.

"Yeah, I think we can get the wood for a frame from nearby and I can go buy the hardware."

"Then it sounds like a plan. I wonder if we can get some jars and lids. Maybe Rona and I can work on canning some vegetables."

"Now, you're thinking." He grinned at me as he stood up to leave. I watched him go, feeling a little bit better about my measly breakfast.

"Ye ken some folk are saying it's you foreigners that have caused the cauldron to stop." I looked to my left to see Willie sitting at the end of the table. He lifted his eyes to mine, and my breath caught in my throat. I'd seen Willie look nervous, embarrassed, even hopeful, but that day his eyes were just cold. "That yer new ways and yer doubts are the cause."

He hadn't said much to me since we were matched. He'd been polite, but I had noticed that where Lachlan and Rab seemed to court Rona and Sheila as normal men would, Willie hadn't sought me out nor paid much attention to me. I had just chalked it up to shyness. Looking at him that morning I wasn't so sure. "And what do you say?"

He dropped his spoon into his bowl and leaned toward me. "I think ye're none too pleased wi' me and you doubt the need for matching altogether."

I was surprised to say the least. I moved down the table to sit across from him and put my hand tentatively on his arm. "If I've ever been anything but kind to you, I didn't mean it. I can't think of anything that I've done to make you believe this."

"Och, I see just fine. I can see what ye think of us, what ye think of me." He shifted uncomfortably and suddenly couldn't meet my eyes.

"Willie, I don't think ill of you or anyone here." I took my hand from his arm and rested it in my lap. Looking down, I said, "It sounds like the person unhappy with this match is you."

"Really?" He looked doubtful. "Ye dinna seek me out. Ye dinna spend any time with me."

I arched an eyebrow at him. I didn't much like this situation, but I was caught in it and I had determined to be open to it. "I could say the same to you. Besides, where I'm from women who seek out men are considered loose and forward. You already think I'm too modern. What would you think of me if I was chasing after you?"

He studied his bowl for a minute, thinking. When he spoke again, his voice was softer without some of the venom of before. "It's different here, ye ken. Our women are leaders. We lads just go along."

I chuckled. "I don't think it's that different. Where I'm from, women run the show. They just do it quietly, so the men think they're in charge."

He laughed, so quiet it was little more than a breath and shaking of his thin shoulders. I hoped that we were finding some common ground.

I held my hand out to him and smiled. "Friends at least?"

He took my hand. "Aye."

"Great. Now, would you like to go foraging with me?"

He sighed, "I think I'd better help the lads with whatever yer steward is planning."

"Alright. I'll see you this evening then?"

"Ye will." He smiled, and I hoped that we had come to an understanding. Still, I couldn't help wondering who it was that was spreading the idea that those of us from outside the village were responsible for the problem with the cauldron.

***

Rab was chosen to propose the smokehouse and canning idea to Aunt Eilidh. Sheila suspected that her mother wouldn't like it and she seemed to favor Rab so they thought he would get a better response. We were all around the table when he said, "Mrs. MacLeod, I've been talking with the stewards and we think that we had best start preparing for the winter. We're going to need food stores."

Aunt Eilidh looked toward the cauldron, where it still stood in its place over the central fire. "I'm sure the cauldron will provide for us. We canna forsake our faith."

"Aye, I'm sure ye're right. Nae doubt the great pot will be back to itself in no time at all." His voice held all the confidence that only Rab seemed capable of. "Still, I'm sure ye'll agree that it canna hurt to be prepared for anything."

She shifted, clearly uncomfortable, and sought out Sheila's eyes across the table. "If we do that, everyone will think we've given up. How can we expect them to keep our traditions if we canna keep our faith?"

Rab made his most dazzling smile. "I think ye would be showing everyone your wisdom in being prepared rather than a loss of faith. Surely, they'll trust ye if ye tell them with the right words. I'm sure ye know how to explain it in a way that everyone will support."

Aunt Eilidh looked at Jock. "What do ye think, brother?"

"I think if we mean to keep the village together, we have to keep them fed." He sighed. "If we canna do that, they'll go off to live wi' the new folk, and you and I will be the only two left to keep the faith."

I could see the wheels turning in her mind. I followed her eyes as she looked around the room, from table to table, at families, stewards, and settled on the cauldron itself. "I canna support it. I am of *na peathraichean*. I canna be seen as anything but the most faithful."

"But Mam—" Sheila started to argue, but Aunt Eilidh silenced her with a raised hand.

"If ye mun prepare, then do it. But I canna speak in favor of it." She planted her hands on either side of her bowl and stood up to lean over the table toward Rab. "If ye're right, then

I will be grateful for the food, and we can see where we go from there. But I canna support it now."

With that, she walked out, leaving us all looking around the table and wondering how she could be so stubborn. Sheila rubbed Rab's arm in support. "She'll see."

"Aye," he said, turning to shake his head at Duff. "She will."

***

The next day, we met after breakfast. The three sisters, Lachlan and Rab, the stewards, and Jock. I had no idea where Willie was, but I couldn't help feeling disappointed that he wasn't there. Duff and Lachlan had worked up a plan to prepare for winter. The first order of business was getting the smokehouse built so that we could start smoking meat as soon as possible. We also needed to build shelves and find space for additional storage. We needed to plant or forage for more of everything that we could dry or can. Once the smokehouse was built, the men would start hunting and fishing to fill our stores.

There was much to be done so we divided up the tasks. Rona and I got to work on a list of equipment and supplies we would need for canning, while Sheila went to harvest enough vegetables for the day's food. Jock began to mark an area in the hall that could be set aside for more storage. Duff and Lachlan set about choosing a spot near the hall to build the smokehouse, and the rest of them went to gather stones for the purpose. We worked well as a team, dividing up the work and getting to it.

It was easy to forget that some people considered us—or at least some of us—responsible. While Rona and I were working on our list, I said, "Have you heard talk about us being the cause of the cauldron stopping?"

"No, I hadn't heard that, but I've been a little wrapped up since the feast." She blushed.

She and Lachlan had been nearly inseparable. I gave her a gentle elbow. "You do seem kind of busy lately."

She giggled. "I know. I really like him."

"You're lucky. Lachlan seems to like you too." I sighed. "Willie can barely stand to be around me."

She looked at me with a pitiful smile. "If it makes you feel any better, I don't think he can stand to be around anyone."

"Unfortunately, I think you're right. Still, he's the one who told me that some of the villagers think that outsiders coming in are the reason the cauldron died."

"Ugh! I suppose you can expect people who have lived all their lives in a place like this to be suspicious of new people coming in." She waved a hand. "This entire village is dedicated to keeping people out. It might be a stretch to ask them to welcome new people with open arms."

"Well, whatever the cause, they don't have much choice now. They're going to need this food whether they like it or not."

"They'll be glad for this once it's cold and they're hungry."

I looked over at the cauldron in its place above the fire. "So you think it's really dead? That it's not just going to start working again?"

Rona looked over there too and sighed. "I don't know. But if we don't know what made it stop doing its thing, then we can't know how to start it again. We just can't afford to count on it."

"Hope for the best, prepare for the worst, right?"

"That's all we can do?" She gave her list a final once-over before handing it to me. "Do you think I've missed anything?"

I scanned the list of supplies. There didn't seem to be anything missing. "Looks good to me."

***

When the men had gathered enough stones to build the smokehouse, we all started working on it together. Duff picked the spot he thought would work best and explained to the others how he thought it would work. The other men and I contributed our own ideas, and we got to building. Unlike most of the dry-built stone houses of the village, we needed to use mortar for the smokehouse to control the smoke. Lachlan built the frame with racks for meat and fish.

Once the frame was in place, we started putting the stones together. It took several days. It never failed that whoever was working would have an audience. There always seemed to be one or two of the villagers watching the progress. Usually it was children, but sometimes they would be joined by an adult. I couldn't help thinking they must be gossiping about what we were doing, whispering behind their hands about the *sluagh ùr* and their strange ways.

I was working one afternoon with Duff and Rab, laying the stones, when Duff got frustrated. He stood up and dropped the trowel into the wet mortar. "Man, you'd think they'd never seen anyone do work before."

Rab glanced over his shoulder at the children watching. This time it was a boy that I only knew as wee Geordie and his little sister, who was probably no older than five. "Aye. They do seem to like a spectacle, but folk here ken well enough what hard work is. They're just not used to working this hard for food."

"Well, welcome to what the rest of the world has to do," Duff muttered. "You seem to understand the situation just fine."

"My parents moved to Inverness years ago," Rab shrugged. "The village canna get much bigger without being discovered. So some families leave, looking for space or a more exciting life. Ye saw some of them come home for the feast."

"Where do they go?" I had to ask.

Rab smiled at me. "Och, mostly nearby towns, but some as far as Inverness, Edinburgh, even America."

"I don't think my mother left seeking a more exciting life," I said, shaking my head.

Rab turned serious. "No, I'm sure that wasna the reason. Still, ye can see why we need to keep our presence here quiet. We canna have just anyone showing up looking for the three sisters or the cauldron."

"Yeah, well," Duff put in, "folks got to eat. We're doing all the work. It'd be nice if they didn't make us feel like the village freak show."

Rab eyed me closely. "Is that how ye feel?"

"Sometimes," I said with a shrug.

"Dinna let them make ye feel like that." He bumped me with his elbow. "This is yer home too."

I smiled. We hadn't talked much after the feast, but I liked Rab. I could tell by his look that both of us remembered how much fun we'd had that night. I might have also blushed a little too. Duff stepped between us and shoved the bucket into my hands. "Will you fetch us some more water from the creek?"

"Right. Sure." I took the bucket off to the burn to refill it.

On my way back from the burn, I couldn't help feeling like I was being watched. This happened a lot around the village. It was tiny and it seemed like everyone knew what everyone else was doing. But you know how isolated the farm can feel in the holler. I was used to privacy when I wanted it. Here I had none. It gets tiring after a while.

Walking back to the smokehouse, I noticed one of the young mothers who lived in the village watching me. She was hanging her laundry under the eaves of her house along the lane that ran parallel to the burn. When I got near to where she was standing, I nodded and said hello in Gàidhlig. She just turned away without saying a word and pretended I wasn't there, that she hadn't been staring at me. Well then, I thought, so that's how it is.

CHAPTER TWENTY-FOUR

June 1968
Làrachd an Fhamhair, Scotland

Willie and I began walking with each other after tea every day. He would wait for me at the door of the hall while the sisters and I helped Jock clean up. For the first few days, he rarely talked. He would wave his hand toward the path in invitation, then he would walk beside me through the village to a lovely spot along the burn. There was a fallen log near a rocky beach where we would sit in awkward silence until one of us got tired and made up an excuse to go back.

After a few evenings like this, I decided to make some conversation. "So, have you always lived in the glen?"

"No, I...lived in Inverness for a while...when I was a boy." He stumbled through his answer, barely glancing at me.

"Do you prefer it here or in town?"

He mumbled his answer, and I had to lean closer to hear. "Here, most of the time...It's quieter here."

"And you like the quiet." It wasn't a question. I didn't need to ask.

"Don't you?" This time he looked directly at me.

I shook my head. "I grew up in the mountains. We weren't as isolated as this, but winters could get pretty lonely. Sometimes I thought the quiet would drive me crazy."

He looked away, his shoulders slumping. After a few more minutes of awkward silence, he said, "I hope ye willna feel so here. This winters can be long."

I sincerely hoped that I wouldn't be there for the winter, but I didn't need to mention that then. "I reckon folks find things to do. At least you have a whole village to be with. It was just me and Mama most of the time."

"Och aye. We gather in the hall and work the wool that we got in the summer. We tell tales and sing." He smiled, looking ahead as if at a memory.

"Do you like to sing?" I asked.

He reminded me of a dog I saw one time in the holler. Mama and I had gone down to Harman's store. Mr. Harman had a basket of peaches and gave me one. I sat down on the steps in front of the store. I wasn't more than three bites into that peach before I noticed a little snout sniffing between the steps. I leaned over and looked down by my feet, but the nose quickly disappeared under the porch.

I kept on eating my peach, and a few seconds later it was back sniffing around my ankle. I must have moved suddenly, because it disappeared again. This time I got up and crouched down to look under the porch. In the dim gray shadows, I could just barely see a little hound dog cowering near the wall.

His head was down, his ears were back, and he was shivering even though it was a hot and sticky day. The dog was so scared I decided to leave it alone. I sat back down on the steps and went back to eating, peach juice dripping between my fingers.

Sure enough, a couple of bites later the nose appeared again. This time I pulled the pit out of what was left of the peach and threw it across the road. I set the rest of the peach down on the step beside my foot.

Soon I saw the snout appear again and grab the peach with its teeth. Then I heard some smacking under the porch as he ate it. Just about the time Mama came out of the store, I felt the dog's tongue flick over my juice-covered fingers.

Willie reminded me of that dog. It was a dance of steps back and forth, and I never knew what would draw him out or cause a retreat. At least I was pretty sure Willie didn't bite. "How old were you when you moved here from Inverness?"

His usual fidgeting began to get erratic. He shifted his feet and rubbed his hand on his thigh. He drew in a breath, and it seemed like he might say something, but in the end he just shook his head and shifted his feet some more.

After a few minutes, he leapt up and said. "We should be getting back."

"Alright." I stood up and he started to walk back. Before we left the beach, though, I grabbed his arm. "Willie, I didn't mean to upset you."

He looked at me and shifted back and forth on his feet. "No, no you didn't. Walk again tomorrow?"

I gave him my kindest, sweetest smile. "After tea."

"Aye, after tea."

***

We walked back, and Willie parted with me in front of the lads' house by nodding furiously and waving awkwardly at the door. I went to the hall to see if anyone else was there who might need some help. Most people had gone to their houses. With the cauldron no longer giving unlimited food, no one tended to linger after tea. I found Gavin, Davie, and Rab drinking whisky and playing cards.

"*A Mhàili bhoidheach,*" Rab sang, rising and swaying a little when I came into the room. "Had a lovely walk, have ye?"

"It was alright." I didn't like his tone. It was clear he'd already had a few. I walked by and went to the back of the hall to get some water.

"Did ye have a nice chat?" he sneered, following me. "Did ye have to do all the talking?"

I decided to ignore him. I made a mental note to stay away from Rab when he'd been at the whisky. The stewards at the table pretended to be focused on their cards.

"Did he try to kiss ye?" Rab whispered, leaning close to my ear. His hand rested on the small of my back.

"That's none of your business, Rab Ballantyne, and I wouldn't tell you if he had," I whispered back angrily.

"Good. That's good. I wouldna want to hear of it." That sounded genuine, and his whisky-scented breath wafted past my nose. I looked up at him, trying to puzzle out what he meant.

He lifted his hand and gripped my arm, his fingers strong. He studied me, especially my lips. He let out a long, whisky-soaked sigh, "Màili."

I leaned back away from him and used my other hand to push his hand off my arm. "Rab, no."

He loosened his grip and stepped back. "Right. Sorry."

He walked back to the table and slumped onto the bench. Picking up his cards, he rejoined the game.

***

By the time we were done with the smokehouse, it was well into July. We were continuing with our plan to put by as much food as we could for the winter. The stewards had gone to Lochinver and picked up some canning supplies. Rona, Sheila, and I set about foraging for berries to make jam and herbs to be dried. We were hanging herbs in the hall early one afternoon while a pot of jam was bubbling on the fire. We were a long way from tea and had moved the cauldron to make room for the jam.

Jock came in with a basket full of vegetables for the day's meal. He plunked down his basket before saying. "It's near August. We should be able to find some mushrooms soon for drying."

August. It was easy in a place where there were no clocks or calendars to forget what day or week it was. Duff and I had been there for over a month. And in a couple of weeks an audition would be happening in New York without me. Not only had I not been practicing, but I had completely forgotten. Maybe I had purposefully not thought about it because it made me angry, sad, and frustrated. Part of me hadn't given up the idea of becoming a dancer, even though another part of me knew it would be much more difficult with a child to worry about, not that I was any closer to having a child. Despite our evening walks, Willie could barely manage to look me in the eye. At this rate, I might be too old to start a dancing career by the time I got out of Làrachd an Fhamhair.

I reached over to stir the jam, trying to hide my sour mood. I didn't bother to turn when I heard the door creak open.

"What can I do for ye, Eithne?" Jock asked.

"I came to get some berries for my weans," a feminine voice answered.

"Sure," I heard Rona say as she went to get a bowl.

Sheila stopped Rona with a hand. Her voice was sharp when she said, "And why should we be giving ye what we've gone and picked? Can ye not pick yer own?"

I turned to watch as the woman named Eithne said, "Well, I've got the bairns to mind. And since when do ye not share food, Sheila?"

Sheila took a couple of steps toward the woman. "Since no one but us and Jock and the young men has lifted a finger to see this village fed. Ye're all so used to having it provided for ye, ye dinna think to work for yer supper."

Eithne took a step back and looked around. Her eyes settled on me stirring the jam over the fire. "Weel, I see ye've given up. Ye even took the cauldron off the fire. It'll certainly never come back if ye dinna use it."

"We'll do as we like, an ye dinna want to starve."

"Stop!" I stepped between them and grabbed a bowl that I filled with berries. I handed the bowl to Eithne. "We haven't given up. We just want to be prepared if the worst happens. We should all be working together." I turned to Sheila. "But we have to share. We are doing all this work to keep the community together."

Eithne took the bowl of berries and nodded to me as she left. Sheila mumbled, "Aye, ye're right. I'm sorry."

"It's okay. I'm frustrated with all the talk too, but we can't have conflict. We just have to keep pushing on."

I was tired of the talk and the looks we'd been getting from some of the people in the village. I had been snubbed by the women, sneered at by the men, and laughed at by the children. Where they had welcomed us at first, the minute something about their lives was disrupted it became our fault. Suddenly, we weren't family anymore. We were *sluagh ùr*, new folk, even though our ways were likely to save them come winter. Unlike Sheila, I didn't feel comfortable confronting people.

So now I didn't fit in at Kettle Holler nor at Làrachd an Fhamhair. This was what I was giving up my dream for, missing that audition for?

"I need some air," I said. "I'm going to see what the guys are doing."

Outside the sun was shining bright and the change in light blinded me. I lifted my hand to shield my eyes and took a few steps toward the lane. Something hit me in the shoulder and fell with a plop. I lowered my hand and looked around, but I was too slow. Looking down, I saw it was a fist-sized clump of dark, wet mud. I pulled on my shirt to see the spot where it had hit, and of course there was a brown smear across my shoulder. That was it. I was done with this village and these people with their stupid superstition and their crazy ideas about destiny and breeding.

I wasn't going to hang around here and let people throw mud at me just for trying to help them. I had an audition to get to. The big question was how to get to it.

I started walking toward Aunt Eilidh's to change my shirt and think my way through an escape plan. I did a mental inventory of how much money I had and how much I thought I would need. I hadn't spent very much on the way there. The transportation had all been paid for, and Duff paid for most of the meals. My stash of money meant to start me off in New York should still be hidden in my suitcase. The real trick was going to be getting to a town, a real town. I could try to go through the mountains, but I just didn't think that would get me far enough, fast enough. And in the village someone was always following me. I glanced behind me just in time to catch sight of the leg of my shadow for the day as he ducked behind the wall of a cottage forty feet behind me on the trail. In a town, preferably a big town, it would be so much easier slip away and blend in. Plus, I'd be that much closer to a train or ferry or some transportation so I could get farther, faster. I wondered if the guys would let me ride along with them on one of their supply runs.

By the time I got to Aunt Eilidh's cottage a plan was starting to form. I climbed up to the loft and dug a new shirt out of my suitcase. While I was changing, Aunt Eilidh bustled in and began puttering around below. She must have heard me because she stopped and said, "Who's there?"

"It's me, Aunt. Molly," I called down.

"Och, are ye alright then?"

"I'm fine. I just got mud on my shirt. I came up to get a clean one."

"That's grand," she said absently. I finished changing my shirt and bent back to my suitcase, thinking it wouldn't hurt to make sure the money was where I had hidden it behind the liner. It was an old box-style case that Mama had picked up secondhand.

I pushed my clothes aside and lifted the panel behind which I'd hidden the money, but instead of finding my envelope all I saw was the frayed edge of the lining and patches of dried glue. With my heart in my throat, I started tossing my clothes out of the way, hoping that it had somehow found its way out of the hiding spot and was mixed in with them. There was nothing. I shoved my hands into the small pockets inside the lid. I picked it up and moved the whole suitcase, hoping it had fallen on the floor. Again, nothing.

"Are ye alright up there?" Aunt Eilidh called.

"Y-yes, ma'am. Be down in a minute." I hoped she didn't hear the panic in my voice. It wouldn't do for her to suspect that I had money hidden. She liked to seem like the gentle matriarch of the village, but I always had the feeling there was more going on with her than she let on. Like she knew more than she said.

"Bring yer shirt down when ye come. I'll set it to soak."

"Right." I put the suitcase back in place and did another quick check to see if it had been dropped somewhere. I grabbed the muddy shirt and climbed down the ladder.

She was stoking the fire when I got down. She turned to me and rested the poker on the hearth. She looked at me, head cocked curiously. "Ye look a mite flushed, lass. Are ye well?"

"Yeah, fine."

You know we MacAlpin girls are good at keeping secrets, but I was sure she saw right through me.

She raised one elegant eyebrow. "Are ye sure?"

"Of course." I admit I couldn't hold her gaze. I turned for the door.

"Wait, *a Mhàili*."

I'm sure it was my nerves rather than her actual tone, but it sounded like she had something significant to say. Maybe something like, "If you're looking for your money, I took it," or, "I found this envelope full of money in the laundry. Is it yours?" I turned back, part dreading, part hoping that she would say something like that. She nodded at my hand. "The shirt?"

"Oh!" I had completely forgotten about the shirt. My fingers were gripped so tight around it, they ached. I held it out to her. "Here."

She reached to take it and her hand gripped mine. She held my eyes longer than made me comfortable before she slid the shirt from my grip. She held it up between her hands and looked at the mud smear. "I'm sure it'll come clean. Mind the weather when ye go. It looks like rain."

CHAPTER TWENTY-FIVE

December 19, 1995
Chapel Hill, North Carolina

Sarah let the book fall to her lap. Everyone in her mother's life had sold her out. Granny had sent her to Scotland without knowing anything about what was expected of her. Duff, despite calling himself her friend, was also her keeper. He had prevented her from running away when she thought she had a chance. Her so-called sisters accepted or even looked forward to their supposed duty. Of course, she wondered if that would have been the case if either of them had been matched with Willie Cross. And of course Aunt Eilidh seemed to be the leader of it all, keeping the village under her thumb under the guise of protecting their traditions.

How much of James's protective generosity was actually a way of keeping her under his thumb? If her situation was as similar to Molly's as it seemed, who could she turn to for help? What if Dermot's profession of love was just a hook to draw her in deeper, to make sure that she followed him to Scotland? Then again, Dermot had actually given her something to work with. He had told her of James's plan, but warned her to keep her knowledge a secret.

Sarah wouldn't be going in blind. By keeping that knowledge from James, Dermot was giving her a choice, even while he was telling her all of the dangers of choosing to leave.

The difference between Sarah and her mother was that Sarah wasn't off in some remote and hidden village. She was still in her town, a town that she knew better than her guard dogs. Maybe she could do what Molly couldn't and find a way out.

She used her gift to verify that Fleming was where she expected him to be. She was starting to recognize the benefits to being able to see things remotely. It was the wee hours of the morning before dawn. No doubt Fleming thought she was asleep or reading. When she came back to herself, she eyed the window. If she wanted to go out the door, she would have to go past Fleming. She should be able to get out the window, though.

Unlike some of the Victorian houses in her neighborhood with their big traditional windows, Sarah's building had been built in the early 1960s. It was a plain brick box divided into eight apartments around two hallways. The windows at the front were large to let in plenty of light, but the side and rear had narrow, sliding windows. Sarah estimated that she could fit sideways through the half of hers that opened.

She didn't remember the last time she had opened her window. Living on the first floor meant they weren't likely to leave their windows open for security reasons that had nothing to do with stalkers and everything to do with living in a college town where theft was pretty common—not that Sarah had much worth stealing. She slowly flipped the lever on the lock, relieved that it opened so easily. Then she tried to pull it open by the small metal handle, which was little more than a metal tab that stuck out about an inch from the frame itself. But the window wouldn't budge.

She glanced over her shoulder, as if she expected to see Fleming standing in the doorway. She took a steadying breath and hooked the fingers of both hands around the metal tab and pulled. It shifted slightly, but stopped. She checked the track to make sure there was nothing blocking it. Then stood next to the opposite side of the window and pulled again. This time she leaned away and used her weight. It clung to its place for a second before squeaking and sliding open. It thunked into the other side of the frame faster than Sarah expected. With all her weight on the window, she lost her balance and her back bumped into the wall.

She froze. Fleming had to have heard one of those noises. There was just no way he hadn't. Sarah held her breath with her back pressed against the wall, waiting for him to come running. She thought about using her gift again to see him, but she was too nervous. If he was coming to investigate, she would know it soon enough. She counted to one hundred, expecting him to burst through the door, but it never happened.

When she thought it was safe, Sarah leaned out the window. It was still mostly dark out and the air had a nice bite to it. There didn't seem to be any movement outside. She listened for a minute for cars on the streets, but didn't hear any. Funny thing about college towns; they're twenty-four-hour noise machines when school is in session, but when it's not they're ghost towns. Sarah pulled her head back inside and set her foot on the window sill.

She dropped out of the window onto some dry leaves, cringing at the rustling sound. She waited again to hear if there was any sign that Fleming had heard her. Having loosened the window opening it, she pulled it back into place without too much trouble. She left a finger's width open so she could get back in when she returned. Sarah turned toward the small parking lot and looked around. She inhaled, and the cold December air burned her nose, reminding her of the mountains.

She had no idea where she was going, but it felt good to be alone. She had been spending plenty of time in her room and the guys had respected her privacy, but she was always aware that one of them was near. It was both comforting and confounding. But just then, no one knew where she was, or what she was doing. It was a heady feeling. She stepped away from the building and crossed the parking lot. This early in the morning she could have walked down the middle of Ransom Street and no one would have noticed, but she stuck to the sidewalk.

She passed the wide grassy lane on the other side of Ransom where the utility lines ran. Looking at the drooping mimosa trees that lined the lane, Sarah wondered if Ryan had used it while stalking her. Or maybe Dermot had. He had been stalking her too after all. Her suspicions hadn't just been paranoia. She guessed she should feel vindicated by that, but she didn't. She walked on until she came to the intersection where she'd been held hostage two weeks ago. It looked so normal, just two narrow side streets crossing, One of them wasn't even two blocks long. Trees and houses stood on the corners. A single streetlight shone on the pavement that had scratched her bare feet and skinned her hands when she fell.

She stood on the corner and scanned the streets. A chill breeze stirred the drying leaves that littered the ground. Sarah decided to take shelter on the porch of the blue house on the opposite corner. Her friends who lived there were gone for the holiday, but she knew they wouldn't mind. She hadn't realized how good it would feel to walk across that street to the shelter of the blue house. That night, her friends had meant safety, help, a call to the police, and an ambulance for Dermot. But she had only gotten to the middle of the street before Ryan had caught her by her hair. She looked down when she reached the spot where he'd caught her. The blood stain was gone, but the spray paint that marked where his body had landed was still bright neon orange against the gray asphalt.

"I'm not the only one, princess. There will always be more," he'd said before raising his gun to the police, before Duff had shot him between the eyes.

Sarah walked on, her head high, to the porch. Ryan Cumberland was dead. As she approached the porch, a lone car passed by slowly. Sarah held her breath as she watched it stop at the corner of Ransom and Cameron. It turned left, and she let out a sigh. The porch might be a little conspicuous. Instead she took a detour around the house into the tiny and overgrown back yard. It sloped dramatically down from the street and was poorly tended. Bushes and weeds grew waist high. Sarah had only been back here once or twice. She thought the girls who lived in the blue house hadn't been back there much more often.

She kicked her way down the narrow path of drying weeds and leaves to the only level part of the yard. There was a plastic lawn chair that looked like it might have been there for a decade and a couple of large stones bordering an algae-covered fish pond. Sarah sat down on the largest stone and eyed the murky pool. It made her wonder just what was in that strange pool in Làrachd an Fhamhair. Was it magic like scrying, or was there a scientific explanation? Was there some chemical in the water that reacted with chemicals in the blood, like a litmus test? Scotland was littered with saint's pools and wells. Some were just legend, but some had chemical properties that would affect certain people who drank the water. Add that to the growing list of things she needed to research.

The wind picked up again, and Sarah hugged her arms to her sides. In the bowl of the back yard, the wind dipped and swirled, kicking up leaves into tiny tornados and blowing some into the pool. They floated on top of the algae, brown oak leaves against the bright green. It drew Sarah back across time to that March morning, when she had made her mother a crown of oak leaves and early spring flowers and then seen the same crown in a puddle on the bathroom floor.

"Tha coltas banrigh an t-sithean oirbh." Those were the words that had taken the light out of her mother's eyes. Until that moment they had been having a wonderful morning. They'd found the first flowers of the year, sung songs, been happy…and happy wasn't something Mama did often. But when little Sarah had put the flowered crown on her mother's head, Mama had immediately tried to take it off. Sarah had no idea how close she had been to the awful truth. *"Tha coltas banrigh an t-sithean oirbh."* You look like a fairy queen.

Sarah stood and brushed off her jeans. She stuffed her hands in her pockets, and with one long look at the oak leaves floating on the green algae, she walked up the slope to the street. She had proven something to herself. She could slip away, and if she chose not to go to Scotland she would do just that. But she wasn't ready yet. She needed to be prepared. And she had some more reading to do.

CHAPTER TWENTY-SIX

Làrachd an Fhamhair, Scotland
July 1968

I forced myself to continue as if nothing had changed. I kept working with the girls, canning and drying. I helped the guys test the firebox in the smokehouse. We made a list of dry goods that we needed and installed storage shelves in the back of the hall. I continued my evening walks with Willie. He eventually became comfortable enough with me that one night he even worked up the nerve to kiss my cheek.

But whenever I was alone, I was searching for my money. I checked under all three pallets in the loft, under Aunt Eilidh's mattress, and in every drawer, shelf, or nook in the cottage. I was starting to think it wasn't there. Maybe whoever had taken it had stashed it somewhere else or added it to some community fund for the village.

One afternoon, I claimed a headache and skipped tea. I was searching the cottage yet again. I got to the wash stand. There was an ewer and basin on top, with a mirror that hung between two uprights, and a small linen cabinet on the bottom. I looked through every inch of that cabinet and felt behind the stand and under it. Nothing. I was so frustrated that I slammed my fist down on the top next to the basin.

The ewer wobbled back and forth, spilling a tiny bit of water into the basin. I watched a drop slide down the porcelain and wondered where else there might be to hide something in that tiny cottage. Then I heard the swish of paper sliding against the plaster wall and saw my envelope drop to the top of the washstand from behind the mirror. I picked it up and tilted the mirror away from the wall enough to see where it must have been wedged into a corner of the frame. I had dislodged it when I hit the top of the stand.

I quickly counted the money. It was all there. I just had to hope it was enough. The way I figured it, whoever took it didn't want the money, or they would have done something with it by then. No, I reckoned their motive was to make sure that I didn't have it, didn't have a way out. I folded the bills and slid them into the front pocket of my blue jeans. Then I grabbed cloth scraps from the rag bin and folded them to about the right size for my little stack of bills. I put the folded rags in the envelope and wedged it back into the mirror frame where it had been.

I had just finished that when I heard voices outside. I quickly stood in front of the wash stand and poured some water into the basin. I was splashing it on my face when the door swung open. It was Sheila and Rona, chatting happily.

"There you are," Rona said as they came in. "The sun's come out and it's a gorgeous afternoon. Take a break with us and spend it in the sun. We've earned it."

Sheila went to the pegs and grabbed a straw sun hat. Her smile was polite, but she seemed distracted. "We just came to get my hat so I willna burn. Come with us."

Through the last weeks working together, I had come to genuinely like the two of them, despite Sheila's occasional prickliness. The idea of spending a relaxing afternoon with them was tempting. Still, I had a lot of thinking and planning to do, and it would be easier to do that on my own. "Actually,

Jock said there was some water mint down the burn. I think I'll go and pick some. It would be nice to have some fresh greens at tea."

Rona shrugged, going for the door. "Suit yourself, but I'm going to go soak up the sun before the wet season gets here."

"Don't work too hard," Sheila said as she put on the hat followed Rona out.

I followed them out and grabbed a basket and knife. I walked downstream, well away from the village and toward the loch. Before too long, I found the mint I was looking for growing at the edge of the water. I rubbed a leaf between my fingers and breathed in the peppermint scent. Between the walk and the mint, my nerves were calmed. I put the basket down and knelt beside the burn to cut some of the mint with my knife.

I had nearly filled the basket when I heard a voice behind me. "D'ye mean to tell me ye're all alone out here?"

I sat back on my heels and squinted up to see Rab smiling down at me. He had several trout hanging from a line. His bag was slung over his shoulder and the sun made a halo behind him. I'm sure my tone wasn't kind when I said, "No doubt there's someone nearby. There always is."

His smile fell. "Sorry to disturb ye. I can go."

"No, no. I'm done." I stood up, wiping my wet hands on my jeans and dropping the knife into my basket. "Are you going back?"

He nodded. "Care to walk with me?"

"Sure." I picked up the basket and fell in beside him.

He lifted his string of trout. "Think ye could smoke some like these?"

They were good sized fish, and I'm sure they would have been delicious fresh. "I've never smoked fish before, but I could maybe learn. We should ask Gavin. He's a fisherman, he might know how."

"Good thinking." We strolled further along the burn. "Some of us were thinking of going hunting. Will the smokehouse do for a whole deer?"

"If we butcher it into the right pieces." I had done a deer before, and our house was certainly big enough. "We might also dry some strips into jerky. And make some sausage to smoke too."

"Use everything, eh? Ye're maybe more Scottish than ye ken." He bumped my arm with his, fortunately not using the arm that was carrying the fish.

"My Mama taught me well. If we need to cure that much meat, we're going to need a lot more salt and sugar, probably some spices too."

"Aye, I think I heard Gavin talking about another supply run. The amounts we need, we might have to go into Ullapool to get without attracting attention."

"Ullapool, huh?" Ullapool was just big enough for me to get away and blend into a crowd, and it had transportation that could get me farther. This might be just the break that I needed.

"Mmhmm," Rab said.

"Wonder if I could go with him. I could see what spices they have and decide what'll be best for the meat." I tried to keep my tone casual, not as if I was desperate to get out of the village.

He tilted his head and raise his eyebrows in question. "Could do, or we could all go. Might be good to get away for a day."

Getting away from one or even two people seemed hard enough. I wasn't so sure about eight. Then again, a larger group might make it easier to get away, and it might take even longer for anyone to notice that I was gone. "Might be fun. Do we have enough cars to get us all there and back with supplies?"

"Och, I think we can manage. Davie's got a truck."

"That's perfect." The more I thought about it, the more excited I got. I wanted to pick up the pace. "We should talk to the others."

Rab took hold of my wrist to slow me down. "Wait, Màili."

I looked up into those deep green eyes and got lost. He looked back at me for the longest time before saying, "Listen, I'm sorry about that night in the hall. It wasn't right to tease ye."

"No, it wasn't," I said. It had been a few days, but I wasn't really angry about it.

"It's just that…" He trailed off. I waited for him to finish, but he just watched me.

"What?"

He shook his head, like he could shake away whatever he'd been thinking. "Nothing. Never mind."

CHAPTER TWENTY-SEVEN

December 22, 1995
Chapel Hill, North Carolina

"Nah, she's been holed up reading in her room for days. We havena even been to the library this week," Sarah heard Fleming's voice coming down the hall, heading for her door. She slid on a pair of sweatpants and smoothed her hair when his knock sounded. She hadn't even bothered to change out of the T-shirt she'd slept in or do anything with her hair. She'd fallen asleep reading the journal and had simply picked up where she left off after opening her eyes this morning.

"Morning," she said as she opened the door. Fleming was standing in the hall with the phone held to his ear.

"It's himself." He extended the phone to her.

"Thanks." She took the phone and shut the door. "James, you really don't have to check on me every day."

"It's me," Dermot's low rumble came across the wire.

Sarah closed her eyes and let it roll over her. "It is so good to hear your voice."

"Careful. Talk like that can go to a man's head." The hint of laughter in his voice had Sarah picturing his slightly crooked smile and a wicked glint in his blue eyes.

"I'm not sure that's a bad thing," she teased.

He paused as if he wasn't quite sure what to say. In the end, he opted to shift the conversation. "I am standing in your flat taking delivery of your new furniture."

"New furniture?"

"Aye, the last tenants were smokers and the place stank. I talked the landlord into a thorough cleaning and makeover." He sounded please with himself.

"That was optimistic of you." Sarah hated to rain on his parade, but she couldn't pretend that everything was proceeding normally, not with him.

"Are ye not coming, then? Have ye decided?" His voice was barely above a whisper.

"I'm still weighing my options. Although if that reporter keeps bothering me, staying put might not be a viable choice anymore."

"Has she contacted you again?"

"Not since the other day, but I also haven't been out much. I've been glued to…" She wasn't sure how much she wanted to tell him about Molly's journal. She'd kept it a secret, not knowing what Molly would reveal. It might be good to read the whole story before telling anyone else, especially anyone working for James Stuart. She had to remember that whatever her feelings for him, Dermot still worked for James. "The books," she finished.

"How's the research going?"

"It's interesting. I'm compiling a list of significant groups of nine and deciding what I want to do a deep dive on. I've found references to nine in everything from sacred woods in Beltane fires to Hebrew numerology, where by the way it is the number of 'immutable truth.'"

His laugh was low but musical. "Well, that sounds important."

"Yeah, but I think I'm going to start with Norse legends. There were the nine worlds in the tree of Yggdrasil and even three women tending the tree. A lot of lines seem to connect there."

"Mmph." She could almost hear his mind at work from an ocean away. "I was talking to my mum about it the other day."

"Your mum?" she teased, mimicking his accent.

"Don't start," he grumbled. "She's a Celtic studies scholar, remember."

"How could I forget?" She had named her son after a mythical Irish hero after all.

"Well, when I told her about the cauldron in your story, she mentioned Ceridwen."

Sarah grabbed her notebook and flipped back a few pages. "Welsh sorceress? Yeah, I had that on my list of things to look into. What did your mom say about her?"

"Well, it's actually a weird story. No doubt I'll say all the names wrong, because they're Welsh, but here goes." He cleared his throat in preparation. "Ceridwen was an ancient goddess or witch, depending on who you talk to, and she had a son, Morfran, who was so hideous to look at that his prospects werena very good. So she decided that if he couldna marry, at least she could make him wise. She went to her magic cauldron to mix up a potion to make her son the wisest of all men. Now this potion was only good for the first three drops. The rest was poison. And to make it, it had to be stirred constantly for…" his voice ticked up a note.

Sarah finished the sentence for him, "A year and a day." That was the typical time period for Celtic folktales.

"Exactly. Since no self-respecting goddess would do her own pot stirring, she set two of her servants to the task."

"Only two?" Sarah asked.

"Who's telling this?"

"Sorry," she giggled.

"Right. Well, when a year and a day had gone by, Ceridwen came to claim the first three drops of the potion for her hideous son. In the excitement of finally finishing his task, her servant lad, Gwion Bach, stirred with a bit too much enthusiasm. As Ceridwen arrived at the cauldron, three drops of the potion splashed up, scalding the boy's thumb. Without thinking, Gwion Bach put his thumb in his mouth to soothe it. And so he got the precious first three drops and the wisdom that was meant for Ceridwen's son. Knowing she would be enraged, he ran away. But the boy's legs weren't fast enough. With the magic from the potion, he turned into a hare, but Ceridwen turned into a hound. He changed into a fish, so she changed into an otter. Each time he changed into another animal, she turned into a predator. Finally, exhausted from the chase, Gwion Bach turned himself into a kernel of grain. And in her pursuit, Ceridwen became a hen and ate him."

"Are we getting off track here?" Sarah wasn't sure what shape shifting had to do with the nine or the cauldron.

"Bear with me," he said. "Instead of just being digested, the magic kernel somehow made its way to her womb and took root. When the child was born, he had all the memories and wisdom of Gwion Bach. Ceridwen determined to kill the baby, but unlike her son, Morfran, this new child was so beautiful that she couldna do it. So she put him in a coracle and pushed him out to sea. But the child's luck held and he washed ashore and was adopted by a prince. He grew up to become the great Welsh bard Taliesin, who I'm sure you've heard of."

"The bard of Camelot?" Sarah was doubtful.

"So they say."

"That's quite an origin story he invented for himself, if he ever existed," Sarah grumbled.

"So cynical," he teased.

"Mmm…so Ceridwen can cook up wisdom in her magic cauldron. Meanwhile Odin gains wisdom by bloodletting and hanging over the Well of Urth for nine days. Does our cauldron give wisdom or sustenance?" Sarah mused.

"And again there's our number nine in the Odin story."

"Right, but no more clues to what's meant in that charm or where these legends come from." Sara flopped across her bed, letting her hair hang off the other side. "Are these elements coming from the Norse to the Welsh or vice versa?"

He made a noncommittal grunt before adding, "Or are they from something even older."

Sarah groaned. "This is why I would much rather study stories that I can collect from people who are alive. This ancient stuff is like trying to find your way around in the dark."

He made a noise that was half assent, half defeat. Sarah had forgotten how much she missed his nonverbal style of communication. He could speak volumes with a single grunt.

Tired of academic discussion, she changed the subject. "Will you spend Christmas with your mom?"

He took a second to catch up to the change, and then his answer sounded. "Mmm? Oh, yeah."

"Have you gotten her a gift?" She wanted to keep him on the line, keep hearing his voice. And she liked the image of Dermot and Seonag celebrating by a fire.

"Och, I reckon I'd better do that."

Sarah wondered what had him so distracted. "It's only a couple of days away. You might want to get on that."

He hummed in thought. "She seems keen on knitting lately. I might get her some nice yarn and maybe a bag to keep it in. Do you have anything planned for the holiday?"

Sarah's throat tightened a little. "I've spent the past couple of Christmases with Amy's family. I guess that's out."

"Has she talked to you at all?" She could hear the concern in his voice.

"I haven't heard a peep from her. Barrett thinks she'll come around eventually." Sarah sighed. "I suppose I will treat my bodyguards to a nice home-cooked meal."

"Haven't ye already done that? Fleming said he doesna want to come home."

She had to laugh. "Well, yeah, but I haven't done the American Christmas classics. Actually, I haven't even cooked in a couple of days. I've been reading so much."

"Ye have to take a break sometimes. We do have books here in Scotland. Ye can research here too," he said helpfully.

"What? You have books? I thought you were all savages who only wear wool, eat haggis, and play bagpipes," she teased, knowing how the usual stereotypes irritated him.

"Och, aye." He let his accent thicken. "And we all talk in Rabbie Burns poems, ye wee sleekit timorous beastie."

Sarah exploded in laughter. She could picture him making a ridiculous face to go with the ridiculous accent. She laughed until her sides hurt. She loved him. "Dermot," she said when she caught her breath.

"Yeah?" he answered. His accent was back to normal, but she could hear the smile in his voice.

"What happens to you if I don't come to Scotland?"

"Well, I'll have a lot more work to do managing this research team. I was counting on your help." He tried to laugh off her question.

"You know what I mean."

He paused. "I would most likely get a stern reprimand for failing to convince you. I would not be invited to the Stuart family Christmas fete for a few years, and I would go back to being a simple folklorist."

He sighed. "I want ye to come because we can keep ye safe. I know it seems like a line, but this is much bigger than you and a few Stuarts. We found ye. Ryan found ye. And they will all find ye again. They've been working toward this for over two hundred years. They're not just going to give up because you don't want to play their game."

"So you've said, but I was asking about you."

"Dinna worry about me. There's naught they can do to me that they havena already done or tried. I'll be fine." His tone was reassuring, but Sarah couldn't help feeling like there was something he wasn't telling her. "But I do need your help with the field team."

"Is that the only reason you want me to come?"

"Well, I am partial to yer cooking." Again, she could picture that crooked smile he got whenever he teased her.

"I miss you," she breathed.

"I miss you too," he whispered.

CHAPTER TWENTY-EIGHT

July 1968
Làrachd an Fhamhair, Scotland

By the looks they gave us when we proposed the outing, I could tell that Aunt Eilidh and Jock didn't much care for the idea of all of us taking off to town. I sat across the table from Willie and Aunt Eilidh when the lads brought up the idea. This time it was Lachlan's turn. It made me wonder if they met in the lads' house ahead of time and drew straws to see who had to speak for whatever new idea was next. Lachlan was a good choice. He was so obviously twitterpated over Rona that no one would have accused the two of them of planning to run wild in town.

"What do ye want to go there for?" Jock asked.

Lachlan looked at the older man. "Well, before we start hunting and fishing for the winter, we need more supplies for curing the meat."

"We're getting low on dry goods like oats and flour too," Rona put in.

"Can ye not make a list and a couple of the stewards go?" Aunt Eilidh looked over to the table where the stewards were sitting. They were talking among themselves. I wondered how they must feel about the trip.

"Weel," Rab spoke up. "I suppose we could, but I think we could all use a change of scenery. Just for a day."

Sheila added her voice. "Please, Mam."

Aunt Eilidh looked around the table at each of us. I tried to look as innocent and hopeful as possible. She stared at me so long that I almost shifted under the weight of it. "Aye, alright. But ye mun be back before dark."

We all sighed and looked around at each other, smiling. I was feeling pretty good until I looked across the table at Willie. He was not smiling. In fact, he looked furious.

Our walk that night was tense and silent. We strolled along the burn, but couldn't manage even our usual stilted conversation. I knew that Willie wasn't supportive of our winter food project, but I was no longer worried about that. It made our walk more uncomfortable, but after the next day, I wasn't going to need to worry about that anymore.

"You know you could come with us," I said. I really had tried at every opportunity to bring Willie along with us. I wasn't sure what he did with his days while we were working, but he wasn't interested in helping or even socializing with the others.

I actually felt a little bad about Willie. He was awkward and shy, but he wasn't a bad sort, at least not that I had seen. I was sorry that he was going to be deserted and even more lonely when I left.

I made the attempt, but he just shook his head and walked on. When he walked me to the cottage, he barely looked at me and just nodded and walked away.

***

The next morning, we piled into cars. Duff, Gavin, and I were in the little green thing that we arrived in. Davie, Rona, and Lachlan took Davie's truck, and Rab and Sheila used his

Beetle. Like everything in Làrachd an Fhamhair, we had to be sneaky about it. We left one by one so no one would notice the sudden traffic on the dirt track that led to the glen. Each car left fifteen minutes after the last. We had arranged to meet by the dock in Ullapool.

For the whole drive through the mountains, I tried to act as normal as possible. Gavin insisted on riding in the back seat, so I spent a good part of the hour's drive sitting on my hands to keep from fidgeting. I watched the Highlands roll by outside the window. It reminded me of that last ride to the bus station in Boone, watching the Blue Ridge Mountains roll by and hoping that it was the last time. As beautiful as the Highlands are, I was feeling pretty much the same thing. I hoped I never saw Làrachd an Fhamhair again.

Ullapool was a pretty sheltered harbor town on Loch Broom, which is more a long narrow bay than a lake. We came down from the hills and drove through the town before meeting the others near the quay. The main commercial street seemed to be Shore Street with its view of the loch. There was a good sized market there.

We spread out through the aisles, looking at what they had to offer and checking things off our supplies list. Sheila and Davie went to look for some specific things that people from the village had asked for. Duff went off after some hardware. The rest of us went to fetch the dry goods.

"I think we should get some of these salt herring too. It's already preserved for us," Rona suggested when we passed a barrel with the preserved fish stacked on top.

"Let's see how much we have left when we get through the list," Rab said.

"I'll go see if there's any room on that price." Gavin walked to where the owner was holding court behind a wooden counter near the door.

Rab looked at me. "We should see about those spices ye mentioned."

We went toward an area that had smaller jars of spices and other groceries. Rona and Lachlan didn't seem inclined to follow us. They would rather make moon-eyes at each other. I was curious about how we were paying for all of the pounds of salt and sugar, oats and flour, so I asked, "Where does the money come from anyway? It's not like there's any industry in the village."

"Och, they do sell a bit of the wool once the sheep are sheared, but mostly it's from people who have left the village. They leave because there isn't room for everyone, but they still give money back to the tribe so the village can go on and stay hidden."

"Like a tithe?" It sounded like the churches I'd seen in the mountains, asking people who couldn't afford food to give 10 percent of their income.

"Aye, I guess it is like that. My parents did it. I'm sure I will as well when I have more income to speak of. I heard it was a bit of controversy when they first started asking for money. The village managed to sustain itself for centuries without money, but the modern world being what it is, we've had to catch up in some respects. The smaller the world gets, the harder it is to hide. The funds go mainly to maintaining the illusion and emergencies like this. That fund is probably what paid for yer ticket here."

"Hmm. I wonder if Mama was sending money back all this time." We had never starved at home, but we also hadn't had a lot to spare.

"I doubt it. That's a long way, and the sisters dinna really need to contribute." He nodded significantly, like he was reminding me that I was one of the sisters. "Now, about those spices."

"Right." I turned to the jars of herbs and spices, focusing on those that we didn't have planted or couldn't forage. I picked up the ones that I thought would be best for fish and venison. Then we caught up with Lachlan, Rona, and Gavin near the sugar.

Gavin got Rab's attention with a lift of his chin. "The owner seems pretty flexible. Considering how much we're buying, wouldn't hurt to negotiate a bit. Eh?"

"Definitely." Rab took the basket of spices from me and headed toward the counter.

Rona grabbed my arm. "Now that our part of the business is done, what do you say we leave the rest to the men? We can get Sheila and browse some of the shops on Shore Street."

"Sounds good to me." Actually, it sounded great to me.

We collected Sheila and were about to go off down the street when Davie caught up with us. "Canna leave on yer own."

Sheila sighed and rolled her eyes. The four of us moved down the street, past cafes, a book shop, a news agent, and one or two dress shops. We hit every shop and did all the silly girl things that silly girls do. Meanwhile, I spotted every alleyway we passed. I looked for back and side doors in every shop.

I watched Davie get more and more bored with us. Eventually, he walked ahead of us with his eyes on the boats on the loch. Finally, he stopped following us into the shops and just waited outside. In one dress shop, Rona and Sheila were having a debate about hemlines when I grabbed a dress off the rack and said I was going to try it on. The shop had one tiny dressing room down a short hallway. It just happened to be across the hallway from a side door.

I pulled back the curtain of the fitting room and hung the dress inside. Then I pulled the curtain closed again, making sure the slide of the metal rings on the rod could be heard. When I was sure no one was watching, I carefully turned the knob on the door. I held my breath, trying not to make a sound, and thanked my lucky stars that the hinges seemed to be well oiled. The door opened into a narrow alley between that building and the next. I crept out and closed the door behind me, still careful not to make a sound.

With my heart pounding, I tiptoed down the alley. It opened into a wider alleyway between Shore Street and the next street. I hustled down this alley, away from the market. When I found an alley that crossed the next block, I took it. At the edge of that alley, I stopped and leaned against the stone wall of a building and tried to catch my breath. My hands were shaking and I could hear my heartbeat. I had gotten away. Now I needed to get out of town before anyone could find me.

On the street, I walked like I didn't have a care in the world. I strolled through the streets for a few minutes until I found another news agent. I ducked in and asked for directions to the bus station. I followed these directions easily enough, trying not to look over my shoulder every few seconds.

It was one of those times when I couldn't resist that urge that I saw Rab's Beetle cruise by slowly on the street I had just crossed. He didn't turn down my street, but I could tell he was going slowly, searching the street. When I didn't see another of our cars, I stepped back onto the street and kept walking as calmly as I could toward the bus station.

I was almost there. I could see the door. It was a long, low building in the middle of the street with a driveway in front for busses to load and unload. I was so close I could smell the bus's exhaust when Duff's little green car screeched to a halt in the driveway. I saw Gavin leap out and head for the door to the station. Duff got out a little more slowly and started scanning the street.

I quickly turned down the nearest street. All the hope that I had been feeling seconds before turned to terror. I didn't want to go back to Làrachd an Fhamhair. Halfway down the next block on my side of the street there was a walled vacant lot. It was overgrown with bushes and grass.

It took me a couple of tries to boost myself over the wall. I scraped my back pretty bad on the stone jumping down the other side. It burned like the devil, but I didn't have time to stop. I burrowed my way through the brush until I found a spot that was shielded from the street. I crouched down in the brush with my back to the wall. I was so tense that I had to remind myself to breath. I sat there under that bush and waited to hear voices I recognized. I hoped that Duff hadn't seen me. But he had spent the better part of the last five weeks keeping an eye on me. I knew it was too much to ask for him to have not spotted me.

Soon enough I heard Duff and Gavin moving down the street, pointing out places they thought I might have gone. They searched every alley and open building. When they hadn't found me, I hoped they would move on and search another area.

That wasn't the way, though. Their voices came closer and then stopped.

"Molly?" Duff must have been standing right by the wall I had jumped over. "Sweetheart, this isn't going to work. I tried to tell you before, honey, they're not going to let you go."

I clapped a hand over my mouth, trying not to make a sound. Duff waited. When I didn't respond he went on, "I know you want to get away, and I can think of a bunch of reasons why, but even if we left you here, you would just end up back in the village eventually. I told you, there are a lot of people with a stake in this."

He waited again. I couldn't believe he thought I would just give up. "Sweetie, if you come out now, we can still get back before dark and no one has to mention this. We won't tell Eilidh or Willie or anyone else. I don't want to make more trouble—"

Just then Gavin dropped down behind me and threw his arms around me, pinning my arms to my sides. I screamed, but he covered my mouth. I put up as much of a fight as I could, kicking my legs and squirming like an eel. In seconds, Duff was in front of me and he took hold of me, pressing my face into his shirt. Gavin backed off.

Duff's voice growled in my ear, "If you scream, the police will come and they will want to know about your family. As soon as we tell them, you'll be returned to the glen. If you get away, some other steward will find you and you'll be returned. If they could get a senator and my colonel, you better believe that they can get to customs officials and will know when you use your passport. I know you don't want to believe it, but you're stuck. I'm sorry, honey. I wish it wasn't true, but it is."

He had told me this before. I didn't know if it was true or not, but that didn't matter. He had caught me, and he wasn't letting me go and neither was anyone else. I stopped fighting. I stopped everything. I stopped feeling. I just stopped.

Duff felt me relax, and he pulled back to look at my face. I couldn't meet his eyes. I didn't want to look at him. I didn't want to look at anyone or anything. I just wanted to curl into myself and keep getting smaller and smaller until no one noticed me anymore.

"Okay," Duff said. I think it was more to convince himself. "You're gonna be okay."

"Over here," Gavin called from somewhere off in the lot. "I found a gate."

Duff tucked me under his shoulder and gripped me tight with one arm. I must have gasped because he loosened his grip and moved behind me. He lifted up the tail of my shirt and hissed when he saw where I had scraped it climbing over the wall. "We'll have to take care of that before we hit the road."

He wrapped his arm around me again, higher than before, and walked me to the gate. We made our way back to the car and drove back to the car park near the quay. The other girls were there with Lachlan. Rab and Davie were still out looking for me. Within a few minutes they arrived. I didn't get out of the car. I could hear the hum of their conversation, but I didn't listen to their words.

Soon, Rona leaned into Duff's car and in a soft, comforting voice said, "Come on. We're going to clean you up a bit and get some food. Okay?"

I didn't answer her, but let her pull me from the car and put her arm around me. Rona and Sheila walked me to a nearby pub and back to the restroom. Sheila pulled a hairbrush from her purse and started working on my hair. Rona wet a towel and wiped my face. Neither of them seemed angry or reproachful. I thought they would be angry that I had used them as cover to run away, but they didn't seem to be.

There was a knock at the door and Rona opened it and pulled in a new shirt and some first aid supplies. She gently pulled my shirt off and cleaned my back before covering it with a bandage. When she was done, Sheila helped me put on the new shirt, a pretty thing with a placket of ruffles in the front. Then they did something I hadn't expected. My sisters. They wrapped their arms around me and held me tight. My hands started shaking. It crept up my shoulders and soon I was shaking all over. Before I knew it, I was sobbing. They just held on to me until the storm passed.

Rona wiped my face clean before smiling at me. "Let's get some food."

The men were waiting at a large table, their faces grim. They all looked at me in question, but I couldn't answer. I was afraid that if I opened my mouth all the misery I was feeling would come spilling out again and this time it wouldn't stop. Duff pulled out a chair for me, and I sat. He ordered me some soup, and we all ate. After a few minutes, the men started talking about the deal they had gotten on the supplies. That led to plans for hunting when we got home. Their conversation buzzed around me. No one tried to make me talk. They just let me be. After dinner, we piled back into our cars and left for the village. Rab had found a blanket in his car, and this time I rode in the back of Duff's car curled up under the blanket.

CHAPTER TWENTY-NINE

December 24, 1995
Chapel Hill, North Carolina

"I still don't understand why we have to go to two grocery stores," Curtis groused as he stopped Sarah and put the grocery bags down by the door. She still wasn't used to the apartment clearing procedure. She doubted she ever would be.

"Because," she told him as he opened the door, "the hippy grocery store has the best produce."

"Seriously?" He gave her a sidelong look and a shake of his head. "Sweet potatoes are sweet potatoes. I don't care where you buy them. Wait here."

He went into the apartment. Sarah stood just inside the door while he opened all the doors and checked all the possible hiding places, making sure no one had broken in while they were at the store. Sarah tried not to be irritated.

He returned, giving her a nod and stepping out into the hall to retrieve his bags. Sarah took her own bags to the kitchen and started putting things away. Sarah wasn't sure if she should be glad he was helping out or freaked out by the strange routine of having bodyguards.

"How many people are you planning to cook for?" he asked when he joined her in the kitchen with his bags.

Sarah looked at a counter that was brimming with turkey, sweet potatoes, pumpkin, stuffing, squash, and soup cans. "Okay, I might have gotten little carried away."

"I mean, I'm not complaining, but you know you're not required to feed us." He smiled over his shoulder as he opened a cabinet and started putting the soup away.

"Ha ha. Of course, but you should get something for being far away from your family on the holiday."

"You should talk to my sisters. They act like I'm choosing to abandon my family for Christmas," he said with a laugh.

"You want me to write you a note?" she joked, bending to shift things in the refrigerator so the turkey would fit.

He let out a bark of a laugh. "I'm not sure it would help. Don't you have someone to spend the holiday with besides us guys?"

She straightened and shook her head. "Nope. I usually spend it with my roommate's family. That's not on the table for obvious reasons."

"The roommate that gave your stalker a key to your apartment?" He raised a skeptical eyebrow. "I can see why you might not want that."

"I can't be mad at her. She didn't know he was stalking me. But she doesn't seem to want to have anything to do with me right now, so Christmas at the Monroe home place is definitely out."

"But you'll miss it, huh?" He looked sympathetic.

Sarah paused in putting vegetables away. "Yeah, I will. I don't really have any family. Amy has a huge one, and they've treated me like one of their own since the first time she brought me home."

"Maybe that's the problem." He shrugged. "Where do you want the potatoes?"

"There's a basket in that cabinet." She nodded toward the far cabinet. "What do you mean?"

"Maybe she's thinking of you like a sister. Sibling rivalries can get kinda crazy. Hell, my sisters are so competitive they'll fight over who gets to serve dessert." He shook his head as he emptied the bag of potatoes into the wire basket.

"Hmm." Sarah hadn't thought about it that way. She only saw Amy's family during holidays, but they were always welcoming. Maybe that bothered Amy more than she realized. "Of course, I've never had a sibling, so I have nothing to compare it to. But that's a much nicer way of looking at the situation."

"And it also probably means that she'll forgive you eventually. My sisters never go long without talking."

"I guess that's reassuring." Sarah folded the empty paper bags and tucked them away in the lower cabinet. "Did you get the mail?"

"Yep, on the table."

She went to the table to comb through the mail. There wasn't much beyond a couple of catalogs and a credit card offer. But there was one gold envelope that looked like a Christmas card. Sarah flipped it over and saw the return address was the Monroe's house in Raleigh. She held it up and showed Curtis, who had followed her out of the kitchen. "Speak of the devil. This is from Amy's folks."

"See? Told ya." He grinned.

Sarah slid a finger under the corner and tore the flap open. Inside was a lovely card with a homey looking snow scene on the front, but when she opened it, it wasn't from Amy's parents.

Taped to the inside of the card was a newspaper clipping. Sarah didn't need to read past the headline to see that it was about the murder of Bridget MacKenzie. Sarah's hand began to shake.

She dropped into a chair and read the handwritten message behind the clipping.

Interesting that you just received a fellowship paid for by James Stuart while Cumberland's other victim was going to take a job with Stuart's company. Did you know her? There's a much bigger story here than you let on, and I'm going to sniff it out. Care to comment first? You know where to find me.

B. Cartwright

"That bitch," Sarah hissed as she read through the clipping. It was a biographical piece about Bridget. In it, a friend of Bridget's mentioned that she had been offered a job with Alba Petroleum.

"What is it?" Curtis looked over her shoulder.

Sarah huffed. "That reporter sent this. She used Amy's parents address to disguise it so I would open it."

"Damn it!" He snatched the card from Sarah's hand. "Okay, we open your mail from now on. Just to make sure it's safe."

Sarah rolled her eyes. "Fine. But I'm more concerned with how she made this connection. The police said they were going to keep the connection to the Bridget MacKenzie case out of the press."

"There's got to be a leak," he said, his eyes hard as steel.

Sarah took a deep breath. "Okay. Here's what we do. I'm going to call my guardian angel cop and warn him there's a leak. You need to call your boss and warn them that this reporter made the connection they didn't want made."

"Right, you go first. I have a feeling it will be a shorter call."

"Yeah." Sarah grabbed the phone. "You're probably right about that."

CHAPTER THIRTY

July 1968

Làrachd an Fhamhair, Scotland

I must have fallen asleep on the way back, because the next thing I knew Duff reached back and shook my knee. "Get ready."

I looked out the window to see the cobalt blue water of Loch Assynt. I sat up in my seat and straightened my clothes. Duff caught my eye in the rearview mirror. "I know it's hard, but you've got to be back to normal now. I don't think anyone will tell Eilidh about you running off, but we can't count on that."

I nodded.

"I don't know how she'll react, so you can't let on how you're feeling."

I nodded again.

"Can I hear you say yes, honey?" He looked at me closely in the mirror.

"Yes," I said weakly. What else was there to do?

"That's better." He gave me a hint of a smile as he turned down the overgrown rutted path to the village.

We pulled in behind Davie's truck in front of the hall. Davie, Lachlan, and Rona were already unloading the things we bought. The three of us fell in with them and began carrying the supplies from the truck to the storage shelves in the hall. A few of the villagers watched us working, but as usual Jock was the only person to help. We were almost done when Rab and Sheila pulled in and parked behind Duff. They both looked angry, like maybe they had been arguing. She walked off in the direction of the cottage while Rab helped us finish up.

When we were done, I reached into Duff's car and got Rab's blanket. Rab was getting into his car to drive it around to the paddock where they were hidden. I stopped him and held the blanket out to him. "Thanks."

He looked at me and I saw a fraction of my own misery echoed in his eyes. "Are ye alright?"

All I could do was nod. He held my eyes and nodded back. Then he took the blanket and got into the car and drove it around the back of the hall.

I was still standing on the green when Aunt Eilidh came up beside me. She put her arm around me and gave me a squeeze. I guess she meant for it to be comforting, but it didn't feel that way. I turned to her, and she studied me for a minute. Her gaze had an edge to it. "I hope ye found all ye needed. I dinna think such a trip will happen again."

She knew. Her eyes drifted down to my shirt. "That's a lovely new blouse. Did you get that in Ullapool?"

"Yes," I mumbled, tugging at the hem of the shirt. "The other one got torn."

"Pity," she said, looking down at the ruffled placket covering my chest. She reached up and fingered the ruffles just where the top buttons were open at the neck. Anyone standing more than a few feet away would think that she was admiring my blouse. I was the only person who felt her fingers slip under the placket and pull out the money I had hidden in my bra strap.

She palmed the money and smiled at me. "Still, I like the ruffles. They make a nice addition."

The twinkle in her eyes dared me to speak up. According to what I was told about my status as one of the sisters, I should have a place of honor here. But thanks to the cauldron situation, I was *sluagh ùr*, new folk, suspect. What I had done that day had only confirmed that, and in a group this small there was no hope that word of my attempt wouldn't spread. If I spoke up about her theft, I would expose my escape attempt and my doubts to everyone, becoming even more of a pariah than I already was.

I felt rooted to that spot on the green. I was stuck in this village until I gave them a child, and somehow I seemed to be the only person bothered by this circumstance. My fellow young people might be sympathetic, but they weren't going to help me.

I looked around the glen at the stone houses with their turf-covered roofs. The cars had been driven into the carport and covered with branches to camouflage them. The gardens spread out in clumpy patches, and the little livestock they had was loose, not kept in barns or coops. Everything was hidden from the outside world, but I could see it. There seemed so much that was still hidden from me. I wasn't of the outside world, but I wasn't of Làrachd an Fhamhair either.

That night at dinner, Aunt Eilidh announced that we wouldn't wait for Lammas Day to move in with our matches. The next day we would start getting our houses in order.

***

Over the next week, three houses were made available to us. One was actually vacant, but two were cleared by moving out the people who were occupying them. We cleaned the houses, outfitting them with linens and crockery, and now were ready to move in. Sheila, Rona, and I picked up our things in Aunt Eilidh's cottage. It felt strange to be splitting up after sharing the loft for weeks. I couldn't help feeling sad about losing them.

I also felt less than excited about what lay in front of me. Since my escape attempt, Willie had only talked to me when it was necessary to be polite. We had continued our evening walks, but only in tense silence. So that was what I thought I would be living with, sleeping with, awkward silences and tense, stilted conversations.

I closed my suitcase and clicked the latches shut. No matter how much I told myself that it wouldn't help to drag it out, I just couldn't seem to make myself move faster. The other girls had already taken their things and climbed down the ladder.

With a sigh, I handed my suitcase down to Sheila. I climbed down the ladder and was immediately wrapped in Rona's arms. Sheila put down my suitcase and joined us. "I'm going to miss sharing a room with you two."

"I know," Rona agreed. "I know we'll see each other every day, but it won't be the same."

I could only nod, trying not to cry. I had never had sisters, and even with the occasional tension with Sheila, I liked sharing that space with them.

"At least ye and Lachlan get along," Sheila groused. "Rab is so hot and cold, I never know whether he wants to do this or not."

"You seemed to be getting along fine when I saw you kissing behind the hall." Rona shot her a look.

Sheila's eyes widened, and she blushed furiously. She lifted a hand to her cheek to cover up how red she was getting. Then I caught her eye. Her face grew serious and she looked at Rona. "We shouldn't be joking. Màili's got to live with the likes of Willie Cross."

"Willie isn't so bad," I said. "He's just shy."

Sheila smiled and stroked my cheek with her hand. "Ye've a kind heart, *a Mhàili*. It's why ye're the right match for our Willie."

I sighed. "I wish I thought he felt that way. I think he sees me as *sluagh ùr*. He says he doesn't blame us for the cauldron stopping. The more things change, the tenser he seems to be around me."

"That's ridiculous!" Sheila leaned back, surprised. "Ye're one of the sisters. They canna question that."

"I wish everyone felt that way," Rona put in. "I've felt it too. As if we're not proper sisters because we've been living with the new folk. I've seen a lot of whispering going on since the cauldron stopped."

"Well then, let's hope that us settling in with our matches will help put an end to that talk." Sheila picked up the basket that held her things and rolled her eyes. "Soon enough they'll all be watching our bellies."

I couldn't help groaning. Sheila opened the door to find Rab, Lachlan, and Duff waiting for us. The other girls' matches had shown up to help them carry their things, but mine was nowhere to be found. I guess chivalry and good manners were a little too much to ask from Willie.

Duff took my suitcase when I stepped out the door. He walked me to the cottage that had been given to us. It was almost directly across the glen from Aunt Eilidh's, though a little further up the hillside. It was one of the houses furthest from the hall, almost as if they could push Willie and me off into a corner and forget about us, the village numpty and his pariah bride. I'm sure Aunt Eilidh would say we were given that cottage for privacy, but I thought I knew better.

I hoped that we would find Willie there waiting for us, but when Duff opened the door we were greeted by nothing but stale air and furniture. The little bit of sunlight coming through the window lit the work table, settle, hearth, and bed. The layout was almost the same as Aunt Eilidh's and the other houses in the village. The main room was open from the hearth to the far wall, with a loft above the bed area for storage or children to sleep. This cottage was small, but empty as it was, it felt huge.

Duff set my suitcase down next to the bed. He gave me a hug. "Are you going to be all right?"

"As you've told me more than once, I don't really have a choice." I wasn't angry. I felt defeated.

"Listen to me." Duff grabbed my shoulders and turned me to him, "I'm here for you. I know it doesn't always feel like it, but your safety is my absolute priority. If he hurts you, if you even think he might, you tell me. Okay?"

"Ha. He can't even manage to look me in the eye," I scoffed.

"That's what I worry about. You're moving in here with someone you barely know, and with the cauldron business things are tense. I know you think you don't have a choice, but that all changes if he hurts you. At least in my book it does. I mean it. You tell me." He punctuated that last statement with a shake.

I nodded. "Thank you, Duff. I know I must make you crazy, but…thanks."

He kissed me on the forehead before he let my shoulders go. Before he closed the door behind him he said, "I'll see you at tea."

When the door closed behind him, I put my suitcase on the bed and sat down next to it. I should have been unpacking, but I felt drained. I propped my elbow on the case and dropped my head into my hand. I told myself after my breakdown in Ullapool that I was done crying over this, but I admit I shed a few tears that day. After I got that out of my system, I got up and brushed my hands down my jeans to straighten them. Then I clicked open the latches on my suitcase and began unpacking my clothes.

***

Willie didn't come to tea that day. There was no awkward evening walk. I waited in the hall for a long time after the things were cleared away, hoping he would show up. When people started looking at me funny, I decided I had better go up to the cottage. Part of me hoped he would be there waiting. Part of me dreaded the very idea. But when I got back to the cottage, it was as empty as it had been earlier.

I stood in the middle of our little cottage wondering what I was supposed to do. I had already unpacked everything. I could see that I was going to need to get something to do at home. I would have to bring up some mending. Maybe I would talk to Sheila about showing me how to use a spinning wheel.

When the other side of the glen was completely in shadow, I got ready for bed. I put on my nightgown and hung the kettle over the fire to make myself a pot of tea. I turned down the bed. There wasn't much to read, so I pulled out the magazine the woman had given me at the airport all those weeks ago.

I drank my tea and flipped through the pages. The people in those glossy images were a world away from where I was now. I started to wonder how I ever thought that I could be like them. Looking at that magazine and waiting for Willie was the most hopeless I had felt so far.

It was at this low point that Willie walked through the door, his eyes downcast as usual. He took off his jacket and hung it on the peg by the door. I stood up and stepped around the little table. His eyes slid up my body slowly, taking in my bare feet and nightgown, which left my shoulders mostly bare. The way he was looking, it felt like I was bare to the skin. His gaze never made it all the way up to my eyes. His mouth formed into a scowl.

"I was starting to worry about you," I tried to sound cheerful, but I felt nothing but.

He grunted.

"Can I make you a cup of tea? I'm sure it's still hot."

"Aye, fine." With the mood he seemed to be in, I was surprised he agreed. I went to our little shelf to fetch a cup for him and poured some of the tea. I turned to set the cup near him at the end of the table and found him looking at the magazine. "What's this?"

"Just a fashion magazine. A woman gave it to me at the airport."

He flipped through the pages. "This is more of yer modern ways."

"It's really just a magazine. It's just pictures of clothes." I kept my voice even. I didn't want an argument.

He held it up to me. It was turned to a picture of a woman in a very short miniskirt. Her eyes were heavily shadowed and her lips painted a bright pink. "Look at these sluagh ùr. This one's got on more paint than clothes. This is what ye want to be?"

"No, I just wanted to see what the fashion was." I stepped closer to him and held out my hand for the magazine. "I was waiting for you and I got bored. That was the only thing I had to read."

He pulled it further away. "Or ye were planning what ye'll wear the next time ye run away."

So there it was. All of this was some kind of punishment for my escape attempt. "That's done now. It won't happen again."

"No, it won't." I watched the muscles in his jaw working while he kept his eyes trained on the top of the table. The magazine was still in his hand. He closed it and rolled it up. I watched his hands twist back and forth, tightening it until it was a compact stick of paper. I remembered what Duff had said to me earlier and wondered if he'd been trying to warn me. Maybe in the weeks they had been living in the lads' house, Duff had noticed something about Willie that I hadn't. His mouth was working like he was trying to form words. Eventually he managed, "D'ye ken what they're saying?"

I shook my head, afraid to speak, but of course he wouldn't look right at me. He shifted the magazine to one hand, lifted it up, and slammed it hard on the edge of the table, "Do ye?!"

I jumped at the noise and stepped back, wondering if I could make it to the door and how far I might get down the trail before he got to me. "No."

"They say that ye ran away because of me. That ye canna bear the thought of being wi' me." His dark eyes looked up at me from beneath his creased brows.

I held out a hand to him. I wanted to reassure him, but I was afraid to get too close. "Oh no, Willie. It's not like that at all. You see, before…before I came here, I was a dancer. I wanted to go to New York to dance professionally. My teacher arranged an audition for me. It was a big opportunity. I didn't know about all of this.

"I had plans for myself, plans that didn't involve staying here this long, much less having a child. I ran because I couldn't stand the thought of giving that up. It had nothing to do with you."

He shook his head and ran the magazine back and forth along the table's edge. "It had everything to do with me."

"I thought I could let it go, that I could give it up and be what everyone wanted me to be." I swallowed past the lump in my throat. "But then the cauldron stopped and people started looking at me and Rona like we had caused it. I figured if these people could watch me work hard every day for them and then still treat me like I didn't belong…Well, I thought that wasn't worth giving up my dream. But there ain't much hope for that now, and I've only made everything worse." My voice cracked and I would have hung my head in sorrow if I hadn't been afraid to take my eyes off him.

"Ye're right. There is no hope for that now." He walked over to the fireplace where the peat fire was glowing orange and dropped the magazine on top of it.

Peat fires burn slow, and I thought I could save it before it went up in flames. I ran to the fireplace and went to grab for it. Willie grabbed my wrist tight and pulled me to his chest. I wasn't worried that he would hit me anymore, but I hated the thought that we might start our duties as mates in anger.

He studied my face, his breath short. His eyes fastened on my lips. At first I thought he was going to kiss me, but then his mouth started working in that way he had, like it was a cold engine that took some warming up before the words could come out. "I ken it's hard to believe, but I do have some pride."

"I know," I whispered. "Of course you do."

"Ye ken why we're here." His jaw firmed and he blew out a breath. "Eilidh willna let ye leave until we've made a child."

I nodded.

"Weel, ye can settle in and long for yer modern ways until ye rot. I willna touch ye." He let me go abruptly and stalked over to the ladder. He climbed up and started taking off his clothes.

I was too stunned to move. I stood there by the fire, not knowing how I should feel. It was true that I didn't want to lie down with Willie. I hadn't been repulsed by him before he had become this bitter, suspicious thing. But my main objection was that I hadn't had a say in it. Now I had gotten part of what I wanted, but I felt even more trapped. At least before I had known what was expected of me. No matter how I had hated the idea, there had been a light at the end of the tunnel, something that allowed me to think about "after." Now, I had been tried, convicted, and sentenced to endless purgatory by the person who was supposed to be my match.

The magazine burst into flames in the fireplace and a couple of sparks landed on my nightgown. I jumped back and beat them out, leaving little holes with charred edges in the white cotton.

CHAPTER THIRTY-ONE

August 1968
Làrachd an Fhamhair, Scotland

The next morning, Willie was gone before I got up. I tried to act like everything was normal. I brushed my hair and teeth and washed my face. I got dressed and washed the tea pot and cups from the night before. I dried them and put them away. When I had done everything I could think of in the privacy of the cottage, I took a deep breath and opened the door.

I walked down to the hall. Everyone was eating their porridge. Well, everyone except Rona, Lachlan, Sheila, and Rab. My appearance in the hall was greeted by raised eyebrows and a few knowing looks. I was sure my face was red as a beet, but I held my head high and went to the cauldron where Jock had made the porridge. I sat down with my bowl at our usual table, but there was no one there except me and Jock.

The old man looked at me kindly. "Morning, lass."

"Morning, Jock," I mumbled.

That was the extent of the conversation. Jock was usually full of news and cheerful chatter, but I think he could tell I didn't feel much like talking. We continued eating our breakfast in silence as the conversation buzzed around us.

It was after breakfast when I went outside to pick vegetables that Duff caught up with me. He fell in step beside me as I walked down the lane toward the farthest of Jock's little garden patches. When he spoke, he didn't beat around the bush. "What's going on?"

I didn't know what to say, but Duff looked like a big old storm cloud ready to break on anyone in his path. Willie hadn't hurt me, but I remembered Duff's warning the day before. If I was truly hopeless, I knew I could always tell him that Willie had hit me and all of this might come to an end. But I didn't like to use Duff like that, and your granny raised me not to lie. So I told him the truth, "My 'mate' refuses to be with me because I'm new folk and he's embarrassed because I tried to run away."

"Did he hurt you?" His tone said that anyone who even thought about hurting me would get the business end of his right hook.

"No. He didn't hurt me." I didn't want Duff going after Willie in any case. I had done enough harm to Willie. "Apparently, the talk in the village is that I ran away because I didn't want to be with him. His pride is sore. I told him the real reason why I ran, but that doesn't seem to matter when it stands up next to what everyone is saying."

"Which is that he's some kind of simpleton and you didn't want to have his baby."

"You can see why he might be sensitive to that kind of talk. Well, he says since I want to get away so bad and I'm stuck here until I get pregnant, he won't lay a hand on me. So I'm stuck here for good."

"Jesus," Duff seethed. "He thinks that's some kind of punishment, huh?"

"I guess. It sure feels like it." We walked on a few steps. "Though when I think about it, now I'm the one that everybody's pitying. Because now even the village idiot won't touch me. I'm not good enough."

"You know that's not true," he said quickly.

"I know enough about how small towns work to know that that's what people will say."

He grabbed my wrist and pulled me in the direction of the bridge. "We have to tell your aunt. The whole point of this is for you to have a child. If they can force you to stay here and do your duty, they can't just let him refuse."

I couldn't help smiling at him. "Don't worry. If I'm stuck here too long, I'm sure you can go back to your life. There's not much need for protection here."

He stopped me and looked at me for a long minute. His mouth was set in a grim line. "I think you need me just as much here as out there. Come on."

He pulled me across the footbridge toward Aunt Eilidh's house, but she wasn't there. He stood outside the cottage and looked around the glen. He must have found her because he grabbed my hand and pulled me back down the hill.

We found her near the small beach. She was cutting bog myrtle. Duff went straight to her. "Ms. MacLeod?"

She stood up and looked at the two of us, giving us a blithe smile. "Yes, child?"

I didn't know how to say it. Unlike Duff, I wasn't convinced that she would do anything for me. She was careful never to seem angry, but I could tell that she wasn't happy with me. I still thought her announcement about moving in earlier was a response to my running away. When I didn't start talking immediately, Duff elbowed me. "Tell her."

I glanced back and forth between the two of them. After a few seconds, Aunt Eilidh looked at Duff. She took my arm and said, "I have a feeling this is woman's talk. Maybe this would be easier if it were just the twa of us."

Duff looked back and forth between us for several seconds before agreeing. "Alright."

He stalked off, his steps eating up the path. Aunt Eilidh turned back to me. Her voice was kind. "Tell me what it is, child."

I took a deep breath. "Well, Willie says that he's never going to touch me." My voice cracked. "He says I'm *sluagh ùr* and he doesn't want to have anything to do with me."

She made a thoughtful "Mmm" sound and drew me toward the path that led away from the village. "Ye ken what people are saying?"

I nodded. "He told me about that."

She nodded knowingly. "Then ye ken that his pride is bruised. Our Willie is a quiet one, but he feels what people think keenly. Has he told ye how he came to live with us?"

"He told me that he lived outside when he was younger, but not much else."

"Ah, weel." She sighed. "Willie's mam grew up here in Làrachd an Fhamhair. She was a good sort of lass, our Deirdre. Knew the auld ways and understood how important preserving our people was. She fell in love with one of our men who lived in Inverness. They had seen each other on feast days all their lives. He came home one year for Samhain, and she was all grown up and bonny. He decided to stay that winter, and by the spring he got her to agree to go with him to Inverness.

"Now, Willie's da was a handsome lad, with a good heart. But there was a sadness about him, like he couldna quite see the good in life. Deirdre showed him what he was missing, that he could be happy. But when they went to live in the outside world, it was harder for him to see that. He took to drink, and the sadness turned to anger. Sometimes that came out as violence.

"After he took Deirdre to the new folk, we saw her light dimming. Each time they came back for feast days, she looked tired. We could tell that instead of her light feeding him, his sadness was draining her. When they had young Willie, we hoped that things would get better. It seemed like they did for a long time. But it didn't last. William continued to drink and things got worse.

"Ye ken Rab's family lives in Inverness as well, and the boys are of an age. Sometimes, when his father was at his worst, Willie would stay wi' Rab's family. But Deirdre would always stay home. She wanted to be there when William cleaned up. Late one night, Willie woke to hear his da shouting and his mum trying to calm him down. He went to see what the noise was about, and he saw his da hit her. We didna ken it at the time, but he had done it before.

"I dinna ken if Willie saw it before that night, but he saw it then. Deirdre saw Willie and told him to run. He ran to the Ballantyne's house in the middle of the night and told them what was happening. When Angus Ballantyne went to see what he could do about it, no one was there. He saw blood on the floor and wall, but the house was empty. He went to the police. They found Deirdre floating in the river the next morning. William was found lying in the gutter. He was alive, but senseless.

"He was put in prison and young Willie lived with the Ballantynes until he could be brought back here. He's been in this glen ever since."

It was an awful story, but not unfamiliar. I'd seen kids like this in the mountains at home. They weren't lucky enough to have a hidden glen full of family to hide away in. "And he's been shy like that ever since?"

Aunt Eilidh nodded. "Ye can see how he might be sour on modern ways. He also worries about talk. When he was in Inverness, he likely heard talk about his parents. Ye ken well how a small community like this talks, and it was no different when he came to live with us. Even here, where everyone is friendly, he withdraws from attention."

"And I brought undue attention and more pity."

Aunt Eilidh patted my hand on her arm. "Ye couldna have kent how it would affect him, but aye. His heart has been sore since he was a boy, and now his pride is sore. He'll come around."

I wasn't so sure about that. "But if he hasn't gotten better in all these years, why would he get better now?"

"Och, well. He hasna had you all these years. Ye've a kind heart, and ye're a problem solver. I've seen that with yer planning for the food, and even with yer determination to leave. Ye can manage young Willie. Ye mun give him time, and be kind." She patted my hand again.

Right. Somehow I was going to heal him, like Deirdre was going to heal his father. I had seen families like this in the mountains, and in my experience violence like that lasted for generations. I thought back to Willie's behavior the night before, the barely leashed violence of the magazine cracking against the table. I'm sure Aunt Eilidh meant for this to make me sympathetic to Willie, but in truth it scared me. "But what if he's like his father? What if he beats me?"

Aunt Eilidh stopped walking and turned to me. Her look was kind and motherly. "Och lass, we would never let him hurt ye. Just look at yer steward, he brought ye to me today. I'm sure he'll keep ye safe. Now, come and pick some herbs wi' me."

I didn't know what to make of my conversation with Aunt Eilidh. I was sorry for what Willie had been through, but I also didn't see how it should fall to me to fix him. And I wondered how Aunt Eilidh could tell me I was safe when she was making me share a house with someone like that. As withdrawn as Willie was, how could anyone know how he was going to react to any of this? I felt like she had just told me to go to sleep with a rattlesnake and hope I didn't get bit.

CHAPTER THIRTY-TWO

October 1968
Làrachd an Fhamhair, Scotland

I lived through months of tense silence in that cottage. Willie ignored me during the day. He went about doing whatever it was that he did. I worked with Jock and the rest of the young people to preserve all the food we could. I got Sheila to show me how to spin wool and took a spinning wheel up to the cottage to spin when I couldn't sleep. A little part of me hoped that embracing something familiar to Willie would soften him a little bit.

I stayed out as late as I could. I worked on smoking, preserving, and preparing until well into the evenings. Our first smoking experiments were fish. The loch was loaded with trout and salmon, and we managed to smoke a pretty good supply, not that the villagers were grateful for it. They still looked at us with suspicion. Still, while they were wringing their hands and wondering how to bring the cauldron back, we stocked the root cellar Jock had been using to keep his potatoes and turnips. The men were forced to dig another, and despite the protests from Duff and some of the other lads, I helped with that too.

It was my goal every day to wear myself out. I learned that if I fell asleep before Willie came in, I would be able to sleep through the night. But if I was awake when he came in, I would suffer from his sneers and hard looks before he climbed up to the loft. Then I would stay up all night listening to every little movement in the loft and wondering when he would change his mind. I didn't know what to think about that prospect. I didn't want him, but I did want out of that place.

I tried to be kind to Willie, bringing his food to him in the hall or having tea ready for him when he came into the cottage. But he never acknowledged me. Whenever we were in public, he ignored me. At home, he stalked about, grumbling and showing me in every way that he considered me unworthy.

One night around mid-September, I fell asleep before Willie came home. I'm not sure if he made a sound or I just knew somehow, but I woke up to find him watching me. He was leaning a shoulder against the wall near the foot of the bed. I couldn't see his face in the firelight so I couldn't read his expression, but I thought I could feel the waves of scorn coming off him. I was starting to estimate the number of steps between me and the door when he pushed away from the wall and went out into the night. I wondered if he had done that before and I had slept through it. I found myself working harder and sleeping less after that.

On the other hand, Rona and Lachlan seemed the picture of happiness. Any time of the day, you could catch them smiling at each other, laughing about something or stealing little touches. She would put her hand on his arm to get his attention. If she were standing near, he would put his arm around her. Moving about their days, each would follow the other with their eyes. Sheila and Rab were less obvious, but they at least seemed to live together happily enough.

I wanted to be happy for my sisters, but it was hard. I was starting to withdraw from everyone. I worked like a dog, but I didn't socialize. The other sisters were wrapped up in their own men. The villagers were too busy whispering behind their hands about me to make friends. The stewards were the only people who didn't make me feel jealous or miserable. So I spent more and more time working with them and playing cards with them in the hall. Duff didn't seem to mind, and I felt safe next to him.

We were unloading a batch of fish from the smokehouse one day when Rab and Lachlan came strolling up the lane. A huge stag was hanging from a branch held between them. The antlers dragged on the mossy ground. Blood coated Rab's shirt, and he grinned like a warrior come home with some great prize. They walked right up to me where I stood outside the smokehouse and laid the deer down at my feet. Rab's teeth flashed white through the filth and sweat and blood. He said, "Think ye can do something with this old thing?"

I was speechless, caught in his green eyes. They were so bright with triumph. The sound of Duff clearing his throat near us brought me back. I looked down at the carcass at my feet. "I think we can manage something."

"That's grand." He nodded at Duff. "Will ye help us string this up so we can butcher it?"

"Yup." Duff leaned down and picked up the end of the branch that Lachlan had been carrying. Rab picked up the other end and the three of them carried it off to clean and butcher.

I finished hanging the fish in the root cellar and went to the hall to start preparing for tea. I was mixing some dough for oatcakes when I heard someone come in. I didn't stop what I was doing.

I jumped when I felt a hand rest on my hip and a solid presence behind me. Rab peered over my shoulder. "Looks good."

I shifted, trying to move away from his hand. "I've had a lot of practice."

He let me pull away but stayed close. He had cleaned the blood off his skin, but hadn't changed his clothes yet. He gave me a speculative look. "I reckon ye have. Ye seem to be doing a lot better than some people expect."

"Hmph. That shouldn't be too hard. People around here seem to expect the worst of me." I kept right on working, adding a little more milk to the dry dough. I hadn't talked to Rab for any length of time since midsummer, but I did like him. In fact, I had kind of avoided him after the time we'd had at the feast.

"I don't, ye ken," he said, bending down to try to catch my eye.

I might have blushed. "Yeah. I know."

He walked around the table to stand across from me. "I ken why ye ran."

That was a subject I didn't really want opened again. Everyone had their ideas about why I tried to escape and nothing I said seemed to change that. "Do you?"

"I'd have gone for it too if I was handfast to Willie Cross." His eyes drifted down to my mouth before flicking back up.

"Really. I would have thought you knew better than anyone what he's been through. Don't you feel any sympathy for him?"

"Of course, it was an awful thing to happen to a wee lad. I tried then to make friends with him, to be kind." He leaned back against the table. "He's so closed off, he canna connect with people. He's been given everything since then, and none of it seems to touch him. I'm not saying he's bad. He just doesna know how to be anything but alone."

"Well, when everything that's done for him is done out of pity, it's easy to see why he doesn't want to let it touch him."

"Ah, but if he doesna behave like anything but a pitiful lost boy, how can he expect anyone to act out of aught but pity?" And that summed up the situation precisely. Willie was locked in this cycle of perpetual offense and reaction that stained his whole life.

"Ye deserve better," his voice was low and he leaned toward me.

That caught my attention, and I looked up at him. He didn't wear his usual rakish smile. It wasn't an offhand comment. He meant it. It was probably the most serious thing I had ever heard him say, and I had to agree. "I deserve to be building the life that I had planned for myself in America. Instead, I'm here up to my elbows in oats and smoked fish, making food for people who'd as soon spit on me."

He looked down, almost like he was ashamed at the way the others treated me. "It's a crime how some of these people treat you and Rona as well. Change is hard for them. And with the cauldron…They're terrified."

"I'm sure you're right about that." I smiled to change the subject, tired of talking about my troubles. "What about you? How are you liking married life?"

He looked at the wall in front of him and blew out a long breath. "Well, I'm here. Doing my duty. Canna say I'll want to stick around after it's done. I've my own life to get back to. Aye?"

Just then, Sheila came in the door with a basket full of turnips. Rona was on her heels with her own basket.

"What's that on your shirt?" Sheila's gaze sharpened on Rab's shirt.

"Rab shot a deer," I said.

Her eyes went wide and she looked up at Rab. He gave a slightly embarrassed smile. It was nothing like the grin he'd shown me when he'd dropped his kill at my feet. Sheila rounded the table and wrapped her arms around his waist, looking up at him with open admiration. "Well, now that's just grand. Well done, love."

"*Mòran taing*," he said with little warmth. He glanced down at her before looking back up at me. His green eyes had gone flat. He looked uncomfortable with Sheila's obvious affection. He disentangled himself. "I'd better go and finish with the butchering. We're almost done."

He gave Sheila a chaste kiss on the cheek and left quickly. For her part, Sheila gazed doe-eyed after him.

***

Our routine continued as the days got shorter and the wind blew colder. I worked myself till I was like to drop. Then I would go to the cottage and try to sleep. Some nights I did. Some not. When I couldn't sleep, I'd sit at the spinning wheel by the fire. Sometimes I would sing to myself while I spun. I reckon I was feeling homesick, because I would sing songs from home. Not the songs Mama taught me, but the songs from the mountains like "Frankie Silvers" and "In the Pines," "'Omi Wise," and "Black is the Color." I'd sing until Willie came home. Then I would keep the music in my head, and the only sound would be the creak of the treadle and the swooshing slide of the brake band.

Some mornings I would be so tired that I'd almost fall asleep in my porridge. Then I would start working. Once you get into a rhythm you can do almost anything for longer than you think. Momentum just keeps you going. But I wasn't always the best tempered person on those days. One such morning Duff and I were tending the fire at the smokehouse when a little boy ran up behind us and started singing a rude little song in Gaelic. This wasn't unusual. Children said plenty of rude things to me, but not usually while Duff was around. I guess this one had figured out that Duff didn't have the Gaelic.

It's a good thing he doesn't speak it too, or he'd have hauled the lad to his mother for a good switching. Of course, that's what I should have done, but I was too tired and short-fused to think of that at the time. Duff grabbed me before I could take a step toward the lad. "Whoa there, Molly." He turned to the boy to say, "You better get, son, or I'll let her go."

The little mite ran, his wee legs pumping, no doubt haring off to tell his mam how the *sluagh ùr* witch had cursed him. Duff hustled me into the hall. He dragged me back to the work area. "God damned little beasts," he swore. "These people make me crazy, bunch of ingrates! But you know we can't go around cursing children in the street."

"Huh. You don't know what he said," I muttered.

He stood me by the work table and started looking around. "I think I got the gist of it." He grabbed a basket and a set of shears. "Listen, I know you're not sleeping, and I think I can imagine why. You're working yourself to the bone. You need a break."

"I don't need a break. I need a distraction." I turned to go back to what we'd been doing.

He stepped in front of me and shoved the basket into my hands. "You need to get out of this village for a little while. Go cut some herbs or greens or whatever it is you forage for. I don't mean go far. Just take a walk where there aren't any people looking at you sideways. Try to go somewhere you can relax and be alone."

"But I won't be alone, will I? You said yourself, someone is always following me," I said bitterly.

"That's for your protection," he said. "And I'll send someone you won't mind. I'll make sure he stays out of sight."

"What are you gonna do?" He had been keeping tabs on me since I moved into the cottage. I was surprised he would let me out of his sight.

"I am going to talk to your aunt. These little incidents have to stop. She's the only one who can get these parents to control the little devils."

I scoffed. "I wouldn't bet on that. They're hearing this stuff at home."

"Well, if anyone can do something about it, it's her. If she won't, I'll take to switching the little monsters myself."

I almost laughed, but I think he was half serious. "Fine, I'll go for a walk."

It was my kind of day, dry but not sunny, nippy but not too cold. I strolled up the path away from the village, and then stepped off the path altogether. I must have walked a lot longer than I thought. When I reached the loch, I noticed that the sun was now to the west. I had been walking for hours. I hadn't been this far from the village since the trip to Ullapool.

When I came to the spot where the burn crossed under the road, I stopped. I could see the loch ahead of me, and the road stretching along the shore. Here it was October and I hadn't seen anything as modern as asphalt since July. It might seem silly, surrounded by all the startling beauty of the highlands, but at that moment, that asphalt was the prettiest thing I had ever laid eyes on. I lifted my foot and put it on the road. It felt so solid through the sole of my shoe that I let out a little cry.

I slapped a hand over my mouth and looked around to see if anyone had heard me. There was no one that I could see. I laughed and picked up my other foot and put it on the pavement. I sighed with pleasure. My heart felt full for the first time since I had arrived in that prison of moss and stone.

I took another look around, and then…well, it might sound crazy. Then again, all of this sounds crazy. I danced. Right there on the edge of the world. Not just a little jig, not a few happy steps. I'm talking perfectly executed pirouettes, arabesques, and damn near anything else I felt like. I don't know how long I was at it. I don't even know where I found the energy, but I did. I kept right on dancing until a horn blared and a truck came barreling down on me. I suddenly knew what a spotlighted deer feels like. I was rooted there in the middle of the road. The truck was coming right at me. I couldn't move, and for an instant, I wasn't even sure that I wanted to.

Then a body slammed into me and I went flying off the road, rolling down the bank on the other side. We tumbled and came to a stop with his body stretched over mine. I opened my eyes only to fall into the green depths of Rab Ballantyne's.

He lifted a hand to my cheek to brush away some grass. "Are ye hurt?"

I shook my head. A bit breathless, I said, "I don't think so."

"Oy! Are ye alright there?" We looked up to see the truck driver standing on the side of the road some twenty feet away.

Rab pushed up from the ground and helped me to my feet. "Aye, fine. Thanks mate."

"Ye might keep yer bird out o' the road, yeah?" the man yelled with a dismissive wave.

Rab looked back at me, his mouth quirked in a half smile. "I'll do that."

The truck driver stalked back to his truck muttering. I couldn't hear what he was saying, but I was sure it was something about dafties dancing in the road.

When he was gone, Rab and I looked at each other and burst out laughing. "What were ye thinking?"

"I wasn't. The road just felt so good and solid under my feet, I had to dance," I said when my laughter died down.

"He's right." He jerked his thumb over his shoulder in the direction the truck driver had taken. "Ye are daft."

I laughed again. "Maybe I am."

"Stay here." He walked back across the road and returned a minute later with a fishing pole and bag. "MacDuff said ye needed a friendly face to follow along today. Ye're no trying to make another run for it, are ye?"

I looked at the bag. "Following along or fishing?"

He tilted his head to the side and gave me a rakish smile. "Using it as an excuse, so I dinna have to explain to Sheila where I've been."

"Sounds like we're both hiding. I just needed to get away from the village for a bit."

"Right. Canna blame ye." He looked around a bit. We were near the loch shore between the ruins of the castle and the house. "Have ye seen the castle?"

I shook my head. He waved me forward, and we walked toward the castle ruin. It stands on a little spit of land that stretches into the loch. There's not much left of Ardvreck Castle. Only a corner tower and a couple of walls are still standing. We walked through an archway into what would have been the inside. Instead the rear and side walls were gone, and it was open to the grassy slope down to the loch.

"I might try fishing over there after all." He lifted his chin in the direction of the point where the land jutted into the water. "Care to come sit wi' me?"

"Sure."

We walked to the shore and settled on the rocks. I looked back over my shoulder and noticed that I couldn't see the road, just the top of the castle tower jutting up above the bank. In front of us was the cobalt blue water of the loch, silver sparks flicking the tops of the small waves. All we could hear was the sound of the water lapping on the rocks. It was like we were the only people in the world.

Rab baited his hook and cast his line. I hadn't seen him doing it this way before. "I thought fly fishing was more your speed."

"It is." He returned to sit beside me. "But it's hard to be good company when ye're flinging a line back and forth."

"Don't let me stop you. I came out here for peace and quiet." I wasn't trying to be rude, but I did want some peace.

He studied me for a few seconds before rising again and pulling his line out of the water. "Alright. I'll just be down the shore."

I watched him as he made his way down the shoreline. In no time he had the line flying back and forth through the air in an elegant dance. After some back and forth, he let it fly and it soared over the water before dropping to the surface. He started drawing the line back in little jumping spurts. After some time in that spot without catching anything, he moved further away.

Content to sit and listen to the water lapping, I leaned back comfortably against the stone behind me. My limbs felt so heavy as I let the sun warm and soothe me. The muscles in my neck and shoulders had been tense for so long, I had forgotten what it felt like to relax. I don't know when I fell asleep. I woke up some time later with Rab sitting next to me again. At his feet was a string of trout.

"How long have I been asleep?"

"Not sure. I was fishing for a couple of hours." He gave me a soft smile. "Ye looked like ye needed it."

He looked back out at the loch, and I took the opportunity to make sure my hair and clothes were straight. "I did. I haven't been sleeping well."

He turned back and studied me. "I can imagine."

I stood up and stretched. "Well, I reckon I better get back. No doubt Jock'll be needing some help."

He stood up as well, stepping in front of me. "No need to rush off. Let me show ye the castle."

I looked up at the castle rising over the bank and then back at Rab. Maybe it was the rest or the dancing before that, but I was feeling easier, less stressed than I had been in ages. I could steal another hour for myself. "Okay."

He gathered his bag and the fish, and we went together up the bank to the castle ruin. We walked past the remnant of the back wall and stood in what must have been the hall. Being open to the elements for centuries meant that the lower level was almost entirely filled with dirt and overgrown with grass. There was enough of the wall left that you could almost tell what the floor plan had been.

I spotted a row of evenly spaced holes in the largest of the remaining walls. "You can see where the beams were that supported the next floor."

"Aye." Rab pointed toward the round tower at the corner. He climbed up the fallen stones to what should have been the second floor and offered me a hand up. "And there ye can see where the supports were for the stairs. If ye look at the heights of the windows, ye can get an idea of where the landings were."

"Wow." I stepped closer to where I thought the landing would be, my eyes on the tower.

"Careful!" Rab grabbed for my arm and pulled me back a step. "There's no floor. Ye dinna want to fall down there."

I followed his eyes down to see an empty pit that at one time probably went down to a cellar. I couldn't tell if the cellar was still there, but the stairs were gone, and it was a considerable drop to the rubble that covered the floor below. "Thanks."

"Aye, ye wouldna want to add to the sad tales about this place." He drew me over to an open window large enough for a person to step through. The other side dropped about fifteen feet to the ground.

"Oh, I don't think I'd need to fall down that hole for that," I muttered, looking across the loch toward Inchnadamph.

"Hmph. Have ye heard the story about the mermaid?" Rab asked, laying his things down on some tumbled stones.

I gave him an arch look. "Mermaid?"

"Och, aye." He leaned a shoulder against the stone of the window and gestured toward the ruin around us. "Ye see, this castle was built by a MacLeod, only he didna have the means to build it here. He couldna pay to have these stones hauled, nor for the labor. So he promised his first daughter to the devil in marriage to get it built. Years and years later, Old Scratch came to collect. But the laird's daughter, Eimhir, didna like the idea of being married to the devil himself. So she jumped." He waved a hand toward where I stood on the other side of the window, then swept it out toward the water. "From the tower here into the water. But she wasna killed. Instead, she transformed into a mermaid who lives in a cave under the loch. They say that the water rises when Eimhir weeps for the loss of her life on the land."

"The devil himself, huh?" I looked out toward the loch and studied the water line, wondering if Eimhir was weeping today. Remembering what Rab said about Willie, I thought I knew a bit of how she felt.

"I do see similarities." He pushed away from the window frame and took a step closer. "Although I hope ye willna do anything so drastic."

"I doubt it will come to that," I turned to him.

"I'm glad to hear it. I would be sore grieved if ye werena here." He stepped closer still, his eyes on mine. He took my hand where it hung at my side and pulled it to his chest. "A Mhàili—"

"Don't. Rab, please don't." I turned my hand in his as if to push him away. I thought I knew what he was going to say. I felt the pull too. I had from that night at the feast. "You're handfast to Sheila, and she's one of the few people from this village who's been good to me."

"Ye do ken that's not my choice. Just as Willie Cross isna yours." He looked serious, and his fingers tightened on mine. "Ye shouldna trust Sheila too much, Màili."

"She's my sister." I had to trust Sheila and Rona. "Things were a little bumpy at first, but we're friends now. Who else knows what it's like to be in my position?"

He slipped his thumb under my palm and held my hand between us. "Sheila and Eilidh are cut from the same cloth.

They're used to getting their way without question, and they dinna let anyone prevent that. Everything they do has an agenda."

"Yes, preserving our people and their way of life."

He shook his head, his voice was softened. "I'm not so sure that's always foremost in their minds."

"That doesn't change anything. She's still your match." I tried to pull my hand away, but he wouldn't release it.

"Not the match I wanted." His eyes found mine, and I was thrown back to that night of the feast months ago when the two of us stood breathless and caught. Then he bent toward me and did exactly what I had wanted him to do then. It started with a slow soft brush of his lips across mine, but soon deepened into the kind of kiss a girl never forgets. I had kissed a boy or two back in the holler, but their awkward fumbling had nothing on this.

He drew away too soon. Too soon and too late. He rested his forehead on mine, and we both fought to catch our breath. When I looked up, his eyes were on mine, but they were full of regret. "I wish it could be different."

"Me too," I breathed.

He stepped back and looked around. "We'd better get home."

CHAPTER THIRTY-THREE

October 1968
Làrachd an Fhamhair, Scotland

The following morning, the porridge lasted longer than anyone expected. Even those who were late to breakfast dipped into the cauldron and found food. We didn't take too much notice then. But when we had a surplus at tea, and again the next morning, people started to talk. By that evening the whole village was buzzing about the cauldron working again. Everyone ate heartily. We did eventually run out, but it took much longer than it should have.

At the end of the meal, Aunt Eilidh stood by the fire and raised her hands to gather everyone's attention. "Children of the auld folk, our patience and faith have been rewarded. Our cauldron is returning to us. It may not be at full strength yet, but I'm sure if we continue as we have been, we will be back to normal in no time at all. I ken well there has been some disagreement about the reason and what we should do about it. I think that tonight has proven that our sisters from across the sea and their efforts to prevent a hungry winter was not the cause."

At this she looked at some of the loudest of our accusers, including Willie. Some of them had the grace to hang their heads. He did not. Aunt Eilidh went on, "Thanks to your faith and their diligence, we have plenty of food in store, and our community has held together. It is time that we celebrate as one. Samhain is just a week away. I say that we make this a Samhain to remember."

This was met with cheers by most, although a few of us at our table looked at each other. Rona and I exchanged a look that said we thought Aunt Eilidh might be jumping the gun. I glanced at Rab, and though he was smiling, I could tell he wasn't confident.

As everyone left the hall that night, Duff pulled me aside. When we were away from the crowd, he bent his head toward me to ask quietly, "What do you think?"

I shrugged. "I don't know. I asked Jock. He didn't put in any more food than usual. But there was definitely more there. Still, I don't think it's time to celebrate yet."

"I know." He looked behind me and nodded. I could tell someone was walking up. "What's to say it doesn't stop again?"

"It's never stopped before this," Rab said, coming up beside me.

"Right," Duff said. "That means we're in unknown territory. I'd rather not spend all our stores on a feast."

Rona and Lachlan walked up hand in hand. He said, "That's a good point."

"So we set aside some rationed food for the feast and keep on as we have been," she added.

Duff nodded. "I think that's probably the best plan. Let's get the others over here and make sure they agree."

Rab turned to wave to Gavin and Davie, brushing his shoulder against my back. I turned toward the crowd as well and looked around. "Where's Sheila?"

Rab gave me that rakish half smile of his. "She's gone to talk to Eilidh. I'll catch her up."

"Alright," Duff said and filled in the other stewards when they got there. We went over our plans for the next day, then split up to go to our homes. As we walked by the door to the hall, I caught sight of Willie inside. He was sitting at a table staring at the cauldron. He looked up, and our eyes met. His were filled with confusion. Just then, whoever had been holding the hall door open moved away and the door swung shut.

Duff walked me home. He made a habit of looking around the house whenever he did to make sure that everything was safe. I didn't have the heart to tell him that the real danger in that house was rarely there when he was. He left me with a fire in the grate and a "Be careful."

***

As planned, we spent the next week preparing for both the feast and winter. For us girls that meant filling basket after basket with turnips and potatoes and dried moss to be put in the root cellar. As we were trimming the greens off the turnips and putting them in separate baskets, I said, "I sure wish I had some fat back to cook these greens with."

"What on Earth is fat back? It sounds awful," Sheila cringed, cutting the greens off the top of another one.

I couldn't help laughing. "It's the fatty part on a pig's back. Sort of like bacon, but it's usually more fat than meat and it's cut thicker. Some people just fry it up, but Mama liked to use it to flavor things like greens and beans."

Sheila made a sour face. "I'll take most anything to make turnip greens taste better."

Rona laughed and started to pick up the basket of turnips she'd been packing with dried moss. "Bacon makes everything taste better. Eh?"

Just as she lifted the heavy basket off the ground, Lachlan ran up and took it out of her hands. "Ye dinna need to be lifting that!"

Rona rolled her eyes but let him take the basket. She followed him to the root cellar. When they came back, they were both blushing pink. Lachlan went back toward where the lads were stacking peat against the side wall of the hall. Rona came back to us.

Sheila studied her for several second before gasping and jumping to her feet. "Ye are. Ye're pregnant!"

"What?" Rona and I said together, staring at Sheila.

She arched a brow at Rona. "I can tell by looking at ye."

Rona blushed even more. "We've just started to suspect."

Sheila shrugged. "Well, I'm nae doctor, but I'm fair sure."

I hugged Rona. "Do you know what you're going to do next?"

She looked behind her in the direction of the men. "We're not sure yet. I kind of wanted to be home near my mom, Lachlan says he might come with me."

"Wow. So he may be a match for real," I said.

"I don't know. But I think we want to try." She seemed to glow brighter every time she looked at the men. Lachlan, for his part, looked up with a mix of pride and adoration.

"Och, ye're lucky. I canna get Rab to look at me like that," Sheila grumbled.

I had to laugh at that, though it might have sounded bitter. "I can't get Willie to look at me at all. You're both way ahead of me in the heir department."

"I wonder why Aunt Eilidh hasn't done anything about that?" Rona went back to packing turnips.

I went back to cutting greens off. "I talked to her about it back in July when he made his feelings clear. She said to be patient that he would come around."

"Aye, I reckon he will then," Sheila put in, not looking up from the turnips.

"Well, he hasn't shown any signs of changing," I said.

Rona sprinkled some moss over a layer of turnips. "You'd think at some point, though, she would want to move on. It doesn't look like he's going to do his duty. Maybe she could find someone else."

"Ugh. Great. Another man I didn't choose."

"Nah, Willie is yer match. Ye saw it in the pool. He'll come round," Sheila said, abruptly standing up and grabbing a basket of greens. She stalked off to the hall to take the basket inside, leaving Rona and I exchanging puzzled looks.

***

The Samhain celebration became a double celebration of the cauldron's return to productivity and Rona and Lachlan's pregnancy. Aunt Eilidh announced the news at the start of the feast. Just as at midsummer, the auld folk who lived outside the village came and brought their own food. To that was added the surplus we had set aside from our stores and whatever the cauldron provided.

There were bonfires and music and dancing. This time I knew what was happening and felt a lot less pressure. I even felt more a part of the community. Since the cauldron had started producing again and Eilidh had made her speech, the villagers had stopped ostracizing those of us who were using our modern ways to preserve food. We were once again part of the community that we had worked so hard to save.

I should say "most" of the villagers stopped ostracizing us. There were a few holdouts who still grumbled about the new folk's ways. Of course, Willie was among them. He skirted around the crowd at the feast, looking dour. I felt his eyes on me several times, especially after the announcement was made about Rona and Lachlan. By that time, I had gotten used to ignoring his brooding and glaring. I had been living with it long enough to realize that it was better not to react.

That night, I wasn't bothered. I danced with the stewards, especially Duff. I played with the children who no longer taunted me. I even drank a little whisky, which is something I never wanted to do at home. I was having a grand time. I went into the hall to fetch some of our jam for the biscuits the children were eating. I figured there wasn't any harm in opening one jar of jam.

I got the jar and was walking back out when a hand reached out of the shadows near the door. I jumped and nearly dropped the jam, but another hand caught it and pulled me into the shadows. I would have screamed but a voice in my ear said, "Shh, it's me."

Rab. We had barely talked since that day by the castle, but we had exchanged more than our share of longing looks. The pull between us seemed even stronger than before. I had to remind myself not to give him the same doe-eyed looks that

Sheila did. It was hard sometimes to watch him with Sheila, especially the way she doted on him. I hated the thought of deceiving her. "You scared me."

"Sorry. I need to see ye." His lips grazed my temple. "Will ye meet me?"

"Rab, we can't," I breathed.

"Aye, we can." His hands gripped my upper arms and held me close to his chest. "They can tell us who our matches should be, but they canna make us care for them, not the way I care for you. Meet me."

His voice was a gentle rumble at my ear. It was as hypnotic as his touch. "Where?"

"At the pool. Just before dawn," he said before brushing his lips feather-light over mine. "Go on then. I'll see ye there."

I slipped back toward the doorway and wrapped an arm around the jam jar before opening the door and stepping out into the party. I tried to go about the rest of the night as if nothing had changed. I continued dancing and laughing. I didn't let on that it bothered me when I saw Sheila wrap her arms around Rab's waist or when she kissed him. I saw it now for what it was: duty. At least on his part. Although that didn't make it hurt any less.

I liked to think of myself as a good person, not the kind to go after another woman's man. Certainly not the kind of woman who would run around behind the back of a friend. I had never done it before, and were it anyone else but Rab, I wouldn't have even considered it then. You might think ill of me, baby, and goodness knows you have a right to. But I hope you believe me that I was troubled by Rab's request.

I looked around the green at the fires and the dancing and I thought that this was what people used to talk about when they talked of fairies. You've probably heard about people getting enchanted and taken away with them. Here we were, living in our hidden glen, coming out to dance and feast through the night on Samhain.

"'Tis a sight. Is it not?" Aunt Eilidh's voice came from my left. I had been so deep in thought that I hadn't heard her come up beside me.

"It is," I agreed. "I was just thinking how easy it would be to call us fairies, feasting all night in our hidden glen only to disappear under the hills at dawn."

That was rewarded with a low laugh. "Aye, the *sluagh ùr* have many names for us, and none exactly right. Though I don't think many folk believe in the auld ways anymore."

I thought of some of the hippy pagans looking for alternative religions back home. Surely there were some around Scotland too. "I think there are some who try, but they usually get it wrong."

She gave me a sidelong look. "Let them. The more they get it wrong, the easier it is for us to stay hidden. We have always been here just below the surface, and we always will be, as long as the sisters remain."

"Right. About that, Aunt Eilidh," I said, "I have tried to be patient, but I don't think Willie will ever do his duty."

"Patience, lass," she chided softly. "Remember, your mother and I waited years before we were able to have you girls."

"I know. But that was because of the war and distance. Willie and I have been sharing a cottage for months and he barely looks at me. I have tried to be kind and friendly to him, but nothing changes. I'm afraid that his bitterness toward the outside world is overpowering."

"What would you have me do? The match was made, the rest is up to you." She kept her tone light for all the words were blunt.

"Could you speak to him? Maybe remind him of what's required?"

"The lad's lived here most of his life. He kens well enough what his job is," she bristled.

"Well, what if we asked the pool again? Could there be another match for me?"

She turned and eyed me closely. Her voice was heavy with disappointment. "So ye still have doubts about this, even when ye're surrounded by yer people, when we see the cauldron working again? I can forgive it when I think of how my sister failed ye. But there is no asking again just because ye dinna like the answer. The match is made, and ye mun live with it."

I could tell she was close to losing her temper. I'm not sure where I found the courage to say, "Even if that means that there are only two sisters in the next generation?"

She narrowed her eyes, and I thought she was going to scold me again, but after a few seconds she thought better of it. Her expression cleared and she smiled. "I'll talk to the lad. Maybe our Rona's good fortune will give him some ideas."

She walked away. Conversations with Aunt Eilidh usually made me feel as if I hadn't quite understood everything, and this one was no different. I felt like there was no good answer. She was right about Mama waiting years for her match, but I didn't think I could make it years under the same roof with a man who couldn't stand me. I was honestly not sure what the right answer was, but I knew one thing: after months of misery and work and barely sleeping, I was tired. I was tired of Willie and his moods, tired of Eilidh and her half answers and manipulations. Most of all I was tired of feeling powerless.

CHAPTER THIRTY-FOUR

October 1968
Làrachd an Fhamhair, Scotland

The night wore on and some of the children fell out and were carried to their beds. A few of the adults went home as well, having had a bit too much of Jock's good whisky. When the sky began to lighten, I told Duff that I'd had my fill and made my way to the cottage. I walked to my own door, then I walked around and back to the trail that led to the pool.

I sat on one of the stones by the edge and looked into the water, which was dark and thick with green algae. I wondered just what this pool was and how its smelly water could make such momentous choices for people. What hold did it have? What wisdom?

"Ye're here," his voice came on the breeze from behind me. He stepped through the trees and into the clearing. The predawn twilight threw the planes of his face into sharp relief, contrasted by the fall of blond curls over his forehead. He looked so handsome that my breath just stopped, like everything in the world but him froze.

"I wasn't sure I could do it."

"Màili, I've something to ask ye."

I had never seen him so serious. "Okay."

"Well," he hesitated and twisted his hands together in front of him, "I want the match that I wanted at midsummer."

"What do you mean?"

"I believed then that it would be you that the pool picked for me. We fit together. I…" He trailed off and stepped closer to me. "I wanted ye then. I want ye now. I dinna ken why the pool picked other people for us, but I havena felt right about it since. I want ye to be mine, Màili."

"What about Sheila? You're handfast to her." I stood and watched him move closer.

"I know, but it doesna feel right. It never has." He shook his head and reached out to me. I let him take my hand. "My heart is tied to yers. It's grieved me these months to watch ye working yerself to the bone and going home to that cold creature."

"He's barely there. He wants nothing to do with me," I whispered urgently.

"I'm glad to hear it." He stepped closer still. "Màili, will ye handfast wi' me?"

I opened my mouth to protest, but he held up his hand. "Hear me out." He pulled me closer until our toes touched on the stones. His eyes held mine. "I ken ye're not a lass to trifle with, and I ken we're both caught fast in a sort of trap. And they might be able to compel us with duty and tradition, but they canna tell us where to love."

He bent down to catch my eye. "I love ye, Màili, and I think ye love me too."

Looking back now, I see it was a girlish sort of love. It was probably the only girlish thing left in me after that summer of duty, and I picked it up and handed it over to Rab Ballantyne. "I do."

He blew out a sharp breath of relief before taking my lips in a brief, urgent kiss. "This is the most sacred place I know. I would have us declare it here, as I wish it had been before."

I couldn't speak. He pulled a small knife from his pocket and looked at me in question. I took a deep breath and nodded. Quick as lightning, he sliced across both our hands. The blood welled and began to run down the side of mine. Rab put the knife away. He pressed his opened hand to mine and held them over the pool.

His other hand caressed my face and he looked into my eyes as he said, "I declare, on this sacred day in this place that you, *a Mhàili NicMhaighread*, are the bride of my heart. I will hold ye there as long as ye allow it."

I could feel the blood dripping from our joined hands into the pool, and for a brief moment I worried what our mingled blood—blood that wasn't matched by whatever the power that pool had—might do. I half expected us to be struck by lightning. But I was in thrall to him, and I repeated the vow, "I declare, on this sacred day, that you *Raibeart Ballantyne* are the man of my heart. I will hold you there as long as you allow it."

"*A Mhàili*," he sighed into my mouth almost before I was done saying it. This time, his kiss was long and slow and full of promise.

He pulled a handkerchief from his pocket and wrapped it around our joined hands. "Will ye lie wi' me?"

I nodded, unable to speak as he pulled me away from the pool. We walked around a ridge to the ruin of an old croft house. It wasn't more than a couple of crumbling walls, but it was cozy. He made a bed for us with his coat and we laid down there in rosy dawn light. I'll spare you the details, baby. But I will say that when your first time comes, I hope it's as beautiful and as full of love as mine was.

***

Rab walked me back to my cottage in the early morning. We came around the ridge to avoid walking through the village, though most folks were asleep after the night's feast. He kissed me behind my cottage. I crept in quietly, hoping not to wake Willie. If he was there, I didn't see him. I crawled into bed and stretched my limbs, feeling languid and well-loved. After a couple of hours' sleep, I got up and fixed myself a cup of tea.

It was late morning, but there was still a bite of cold in the air. It reminded me of home in the fall, and I opened the door to let the fresh cool air in. If Willie had been there when I got back, he was gone now. I was alone and I hummed a bit to myself as I got dressed and waited for the water to boil. I actually felt more cheerful than I had in ages. I could have gone down to the hall to get something to eat, but I decided against it.

As long as I stayed in my cottage alone, I could continue to enjoy the feeling of loving and being loved. I didn't have to worry about loving the wrong man, or going against whatever magic had told us he was the wrong man. I could just think of Rab and how it felt to have him beside me. The rest of the problems that came with loving Rab could wait. I would just enjoy what was left of the morning.

I took my cup of tea and leaned in the doorway to drink it looking out over the glen. We could see most of the glen from our cottage high up on the hillside. The village was quiet that morning, no doubt there were a few folks hung over from the night before. The damp chill air left patches of mist clinging to the lower part of the glen near the burn.

Suddenly, the door to the hall banged open and Jock came running out with a ladle in his hand. He shot across the burn and up the hill to Aunt Eilidh's house, where he banged on the door with a meaty fist. She came to the door in her nightgown, still rubbing her eyes. I couldn't hear what was said, but Aunt Eilidh grabbed a shawl and hurried down the hill and to the hall.

Jock's ruckus had awakened some people in the houses near the hall, and some people began to drift over. When those early arrivals came running back out and started knocking on cottage doors to rouse their families and neighbors, I put my teacup down and went to see for myself what was going on.

I pushed my way through the buzzing crowd in the hall to find Jock standing triumphantly in front of a table that held every available pot full to the brim with stew. It smelled like the venison stew that we'd had the night before. "Get ye a bowl everyone and test it for yerselves. It's back!"

People were taking bowls and spooning stew from the cauldron, the whole crowd of them. I went to Jock. "Did this all come from the cauldron?"

"Aye lassie, it did," he beamed, and the twinkle in his eyes put me in mind of Santa Claus. He stepped away from the table and turned to me. "I came in to make some porridge, thinking that the early risers might need something hearty in their bellies after last night. I went to scrape out the cauldron of what was left of the stew and it just kept coming. Every time I put my spoon in, it came up full. I filled all those pots, and it's still got plenty."

His joy, everyone's joy, was contagious. I looked around the hall, and everyone I saw was smiling and laughing as if last night's party had never ended. Well, nearly everyone. Aunt Eilidh looked puzzled. Oh, she smiled and ate and laughed with the others, but when she thought no one was looking I saw her staring at the cauldron in confusion.

***

Willie didn't know what to make of this miraculous recovery. After everyone had eaten their fill and drifted away to celebrate on their own, I found him in the hall examining the cauldron. Several of us watched as we cleared away the dishes. He walked around it. Rapped on the outside with a large spoon. He crouched down to look beneath it. He stood over it, shifting its contents around as if he were looking for a hole.

I actually felt a little sorry for him. When the cauldron was not at full strength, he could cling to the idea that the outsiders in his village were the cause of the trouble. Now, with the cauldron working as it had before, some said it was even better, and the outsiders still present and still employing their modern ways, there was no support for his belief that we were responsible. I wasn't sure what he would do when he fully understood that what he believed was not the truth.

When we were done cleaning up, he was sitting at our usual table looking at the cauldron. I took him a cup of tea. "Here. You look like you could use this."

He took the cup without a word and without looking up. I sat down across from him, and we stayed there in silence for a few minutes. Eventually he spoke softly, almost like he didn't want the cauldron to hear. "I canna understand it."

"You're not alone there. I think everyone is as puzzled as you are." For the first time in months, he was talking to me rather than scowling and hurling insults.

His mouth worked in that way he had of working up to speaking. "The legend is clear. If we keep to the auld ways," and he brought the side of his hand down on the table in a soft chopping motion, "we will live in plenty. The cause must be from the outsiders with their modern ways."

This was tricky territory, I knew. This had been his beef since the cauldron stopped. "Well, even in America, my mother and I kept to the old ways the best we could. We kept the feast days and lived in harmony with the mountains. I don't see the things we've done here as so modern. People have been doing these things for hundreds of years."

"I ken that," he said, nodding, his eyes still on the cauldron. "Ye would have saved us. If it hadn't come back, yer food would have saved us. I hated ye. Thought ye..." He shook his head, never taking his eyes off the cauldron. "Everything I believed was wrong."

"You were just trying to find an explanation and you picked the simplest one. That's perfectly natural."

"I was wrong." His eyes shifted to mine, and they were so full of confusion that I hurt for him.

I reached across the table and laid my hand on his. "You were caught up in why it stopped. It's normal to want to understand and to want to blame someone. But understanding doesn't put food on the table. We were just worrying about how to deal with it and what to do next. We didn't change our ways, we just dealt with the situation at hand."

"Don't you want to know why it stopped?"

"To be honest, I have a hard time believing that it does what it does in the first place. I don't understand how it works. So how could I even think about how it got broken? I was just trying to help hold the community together." I paused. "Back where I'm from, a little boy wandered off from a trail and got lost on the mountain. Everyone helped with the search. When no one had found him after a day, his family started pointing fingers at each other. His daddy wanted to know why his mama hadn't been watching him. His mama said it wouldn't have been a problem if his daddy had taken him fishing like he promised instead of going out drinking with his buddies. The sheriff didn't think people were looking hard enough, and the preacher didn't think people were praying hard enough. Eventually, I got so tired of all the bickering and fighting that I used my gift to figure out where he was. He had fallen down a ravine and hurt his leg so he couldn't climb back up. I was only a kid, so I couldn't be part of the search. But I told my Mama what I saw and she worked it out so that he was found soon enough. I guess what I'm saying is that if you worry too much about why a problem happens, you'll miss finding the solution. Knowing why only matters for making sure it doesn't happen again."

"How do we make sure this doesn't happen again?" he asked, his voice hoarse with emotion.

"That's a very good question. I'd say we solved the immediate problem, so now we can try to figure out why. Have you thought of any other reason why it might have stopped?"

"Someone broke faith." He looked down at the table, scraping a blunt thumbnail back and forth along the grain of the wood. He was deep in thought. "For the cauldron to stop like that, someone had to break faith."

"Okay." I wasn't so sure of that, but you know I was never one to stand on religion. "I can see why you might have thought the outsiders were the cause. But if we eliminate that, what's left?"

He continued worrying the same spot on the table. His mouth worked like he was chewing on a question. "Dunno."

"Was any other incident around midsummer that could have made the cauldron stop, or made someone lose faith?"

Willie shook his head slowly, thinking. "I think I might know someone who can help."

He stared at the cauldron, deep in thought. After several minutes, he rose and started walking toward the door muttering. I couldn't really hear what he said, but I thought I heard the words "green man."

It was near to a week before I saw him again.

***

Rab and I began meeting regularly in the ruins near the pool, at the castle, in the root cellar, just about anywhere that we could steal a few minutes alone. There wasn't much opportunity for us to scrape together more than a few stolen kisses.

We were at the ruined croft late one night, snuggled up under our coats on a bed of moss when he said to me, "I saw ye that day, ye ken?"

"What day?" I asked, my eyes heavy with satisfaction.

"That day in Ullapool, when ye ran from us." He brushed some of the hair back from my face. "When we were looking for ye in my car, I saw ye behind me on the street. I didna say a thing. Part of me hoped ye got away."

"And the other part?" I snuggled closer, resting my head on his shoulder.

"The other part wondered if we couldn't both get away." He squeezed me to him.

"Is Sheila really all that bad?" I sometimes bristled at the way Sheila acted like she owned the village, but she wasn't a bad person.

"I dinna suppose so, but I've known her all my life." I felt his shoulder lift in a shrug under my head. "And she isna you, bride of my heart."

Late one afternoon, I was walking back to the village after meeting Rab at the castle. We were always careful not to walk back together. Near the ridge that led to the village, an arm snaked out from a rocky outcropping and pulled me off the trail. He scared me half to death. "Do you think I don't know what you're doing?"

I sighed and looked up into the angry face of Grant MacDuff. "Well, I did hope you were busy, but I guess that would be too much to ask."

"Oh, I've been busy. Busy following you to every hidey hole you could find. It's my job, remember?" He hovered over me like an angry big brother.

"Fine. So you know." I made to go around him back to the path, but he blocked me.

"I've got news for you, sweetheart. I've known all along. And if I could figure it out, you better believe your aunt and cousin are gonna figure it out too. I wouldn't want to be you when they do." He gave my shoulders a good sharp shake.

"I know." I let my shoulders slump under his hands, deflated. "I hate lying to them, but…I love him, Duff. And I'm tired of everyone else making choices for me. I choose him."

His face softened and he let go of my shoulders, smoothing his hands down my arms, "Oh, honey. There's no question you drew the short straw here, but I don't think you can trust Rab."

"You're wrong. He loves me."

"I'm sure he says that, and maybe he does. But do you really think you can count on him when somebody other than me finds out about the two of you?"

"What's the worst they can do, Duff?" I gave him a pointed look. "Oh please, don't let them throw me in *that* briar patch."

He blew out a breath and turned away. He looked out over the hills with his hands on his hips. "Just be careful."

"I will." I moved away from the rock and stood close to him. "I may not like this situation, but I don't want to hurt anybody. I don't like going behind Sheila's back and neither does he."

"Hasn't stopped you from doing it," he muttered.

It hurt to hear, but he was right. I knew it was wrong, but I couldn't help myself. "You know what the last few months have been like for me. I've been miserable. All my plans were ruined. I've been living with someone who hates me. Can you blame me for wanting just a little bit of happiness? I really love him, Duff. I wish it wasn't like this."

"I'm just afraid that little bit of happiness is going to cause even more misery." He put an arm around me. "I don't want to see you get hurt."

I leaned my head on his shoulder. "I'm already hurt. I'm just trying for something better."

CHAPTER THIRTY-FIVE

December 25, 1995
Chapel Hill, North Carolina

Sarah straightened her shoulders and took a deep breath before ringing the doorbell. This would either go well or terribly, but she couldn't stand the idea of spending Christmas alone when there was family nearby. She had already fed Fleming and Curtis. Fleming had promptly gone back to their flat on Rosemary Street to sleep. Curtis had wanted to spend the rest of the day on the couch watching football, so he hadn't liked it much when Sarah announced that she wanted to take some food to a friend.

"But it's Christmas," he had said, as if that was enough justification for sitting on the couch all day.

"I know that." She knew he was due for a day off, but there was something she had to do. "I'm sorry to drag you out of your turkey stupor, but a friend of mine is all alone today. I thought I would take him some food. What could be more Christmas-y than that?"

He hadn't offered an argument. He had risen from the couch and given her a narrow-eyed look as he reached for his coat.

His reaction to going out on Christmas Day was nothing compared to his reaction when she had told him that he couldn't come inside with her. When she had told him that she wanted to stay out of sight, he exploded, "Aw, hell no!"

"Shh, I don't think people on the next block heard you," Sarah whisper-yelled.

"I don't care." He shook his head and leaned closer. "You want me to let you walk alone up to a house, and go inside with a man I don't know? That would make me the worst bodyguard in the history of bodyguards. If anything happened to you—"

"Nothing is going to happen to me. The man in that house is the cop who saved my life three weeks ago. He is the last person in this world who would hurt me."

His eyebrows drew together. "You don't know that."

"I do," Sarah whispered, leaning closer to him. "I've actually known him for a long time. He doesn't like a lot of attention for what he does and he's very private, which is why I need you to stay in the car. He won't hurt me, but he also might not answer the door if he sees someone he doesn't know standing on his porch."

"Sarah, I've already screwed up once with that reporter. You're asking me to take too much of a chance here," he said, his head shaking.

In the end, they compromised. Curtis walked her to the door with the box of food and then retreated to the car before she rang the doorbell. Sarah supposed that made him feel better. At least she wouldn't be accosted on the completely empty residential street.

While she waited, she let her eyes drift around his little porch, which wasn't much more than a covered stoop. Duff lived in a little mid-century brick-front Cape Cod on a street lined with other mid-century Cape Cods with striped aluminum awnings over their concrete iron-railed stoops. The bench that

Curtis had set the food on seemed to have been made from a shipping pallet and bicycle parts. There were wind chimes made of copper pipes hanging from the awning.

The wind chimes reminded her of Duff's cabin in the holler. He had always loved to build things out of the junk he collected on his summer rambles. The wide porch of the cabin had been lined with gadgets and things that he'd made out of anything he thought would work together.

This little house didn't look much like that ancient rough cabin, but it had touches that were definitely Duff. If she had seen it before today, she might have guessed he lived there. But she suspected that he lived just far enough off campus to be comfortable without having to worry about her walking by one day and figuring it out.

She heard the door open and turned to find Duff giving her a wary look. He stepped out and looked up and down the street. He was wearing jeans and a flannel shirt that looked more like what she was used to seeing him in than his police uniform. Of course, now he was clean-shaven and his hair was cut short, not at all like the Duff of her childhood. "Are you alone?"

"My protection is in the car over there." She jerked her head back in the direction of the car. She did feel bad about leaving Curtis out there, but she had some things to ask Duff that didn't need an audience.

He gave her a wary look. "I don't want to get caught up in that mess again."

She smiled and batted her eyes in a show of mock innocence. "Well, when I heard that the police officer who saved my life was spending Christmas alone, I just couldn't stand for that."

"Hmph." He glanced into the house and then back at her. "I'm not really prepared for company."

A grin spread across her face. "I'm not company. I'm family." She waved to the box on the bench. "And I brought dinner."

Sarah held her breath, hoping he would invite her in. He looked at the box, but didn't make a move.

"Please, Duff." She hated the crack in her voice and hoped he hadn't noticed it.

He looked up and she saw that his warm brown eyes were swimming with emotion. They were full of fear and joy and everything in between, but above all there was a longing that matched her own. This man was her father by love if not by blood, and he wasn't going to deny that. He cleared his throat and bent to pick up the box and carry it inside.

Sarah took a second to catch her breath. She tilted her head back, willing the tears not to fall. A breeze blew by and the clapper for the wind chimes hit a large copper pipe with a resonant bong that she felt in her heart.

She turned back to the car and gave Curtis a thumbs-up before following Duff inside. She found him in the small kitchen. His house was neat and orderly but utilitarian. His cabin had always been that way too. Now that he had invited her in, Sarah found herself chattering nervously. "I brought turkey and stuffing, sweet potatoes, green beans, collards, and blackberry pie."

"You made all of this?" He looked shocked.

She wrinkled her nose. "I got used to Christmas with a big family. I might have gotten carried away."

"You usually spend Christmas with that friend of yours, don't you?" he asked as he started unpacking the food.

"Amy? Yeah, but then my stalker pretended to be her boyfriend for months. She really thought they had something, so reconciling herself to the idea that it was all a lie is taking some time. Plus, her grandfather had a stroke a couple of weeks ago. They've got their own family drama going on without me bringing mine to their door."

He stopped in the act of getting the plates and studied her. "It's not your fault, you know. You didn't do anything wrong."

She couldn't stop the short laugh that bubbled up. "So everyone keeps telling me, including my steward."

He went back to assembling the plates and silverware. "He seems capable."

Sarah started lifting the covers off the food. She had gotten up early to cook everything but the pie, which she had made the night before. It was all still warm. "Hmm, that's one word for it."

Duff looked like he might pursue the subject, but didn't say anything else.

Sarah ducked out of the kitchen and carried some food to his small dining room table. She stopped a minute to look around at his sparse furnishings. The dining room opened through a wide archway to the living room. His furniture looked secondhand, but it all had his stamp. As different as he looked from the outcast drifter who had helped raise her, she knew the man who lived here.

Still, it was so hard to know how much to say and how much to hold back. It had been almost seven years since they'd really talked. There was this familiarity that made her want to confide everything to him, but given everything she'd been reading in her mother's journal, there was also a strangeness that caused her to hold back.

She went back to the kitchen to get more food. Duff had stopped what he was doing and braced his hands on the counter. His face was raised to the ceiling and she could see the muscles in his shoulders bunched with tension.

"Duff?" Was having her there hurting him? "I can g—"

He didn't let her finish. He reached her in one stride and wrapped his arms around her tight. His voice was thick with tears. "Don't even think about leaving me now."

Sarah felt herself dissolve into tears. The warmth of his arms, something that she hadn't felt since she was a child, melted her nerves.

By the time their tears slowed to a trickle and the sniffling stopped, the food had gotten cold.

***

"Have you had any luck trying to find the leak in the police department?" Sarah asked as she grasped the coffee cup. For the first time in years, Sarah was with someone who knew her history because he had been there. She didn't have to hide anything from Duff. She didn't have to choose what to tell him about her past, or what to filter out. Above all, he didn't have an agenda for her. He didn't want her to do anything or be anything that she wasn't. Sarah shifted her grip to the handle of the mug and leaned back on the couch, relaxing for the first time in weeks.

Duff settled down with his own coffee, crossing his legs and resting the mug on his knee. He stretched one arm across the back of the sofa and shook his head. His mouth was a grim line of frustration. "No. Our captain has read the riot act to the whole station. He's questioned everyone who had access to the information connecting your situation with the murder of Bridget MacKenzie. They're all afraid to talk to reporters about the weather now, let alone an actual crime."

"Well, let's hope that at least plugs the leak, even if that particular horse has already left the barn."

"Let's hope so," Duff agreed, though he didn't sound optimistic. He fidgeted with a quilt that was laid over the back of the couch.

The quilt was in the geometric tree of life pattern and from the different stripes and plaids looked to be made of men's shirts. "Is this one of Granny's?"

"Mmhmm, she made it for me the second winter I was on the mountain. You were just a baby when we came up with our distribution plan, and that November when I came back after my first summer away, she had that waiting for me. I think it was my reward for coming back."

Sarah rubbed a hand along one of the triangles. "I wonder where she got the shirts."

Duff studied the quilt as if the answer would be there. "I think some of them belonged to her steward. She probably traded for the rest. You know Maggie wouldn't have bought them special just to quilt."

Sarah gave an amused snort. "If nothing else she was always thrifty."

He laughed. "I think that's putting it mildly."

They enjoyed their coffee in silence for a few minutes. Finally, Sarah had to ask, "Why did you come back all those years?"

He let out a long breath, weighing his words. "At first I admit it was kind of selfish. I just kept hoping that your mama would snap out of it." He shifted uncomfortably. "You know, that she would wake up one day and see that I was someone she could count on, maybe love. After she…" He stopped again and took a longer breath. "By the time she left us, I stayed for you. You've been my baby girl in everything but name since you were born. I couldn't leave you when you still needed me."

She watched him and saw the truth in his eyes. "I'll always need you, Duff."

"Not as much as you think. Besides, I was afraid that me being around would lead the wrong people to you. It's easy to live off the grid when you work day labor and live in the hills. It's a lot harder in a town like Boone or Chapel Hill. I had to lay low so no one who knew what I was could follow me to you."

Sarah shook her head. "They found me anyway."

"I know, baby." He rested a hand on her knee. "I think that it would have happened no matter what your mama or I did."

"Well, you had a much nicer way of preventing it." She shrugged, studying the rim of her mug.

Duff gave her a look that had her stomach curling with guilt. "Don't be hard on her memory."

"Could you help me?" she asked, running her thumb along the rim of her mug. "I mean, if I want to disappear like you did?"

He leaned back, eyebrows raised. "It's been a while since I've done something like that."

"I'm not looking to get you in trouble. I'm sure it's not something a cop should be doing. I just thought maybe you might know where I could go, Doug." She emphasized the fake first name he was currently using.

He arched an eyebrow at her in warning. "I didn't say I wouldn't help, just that it had been a long time. But I'm not sure running is your best option. Have you read the journal I gave you?"

"Some of it." She turned away and scanned his bookcase, unable to meet his eyes.

"How far have you gotten?" He looked tense.

"She just started sneaking around with Rab Ballantyne." Sarah kept her voice carefully even. "And the cauldron just started working again."

"You see how trying to run worked for her." Duff scooted forward on the couch and braced his elbows on his knees. He looked straight ahead at a point behind the dark television screen. "I'm surprised you're even talking to me. I'm not real proud of the role I played that year."

"The way Mama tells it, you didn't have much choice." Sarah watched his shoulders tighten and wished she could comfort him.

"That's what I told myself." Duff shook his head. "I thought at the time that I would be able to go back to the life I meant for myself, so did your Mama. When you're young like we were, it's a lot easier to cling to an idea so much that you don't recognize reality. People I looked up to told me I didn't have a choice, and I believed them."

"You don't think that now?"

He let out a long sigh. "I believe there's always a choice. Your mama taught me that. But every choice has a price. You have to decide whether what you want is worth the cost."

She let that idea settle in. She had seen the cost of her mother's choices and her mother's effort to swim against the stream. Had it been worth it in the end? It had only brought her misery. "Where are they, Mama's people?"

He shook his head with regret. "Near a place called Inchnadamph, in the hills. If your Granny didn't tell you more than that, I can't either. That's for your protection and theirs. When you go to Scotland, you'll find them or they'll find you."

"Well, that's very cryptic. Thanks," she huffed in frustration.

"I'm sorry." He looked it. "That's just how it is."

She didn't ask another question until she felt her frustration was under control. She didn't want to argue. When she was calm enough, she broached the next question. "What can you tell me about Rab Ballantyne?"

He arched an eyebrow at her. His voice was flat. "Not much. He was handsome. I guess he was kind of charming. Your mother loved him."

"You don't sound like you thought very much of him." She watched a wave of bitterness pass over his face like a cloud.

He shook his head. "Keep reading. You'll see why."

She squeezed his arm. "You stuck by Mama."

He covered her hand with his. It was warm. His blunt fingers were strong, nails clean. A memory flashed in her mind of watching him working on his old pickup truck, his hands covered in grease and dirt. He had been a chameleon and she had never known. He smiled softly. "I did. I was sworn to."

"You said you loved her. Did she ever…" She let her voice trail off, not finishing the question.

"No." He leaned back and fidgeted, rubbing a hand over his knee. "I don't think she thought of me that way. I always hoped. But by the time I think her heart healed, her mind was broken."

Even then, he hadn't left her. He had stayed longer than usual that awful year, when all of their lives had revolved around Molly's breakdowns. He had always been there and had always been patient. Sarah couldn't think of a more dedicated love. She wondered if Dermot would show that kind of dedication.

"Do all stewards fall in love with the women they protect?"

"Aw damn." He leaned forward and put his cup on the coffee table before turning to face her. He pinned her with a grave look. "Is he in love with you?"

She nodded, afraid to speak.

His voice turned gentle and he leaned down to meet her eyes. "Are you in love with him?"

Another nod and Sarah started to feel the all-too-familiar burn of tears.

"Listen to me, baby girl, and listen good." He held her hand in both of his. "They've found you, and they're not going to let go. If you run, you'll be running for the rest of your lives, and that will very likely ruin what you have. You have to choose whether or not you want that life."

Sarah tightened her jaw and lifted her chin. "Haven't I been running for the last twenty-six years? The only difference is now I know it."

"You don't know it all yet." He looked resigned. "Hell, I don't know the whole story, and I was there. I reckon the only way to learn the whole story is to talk to the other folks involved."

"And that would mean going to Scotland, which is exactly what the Stuarts want," she said grimly.

"How much is it worth to you to know the whole story?"

"Seeing as I just found out, I think I can live without that. The real question is, can I live without him?" Sarah leaned back and rested her head against the back of the couch, suddenly feeling very tired.

Duff picked up their coffee cups and rose to take them to the kitchen. He stopped in the doorway and turned back. "Like I said, there's always a cost."

CHAPTER THIRTY-SIX

November 1968
Làrachd an Fhamhair, Scotland

The creaking of the ladder woke me. In the orange glow of the peat fire, I saw the outline of a person coming down from the loft. My heart was in my throat. I hadn't seen Willie since the day after Samhain. To my knowledge, he hadn't been home in all that time. Our last conversation had been relatively peaceful, though he had been troubled. He was hard to read on a regular day, but when he'd been gone for days and upset before that, there was no telling what he might do.

I sat up in the bed and pulled the quilt up to my neck. He reached the bottom of the ladder and our eyes met. He was half in shadow, but unlike the times he had watched me before he didn't seem angry. He had a bag slung over his shoulder. "I'm leaving."

I didn't know what to say to that. I didn't want Willie, but I didn't want to hurt him either. I just nodded.

"I'm not your match. I think you know that." He didn't come closer, so it was hard for me to read him. He held a hand up. The meager light from the fire glinted off something metal dangling from his fingers. "I just came back for my locket. It was my mam's. She died."

"I know," I breathed, afraid to startle him.

"Right. She was a good woman. But she lost faith in the auld way. I thought you had too. I was wrong." He paused, his brows drawing together as he forced the words out.

I relaxed a little. I didn't think he was going to hurt me. "It's okay. We're all wrong sometimes."

"Sometimes people get in our way. They're wrong." He closed his hand around the locket and gripped it tight. "I'm sorry."

He opened the door and gave me a last look. When he had closed the door, I counted to ten. Then I got up and climbed to the loft. All of Willie's things were gone: clothes, shoes, everything but the sleeping pallet. He had really left. The question is, where was he going?

When I climbed back down the ladder, I noticed the light was different, brighter. I looked around. I looked out the window across the glen to see bright light coming from Aunt Eilidh's cottage. I went closer to my window, thinking maybe she was up late. My stomach clenched when I realized the flames were too bright to be from the fireplace or a lantern. My aunt's house was on fire. I grabbed a shawl and ran into the frigid night.

As I ran, I knocked on every door I passed, shouting for help. The villagers sprang into action, with me grabbing buckets and running down the hill to the burn. We ran across the bridge and up to Aunt Eilidh's. She was coming out of the cottage, coughing and sputtering as the moss roof began steaming.

"She broke it!" Willie screamed from just up the hill. He was holding a torch that lit up his wild eyes. He pointed to Aunt Eilidh, who was huddled and coughing with Jock and Sheila. "She's the one. She broke it."

Davie and Gavin shot up the hillside after him. He dropped the torch and ran. He was smaller than them, but quick. He ducked around some rocks and skipped up and down, back and forth. All the time he kept shouting, "She broke it. Eilidh broke it."

The rest of us quickly formed a bucket brigade from the burn to the cottage. It was apparent that not much more than the walls would be saved. However he had started the fire, it had spread too quickly for our buckets to stop it. Everything inside was a loss. The wet weather meant that the turf and moss of the roof wouldn't burn, but the timbers inside were so weakened that part of the roof caved in.

By the time we gathered in the hall, the sun was coming up. We handed out water for everyone's smoke-raw throats. Sheila was treating Aunt Eilidh's burned feet and ankles. When she was asked what happened, her voice sounded like tearing paper. I could tell by the way she hesitated and grimaced that it hurt to speak. After minimal talking and lots of pointing and gestures, we got most of the story.

Willie had snuck into the cottage and poured the contents of an oil lamp onto the floor while Eilidh slept. When she woke, the floor and curtains had been on fire. No one had heard him shouting or even seen him until we were all gathered trying to put out the fire. He had eventually made it over the ridge. When Davie and Gavin thought they were close to catching him, he disappeared.

Almost everyone agreed that Willie was mad, though I wasn't so sure. I told them he had come to the cottage earlier and taken his things. He had seemed calm and regretful, but not upset or deranged. I had seen him upset before. He had made me afraid before, but not that night.

"You said last week that he was upset by the cauldron coming back," Duff said.

"I don't know if I'd say upset, more confused," I answered. Everyone within hearing was listening closely. "He was so sure that he knew what had caused the cauldron to stop. When it started again, I mean when it really took off after Samhain, it proved him wrong. He couldn't quite understand that. I think it had him questioning a lot of things. I tried to talk to him to get him to just appreciate that it was working again, but he left. I didn't see him again before tonight. Did anyone else see him?"

I looked around the group, but everyone was shaking their heads. Willie had left the village a week ago and had come back only to get his things and set Aunt Eilidh's cottage on fire. And he was still out there.

The men decided there would have to be watches set up, and that teams would go out during the day to search for Willie. Aunt Eilidh was carried to Sheila and Rab's cottage. We girls went with her to make sure she was comfortable and help Sheila. I was making some tea to mix with honey for her throat when I felt Aunt Eilidh's eyes on me. She didn't look angry, more thoughtful. I don't know what she was thinking, and I didn't want to ask her to talk. I figured if it was that important, she would make the effort or write it down. She didn't.

***

The next three months were spent in a state of constant watchfulness. Everyone was looking for Willie outside the village and in. It was like he stalked us, though he didn't do anything else to harm anyone after burning Eilidh's cottage. Sometimes people would go out to get peat for their fires and find their stacks smaller than they should be. There were a couple of times that one of us would go to the root cellar to see empty spots on shelves that should have held food. Several times I tried to find him with my gift, but it never worked. It was like he just wasn't there anymore.

Occasionally, he would play with the men on watch. He might appear and lead them on a chase, only to disappear before he could be caught. Rab soon learned this was the best time to come and find me. The watches made it difficult for us to meet, but Willie's harrying of the watch gave us a few opportunities.

"Ugh! I thought I'd never see ye alone," he groaned as he pushed me against the wall in one of the root cellars. His mouth came crashing down on mine, and he kissed me with a hunger that only comes from absence.

"I know," I said between kisses and gasps. "Be quick, I need you."

I did. The winter was starting to make me feel even more alone. I was isolated in my house, with no one but the watch to check on me. They did that regularly, wondering if Willie would come back to the cottage. But the rest of the time there was little work to do. Rona was suffering from terrible morning sickness and spent a lot of time in bed. Sheila was tending to her mother. That left me alone to spin yarn, knit, and help Jock with the meals. There wasn't much else to do in the winter. I needed the connection that I felt with Rab, with anyone.

After we had stolen some time together, I got to hear about the state of things in his house. Aunt Eilidh was a demanding patient, but she was also afraid. "Every sound outside the cottage makes her skittish. She's sure Willie will come back for her. It doesna help to hear the watch calling out when he makes his little forays around the village. He's got her fair fleggit."

"I know how she feels. I woke up quite a few times and caught him watching me while I slept." I hadn't told anyone about those times, not even Duff.

Rab leaned back and looked sharply at me. "Not recently? He hasna come to ye since he ran off has he?"

I shook my head and nestled closer to him. "No, not since the night of the fire. I don't think he wants anything from me. I'm still not sure what he wants from Eilidh."

"Me neither." He rested his cheek on the top of my head. He must have been thinking of it, because a minute later he said, "I think she knows, though. And maybe Sheila does too. I catch them whispering sometimes. They dinna do it when I'm near, but when I catch them at it, I can see the guilt in Sheila and she willna look at me."

"I wonder what that's about."

"Aye. I'll have to listen a mite closer."

If he ever learned what they were whispering about, he never said. I did wonder about it, especially when Aunt Eilidh finally emerged from their cottage one day to come to tea. It was almost Yule. She had been inside and out of sight of most of the village for weeks. Her feet were mostly healed, but the burns seemed to have done some damage to the muscles. Now she walked with the help of a wooden cane that Jock had made her.

Bent over the cane and having spent weeks inside, she came out paler than usual. Dark circles of worry sat below her eyes, and she was thinner, gaunt. Her hair was still fiery red, but now there were a few streaks of white, and she had pulled it back away from her face to hide them. Where she had been willowy and ethereal before, now she was bent and haggard.

She walked with an awkward gate, leading with the cane and following with a shuffle of her sore feet.

Her reappearance was greeted with a mix of joy and horror. We were all happy that she was with us, but horrified by what happened to the beautiful, benevolent matriarch we all knew. Just as stark as the change in her appearance was the change in her demeanor. She was no longer the mother figure who organized and led with her kind words and gentle wisdom. Now she barked and grunted and demanded things. She looked at everyone but Sheila and Jock with suspicion, especially me.

I would often catch her watching me from across the table as if she was waiting for me to give something away or confess something. It was like she thought I sent Willie to burn her out. I found it very unsettling and made a conscious effort to avoid her.

***

"When are we going to be able to stop sneaking around?" I asked Rab one day after we'd had a tryst downstream from the village. Our opportunities to meet were dwindling as the weather grew colder. We were lying in a patch of brown reeds near the water. Even with his coat underneath us and mine over us, we were freezing and huddled close to each other. If anyone came upon us, there would be no mistaking the situation, but people didn't wander about as much now.

"Och, that's not an easy question." He looked in the direction of the village. "I'm here until Sheila…well, ye know."

"I know." I tried not to sound hurt by it. I knew he was likely still sleeping with Sheila, but I didn't have to like it.

376 · MEREDITH R. STODDARD

He tightened his arms around me and kissed the top of my head. "Aye, well. We havena had many chances for that with Eilidh sharing our little cottage. There isna much privacy with only a loft to separate us. I dinna fancy making love with my mother-in-law a few feet away. And Sheila? Well, she hasna felt much like it since the fire. Even when we're not around Eilidh, she doesna want to."

"Hmm…It's funny. Part of me is glad to hear that, because I want you all to myself, and part of me hates hearing that because it means you're stuck here even longer."

"What about you? They canna expect ye to have a child with Willie now, but there have to be three sisters."

I blew out a breath and rested my head on his collarbone. "I wish I knew. When I talked to Aunt Eilidh about choosing a different match she wouldn't hear of it. I have no idea what she'll say now, but I think you're right. They can't expect it to be Willie anymore."

He smoothed the hair back from my temple and sighed. "I ken what ye mean. I'm glad ye are na sleeping with anyone else, but I know it may need to happen."

"Yeah," I grumbled. "At least you don't have to look every day at the person I'm supposed to be sleeping with."

He pushed me away so he could look into my eyes. "But I did. I might not have told ye how I craved ye then, but thinking of ye and knowing that he might have his hands on ye. It was eating me alive."

I could tell that he meant it. I thought about those months of misery when he hadn't said anything about how he felt. We had lost so much time and were losing more. "You haven't answered my question. When can we be together without having to sneak around?"

"I can't tell, but we'll make a plan. Whichever of us leaves here first should wait for the other. Once we're away from here, we can live how we like and no one can say aught about it."

"Where? Where should we meet out there?" I needed to know, to have something to look forward to. I needed something to cling to so my heart wouldn't break every night he went home to Sheila.

"Inverness," he said after a minute's thought. "There's a statue of Flora MacDonald in front of the castle. We can meet there."

"When?" I pressed.

"What d'ye mean, when? We canna tell that now." I could tell he was getting impatient, but we needed to have a plan.

"We should set a time, every week. So whoever leaves first should just wait there every week for…an hour, eventually the other will meet them there."

He thought about that for a bit before nodding. "Aye, that's fine. Say every Monday at four o'clock."

"There you go." It was a small thing. Just a day and a time with no specific date, but something to hand on to. "Mondays at four. Until we're both free."

He kissed me slowly. "Until we're both free."

CHAPTER THIRTY-SEVEN

December 25, 1995
Chapel Hill, North Carolina

Sarah yawned hugely, feeling her ears pop and the muscles down the back of her neck tingle. Cooking all that food had worn her out. Her eyelids were getting heavy, and Molly's handwriting was starting to blur. She put the journal on the nightstand and turned off the lamp. It was the earliest she'd gone to sleep since she started reading Molly's account of her time in Scotland. She might actually get a good night's sleep for once.

She fluffed her pillow and laid down on her back, hoping sleep would come quickly. Closing her eyes, she took a few deep breaths. Then she started thinking. It was just like her busy brain to start churning as soon as she closed her eyes. Usually it was about things she needed to do the next day. This time it was Willie Cross and his campaign of harassment. She could sympathize. After Beth Cartwright had accosted her in the bathroom the other day, she had begun to worry that the reporter might be hidden around every corner.

She hadn't been going to the library as much. Molly's memoir had been enough to keep her occupied. But the few times she had ventured out, she had been on edge, like having her own personal boogie-woman. So close on the heels of Ryan Cumberland, Sarah was starting to think she would never be free of someone dogging her heels. She vaguely wondered what Cartwright was doing now. How did she sleep at night?

Of course, Sarah didn't have to wonder. She could see what Beth Cartwright was doing if she wanted to. She could use her gift, although she hadn't used it before without knowing where the person she wanted to look at was first. Mama had, though. Maybe it was time she tried. She was already halfway there; her body was relaxed at least.

She took a deep breath and tried to focus her mind. With each exhale, she grew lighter, until she felt like she might float away. She first thought of Fleming in the other room. She could see him on the couch, watching American football with the sound turned way down. As a test she focused on Curtis and breathed. Soon she could see him brushing his teeth in the tiny bathroom in Dermot's old apartment.

Of course, she could have imagined what the guys were doing. After a couple of weeks of living in each other's pockets, she knew their routines pretty well. Would it work for someone like Beth Cartwright who she barely knew? There was only one way to find out.

Sarah took a deep breath and pictured the reporter's face in her mind. She could almost feel herself being pulled toward something. The lights of the town sped past her in a blur. Things went dark, and Sarah felt herself slowing down. Light began to filter into her vision, ghosts of shapes rimmed with a warm glow. Ambient sound hummed, punctuated by occasional sharp noises of laughter or a musical clinking. Slowly the shapes resolved themselves into people. The glow was coming from behind a bar with liquor bottles arranged in front of a mirrored wall.

A woman in a black cocktail dress leaned provocatively to whisper into the ear of a man on the stool next to her. Dressed up and wearing dramatic makeup, Sarah almost didn't recognize Beth Cartwright. She watched the reporter put an arm around the shoulders of the man she was flirting with. She said something to him and he drank from a glass of amber liquor. He shook his head. He was wearing a very nice cashmere sweater over a collared shirt. His hair was dark and combed neatly. Sarah felt a tingle of recognition, but couldn't see his face. He put the drink down on the bar and turned to Cartwright. He slid an arm around the woman's waist and leaned close to whisper back to her.

Cartwright laughed loudly and leaned her head back, thrusting her breasts toward him in obvious invitation. He responded by ogling her cleavage, and Sarah saw his face in profile for the first time. That tingle of recognition became a full blown wave that crashed over her. It was no wonder she had made the connection between Sarah and Bridget and James. She'd gotten that information from the very man whose job it was to make sure it wasn't public knowledge. The man standing at the bar ogling the reporter who had been dogging her for weeks was none other than Martin Carol.

Sarah wanted to smack him, but of course she wasn't really there. She felt fury rising inside her. The strong emotion seemed to have her pulling away, as if it were drawing her back into her body. She looked around quickly, trying to find something to show where they were, something she could use to verify that what she was seeing was real. As she pulled away and up she spotted the tables in the bar. The napkins were printed with a gold letter T inside a circle. She had been in Chapel Hill long enough to know the logo of the Tryon Hotel.

Sarah slammed back into her body and sat up with a gasp. She struggled for a couple of minutes to catch her breath and wait for the room to stop spinning. When she got her equilibrium back she checked the clock. Twelve-thirty would be six-thirty in Edinburgh. She jumped out of bed and practically ran to the phone. Fleming was on his feet in a flash and beside her in one stride.

"It's okay." She held up a hand to stop him. "There's no danger, at least not to me. I think I know who our leaker is."

"How?"

"Just trust me," she said and dialed Dermot's number.

"Hello?" he answered on the second ring, sounding perfectly alert. She was glad he wasn't groggy.

"Hey, I know who the leaker is." The words tumbled out so fast she wasn't sure he'd understood her at first.

"What? How?"

"It doesn't matter how." She couldn't very well tell him it was because of a vision she'd had or astral projection or whatever name you put on her gift. "Just tell me this. Do you remember what hotel Martin Carol was staying at?"

"Why?" Still confused.

"Just…do you? Can you find out?" She had to verify that before she accused the man.

"I think I wrote it down," he said. "Hold on."

She waited, listening to some rustling and shuffling on the other end of the line. Fleming watched her, his brows drawn together halfway between confusion and irritation.

After what seemed way too long to Sarah, Dermot came back on the line. "It's the Tryon. Is that the one on Columbia Street?"

Sarah closed her eyes and gritted her teeth. "Yeah, it is. It's also the one where he was seen in the bar talking to Beth Cartwright."

"No," Dermot sounded incredulous. "Could he really be that stupid?"

"I have no idea. Maybe he doesn't know she's a reporter. It didn't look like they were talking business."

"Who did you say saw them?" She could hear the caution in his voice.

"I didn't, but it's someone I trust."

"Sarah, this will ruin his career. You dinna want to do that based on a rumor."

"Do you want this leak plugged or not? Listen, I hope I'm wrong. Ask him before you tell anyone else." Let him verify what she saw. "Tonight, he met a woman in the bar of the Tryon Hotel, a blonde in a very low-cut black dress. They looked very cozy, arms around each other. He was drinking something neat, whisky maybe."

"How do you know this?" he breathed in shock.

She sighed. "Maybe I'll tell you one day. Just ask him."

"Right. I'll ask him. Tryon Hotel, blonde, tits, black dress. Anything else?" He still sounded like he didn't believe her.

Sarah thought about any other information she could use to verify. "He was wearing a nice burgundy sweater. I think it was cashmere."

"Cashmere jumper, burgundy." She could hear his pen scratching as he wrote down the details. "I'll get in touch with him. What time is it there?"

"Around twelve-thirty." Having passed on what she saw, Sarah felt the energy drain from her shoulders. There was nothing else she could do about it short of going to the hotel herself.

"Alright, I've got the information. You should get some sleep, and tell Fleming he can relax. I've got it covered."

Sarah looked up at Fleming, who was still standing in front of her and watching closely. She gave him what she hoped was a reassuring smile. "Okay, thanks."

"No worries, cheers." The line went dead.

"Relax, there's nothing wrong. Just needed to pass that information along," she told him.

Fleming arched an eyebrow at her before stepping back. "Where did that information come from?"

She gave him a shuttered look. She didn't want to answer any more questions about that until what she had seen was verified. "A reliable source."

CHAPTER THIRTY-EIGHT

February 1969
Làrachd an Fhamhair, Scotland

Yule passed by and the weather grew even colder. Willie's harrying of the village slowed to only the occasional theft. There was a feast on a much smaller scale than we'd seen on Samhain, but we still had plenty to celebrate. Rona was starting to feel better, and she and Lachlan were planning to return to Canada come spring. Aunt Eilidh's walking improved the more exercise she got, but her temperament was a different matter. After weeks with her mother underfoot, Sheila's mood was foul just about all the time.

I took to spending even more time in my cottage. There wasn't much reason to leave. I would have thought that people would be friendlier to me after the cauldron started working again, but Willie and his antics had taken care of that. Now the whispers said that I had driven him mad. No one seemed to remember what he had been like before. I was tired of the whispers and tired of defending myself. I ate my meals and took hand work back with me to the cottage and spent my winter quietly working by the fire.

If the weather was good, Rona would come and visit, but when the snow and ice came she didn't want to risk the slippery path up the hillside. Eventually, the only daytime visitor I got was Duff. He would come by and make sure I had enough peat for the fire and nothing needed repairing. He'd try to get me to come down to the hall more often, but I didn't see much point.

I wasn't completely unhappy, though. With the nights longer and colder, fewer people were outside after dark, and some nights Rab managed to sneak away from Eilidh and Sheila's bickering to visit me. He took a roundabout route so no one saw him, and he'd come in after I'd put the lamp out. Those nights were magical. I much preferred making love in a bed than on moss or stone. Of course, he always left well before dawn. I longed to one day spend a lazy morning watching the sun rise in his arms like we had that first time.

Near mid-February, I began to suspect that you were with me. It started as a little nausea and a dizziness whenever I stood up. Finally, one morning, I couldn't get out of bed for feeling so sick. It passed eventually, but I decided that I didn't need to go down to the hall that day.

By evening, Duff was at my door. "Molly ?"

I opened the door. His worry showed on his face. "Hi, don't worry. I just wasn't feeling well."

He pushed his way in and put a hand on my forehead. "Are you sick? You don't feel warm."

"I'm not sick," I protested. "It's probably just something I ate."

He looked at me sharply. "You been eating something the rest of us haven't?"

"No, but that doesn't mean everything agrees with me." I rolled my eyes, hoping to brush off his concern. "I'll be fine."

He gave me a look that said he wasn't sure he believed me. "I'll bring in some peat bricks."

"Thank you," I said, turning away to hang the kettle over the fire. I usually made tea and he would visit for a little while.

I didn't want to break that routine. I wasn't quite ready to admit what I thought was going on. I didn't want him getting suspicious.

He came back and stacked the peat near the fireplace. I made cups of tea, and we sat talking quietly about nothing important. It was good to get my mind off of things for a little bit.

Duff got up to leave, and I took the teacups to the basin to wash. I was just putting them in the basin when he said, "I think Eilidh is about ready to live on her own again."

I turned to look at him and must have missed the basin. One of the teacups fell to the floor. I bent quickly to get it. Fortunately, it only appeared to be chipped. When I stood up, my vision turned black around the edges, and I felt myself start to fall. I caught myself on the worktable, but not before Duff saw me.

He threw his arm around me and helped me to the settle. "That's it. I'm getting Eilidh."

"No!" I grabbed his arm.

He squatted in front of me until I met his eyes. "You're not sick, are you?"

Tears welled in my eyes, and I couldn't talk past the lump in my throat. It was the first time I had admitted it, and I just knew how disappointed he would be.

He shot to his feet and turned away from me, hands braced on his hips. I listened to him breathe for a minute, trying to calm himself down. He didn't turn around when he asked, "Does Rab know?"

"No." I looked down at my hands twisted together in my lap. "I just realized it myself."

"I'll tell him you need to talk to him," he said softly.

I don't know what I expected from Duff…the angry big brother routine from before, disappointment, judgment. But after that first burst of emotion, he didn't treat me any different. He helped me to a comfortable place by the fire and made sure I had everything I needed. "You can probably get away with staying up here today without raising any eyebrows, but you're going to have to come back down to the hall sometime tomorrow, or folks are going to get suspicious."

"You're right. I'll be down tomorrow if not for breakfast, then for tea," I said, feeling a little better.

"I'll talk to Rab," he said, resting a hand on my shoulder. "We'll figure it out."

***

I was feeling sick, and not from hormones. I had no idea how I was going to explain being pregnant. Rab had not come to see me the night before. I guess he hadn't been able to get away. I hoped I could keep the secret long enough to talk to him.

Keeping the line pure was so important to the whole community. How was I going to explain that I was pregnant when my designated match was nowhere around? No one would believe my baby was Willie's. Everyone knew we'd never been together, not really. Duff was right, though, the longer I stayed away, the more people would suspect something was going on.

I did my best to make myself look presentable and went down to the hall. I thought I had done a good job of looking and acting like everything was normal, but throughout the meal Aunt Eilidh kept staring at me. It made me even more nervous, and I definitely didn't need that. Other people at the table noticed her staring and started looking back and forth between us. Rab's brows were creased in concern.

I finished my meal and carried my bowl to the dry sink at the back of the hall. Within seconds, I heard the odd thump-shuffle sound that Aunt Eilidh made with her cane when she walked. I turned around and she stumped toward me. When she was close enough, she used her free hand and gripped my arm. She stared hard into my eyes for several seconds.

"Whose is it?" she ground out. Her green eyes were fierce.

"What?" I tried to move back, but her grip tightened like a vice.

"Ye ken well enough what I mean. Whose child is it?" She pulled me closer.

I was shocked. I had only told Duff, and I knew he wouldn't have told her. "How can you know?"

"I can see it on your face," she spat. "It's not Willie Cross's, ye whore. Who is the father?"

I wasn't about to tell her. I was sure Rab would stand up for me if the need arose. Still, if she hadn't called me a whore, I might have been more respectful in refusing. Instead I leaned forward until our noses almost touched and I looked her right in the eye and said, "I'm not telling you."

Her grip tightened until I thought she would leave bruises. She pulled me back toward the tables. We stopped by the fire near the center of the hall. She got everyone's attention by banging her cane on the side of the cauldron. At the clanging, people who were eating looked up. I turned as much as her bruising grip on my arm would allow. Duff rose, and the look in his eyes was dangerous.

"This brazen whore is with child," Aunt Eilidh said loud enough for every corner of the hall to hear. "She willna say who the father is. I think we all ken it's not the match that was chosen for her. Which one of ye is it?"

She looked around from man to man, but none answered. Some of them cringed. Some of their faces turned red as if they were embarrassed, but no one stepped forward.

"I will ask ye again." She let go of my arm and started thump-shuffling her way down the aisle, pinning each man she passed with a glare. "Who is the father of this woman's child?"

When her back was turned to me, I glanced at Rab. He was looking at the table in front of him. His hand was wrapped in a fist around his spoon. His knuckles were white. Aunt Eilidh turned to stump back toward me, and I shifted my eyes to the floor. "I ask ye all a third time. Who is the man who denied our prophecy, who broke our covenant, and made a child with this woman?"

This time some people whispered and mumbled. I looked around at people who had eaten food that I preserved, people who had cursed and scoffed at me before. If that cauldron hadn't come back, they might have starved but for my efforts. That meant nothing in the face of this. None of them would look me in the eye. I looked to the table where my sisters and the men sat. Rona and Lachlan looked at me, but their eyes were full of pity. I watched a slow, fat tear roll down Rona's cheek. Sheila just looked shocked, like she couldn't quite believe what she was hearing. Jock's head hung from his shoulders in disappointment. And Rab...Rab lifted his eyes to mine, but his look was so full of apology that I knew he wouldn't speak up.

Aunt Eilidh turned back to me. I was reminded of that first time I saw her and thought of her as half-fairy, half-gorgon. This day it must have been all gorgon because I felt frozen to the spot. She lifted her cane and pointed it at me across the fire. "This *sluagh ùr* trash has come into our community with her modern ways and her lack of faith. Her resistance caused our cauldron, which kept us fed for thousands of years, to stop giving food. She tried to escape us. She drives young Willie Cross mad rather than do her duty. She is poison in our well and should be cast out before she sickens us all."

"Now hold on a minute!" Duff's voice boomed out. He stepped around his table by the door and strode over to me. He placed his hands on my shoulders. "This woman doesn't know any more than you or I do about why that cauldron stopped working. And if it stopped working because of Molly, then why did it start again? That's the question that drove your Willie mad. Most of you know he was halfway there to begin with."

He shifted his eyes from one villager to another before holding up one finger and walking quickly to the shelves at the back. He returned in a flash with a jar of canned peas. "Now, you can cast her out. But if you think she's poison, you'll have to cast out every one of these jars of food, every piece of meat, every fish that she smoked. I watched her work like a dog for months while you," he pointed at Eilidh, "made her live with a madman who stalked her.

"If that cauldron weren't working today, this village would be surviving on the work that she did, even though you made her an outcast for it." He pointed at me. "You can call her poison, but she could have been the glue that held this bunch together. You would have had to crawl out of these hills to live on the charity of the new folk if it weren't for her. Some of y'all have done nothing but be hateful to her. You threw insults and even mud at her, and she still worked for you." He swung around to confront Aunt Eilidh. "How dare you call her poison? How dare you say she's not good enough?" He turned to Rab with a sneer. "How dare you?"

I could tell by looking at their faces that Duff's words were only working on a few people. Most of them looked stone-faced at me. I stepped forward and gently took the jar from his fingers. I set it on the nearest table. "It's alright, Duff."

I turned to the room and said calmly. "You can cast me out. I might not want it now, but the truth is I wanted to leave here for a long time. And maybe I don't have enough faith. Maybe I like some of the new folk ways, but I've tried to do my best here."

I looked at Rab and let my hand cover my still flat belly. "I might be leaving, but I'm taking a piece of this place with me. Y'all can't take that from me."

I turned to Duff and whispered. "Get my things and meet me at the castle."

I walked out the door and into the cold January day. I managed to hold my head up as I passed the ridge and out of sight from the village. I kept walking until I reached the sheltered loch side of the castle ruin. That was where the tears took over. I fell to my knees on the stones of the castle and wept great heaving sobs.

***

I don't know how long it lasted but my storm of emotions was interrupted. "Shh. Dinna greet, *a Mhàili.*"

I looked up to find that it was dark and Willie Cross was there. He was patting the air near me as if he wanted to touch me but was afraid to. The moon was bright and it reflected off the water enough for me to see that he was filthy. His hair was a matted mess of twigs and mud. His eyes were wild. He looked like the madman he'd been playing for the last couple of months. I scrambled to my feet and backed away from him. "You should go, Willie. Duff will be here any minute."

"Shh…shh…Ye mun go back." He took a step toward me.

"No, Willie. I can't go back. They cast me out." I stepped back, climbing the stones behind me.

"But they dinna understand. What ye have there," he nodded, his eyes on my belly. I covered it by reflex with my hand. He stepped closer and I stepped back and up again. "It's so precious. She belongs here. She needs to be here."

"I'm not going back, Willie. You need to go." He continued advancing on me and I stepped back, but this time there was nothing solid under my heel. I had backed up to the open hole of the old stairwell. I nearly lost my balance and waved my arms. Willie grabbed my arm and pulled me away from the edge. I stumbled, but he kept me on my feet.

He started pulling me down toward the arch that led back to the road. "Ye have to go back. She needs to be here."

Once my feet were under me, I started pushing back against him. He kept trying to drag me back down the tumbled stones. I pushed against his chest, tried to pry his fingers from my arms, anything I could think of. He meant to take me back to the village no matter what.

I finally succeeded in prying his hand off my arm and pushed away from him. He whirled back to me and I felt the back of his hand crack against my cheek. "Ye'll go back."

My face stung. He used the moment to grab my arm again, but this time I fought harder. "No!"

I yanked and almost got free but he came back with a closed fist. It pounded into my jaw and I tasted blood. I was stunned, but I kept pushing against his chest. He rained blows around my head and shoulders. All I could think of was you, baby, and my fear of losing you. I put my hands down to protect you and let him batter my face and head. I thought that he might actually knock me out and drag me back.

Then a soft, meaty thunk sounded, and the hail of blows stopped. I looked to see Willie clutching at an arrow that was sunk deep in his neck. He stood over me and leaned back. His hand was wrapped around the arrow and his mouth was working like a landed fish. He stumbled backward a few steps. In seconds, he lost his balance and went tumbling down into the open stairwell.

I crumpled to the stones and rolled onto my back. The world was spinning, and my eyes were beginning to swell. Before everything went black, I looked up to see where the arrow had come from. On the partial back wall, outlined by the moonlight, I saw it. The same crouching figure I had seen by the pool six months ago. The figure of a man with a stag's horns. In one hand he held a bow. I didn't know if I should be afraid for myself or not, but I felt my energy draining away. I rolled onto my side and curled around you before the world went black.

CHAPTER THIRTY-NINE

December 26, 1995
Chapel Hill, North Carolina

"Freeze!" Sarah heard Curtis bark from the front room.

It was immediately followed by a feminine voice shouting, "I live here!"

Sarah dropped the summer clothes she was packing into a box and followed her ears. She found Curtis standing near the door, holding a yellow and black stun gun at the ready. It was pointed directly at Amy, who was in the doorway with her arms in the air and her eyes spitting fury. There were a couple of empty boxes and a suitcase at her feet.

"Curtis, it's okay." Sarah put a hand on his arm and pulled it down until the gun was pointing at the floor. "She really does live here.

"What the hell is going on?" Amy lowered her arms and set her fists on her hips.

"Amy, this is Curtis Blake. Curtis works for James Stuart. Curtis, this is my roommate and friend, Amy Monroe," Sarah said, trying to sound as calm as possible in the hopes of diffusing the situation.

She could see the muscles jumping in Amy's jaw as she nudged the boxes aside with a foot and pulled the suitcase into the apartment. She closed the door none too gently. "What exactly does he do for James?"

"He's a bodyguard." There was no beating around that bush.

"What for?" Her face looked thunderous. "Ryan's dead."

Sarah let her shoulders slump. Obviously, Amy was still upset. Sarah struggled with how much she could tell Amy and how much to keep secret. "I told you that Ryan killed Bridget MacKenzie in Nova Scotia, right?"

Amy's reply was curt and bitter, "Yeah."

"Well, Bridget was a geologist, and as it turns out she had been offered a job by Alba Petroleum shortly before she was killed. James is concerned that I could be a target for anyone else who might be obsessed with him if word gets out. Also, they help keep reporters away."

"That's what he's really worried about," Amy said, rolling her eyes. It was clear that Amy was still angry. A week ago, Sarah might have been inclined to try to talk to her and find some kind of common ground, but between Beth Cartwright and Molly's memoir she was feeling more than a little raw. She found that she couldn't muster up the energy to face Amy's anger, no matter how misguided it was.

"I'll be packing things up. Let me know if you need anything," Sarah said and went back to her room, leaving Amy by the door with her empty boxes.

For the next couple of hours, they seemed to be tripping over each other. When Sarah was returning from taking a box of clothes out to her car, Amy was on her way out with a box. When Sarah went to pack up her pans in the kitchen, Amy came in to grab her blender. Each time, her friend seemed more tense, more agitated.

By the time she joined Sarah at the bookcase that ran under the front window, Amy seemed ready to pop. They sat on the floor in front of the bookcase silently divvying up the books. When Sarah came across one that belonged to Amy she would add it to a stack next to Amy's box. Sarah couldn't entirely understand why Amy was still mad, but she also couldn't bring herself to ask her friend what was wrong. No doubt that was part of Amy's problem.

Sarah found herself falling into an old habit of pretending the problem wasn't there. In the last few months of her life, Sarah's mother had been erratic and prone to violent outbursts. Granny wouldn't consider sending her to a hospital, so little Sarah had learned to ignore her. Reacting to Mama's outbursts had only made them worse. So whenever Mama lost control, Sarah would hold onto hers with both hands and eventually Granny or Duff would drag Mama away or she would run out of steam. That's exactly what Sarah was determined to do with Amy. Her roommate was spoiling for an argument, but Sarah was determined not to take the bait.

She would sit there sorting and packing up her books in peace if it killed her. She added a copy of the *Songs and Poems of Robert Burns* to the stack beside Amy's box. Amy glanced at the book, "Isn't that one yours?"

"Nope. Mine is in my room." There, perfectly calm.

Amy shrugged and turned back to the shelf she was working on. Several books later she held up a textbook of Sarah's. "I'm taking Johnson's art and anthropology class this semester and this is on the list. Do you mind if I keep it?"

Sarah shook her head and gave Amy a brief smile. "Not at all, as long as you don't mind my annotations in it."

Amy added the textbook to her box. "So, Hottie MacMoneybags is paying for your security detail. I'm sure he does that for all the girls."

Calm, Sarah was going to stay calm. "Yeah, it seems like overkill, but they're good guys, and it's better than being here alone."

"Guys?" Amy asked, glancing back toward where Curtis was seated at the table in the dining area. He appeared to be reading the paper. "I only see one."

"Oh, Fleming has the night shift. You met him before." Sarah didn't really want to remind Amy of the day after Ryan's attack.

Amy arched an eyebrow. "But he was here before."

"He works for James. He was on vacation before and came to visit Dermot. Now he's working." Sarah hoped Amy wouldn't dig deeper into that story. She hated hiding things from Amy. Just like she had with Barrett, she wanted to tell her friend everything and get counsel on what she should do. But in Amy's current post-Ryan mood, Sarah just didn't know what her friend might do with the information.

"Well, this certainly seems cozy, you and your guard dogs in our apartment," Amy snarked. "I guess one hot Scot and a billionaire weren't enough."

Sarah went back to her shelf. She was not going to let this escalate. "You know it's not like that."

"Oh?" Amy stopped sorting and turned to Sarah. "What's it like then? Because I feel like all this stuff is happening around me and I'm the only one who's not clued in."

"I'm sorry." Sarah didn't know what else to say. She was sorry…sorry that Ryan hadn't been the man he said he was, sorry that he had come between them. She was sorry that she couldn't tell Amy the truth, but the truth was even harder to believe than the story Amy already knew. Sarah turned back to the bookcase and sorting the books.

"That's it?" Amy snapped. "That's all you've got to say?"

Sarah sat back on her heels, shoulders slouched. "What do you want me to say? Ryan's motivations are just as big a mystery to me as they are to you."

"Well, it sounds like his motivation had to do with James. I would think you would be running as fast as you can away from him, but it looks like he's running your life now. You're as much a hostage today as you were three weeks ago. These guys are just friendlier."

Sarah bit her tongue on a nasty retort. Instead she said through her teeth, "This from the person who told me to encourage him."

"I didn't know he was going to turn you into flipping Cinderella." Amy threw up a hand in exasperation.

"Does that make you my wicked stepsister?" Sarah's determined calm was starting to fray.

Amy gave her a withering look and waved a hand at the boxes. "Well, apparently it makes me homeless."

"Now you're being melodramatic. Barrett told me that you already have a place lined up. And what are you talking about, making me Cinderella?"

"Come on! The gifts, the fellowship. He even sent knights to protect you." She shot an arm out in Curtis's direction as if he were Exhibit A.

"Knights. Really?"

"What the hell do you call them?" Amy rolled her eyes and Sarah got a flash of what she'd been like as a cranky teenager. "God, I can just picture you holding court at the Daily Grind."

"Oh yeah, that's exactly what the last three weeks have been like, me and Sir Curtis of Atlanta over there gadding about town from one party to the next. Right, Sir Curtis?"

"Uh-uhn, I'm not getting in the middle of this," he said from behind his newspaper.

"Some knight you are," Sarah said. Turning back to Amy, "Sorry. I'm afraid I missed the ball because I've been busy trying to rescue my floundering dissertation. Oh, and keeping reporters away from you."

"I think I can handle reporters just fine," Amy snapped.

"Well, feel free then. I've been fighting everyone from the police to James's PR people to keep your name out of this, but I'll be happy to stop. Just remember you said that when a reporter hides in a bathroom closet so she can get you alone."

Amy stood up, feet planted wide. "Oh, boo hoo! Let's add pushy reporters to the long list of traumatic shit that's happened to Sarah."

"What?" Sara shot to her feet.

Amy held a hand to her mouth as if she was whispering, but didn't lower her voice. "Poor Sarah, her family's all gone. Poor Sarah, nobody in the holler would be her friend."

"You know, you sound just like him," Sarah hissed.

"Poor Sarah, her mother never loved her," Amy sneered.

Sarah stopped short, feeling like the wind was knocked out of her. When she caught her breath she asked, "Why would you say that?"

"Because I'm tired of it," Amy spat. "I have spent the last five years in the shadow of your damage, dealing with the sleepwalking, the paranoia, and the bathtub nightmares."

"I had no idea being my friend was such a trial," Sarah said.

"You just suck all the oxygen out of any room. Everyone gets taken in. You're like some baby chick with a broken wing. Anybody with half a heart wants to fix you and nobody else can compete."

"Because it's not a competition!" Sarah pleaded.

"Isn't it?" Amy shot back.

"I didn't think it was, but someone seems to have convinced you otherwise."

"What are you talking about?" Amy looked incredulous.

Sarah took a deep breath, trying to reel in her temper. "I'm talking about Ryan Cumberland pouring poison into your ears for months, until you sound more like him than the friend I know and love."

"He didn't put anything in my head that wasn't already there," Amy said, stone-faced.

Sarah gritted her teeth as she stared down the woman she had thought was her friend. "Good to know."

Emotions roiling, Sarah dropped to her knees and went back to sorting books. Tears clogged her throat, but she was not going to let Amy see how hurt she was just so she could accuse Sarah of another plea for attention. They had been looking out for each other for the past five years. Sarah didn't think it had been as one-sided as Amy was portraying it. She promised herself that later she would think about their relationship and whether she had taken Amy for granted. But right now, she needed to keep it together. Shields up, focus on the task at hand.

She carefully read the title of each book and sorted them accordingly. And if the titles began to blur from tears in her eyes, she blinked them back and kept going. She could feel Amy's eyes boring into the back of her head. Amy hadn't moved from where she'd been standing. When she finally spoke her voice was much more subdued, "Sarah."

Sarah kept on sorting and packing books. She was done with this conversation. Her emotions were too raw to continue talking without saying something she would regret.

From the corner of her eye, Sarah could see Amy shifting from foot to foot, as if she couldn't decide what to do next. Amy sighed in exasperation. "I just get so frustrated with you sometimes. Everyone tries to help you, and you push us away. And now our apartment is like a fortress and you don't trust anyone."

Sarah let the hand that was holding the next book drop to her lap. Her voice was deadly quiet. "I trusted you."

"And look where that got me," Amy muttered.

"That's it!" Sarah sprang to her feet, the book dropping to the floor unheeded and whirled on Amy. "I'm really struggling to understand the level of self-deception that has you still blaming this on me. YOU brought Ryan Cumberland into our home. YOU ignored my misgivings about him."

Sarah advanced on her friend, eyes blazing. Amy retreated as Sarah pressed on. "When I caught him in my room, YOU dismissed it, and then YOU GAVE HIM A KEY! When I brought you proof that he was lying, YOU told me I was the problem. I warned you about Ryan more times than I care to count and you did nothing!"

Sarah continued her advance, and Amy retreated until her calves hit the chair and she dropped into it. Her face showed her shock at Sarah's outburst. Sarah braced herself on the chair's arms and leaned closer. "And after he attacked me in my bed after letting himself into our apartment with a copy of YOUR KEY, somehow you've turned this around to be my fault. I have let you accuse me and berate me when all I have done is tried to spare your feelings. THIS IS NOT MY FAULT!"

Sarah stopped, not believing that she had let her temper loose like that. She straightened up and backed away from her friend. She couldn't imagine them returning to their old dynamic after this.

Sarah turned to look out the front window, anywhere but at Amy's horrified face. The silence was crushing. Sarah stood there, trying to rein herself in. She watched a car go by on Ransom Street and a neighbor walk by with their dog. She counted her breaths, waiting for Amy to come back with another wave of recriminations.

"I'm going to go," Amy's voice was barely above a whisper and clogged with tears. She sniffed wetly. "Let me know a time when you'll be out and I'll come and get the rest of my stuff."

Sarah squeezed her eyes shut, sick with guilt and fighting back her own tears. She worked so hard most of the time to stay in control, to not lose her temper, to not be like Molly, and here she was screaming in her best friend's face. "You're wrong, you know."

Amy stopped, her hand on the doorknob. "I think that's obvious."

Sarah sighed and looked over her shoulder. Amy's shoulders were around her ears, like she was expecting another outburst. "No, about my mother. She did love me. She just couldn't stand to watch me become what she was."

"Sick?" Amy's voice wasn't as bitter as Sarah expected. She sounded almost contrite.

"Alone and trapped." Sarah turned back to the window. "And that wasn't my fault either."

It wasn't. Sarah had blamed herself for almost twenty years. She thought she had caused her mother's misery, her madness, and her suicide. But reading Molly's account had shown her that it wasn't her fault. Molly had been on that path before Sarah was even born. There was irony in the fact that Sarah wouldn't have the journal if Ryan hadn't attacked her and brought Duff out of hiding. He had tried to kill her, but he had helped her find her mother again.

"Take care of yourself, Sarah," Amy said and closed the door behind her.

CHAPTER FORTY

February 1969
Ullapool, Scotland

When I opened my eyes, I saw the sun reflecting off a cracked plaster ceiling. I should say I opened one eye because my left eye was swollen shut. I could hear voices talking softly somewhere nearby, but I didn't understand anything they were saying. I was lying on a bed with my arms at my sides. Everything hurt. My limbs felt like lead and my head throbbed. I started feeling around me, and one hand bumped against something hard and cold. I wrapped my fingers around a metal bar that must have been a railing. A hospital or clinic then. I had no idea how I had gotten there, but there was really only one thing I cared about.

I tried to call out, but my voice came out as little more than a croak. I swallowed hard and tried again. "Rab?"

There were some quick footsteps nearby, and Duff came into view on the side where I could see. He gave me a gentle smile and took my hand. "Hey. You're awake."

Another hard swallow. "Baby?"

His smile spread. "The baby is fine. The doctor says most of the…"

I didn't care about much else at that point. Duff kept talking to me, but I stopped listening. I closed my eyes and drifted away.

When I woke up again, it was dark. The room was lit by the light coming in from the hallway. This time I noticed the antiseptic smell. Everything was quiet except for the soft snoring going on to my right. Duff was sitting next to my bed, his head leaned back against the wall behind him, eyes closed.

I had no idea how long I had been out, or how long it had been since we got to wherever we were. All I knew was that I was not in Làrachd an Fhamhair anymore, and Rab wasn't with me. He wasn't with me because he hadn't stood up. When I had needed him, when he'd had the chance, he had kept silent. Willie Cross had battered my face, the village had hurt my pride, but Rab's betrayal broke my heart.

The truth is, the whole situation broke something else inside me. I had kept it together for months, but there in that dark, cold room it all caught up with me. It was like I had taken every betrayal from Mama's to Rab's, every insult, every slight, every hour of unappreciated work, every terrified night in the cottage, and stacked them all off to the side so I could keep going. But now it was all crashing down on top of me in an avalanche of pain and bitterness. It was suffocating. I laid there counting up all my hurts, like an insomniac counting sheep. Eventually, it exhausted me and I fell asleep again.

I woke again in the morning, and by woke, I mean I opened my good eye and listened to the things going on around me. There wasn't much else to do. I was numb. I heard the squeak of nurses' shoes on the hall floor, the rattle of a supply cart, and the brush-whomp of swinging doors. I was alone.

Alone. Where was Duff? I began to panic. Everyone else had abandoned me or pushed me away…everyone but Duff. Now he had no reason to stay with me. His obligation had expired when they had kicked me out of the village. I wasn't a sister anymore. I wasn't a child of the auld way. I was *sluagh ùr* and there wasn't any more reason for him to protect me. As this realization dawned on me, my heart started racing and breathing got harder. I sat up in the bed and looked around the room. It was empty but for the bed and a single chair.

The bed had railings on both sides. I started pushing one side back and forth, trying to lower it, but it wouldn't budge. I rattled it back and forth, thinking it must be stuck and there had to be some catch that was keeping it from going down. My heart beat faster and faster with my frustration. I had to see where I was, if I was truly alone this time. I scooted down to the end of the bed and climbed down. I went in to the hall and looked both ways.

There was a desk at one end and a solid wall at the other. I hurried toward the desk looking for Duff.

"Where is Duff, Grant MacDuff? Where did he go?" I asked the nurse. When she looked at me dumbly, I asked louder. "The man who was with me, where did he go?"

"Miss." The nurse stood up and put out a hand to me, saying, "Let's calm down now."

"The tall American, I need to see him. Where did he go?" My breath was short. I kept looking around for Duff. I was so sure he had left me. "Where is he?"

"Now, miss." The nurse came around the desk and approached me. She reached for my arm, but I pushed her hand away and turned back down the hall.

"Duff! Grant MacDuff!" I called out, hoping he was in one of these other rooms. He had to be. I was terrified he had left.

I was halfway back down the hall when the double doors near the desk opened and Duff and a man in a white coat came

408 · MEREDITH R. STODDARD

rushing toward me. I had worked myself up so much, though, that I didn't notice. I kept on calling for Duff.

"Molly." Duff reached me and put his hand on my back. "Molly, I'm here."

"Duff!" I looked at him, doing a visual inventory, light brown hair, warm, chocolate brown eyes, prominent cheekbones…I drew in the first good breath since I had noticed he was gone. "I thought you'd left me."

He smiled that same gentle, understanding smile he had given me back in June after I had pounded him with all my frustrations. "Never."

I collapsed, weeping with relief. He caught me just like he always did and hefted me up into his arms. "Shh, Molly. I'm not going anywhere."

***

I must have fallen asleep again, because the next time I opened my eyes, I was in bed. Duff was sitting in the chair beside me. He was leaning forward with his head resting on the mattress. He had his hand stretched through the railing and wrapped around mine. My throat was raw from crying, but I didn't have much to say anyway. I turned my hand over and threaded my fingers through his.

He lifted his head and drew in a deep breath. His eyes found mine. "Hey."

I couldn't quite make my voice work, so I nodded at him.

"I need you to listen, baby. I need your help." He leaned closer to me and lowered his voice. "We're in the clinic in Ullapool. Physically you're fine, but after your outburst earlier, they want to move you to a mental hospital. Now, I know you've had a hard time, and I know you're hurting, but I can't help you get home or do whatever you think you need to do next if they separate us. Do you think you can keep it together long enough for us to get you out of here?"

I wanted to help him, but I just wasn't sure I could. I couldn't give him an answer.

He brought up his other hand and wrapped it around where ours were joined. "When we get out of here, you can fall to pieces if you need to. I'll try my best to make sure none of those pieces get lost. But I can't do that if I'm not there. We've been cut loose from whatever resources we had, but we're together. I swore an oath before I met you that I would protect you, and I'm not going to stop now. Where you go, I go. I just need you to be well enough to tell me where."

I took a deep breath and nodded.

"That's my girl." He smiled and kissed my hand. "Now, here's our story. We're on our honeymoon and we separated just for a few hours. I went on a hike, and you went to see some ruins. You were attacked there by a strange man who ran off with your purse after he knocked you out. I found you and brought you in. Okay?"

I nodded again. Of course we needed a story. We couldn't have anyone looking for the village. I swallowed past the rawness in my throat. My voice came out as little more than a whisper. "What ruins?"

He sighed. I think he was relieved to hear me talk, to realize that I was listening. "Calda House. It's as close as I could get to the truth without sending them to the castle. I didn't want them to find the body if it was still there. That would open up all sorts of questions."

I nodded.

"Molly, I need you to convince them that you're okay. I know it hurts, but we've got to stick together. Alright?"

And we did. A doctor came back with a nurse to interview me, and I did everything I had to do. I pulled it together one more time. I looked adoringly at Duff and repeated the story he'd told me. I made myself sound as smart and clear as I could. I gave a description of the person who attacked me. I watched them check the right boxes. The doctor seemed nice enough. The nurse never took her eyes off of me, as if she was afraid I might jump up and start raving at any moment.

In the end, the doctor slid his pen into his pocket, flipped the cover over on his clipboard, and smiled at us. "Well, I think that'll do it then. Let's get ye out of here. Shall we?"

Duff gave my hand a squeeze and kissed my forehead before following the doctor out to finish the paperwork.

Left alone for the first time since my outburst, I swung my legs over the side. They had put the railing down. I padded over to a little sink and mirror in the corner. The swelling was starting to go down. I could see a little out of my left eye now. The rest of what I saw was just awful. There was a huge bruise on my jaw where he had hit me the first time. My lip was split and held together with a couple of stitches. There were also a couple of stitches closing a cut over my cheekbone. My left eye was a ring of purplish black, and there was a knot on my forehead near my temple. I pulled the top of my gown aside to find some bruising around my collarbone.

I guess I should be thankful that Willie only hit me around my face and head or you might have been in more danger. I knew I needed to hold it together, but seeing all that damage drew me right back into the moment. My eyes started tearing up and my hands started to shake. Willie had been mad to get me back to the village. He didn't know his strength, and he could have, probably would have, bashed my head in trying. That horned figure saved my life.

I put my hands down to grip the side of the sink for support and took a few deep breaths, remembering what Duff said. I could fall apart later. We had to get out of here. I was making some progress getting control of myself when he came back in. He wrapped an arm around me and helped me back to the bed.

"Just a little bit longer, baby. I know you can do it."

***

I did do it. I held myself together and acted the part of the damaged but devoted wife until we closed the door on a rented room just off Market Street. In fact, I kept it together a lot longer than that. Duff will probably tell you that he wishes I hadn't. But I had a plan. Rab and I had made it that afternoon when we were hidden in the grass by the burn. We had a meeting place, a place where I was supposed to wait for him.

You will learn, baby, that when you have something to hang on to, you can endure a lot more than you think. All you need is hope, and I had it. I believed that we had a plan, that words had meaning, that love mattered. I still believed in your father.

Duff set our bags on the bed. He pulled a train schedule out of his bag and spread it out on the little table by the window. It was a gray and dreary day as any February day in Scotland. I was sitting on the bed watching the foot traffic out on the street. I hadn't bothered to take my coat off.

"Okay. There's a train to Glasgow leaving tomorrow. I figure we've got enough money to get us there. And get us a place to stay. I'll need to find some work if we're going to save up enough to get us home."

I was only half listening, so it took me a while to realize what he was saying. When his words broke through I stopped him. "We can't leave."

He looked at me surprised. "Well, we can't stay here."

I shook my head. "Of course not. We have to go to Inverness."

"What for?" he asked softly. I could tell he already suspected he knew the answer.

"For Rab," I sighed. "We made plans that whichever one of us left the village first would wait for the other in Inverness."

Duff came over to the bed and knelt down in front of me. He laid his hands on mine. He took a while to speak, choosing his words carefully. "Shug, he didn't stand up for you when that woman shamed you in front of the whole village. Do you really believe that he's going to come for you?"

It hurt to have it put that way, but I understood his point. Still, there was more to it than pride and shame. "You've been telling me for months that this is a complicated situation, and there's no easy way out of it. Do you think that's any less true for him?"

He drew away from me and stood up. He faced the wall with his hands on his hips. "Do you know how hard this is for me? Watching you getting kicked in the teeth all these months? Now you're asking me to do it again."

"No, I'm not." I stood up and went to stand next to him. "I'm not one of the sisters anymore. I'm just a girl. I don't need a bodyguard anymore."

"Don't insult me." He turned away, shaking his head. "I told you before. Where you go, I go. You might not be a sister anymore, but that doesn't mean everybody knows that. Besides, I don't think it's that easy. Eilidh can kick you out of the village, but she can't take away who you are. She can't take away your gift."

He had a point. I would rather not be alone, but I also didn't want to feel like I was dragging Duff all over the country for my own agenda. "Alright. Will you stay with me until Rab comes? Then you can go on about your life."

"Of course I'll stay." He put an arm around me. "But I don't think Rab is coming. I know you don't want to hear that, but I've got to be honest with you."

"I understand. And I see why you might think that." I leaned my head on his shoulder. "I just have to believe in him."

CHAPTER FORTY-ONE

December 26, 1995
Chapel Hill, North Carolina

Sarah felt emotionally raw for the rest of the day, like she was hung over from the release of telling Amy how she felt. What could have been cathartic only left her feeling guilty and tired. She wished she could take it back, fix things. But maybe it was for the best. She was leaving anyway. Whether she went to Scotland or somewhere else, she might as well make a clean break. At least Amy wouldn't miss her.

Not wanting to let her hurt show, Sarah threw herself into cleaning house. Curtis mostly stayed out of her way, but helped where he could. She finished packing everything that wasn't supposed to go to Scotland plus a few essentials for the next week. It actually took less time than she thought it would.

Curtis helped her load the boxes into the back of her little Honda. Surprisingly, everything fit in the car with a little room to spare.

"Is that it?" he asked, straightening up from putting the last box in the back seat. Sarah checked the notes on the sides of each box: summer clothes, books, junk. "One more thing. I'll get it."

She turned back toward the building and started walking. Curtis jogged a few steps to catch up with her. "Not without me you won't."

"You know I like you, Curtis, but I'm not going to miss having you on my heels all the time."

"Just doing my job," he said as they walked into the hallway. He unlocked the door and went in to check the apartment. Even when they had only been outside for a minute, he didn't let up on the routine.

"Where is it?" he asked.

"It's in my room. I'll get it." She hurried back to her room. The trunk was sitting in the mostly bare closet. It was Granny's trunk, where she had found the picture that had put her in an academic tailspin. She had held on to it since Granny died, dragging it with her from Kettle Holler to Boone to Chapel Hill. Now she was leaving it behind. Sarah told herself it just wasn't practical. She had the photo of Granny and Isobel MacKenzie tucked into Mama's journal. The rest was just memories, and she could hang onto those without the trunk.

She slid it out of the closet until she could reach both handles and carried it to the front room. "This is it," she said. "Let's go."

"Okay. Want me to carry that?" Curtis offered.

"Nah, I've got it. It's a family heirloom." She shifted to get a better grip on the handles.

"Okay." Curtis opened the door and checked the hallway. He led the way to the car, scanning the street and the parking lot. Sarah put the chest on the back seat and even buckled a seat belt around it.

They drove to a storage facility near Durham, where Sarah shelled out a year's worth of rent on the smallest locker they had, which was only slightly larger than her closet but still bigger than she needed. She hated dipping into her savings, but they gave her a discount for paying up front. So she gulped and wrote the check. She wasn't sure what she would do after a year, but that had her covered for a while.

When they had finished unloading her things, Sarah stepped back to look at it. The boxes were neatly stacked in the back of the unit, her granny's chest resting on top. For a minute she couldn't move. Twenty-six years, and this small stack of boxes, a couple of suitcases, and a beat-up Honda hatchback were the only tangible things she had collected. She had sold one home and was now being run out of another. Everywhere she had lived in between had been temporary.

She felt hollowed out. It wasn't the lack of possessions that mattered. They were only things. But seeing them stacked there and going back to a nearly empty apartment made it all seem final, and she didn't like that. She had felt more at home here than anywhere else. She loved Chapel Hill, with its special blend of Southern culture, intellectualism, and plain weirdness. She had people here, even if they weren't related. She had a position here. She had plans…but now that was all up in the air.

Curtis gently touched her back. His voice was low. "C'mon. We don't have to go home, but we can't stay here."

It was just a figure of speech, but Sarah couldn't help thinking how right he was. When they went back out to the car, a frigid, drizzling rain had started to fall. Curtis drove while Sarah watched the town she loved roll by between the tracks of raindrops on the window. The lights of the businesses along Franklin Street refracted into bursts of color before bleeding jagged paths down the glass. Each drop sliding down and fading at the bottom had a name: Amy, Barrett, Donald, Duff, Jon, Meg, Jane…She hated leaving them all. She hated James, Dermot, Ryan, and anyone who was pushing her away from her adopted home.

By the time Curtis pulled into the tiny parking lot behind her building, she had almost decided that she wasn't going anywhere and she would fight anyone who tried to make her. The rain had picked up, and after a quick survey of the area, they hopped out and made a dash for the door. Curtis stepped in front of Sarah and began the usual routine for coming home. He checked the outer hallway that ran down the center of the building before leaving her by the door to clear the apartment. Sarah stood in the open doorway to her apartment, waiting for the all-clear when she thought she heard someone call her. After the day she'd had and the rain, she didn't trust her ears. She turned back to the apartment. Curtis wasn't quite done.

"Sarah," a feminine voice whispered. This time she was sure she'd heard it. She stepped back into the outer hall.

"Amy?"

A thin figure stepped into the doorway that led to the street. The porchlight shone on Beth Cartwright's ghost-white face. Her blonde hair was soaked and several strands clung to her face. She was shivering from the cold. "Not Amy. You can call off your dogs."

"Sorry, what?" Sara backed away, toward the apartment door.

"I've dropped the story. You can call them off," she said bitterly, not following Sarah.

Clueless, Sarah shook her head. "I don't know what you're talking about."

"Clear," Curtis's voice came from inside the apartment.

"Don't you?" Beth gave Sarah a skeptical look. "After our little meeting in the restroom, someone called my editor and threatened a lawsuit that would bankrupt the paper. Then someone broke into my apartment and ransacked it. They stole my computer and anything I had on the MacKenzie case."

"So you got robbed. It happens around here," Sarah scoffed.

Beth arched an eyebrow. "That's all they took. They left my stereo and TV. Why would they take a folder of newspaper clippings and leave a TV?"

"Sarah!" Curtis called sharply.

"It's okay. I'm just checking the mail and talking to a neighbor." She turned back to the woman. "He's going to be out here in a second."

"Listen." Beth stepped closer and lowered her voice. "I don't have anything against you, but I think you're mixed up in some dangerous stuff. It's not just the break-in. My source that tipped me off to the Canadian connection hasn't been seen in two days. I checked his hotel and they said he hasn't checked out."

Martin Carol had disappeared? Sarah had little doubt he'd been called back to Alba Petroleum headquarters for a good talking-to. "Maybe he just left and forgot to check out."

Beth shook her head. "I talked my way into his room. His things are still there. It's too much to be coincidence."

"Sarah." This time Curtis did step out into the hall. Sarah looked back over her shoulder and he looked furious. "You can't just stay out here like this without me."

"I'm coming." She turned back to the open door, but Beth Cartwright was gone. Sarah leaned out into the rainy night and caught a glimpse of her jogging away, shoulders hunched and head down.

CHAPTER FORTY-TWO

1969
Inverness, Scotland

We used what money we had left to take a train to Inverness and rent a flat. Duff got a job at the docks, working under the table. I wanted to get a job too, but he wouldn't hear of it. I started taking in mending for some of the folks in our building. Just like in Ullapool, we had to pretend we were married to get people to rent to us. So I had to get used to being called Mrs. MacDuff.

Every Monday at four o'clock, I spent an hour sitting on a bench in front of the castle. With the statue of Flora MacDonald behind me, I watched the water of the River Ness roll by and the rabbits hopping along the bank. I sat there every week through March, April, May, and on into June. I watched the days grow longer, the trees grow leaves, flowers bloom and wither, and countless people visit the castle. And I watched you grow. My clothes started fitting tighter. Soon enough, you were a round bump underneath my skirt. Then I started to feel you move.

That hour, every Monday, became our time. I would sit at the bench with my eyes on the river, but my senses turned inward. I could feel you growing. It was like our own conversation. I thought about all the things I wanted to tell you, all the things I'd teach you. I couldn't wait to see your face. I hoped that you would have your daddy's eyes, and you do.

One day almost a year after I had come to Scotland, you and I were spending our usual hour together on the bench when someone sat down next to me. I didn't pay much attention. People came and sat near me sometimes, but no one ever spoke to me unless I spoke to them, which was rare. I had no reason to expect this person to be any different until she spoke. "Ye know he isna coming, don't ye?"

I turned my head and took in my cousin Sheila. She wore a pretty flowered dress and shiny new boots. No one would ever guess that she was anything but a typical girl from any Scottish town. She also wore that same smug look she had when she told me about the matching and what was expected of me in Làrachd an Fhamhair. It reminded me that Rab had told me not to trust her. "I reckon he told you, huh?"

"Didna have to. Did we never tell ye what our talent is?" She tilted her head and gave me a condescending look, like I was simple. "You and yer mam see the present, where things stand. Rona and her mam see the future. Mam and I? We see the truth when we look for it. Of course, I didna look for it then, because I couldna believe that sweet, suffering Màili would do such a thing to a sister."

I didn't say anything. There wasn't much to say. I had done a terrible thing. I wasn't proud of it. But that didn't change the fact that I loved your father.

"Then after ye left, I thought I should take a closer look at my man and see what was in his heart. And that's when I saw it, you and Rab and your wee plan. I have to hand it to ye. I didna ken ye were capable of this kind of deception. But I see it now."

"Do you?" I bit out.

"Aye, ye're a sharp one. I underestimated ye."

We sat there in silence while Sheila planned her next verbal twist of the knife. I felt the cool breeze blowing off the river. I always found strength in the wind. I thought of those windflowers that bloom first in the spring on the mountains, the ones we were picking that morning. "So you always see the truth, but you don't always tell the truth, do you? Rab said you and your mother are hiding something. What is it?"

She waved a dismissive hand. "Och. That's naught to fash about. Just a theory about what stopped the cauldron."

"Oh?"

"Doesna matter now. We found poor Willie, killed by hunters. Such a shame, lad never was quite right."

"I didn't make him that way," I said.

"Of course ye didn't. He went mad when he was a boy. But the story that everyone will tell is that the *sluagh ùr* lass who tried to be one of us drove him mad. That's what's in people minds. There's no changing it now."

"There are worse things than being thought bad of by thirty or so people hiding in a glen in the highlands. I think I'll survive."

"We're to be marrit, ye ken? Rab and me." I could hear the sneering grin in her voice.

I kept my eyes on the river. I wasn't interested in fighting with Sheila, and I wasn't going to rise to her bait. I kept my voice carefully even. "Is that so?"

"Aye. We've come back here to earn some money and to get the rest of his things." She was loving this. "We've been in town for weeks."

Weeks. Rab had been in Inverness for weeks. I had been sitting on this bench every Monday afternoon for all that time, and he hadn't come. That was like a knife to the gut. I laid a protective hand over my belly. Struggling to keep my breathing even, I blinked rapidly to keep the tears from falling.

"I reckon we'll settle near the village, but not in the glen. We dinna want to be too close to Mam. Maybe Lairg or Lochinver…" She began to ramble on about her plans for Rab and their life together, twisting the knife a little deeper. I expect she thought I deserved it. The truth is I had stopped listening. She had done all the damage she could.

I sat there with my eyes on the river until the hum of Sheila's voice stopped. I guess she decided she was done. Before she left, she leaned over and whispered in my ear, "Go home, *a Mhàili*. No one here wants ye anymore."

I was paralyzed. I was sunk so deep in hurt and uncertainty that I honestly couldn't move. At least I couldn't make my legs pick me up off that bench. I couldn't trust Sheila. I knew that much. Maybe Rab had been there for weeks like she said, or maybe he wasn't there at all. There was only one way to find out.

If Sheila could use her talent to find out about Rab, so could I. So I closed my eyes and took a deep breath. It took a few minutes for me to relax enough to cast out, but I did it. I found him in a pub sitting at the bar. He was drinking a pint and had his fiddle on the stool beside him. He rested his head on his hand.

I couldn't tell if he was sad or just tired, but I could see that he wasn't happy. It made me wish for a second that I had Sheila's gift of seeing the truth. Then again, maybe not. I knew she enjoyed hurting me. I thought she was a liar, but I had no way of knowing how Rab felt without asking him.

"I'll be expecting ye to be mite more lively tonight, eh Rab?" the barman said. He was right across the bar from Rab, but it sounded to me like an echo from another room.

"Aye. Aye. Pour me another pint and I'll be fair sprightly, ye'll see," Rab grumbled, barely lifting his head. He pushed his glass toward the barman, who took it and poured a pint with practiced ease.

"Will your Sheila be here tonight?" the other man asked, setting the pint in front of Rab and bracing his meaty hands on the bar.

"Don't think so," Rab muttered, looking into the glass as if it held the answer.

"Good." The barman leaned back as if he was satisfied with that answer and began wiping the counter with a dingy towel. "She scares away the other lasses."

A bitter chuckle bubbled up from Rab as the barman moved on down the bar. "Ye dinna know the half of it, mate."

I pulled back into myself. I had seen enough to know that Rab was in town and had been there long enough to be playing at that pub, long enough for Sheila to be causing problems there. More importantly, I knew where he would be that night.

I didn't have to take Sheila's word for it. I could go and find out for myself why Rab hadn't met me by the castle, and I could make him see that it was a mistake. I was sure that when he saw me again, he would be mine. I knew he wouldn't be able to abandon us. He couldn't choose someone I knew he didn't love over us.

I went back to the flat I shared with Duff. I felt a little guilty about it, but I was glad he would be working late. That way I wouldn't have to explain where I was going. Duff never thought much of Rab, and the months we spent in Inverness only made matters worse. I was hurt that Rab hadn't contacted me, but I knew that Duff would be furious. It was better if I didn't have to lie about where I was going.

I put on my best dress, a cute A-line number in pink that Mama had made me. The cut of the dress was generous enough to look alright with my growing belly, but it also didn't hide it. I tied a wide pink band around my hair, just like the white band that posh woman had in the airport in New York. I even used the little bit of makeup that I had. I was determined to look my best, and as far as I could tell, I did. I had that glow they talk about when you're pregnant. You just shine from the inside. I felt better, more hopeful, than I had in months, hell, probably better than I had in a year.

I pulled the door closed behind me and locked it. Even the dark, dirty hallway of our building seemed brighter that evening. I practically skipped to the Bent Arrow Pub I had seen earlier. I must have taken longer to get ready than I had planned. The pub was buzzing.

The golden light spilled from inside onto the twilit street. I could see the band playing through the window. It was a ceilidh, much like we would have had for the feasts in the glen, although the dancing was a bit more modern. Rab and whoever he was playing with certainly seemed to pack them in.

I could see them on stage, though I couldn't hear the music from outside. They were having a grand old time, though. I figured I better head in there and join them. The door was a great heavy black thing with arches and millwork that would put any church to shame. I took a deep breath and pushed it

open. I was immediately hit with a wall of music that made my
heart leap for joy.

***

There was a little courtyard across the street from our flat
in Inverness where the neighborhood children would go to play.
It wasn't much, just a few trees and a grassy lot. I could hear
them laughing even with the windows closed. There was this
one tree in the courtyard that was dead. It stood there
surrounded by the green leaves of the others in the fullness of
summer. But its bare black branches forked from its trunk like
skeletal arms opening to the sky, begging.

That was how I felt that night in the pub. I was surrounded
by life and laughter. People were dancing. Rab was there on the
little stage, playing his fiddle. And I stood there, hoping to
catch his eye, hoping he would see me and stop as he had at the
feasts in the glen. I barely heard the noise of the pub, barely
noticed the dancers jostling me.

I just needed for him to see me. If he saw me, he would
come and talk. We would dance. We would be in love again
and he would come with me. I was sure of it. He just needed to
know I was there. Me, Màili NicMhaighread, the bride of his
heart.

Something on the other side of the room caught his
attention and his face brightened, glowed. I followed his eyes
and watched Sheila making her way through the dancers to the
stage. He reached a hand to her and she stepped up next to him,
laughing. She wrapped her arms around his neck. He pulled her
close. Over the top of her head, his eyes finally met mine.

He knew I was there. He had known. He had chosen not to stop for me. He hadn't come to meet me at the castle because he really had forsaken me. All those months I had been keeping vigil on my bench by the castle, but he was never coming. I had been holding it together because I believed in Rab. I believed in us, but he didn't.

That, baby, was when I fell apart, the moment when I knew your father either didn't care, or wasn't man enough. That was when the combined weight of the last year finally dragged me down. Mama's lies, Eilidh's manipulations, Willie's suspicions, bullying, abuse, being beaten and shamed. I might have had a few weak moments, but I had always come back. I had survived them all until I saw your father's eyes that night. They were still the same green that you see in the mirror every day, but they were cold and flat. I don't know how I got out of that pub or where I went after that. I just started walking.

I've heard people say that a broken heart feels like a hole in your chest, but I don't think that's exactly right. It's true your chest feels hollow, but it's more like someone punched through your chest and left your heart hanging out the back of you. Like you're dragging it behind, raw and sore and open to catch on every splinter and rock. I hope you never feel it, baby, but I know you probably will.

***

Duff found me sometime the next morning. I'm sure he'll tell you how he was frantic with worry, but I barely heard anything he said to me. I only remember waking up the next evening and sitting at the foot of my bed staring out the window at that poor dead tree.

You and Duff were the only things keeping me alive after that. I didn't leave the flat again until I left it for good. I stopped taking care of the flat, of myself. I slept sometimes. Most of the time I just stared out the window. I would have stopped eating, but you made me so hungry that I had to.

I didn't talk, not even to Duff. He never asked what happened. I reckon he had an idea. He just carried on like he was sure that, eventually, I would snap out of it. He talked to me, dressed me every day. He brushed my hair and made sure there was food for when you got hungry.

"You won't believe what happened at the docks yesterday," he would say to me while he brushed my hair. Then he would tell me some story about a near accident or a funny thing that one of the other men had done or some ship that had come in.

When he came home in the evening, he would come bustling in the door with hot food that he had picked up on the way home. We didn't have much of a kitchen, and Duff wasn't much of a cook. But he tried to bring me the best food he could find. "I got that meat pie you like."

He tried to sound cheerful, like he hoped I would catch it and smile despite myself. Sometimes I could tell it was getting to him. He would come in a little later, and though he always brought food, he would put it on the table quietly without the usually cheery invitation. Then he would gently pull me up from the bed and walk me over to the tiny table. Some mornings he would leave without saying good-bye.

I felt like I was dragging him down with me. I didn't want to, but I also didn't know how to stop it. I wanted to tell him to leave me and go home, but I couldn't make my mouth form the words. I always felt like there wasn't enough breath in me to make the sounds, like the muscles in my face had forgotten how to work. I felt like I was trapped inside myself. Every day when he walked out the door, I half expected him not to come back. I wouldn't have blamed him. In fact, part of me hoped he would just go. I was dragging enough grief. I didn't need to drag him too.

I was sitting on the end of the bed one day when Duff came bustling in the door. He didn't say a word to me, but he looked excited. He glanced around the flat and started straightening things up. I don't know how long it had been since I had seen Rab, but you had grown. Duff had brought me some new clothes from the charity shop around the corner. I don't think I had moved from that spot since he had left that morning. When he was satisfied with the state of things, he went back out the door.

He reappeared a minute later and he wasn't alone. Duff knelt in front of me and took one of my limp hands. I didn't take my eyes off the window. I had been relatively safe in the flat. No one expected me to talk or act like I was okay. I didn't want to meet anyone. I may have wanted to talk to Duff, to tell him to leave me alone, but Duff was safe. The world outside that window wasn't safe. New people were not safe. "Molly, this is Mr. Green. He's going to help us get you home."

I felt my head start to shake. I didn't know if the movement was even big enough for them to see, but I felt it. I didn't want to go home. Home was where Mama was, and she had lied to me. Even worse, I didn't want to face her and tell her what had happened. She might reject me just like the people of the glen had. I was near to panic.

Some of it must have shown on the outside, because Duff's eyebrows drew together in concern. He looked up at the other man, who was somewhere near my shoulder. I don't know what he saw, but Duff stood up and stepped aside.

The man quietly pulled a chair over from the table and placed it between me and the window. He lowered himself onto the chair. I closed my eyes tight. I didn't want to look at him. I didn't have any room for new people in my world full of hurt.

"Miss MacAlpin." His voice was like warm honey and my name dripped onto some raw place inside me. "Will you look at me, my dear?"

Something in that voice was impossible to resist. I slowly pried my eyes open. The man in front of me was polished like those stones you find in the river. Smooth and cool, he wore a fine tailored suit of dark green and shoes so shiny I could almost see myself in them. He sat relaxed, even regal in our plain, slat-backed chair. His eyes were the brown of rich, fertile earth and they smiled at me warmly. His hair was cut perfectly, but the thing that stopped me short was the tree.

The dead tree that I had been looking at for months, the one that looked like pleading arms open to the sky, was behind him. Those bare, black branches seemed to rise out of his head like antlers, just like those on the horned figure I had seen in the glen, at the castle. I felt a jolt of fear, like a chill leaping in my blood.

He quickly took my hand. His hand was so warm. Our eyes met, and he read the question in mine. He answered with small but unmistakable nod. "I am your friend, *a Mhàili*."

I couldn't say anything. After all that time, it was like I had forgotten how. I didn't pull my hand from his. Somehow, I knew he was telling me the truth. "My dear, I'm afraid there has been a misunderstanding."

He took my hand and turned it over. He began gently rubbing the web between my thumb and index finger. I felt the icy fear begin to melt. "I would like to help you and your child. We need to make sure you are safe. By what your friend Mr. MacDuff has told me, that doesn't seem to be the case here. Would you agree?"

I don't know how I did it or even why, but I nodded. "I think that your home in North Carolina is the best place for you and your child. Don't you agree?"

No, I didn't. I was both angry at Mama and afraid of her rejection. My eyes began to sting. The words fought their way to the surface. It reminded me uncomfortably of Willie Cross and that way he had of chewing on his words before they came out. "No. Mama, will send me away."

I heard Duff's sharp inhale to my right. It was the first time I had spoken in weeks. Mr. Green looked at me kindly. "No, lass." He laid a gentle hand on my belly. "Could you send this one away?"

I shook my head. I felt a tear drop onto my cheek. He went on, "No, nor could she turn away her own daughter. You are something very special, *a Mhàili*, and so is your daughter. We must work together to keep her safe. Hmm?"

I nodded.

He lifted his hand and stroked my cheek, smiling at me. "Let's get you home."

He rose, pulling an envelope from his jacket pocket and laying it on the table. When he looked at Duff, his gentle demeanor was gone. In its place was a sure command of everyone around him. "This should be more than enough to get the two of you home and back to Margaret. She will know what to do then."

Duff walked him to the door. "I can't thank you enough, Mr. Green. I've been worried sick."

Mr. Green cast another look at me. "She'll be alright once she gets some distance. The babe will help as well. Take care of them, MacDuff."

Duff glanced over his shoulder at me. "I will."

CHAPTER FORTY-THREE

December 26, 1995
Chapel Hill, North Carolina

Freedom. Sarah took in a deep breath full of wintery mist and bus exhaust, but the air couldn't have been sweeter. She was on her own. No bodyguards, no stalker that she knew of. Just a girl taking the bus to talk to her foster dad. The rain tapered off to a mist that was just heavy enough to keep everything wet. She pulled the collar of her coat up against the chill and made sure her hood was still in place.

She had used her gift to watch Fleming settle in for the night. When she was sure that he thought she was asleep, Sarah had cast out to locate Duff and made sure the area around her building was clear. Then she threw on a hoodie that hid her face from anyone who wasn't directly in front of her. She slid open the newly oiled window in her room and climbed out, pulling her jacket behind her. She walked a couple of blocks before catching the bus across town to Duff's neighborhood.

She made her way down the street that ran parallel to Duff's, before cutting between houses. She went that way in case anyone was watching the front of the house. It was hard to jump the chain link fence around his yard without making noise, which she suspected was the reason he had it. Still, the noise she made was minimal. She didn't think Duff knew anyone was there until she knocked on his back door.

The light in the kitchen came on, and Sarah caught a glimpse of irritation on Duff's face through the window just before he opened it and looked out. She was standing in the shadows and noticed that Duff had one arm carefully tucked behind his back. She didn't doubt there was a gun in that hand. Before he got too nervous, she stepped into the light from the open door and looked up at him.

"Sarah?" His eyebrows drew together in concern. He leaned out the door and looked from side to side.

"How much did you know?" She probably should have exchanged pleasantries, told him not to worry, maybe asked if she could come inside. But that question had been on the tip of her tongue since she'd finished reading Molly's story. And when she met his eyes, it had just spilled out.

His lips formed a grim line and the muscles in his jaw flexed. "Not enough."

"Please don't be cryptic." She took a step closer and lowered her voice. "I need to know."

"Alright. Come inside and sit down." He stepped back to let her in.

Sarah came inside and closed the door behind her. She pulled the hood back from her face and took off her coat. Duff set the gun down on the counter and moved to the refrigerator. "I'm starting work in an hour. I was just about to have some coffee. Want some?"

"Yeah, thanks," she said quietly as she took a seat at the kitchen table.

"I'll be back in a second." When he came back, he was carrying a manila envelope. "That should be all the documents you need for a new identity."

Sarah opened the envelope and looked in to find a birth certificate, driver's license, even a passport. "That was fast."

He gave an acknowledging tilt of his head. "I called in a favor."

Duff fixed her a cup of coffee while she looked over the documents. He joined her at the table, and when he spoke his voice was low and flat. "Back to your question. I knew that at some point, the Stuarts would want to reestablish the monarchy and that your Mama's people are important to that. I knew it was a...matchmaking trip."

"You mean a breeding program," she said flatly, laying the envelope back on the table.

He wet his lips and leaned back in his chair. "I suspected. I didn't know how...specific it was."

"Did you know about the gifts?" she asked.

"What gifts?" By the look on his face, Sarah believed that he genuinely didn't know what she was talking about.

"Our abilities," she tried again. She had to be clear, without revealing too much.

"What is this about?" He leaned forward and rested his forearms on the table.

Sarah shook her head in frustration. "I just need to know."

He looked at her closely. "Why?"

"Because I need to know how much *he* knows." She brought her hand down on the table. "I need to know how much he's been lying to me."

Duff reached across the table and took her hand. His fingers wrapped around hers and he gave them a reassuring squeeze. "Okay, baby. I'll tell you what I know."

Sarah nodded, her eyes on their joined hands.

"Your mama's people have been around longer than anyone really knows." He spoke slowly and clearly as if he was giving evidence in court. "And they have something that is important and needs to be kept hidden."

"The cauldron?" she asked. Could this really all hinge on some magic object?

He shook his head. "I don't think so. The cauldron is special. Don't get me wrong, but I think it's just there to help them with what is really important. I think they have some knowledge, or a way to see things that the rest of us don't."

"Like what?"

"It's hard to explain. But your mama figured out how to get to their hidden glen without a map or anything. And your granny could get a message to me whenever she needed to, no matter where I was. She would call someone she knew who had a phone and get them to pass on whatever news she wanted me to know."

Sarah could imagine Granny casting out, just as Mama had described, just as she had done. Sarah hadn't tested her gift outside of town, but maybe Granny was stronger. She probably had more practice.

"Long ago, your people made a pact with the Scottish kings. You would use your skills to help them, and they would help keep your people hidden. They were supposed to work together."

"What happened?" The Stuarts had been out of power for centuries.

"I'm not sure." Duff shrugged. "I reckon your people could tell you more about that. I do think it happened around the time of James IV. I guess when the Union happened, he forgot the importance of your people."

"So why are the Sinclairs still working for them?" The secret alliance between her people and the Stuarts seemed pretty much broken, but the Stuarts seemed to have a lot of control over the Sinclairs, at least the ones she knew.

"Because there are still some Stuarts who remember the alliance with your people," he said through gritted teeth. "And the Sinclairs are the king's stewards."

"In the twentieth century?" She looked doubtful. "They still are?"

He nodded, his mouth grim. "Obviously some Sinclairs have forgotten, but some of us still are."

Sarah had a hard time understanding how that kind of loyalty to a lost cause could last for generations. She carefully set her mug on the table. "You were coerced into helping them. Do you think maybe Dermot was too, maybe he still is?"

"I can't speak to the man's motivation, baby," Duff sighed and gave her a pitying look. "But I can tell by the way he looks at you and the way he screamed when he saw you in the arms of that killer that he cares a lot about you. And it's not just about duty."

Sarah felt tears pooling in her eyes, and she turned her face away so Duff wouldn't see. "This is going to hurt, Duff. It's going to hurt bad."

Duff's hands surrounded hers where they cradled her cup. "I know, baby girl. But it's when you stop loving that hurts the most. That was your Mama's problem. It wasn't that she fell in love with somebody else's man or that her people treated her bad. It was when she realized that she gave everything to a coward that broke her. It made her doubt every choice she'd ever made and every one she made after that. She couldn't trust herself anymore, and she couldn't trust anyone else."

"She could trust you." Sarah turned her hand to grip his.

"No, she couldn't. Remember, I took her there, and when she tried to escape, I took her back." Sarah could see the decades of guilt and pain written in the lines on his face. "I won't do that to you. That's why I got you those papers, even when I'm not sure running is the best idea. Whatever you decide to do, if I can help you, I will."

"Thank you." She squeezed his hand and smiled through her tears. "And for what it's worth, I know she didn't blame you."

He nodded jerkily, then stood up and wiped a hand down his face. "Come on. My shift starts soon. I'll drive you home."

"Okay." She poured the rest of her coffee into the sink and left the cup inside. As they were walking out the door, she thought of another question. "Who was Mr. Green?"

Duff blew out a long breath as he pulled the door closed and locked it. "That is a much bigger question than we have time for tonight. Let's just say he's a very good friend to have."

The ride back to Ransom Street was silent. Sarah just enjoyed being with Duff for however long she could. They drove past her building, and everything looked quiet. The lights were off and Sarah could see the glow of the TV through the front window. There was no uproar, no police lights. It didn't look like Fleming had realized she was gone.

"Looks like you're good, although I don't condone you running around without protection," he said as he pulled to the curb down the block from her building.

"I have all the skills you taught me." She smiled at him, her hand on the door latch. "I just used them a few weeks ago, remember?"

He made a noise in his throat, and she could almost see his disapproving look through the darkness. It was such a Dad moment that she couldn't help giggling.

Sarah took a key out of her pocket. "This is the key to a storage unit at that place on Route 15 by the Greek restaurant." She hesitated. "It's paid up for a year. If I'm not back by this time next year, can you pick up my things?"

It was a minute before he answered. His face was turned to the window. When he spoke, his voice was thick with emotion. "Yeah. I'll keep it for you."

She held up the envelope. "Thanks for the papers, even if I might not use them."

"Keep 'em. Even if you don't use them now, you might need them someday."

She studied him, letting several seconds stretch through the darkness between them. "You're not going to disappear on me again, are you?"

He reached across the console and gripped her hand. "No, I can't go back to that. That world and what it did to your mother tore me apart. But I won't leave you, baby. I'll be right where you can find me."

She leaned over and wrapped an arm around him, squeezing tight.

"I love you, Duff," she whispered in his ear and kissed his cheek before opening her door.

"I love you too, Sarah girl." The interior light came on, and he was washed in a warm glow. He stopped her from getting out with a hand on her arm. "Listen, if loving your mother taught me anything, it taught me that it's better to have some of that person than nothing at all. Yeah, it hurts. But once you accept there's going to be pain at the bottom, you can sit back and enjoy the fall."

In that moment Sarah didn't see the man in front of her, the weathered, world-weary one in his late forties. She didn't even see the unkempt drifter disguise he had worn when she was a child. She saw the young Duff, the one her mother described who looked like a cowboy. The one who let an angry girl beat on his chest and held her when she wept. She saw the man who loved her mother even through the worst of her madness. The man who was so hurt at the bottom of his fall that he had stayed in the shadows watching her for years. She didn't say anything. She couldn't talk. She gave his hand one last squeeze and got out of the car. She closed the door as silently as possible and headed for her window.

CHAPTER FORTY-FOUR

Once she had climbed back through her window, Sarah looked around her nearly empty room. She had whittled her things down to fit into two suitcases and her backpack. The few clothes she had now were hanging next to empty hangers in her closet. The furniture had come with the apartment. She had the bedclothes and a couple of pans in the kitchen. And her coffee maker, but Amy could have that. Almost seven years out of the holler and she didn't have much more than she'd had then.

They had never needed much. Granny had mostly lived off the land. Whatever money she'd had, she'd been thrifty with it. Reading about their village in Scotland explained a lot about why Granny lived the way she did. She hadn't been used to having things or the constant need to grow, expand, and consume that most Americans seemed to suffer from.

Growing up, Sarah had always thought that was just Granny's way. She hadn't asked why, but maybe it had been Granny's way because Granny was hiding. According to what Jock had told her mother, Granny had left Scotland to avoid detection by the Nazis. Had they been looking for the cauldron or for the sisters who had the kind of skills that might help them win a war? One who could see and find things at a distance, one who saw the future, and one who saw the truth? If the talents the sisters had were true, they would be invaluable to someone trying to take over the world...or take back a throne.

Except there weren't three sisters in her generation. Bridget, Rona's daughter, was gone. Sarah wondered if she had another cousin, or half-sister, somewhere who was gifted, one who saw the truth like Sheila. Ryan and Dermot had both called her "the one." Did that mean the other girls didn't have gifts? Or that hers was something different? Ryan Cumberland had gotten to Bridget first. Did that make Sarah the alternate?

She kicked off her shoes and laid down on the bed. Tucking her hands behind her head, she stared up at the ceiling. She had a decision to make. She had been avoiding it for weeks, researching and cooking and reading instead of coming to some conclusion about what to do next. The trouble was, whenever she tried to think about the situation, she was swamped with so many emotions and questions that they all just ended up in a jumble lodged somewhere in her chest. If she wanted answers, she had to go to Scotland. If she wanted Dermot, she had to go to Scotland.

Her plane tickets were in an envelope tucked into the frame of the mirror over her dresser. The date on them was January fourth. It was December twenty-sixth. That left her a week of bare-bones living to look forward to. Correction: a week of bare-bones imprisonment. The guys did a good job of making things as comfortable as possible, but it was hard to think of her current situation as anything else. She was also sure that her every move was being reported back to James Stuart.

James could give her the world, but it would be on his terms. A patron like James could fund a lot of research trips and make a lot of connections for her. However, courting that support meant dealing with his dynastic intentions. She had seen over the last few weeks just how powerful he was and how far he could go. She sincerely hoped that Martin Carol had hopped the first flight back to Edinburgh, but somehow she doubted it. Did she really think that she could take advantage of the opportunities James offered, while still holding him at arm's length?

If she ran, just took off and started a new life, she would have to choose freedom over everything she'd been working for, over finding answers about her mother, over love. What good was freedom without that? Maybe Duff was right. Maybe it was better to have some of the person you loved than nothing at all. She had sent Dermot away in the hopes that distance would bring clarity, but whenever she thought of him she was struck with an overwhelming need to be near him again.

***

...white and pink swirled around in a bright kaleidoscope. And Sarah heard her mother cooing in her ear.

...They won't have you. Keep yourself...

Mama's arms cradled her as she floated in the warm water.

...Don't let them make...

...Mama?...

...Not my baby...loved your father...

...Mama, I can't breathe...

...won't do it to you...I'll protect...

She knew it was a dream. She wasn't actually under the water. The flowers weren't really floating above her. Molly wasn't really there.

"You're not here," she said in her dream.

"I'm always here."

***

December 27, 1995

Sarah put the notes she had written for Amy and Barrett in two envelopes on top of the now-empty dresser. Then she picked up the necklace with the boar pendant that Dermot had given her and fastened it around her neck. She had stripped the bed and run the bedding through the wash earlier that day. The sheets and quilt were folded neatly on top of the mattress.

It had been a quiet day. Most of the university buildings were still closed for the holiday, so she had spent it doing laundry, reading, and lulling the guard dogs into a false sense of calm. She had offered beer and a high fiber dinner. She had even stayed in with them afterward and watched a football game on TV. When it was over, Curtis had gone off to rest and Fleming had settled in to watch some Andy Griffith reruns. He had discovered the show late one night and become quickly addicted. When Sarah had left him, Opie had just found a change purse full of money.

Sarah bided her time, folding the rest of her laundry and putting it into her suitcases. She hoped she was making the right choice. She checked the clock again. Ten-thirty was still too early to begin her plan.

She finished folding the clothes and zipped up the larger of her suitcases. Then she sat on the bed to wait. She thought about all of the memories she'd made there. She had really found her feet in Chapel Hill. She had decided on a career, made friendships that would have lasted if it weren't for her current situation, and fallen in love. This had become a home of her choosing, and she had fit here as much as she could anywhere. Now she was being forced to leave it.

As she had with her previous homes, Sarah cast out to view the memories of the place. She took her time reviewing all of her favorite spots as if she were taking a walk. She saw the blue house on the corner where her friends lived. Tree-lined Cameron Avenue, the quad, Wilson Library. She could see Greenlaw Hall and The Pit. Beyond them were the Arboretum, Donald's house on Boundary Street, and Gimghoul Rock, where she had told Dermot of the love triangle that had ended in a duel. She hoped that story wouldn't be prophetic.

Even with the trees winter-bare, Chapel Hill was a beautiful town. Her heart hurt to leave it. She had no idea if she would ever make it back here, back to her friends. When she thought she had soaked up all the memories she could, she drew herself back to the apartment.

It was near two o'clock when she opened her eyes. It was time. Sarah slid open the window. The first thing to go out was the smaller of her suitcases. It was bigger than her backpack, but she was relatively sure she could get it through the window sill and got the end with the wheels on it over the track without making any undue noise.

She wiggled it back and forth, pushing it through the window inch by inch until it was nearly out. Then it caught on the foot at the end opposite from the wheels. Sarah slid her arm out the narrow opening between the window and the suitcase. She wrapped her fingers around the bottom edge of the case and lifted at the same time that she pushed with her other hand. The suitcase slid the rest of the way out and fell out of her grasp. Fortunately, it only had a few feet to fall, but it landed with a thud.

She froze and held her breath, listening for Fleming's footsteps coming down the hall. Sarah waited for several minutes for him to investigate, but she didn't hear anything. She leaned out the window to see what state her suitcase was in. It lay on the ground a few feet below, but didn't seem to have been damaged. She breathed a sigh of relief.

Now for the hard part. There was no way the larger of her suitcases was getting out that window. She was going to have to take it out through the main room. Which meant she would have to be sneaky and wait until Fleming went to the bathroom or fell asleep, which was highly unlikely. She prepared by putting her coat and backpack on, but leaving her shoes off. Then she took a deep breath and cast out again. This was quickly becoming old hat.

She had no idea how long she watched him, but it seemed like an eternity. Like a watched pot, he puttered around the kitchen, read the newspaper, flipped channels through a series of infomercials…Sarah tried to have patience. Eventually, all that broccoli she had served at dinner would pay off. Finally, he went to the bathroom. Sarah was back to herself before the door finished closing behind him.

She softly opened her door, easing the knob back into position so there wouldn't be any sound. Then she lifted her suitcase in one hand and shoes in the other. Once she had cleared the hallway without bumping the case into the walls, she made a bee line for the door. In less than two seconds she had undone the chain and deadbolt as quietly as she could. She slipped out, somehow managing not to hit anything with the unwieldy suitcase.

She pulled the door closed behind her and relocked the deadbolt as quietly as she could from outside. She had to turn the key slowly so it didn't make its usual thunk. When she had locked it, she stopped again to listen. From inside the apartment, she heard the toilet flush and thanked her lucky stars she had made it out.

She slipped on her shoes and grabbed her suitcase. She made her way to her car and opened the hatchback as quietly as she could. She tried her best not to make any noise as she put the heavy suitcase into the trunk, then went to retrieve the smaller one. Creeping as quietly as possible to her window, Sarah picked it up again, stopping to listen for any sound that Fleming had noticed she was missing. All quiet.

Sarah scuttled back to the car and loaded the small suitcase into the back. Then she picked up her backpack and slid into the driver's seat. She closed the door with just a soft click. Keeping her fingers crossed that he wouldn't notice the engine starting, or that he would assume it was one of the few other residents still in the building, Sarah started the car. She didn't bother turning on the lights. The streetlights were enough to see by, at least until she got further away. She turned out of the parking lot and took a left onto Ransom Street. When she was turned fully away from the building, she turned on her lights and drove away with her life as she'd known it in the rearview mirror.

***

From Molly MacAlpin's Journal

From the moment I knew you were with me, baby, I hoped with all my heart that you wouldn't have to go through what I did. A part of me tried very hard to believe that because your father and I weren't the right matches for each other, you and I had broken free. Maybe because we chose each other instead of just doing what we were told, you would be safe. But then I've hoped hundreds of things from that day to this one. I hoped that you would be a boy so you couldn't be one of the sisters. I hoped that the glen would be discovered and someone would put a stop to the whole thing. I hope that you will be able to make your own choices. You're the smartest person I've ever seen, and I want your future to be determined by your will, not by your womanhood.

I tried my best to be a good mother to you. I have loved you more than I thought I could love a person. I took all those fears about the future and what might be waiting for you, and I locked them in a little box and buried them way in the back of my mind. They were a problem for another time, another day.

But then that day in the bathtub, when you told me about your dream, you blew that box wide open and all my worst fears climbed out. I worried that you might be one of the sisters, but I think you're much more. Listen to the song and the legend of our people. You are the queen they've been waiting for. However hard it was for me, I'm afraid it's going to be even harder for you. That's why I did what I did. I hate thinking about what's coming for you. I can't stop it. I know that now. But I can't watch it happen either, and there's nothing in this world I can do to protect you.

This is where I say good-bye, baby. Don't blame your Granny or yourself. There's no one to blame for this but me. I'm weak, but I hope that what I've written here can help make you strong.

Pay attention to what Duff tells you. I've never met a better man than Grant MacDuff. He's the best father I could give you.

I wish I could have loved him better. I hope that if you get a steward of your own, he is as good a man as our Duff.

I wish I could have been a better daughter. I wish I could have been a better mother. Hell, there's a lot of things I wish were different, but there's no helping that now. I'm going to cast out one more time, baby. This time I won't be coming back, but I'll always be with you.

AUTHOR'S NOTE

Some of the folklore in the series is invented and some is authentic, and some is a little bit of both. The Scottish, Irish, Norse and Welsh legends that Sarah finds in her research are authentic. The origin story of Sarah's people and the story of The River Maiden are invented, but are based on existing archetypes that appear in Celtic and British folklore.

One area where things cross over is in the case of the Gaelic charm that Sarah goes to see in the North Carolina State Archives. Dugald MacFarlane's charm is a rare document from a Scottish immigrant in 1750. It is in fact in the state archives in North Carolina. The text used in the book is invented following the form of actual charm, but with different content that fits the story. Although, Dugald MacFarlane's charm does mention "nine miraculous elements" and Saint Columba. If you are interested in more information on Dugald MacFarlane's Charm, I recommend Ronald Black's article for The North Carolina Historical Review, "The Nine: A Scottish Gaelic Charm in the North Carolina State Archives."

Làrachd an Fhamhair is an invention for the sake of the story. However, there are many legends about disappearing and reappearing villages and islands in Scotland. Our little village is in the hills east northeast of Ben More Assynt near the village on Inchnadamph.

GAELIC PHRASES

Wallace Purdy's Charm

Na naoinear de an Làrachd	The nine of the Footprint
Bha sgath air Calum Cille	That Saint Columba feared
Air lèirsinn den fhirinn	Upon vision of truth
Air an bean-luirg	Upon the finder-woman
Seun sibh fo-duine agaibh	Put them under your protection
Thoir luathachadh air turas	Hasten their journey
Le dùrachd tri-fhillte triuir	With the goodwill of the threefold three

A bheil Gàidhlig agaibh? (uh vel GAH-lik AH-giv?)– Do you speak Gaelic?

a Dhiarmuid (uh HAR-mooj) – Dermot direct address

a graidh/ mo ghraidh (uh GREYE/mo HREYE)- Love, my love

a leanabh (uh LYEHN-iv)- baby, young child direct address

A Mhàili bhoidheach (uh VAH-lee VOY-yuhk)– Pretty Molly from a popular Gaelic song

a Mhami (uh VAH-mee)– Mommy, direct address

a nighean (uh NEE-yun)– daughter direct address

an righ air chall's a... (uhn ree ar hawl sah) – the king lost...(fragment)

Beanachd leibh (BEN-uhk layv)– Blessings to you (formal) commonly used for goodbye

Cailleach (CAHL-yahk) – Old woman, hag

ceart (kyarsht) – Right, correct

cò (coe) - who

Cò às a tha sibh? (Coe ahs ah hah shiv?)– Where are you from?

Eirichidh e a-rithist (AYR-ee-hee ay ah REE-isht) – He will rise
again

Làrachd an Fhamhair (LAHR-uhk uhn AH-var) – giant's footprint

Màili/A Mhàili (MAH-lee, uh VAH-lee)– Molly/direct address

Mar sin leat (mar shin laht)– Goodbye, common response to
Beanachd leat/leibh

mo chridhe (moh HREE-yeh) – my heart

Mòran taing (MOE-rahn tangk)– Much thanks

Na bith eagail ort. Cuir earbs' annam. (Nah bee EK-guhl orsht.
Coor AIR-uhb sa OW-nahm) – Don't be afraid. Trust me.

na peathraichean (nah PAYR-uh-hen)– The sisters

na triuir peathraichean (nah TREE-ur PAYR-uh-hen) – the three
sisters

puirt a beul (POORSHT uh BEE-uhl)– mouth music

Tha coltas banrigh an t-sithean oirbh. (Ha COLT-uhs BAHN-ree
uhnt SHEE-uhn EHR-iv) – You look like a fairy queen.

Tha gaol agam ort/ Tha goal agam orbh. (Ha gool akahm orsht/Ha
gool akahm EHR-iv)– I love you (informal/formal)

Tha, gu dearbh! (Ha GOO JER-uhv)– I do, indeed.

Shnàmh mhaidean air an (NAHV VAH-jehn ehr ahn) – A maiden
swam upon…(fragment)

sluagh ùr (SLOO-uhg OOR) – new folk, new tribe

ACKNOWLEDGEMENTS

Writing can be a lonely business, and hard to do without the support of a lot of great people. I would love to thank everyone individually, but no doubt I would forget someone. There are however a few standouts. Once again, Jon VanZile of Editing for Authors has been my manuscript whisperer. Caroline Root of Daily Gaelic has been teaching me Gaelic for over a year, and her help is invaluable.

Since publishing The River Maiden, I have been on the receiving end of an incredible amount of support from some wonderful readers. They have turned out to singings, invited me to speak, written reviews, given my book as gifts and recommended it to their friends. They have reached out to me to tell me how they felt about the book, often in moments when I was sunk in the morass of self-doubt that most writers suffer from. Some were my friends before the book came out, some have become my friends since. All are precious to me.

Last but far from least my husband and kids for tolerating the many hours that I've spent working on this. Also, my extended family for their lifelong support.

ONCE & FUTURE SERIES

Unfit (ebook short)

When she left Kettle Hollow, Molly MacAlpin hoped never to see her remote mountain home again. She returned eighteen months later angry, pregnant and abandoned by the man she loved. So, she threw all her energy into making sure her daughter had the best life possible.

With the help and sometimes interference of her mother, she is raising a bright, sweet child she they hopes will have every possible opportunity. Until one spring day a brief conversation with her little girl brings her world crashing down around her.

The River Maiden

Sarah MacAlpin has always felt like an outsider. Raised by her Scottish grandmother deep in the Blue Ridge Mountains, Sarah grew up with one foot in the old world and one foot in the new world. Her childhood friends were the stuff of ancient Celtic legends. But Sarah's seemingly idyllic past hides a horrifying secret. As a little girl she watched her mother's inexorable slide into madness. But she hasn't let her past stop her from reaching for her dreams. She has managed to put together a pretty good life for herself. She has great friends, a boyfriend, and her career as a folklorist is all planned out. That is until she meets Dermot Sinclair. The handsome Scot seems to be dogging her every step. At best he's a fellow folklorist who can help her research. At worst, he could be there to steal her work. All she has to do is find one song that proves her thesis and her dissertation will be done. Unfortunately, unlocking that song may also mean unlocking some buried memories and a dangerous destiny set in motion generations ago.

Buddy (ebook short)

As the youngest of the contentious Corbett clan, Buddy has spent most of his life trying to get away from the remote mountain hollow where they all grew up. Now at the end of a long day, he can't avoid talking to them. When one of his brothers mentions their old neighbor, Maggie MacAlpin, he can't help thinking about Old Maggie's granddaughter, Sarah. She was as tough and wild as she was beautiful. And she was the first girl that Buddy ever loved.

One summer when they were barely old enough for kissing, Buddy learned just how much that love could cost them.

ABOUT THE AUTHOR

Meredith R. Stoddard writes folklore-inspired fiction from her attic hideaway in Central Virginia. She studied literature and folklore at the University of North Carolina at Chapel Hill before working as a corporate trainer and instructional designer. Her love of storytelling is inspired by years spent listening to stories at her grandmother's kitchen table. She also advocates for the preservation of traditional fiber arts and the Scottish Gaelic language.

You can also follow @M_R_Stoddard on Twitter.

Printed in Great Britain
by Amazon

79117343R00274